lot America, 7⁵⁰

EGGS AND BAKER

or

THE DAYS OF TRIAL

EGGS AND BAKER

or

THE DAYS OF TRIAL

By

John Masefield

NEW YORK

THE MACMILLAN COMPANY

1936

PRINTED IN THE UNITED STATES OF AMERICA
BY THE STRATFORD PRESS, INC., NEW YORK

EGGS AND BAKER

or

THE DAYS OF TRIAL

EGGS AND BAKER

On the last Saturday of September, 187–, Robert Frampton Mansell, the baker, sat in his kitchen, with his wife, Tryphena, his son, Bob, and his guest, Adolf Engels, snatching his middle day dinner as best he could.

The kitchen lay behind his baker's shop, which opened on the broad street of the village, or little town, of Condicote. Through the glass door, which shut the kitchen from the shop, Bob could see across this street, to a blue blaze of summer sky above the roof of what was called the Pilgrimage. This was a long, fifteenth century building, once the hostel for pilgrims visiting the shrine at Condicote Monastery. No pilgrims lived there now. What was not ruinous was used as a warehouse. On the roof of it Bob saw a dozen tumbler pigeons preening or dozing in the sun. Sometimes they slithered an inch or two upon the steep pitch of the roof; then they fluttered and struggled back to their position, but plainly they loved the sun too well to wish to rise aloft and tumble.

Though the tumblers held Bob's interest the most, he was not forgetful of duties. Often he glanced in the other direction, into the baker's yard at the back of the house, to make sure that no little boys were creeping in to raid as was their Saturday custom. It was sometimes possible for them to steal little bits of hot bread when everybody was so busy, and if they could not steal, they still could torment the cob Marrowbones who drew the baker's van.

"Here's Joe", Tryphena said, rising from her seat and

taking a thick sandwich from the dresser. "Here's your dinner, Joe".

Joe was a big, stooping, good-natured and slow-witted man, who was the journeyman of their bakery. He was used to drudgery, and did not mind the hard work of mixing and kneading. As his wife was a violent shrew, with a habit of knocking him over the head, he liked the life of a baker, which kept him much from home, with irregular hours. He could stay away from home at nights, with the fair excuse, that he was wanted for the work. Often, he slept at odd times in the corners of the bake-house, and only rose to tend the work in hand. The work had bent him, but had not given him the baker's pallor; he had colour in his cheeks. He often sang at his work, in a sweet gentle voice, the fragments of hymns which he could both remember and understand. He had been a farm-boy in his childhood, and still trembled at the cruelty with which the farmer had beaten him. From his farm days, he kept also a curious skill in setting wires, for rabbits, hares and pheasants, of which he got a good many every year, without drawing suspicion on himself.

Joe now drew forward, smiling, as his way was, to touch his forelock and take his dinner from his mistress, with his usual words of, "Thank you kindly, Ma'am, as I'm sure". This time he hesitated, and seemed unwilling to go.

"What is it"? Tryphena asked.

"If you please, Ma'am", he said, "the Magpie has been here all this forenoon, in case you could spare a bite for him".

"Ah", Tryphena said, "I must cut for him, too, I suppose".

She took the loaf as though she had a grudge against it,

cut its throat, so to speak, slashed a piece of mutton from the bone, jammed the two together, and handed the two, roughly bent, to Joe.

"Here's the Magpie's dinner", she said.

Joe thanked her, and turned back to the bake-house, where the batches of loaves were now being put in and drawn.

"I forgot that poor mad lad was here", she said. "I don't know that he does much good".

"He's a help on a Saturday", the baker said. "If he didn't get odd jobs of the sort, he'd soon be in queer street, the poor old Magpie. There he goes, Adolf, the Magpie. He works here for us from time to time, but he isn't quite all there".

The Magpie came suddenly to the kitchen door, opened it, looked with bright eyes at the party, waved his sandwich and said,

"Thanky, Mrs. Baker, for very nice din, all so good".

He might have been thirty years of age or more. He was dressed in an old pair of trowsers given by the baker, a rough Crimean blue shirt and a coat all in rags, taken from a scarecrow. His hair was streaked with white in a magpie fashion. He laughed at them, took a bite of his sandwich and went out.

"That's right, you run along, Magpie", Tryphena said.

Though the meal was as harassed as a Saturday dinner always was at the bakery, it was a feast, not a regular meal, because of the guest. Tryphena had added to the cold mutton her best red currant jelly, a dish of chocolate éclairs, and a plate of blue plums. It was a special day for them, because of Engels, for whom both she and the baker felt something of what her namesake may have felt for St. Paul in Rome. To them he was a martyr for the cause, and an apostle bringing light into dark places. Bob did not share their feeling about him. He resented the stranger's presence on this particular Saturday, when so much was to be done, and he had had for a long time a dislike for the man and his ways.

He was a somewhat sinister-looking man. He had dark, restless, sharp eyes set closely together. His nose was prominent; his face of a dead white, clean shaven, with thick, closely cropped hair above it, of an ugly dark brown. The eyes looked at you sharply in a sergeant's way, to find fault or to bully. Like the baker, he was about forty-three years old. There was an air of force about him. He was built to make his presence felt. He had a bullet head, and a compact, active, well-knit, bullet body, designed for impact. Most people, looking at him, would have set him down as a teacher in some very bad school engaged in the spreading of darkness by the exercise of petty tyranny. He ate greedily, and plainly liked being flattered by the attention and respect of his host and hostess.

"By the way", he said, "your wife was saying that you've been coming out as a writer for the cause. I seem to have heard of it, too, at Stanchester".

"Yes", the baker said. "For these last few weeks, I've been having a letter in the *Yockford Times* every week, about the slums just down the road. You might like to cast your eyes down the letters. Tryphena will give you the file after. There are two rows of pigsties there with three hundred people in them, all paying rent which gets, sooner or later, to the Church. I've drawn a pretty hornet's nest about me; but I'm going on till something gets done about them".

"It's wonderful, what folk will permit, without asking into it at all", Tryphena said.

"You're right, if there's money coming from it", Engels said.

He did not show any interest in the baker's letters to the paper; he did not ask to see the file. The baker was a little abashed, perhaps, at his lack of interest, but returned to the charge.

"What me and the wife were hoping", he said, "was, that perhaps if you took the letters up to Town with you, when next you go, you could get head-quarters to look at them for *The Banner*, in case there should be a free column any week".

"They would be too provincial for *The Banner*", Engels said. "They'd want only town topics in *The Banner*. They'd want something nearer home".

The baker sighed; after all, he had hardly dared to hope that *The Banner* would look at his things; Tryphena had said that it would, and ought to, but he had hardly hoped for such glory. He covered his disappointment by a more generous praise of his guest.

"Speaking about *The Banner*", he said, "you're a wonder in it, month by month, keeping us provincials rallying to the cause. Your Calls, as you call them, are just like so many trumpets. They stir one up to the fight. And, by the way, you never wrote a better call than last month's in *The Banner*. That bit about the ground landlords must have made some of them squirm. It got them through the fat, as your father used to say".

"Ah, you saw that, did you? I liked that one myself".

"That one that I like so much and keep reading", Tryphena said, "is that one about the difference between what

the rich do to the poor now, and what the poor would do
to the rich, if the change were to come".

"Ah, yes", the baker said, "the wife keeps reading that
one, over and over".

Engels swallowed the compliment as though it were
something to eat, but Bob, who was watching him saw, at
the same time, a tiny curl of contempt on the man's lips.
He was eating their food and their flattery and at the same
time despising them. Bob, who always disliked him, longed
to kick him.

Engels noticed Bob's face, and resolved to punish him.

"I don't think Young Hopeful quite approves the cause
of the Poor", he said. "Is that the result of the Rector's
Latin"?

"Bob is still too young to bother about politics", the
baker said.

"His heart hasn't been opened yet", Tryphena said. "It's
all stuffed up with these books".

"I know that when I was his age I had taken to the
cause", Engels said. "But in my case the enemy hadn't tried
to bribe me away from my own class. Now I warrant your
son can tell us who crushed out the light of Napoleon? I
thought so. And who ordered the massacre at Peterloo, and
the one at Tolpuddle? His own classes' sufferers are passed
over. Does your Rector never tell you to beware of men
like me, I wonder"?

The temptation to be outrageously rude was very strong
in Bob, but at that instant someone went with a quick step
past the kitchen door and up the yard. It was a welcome
break in the talk.

"There's that boy Gregory at last", Tryphena said, peering out and calling, "Ho, Gregory, this way. In here. Ah,

bah, none so deaf as those who won't hear. There he goes, back to the stable. He's bringing the fish, for tonight. Run and get it from him, Bob".

Bob was delighted to get away from the constraint of the feast. He leaped out into the yard and after Gregory, who by this time was at the bakery door, looking in at the work in hand. Joe, the journeyman, was handling the batches of buns with the peel.

Gregory Rawson was the son of a woman who kept a little shop for fish, fruit and vegetables further up the street. He was nearly three years older than Bob. He was a somewhat loutish-looking boy. He had taken Bob under his wing when they had been at school together at Mr. Uley's Academy (as it was called) off the Tatchester Road, and the friendship continued, though they had had little in common. Gregory was now a big fellow, earning money, smoking, singing in the choir on Sundays, and sporting a malacca cane and a very bright tie on Sunday afternoons. He was not nearly so clever as Bob, yet they got along very well, and were close companions.

"Ah, Bob", he said, "I've brought you some mackerel. Mother says she daren't send the plaice, it's been so hot".

"Is it all right, your coming this afternoon"? Bob asked.

"Yes. I and Polly will be there. It'll be a good day for it".

"Goody", Bob said.

"I see you got somebody to dinner", Gregory said. "Who is it"?

"Adolf Engels", Bob said, "the radical, who will be speaking at tonight's meeting".

"Gummy".

"You might well say 'Gummy' ".

"Diggory says that that man Engels has been in prison more than once, and will be put there again, if he doesn't mind his tip", Gregory said.

"He has been, and will be", Bob said.

"Well, don't let him stop your coming this afternoon".

"No fear".

"I met young Mr. Wye, of the Steam Bakery, just now", Gregory said. "He said that the way your father was shaping, he would be in the bankruptcy court within two years, what with radical meetings, and not facing to the times".

"Tell him to put his head in a bag and ride to Putney on a pig", Bob said. "Did he say that to you"?

"No, not to me exactly; but he was in his yard as I was delivering, and he was talking about your father's meeting, to old Files and his son. That was what he said".

"Did he say anything else"?

"He said that, of course, he didn't complain; it all benefited him".

"Well, don't let him laugh too soon", Bob said.

He was abashed, none the less, by what Gregory had said. Gregory had a way of overhearing all the horrid things that were said, and then retailing them in all their baldness. Young Mr. Wye was a dangerous rival and a very shrewd man. He had begun as a baker in Condicote only two years before and had already halved the Mansell business. If he said that Mansell would be bankrupt within two years, then there was more than a chance that Mansell would be, "what with radical meetings and not facing to the times".

"You've got all your things for this afternoon"? Gregory asked.

"All done up and in the van, all ready", Bob said.

"Well, I'll be getting on back", Gregory said. "And I'll go over the wall if you don't mind, so then your mother won't row me for not bringing the plaice".

He nodded to Bob, and at once hoisted his lanky body over the low wall which fenced the baker's yard from the untidy overgrown waste, stuck about with stumps of ruin, which had once been a part of the monastery. Bob went back to the kitchen with the mackerel.

"Gregory has had to bring mackerel", he said, "owing to the heat".

"Wait a moment", Tryphena said, "I will speak to him about that".

"He's gone, Mother", Bob said.

"Gone. How"? Tryphena asked.

"Over the garden wall".

"It's a wonder some folk can't ask leave before taking a liberty like that, going over the yard wall", Tryphena said. "I suppose I shall have to put up with it as I shall with the mackerel, but that boy Gregory is getting to be a big lout, and he and I will fall out one of these days".

"He said he hoped I wouldn't mind", Bob said. "He's always rushed on a Saturday, and a short cut saves a lot of time".

She took the mackerel, and put them into a basin of cold water diluted with vinegar.

"The less I see you going about with that big lout Gregory", she continued, "the better I shall be pleased. And it's like his mother, too, to send the mackerel, when she knows I'll have to take it or leave it. It's always on a day like this that these things happen. Now get your dinner, and be off, Bob. You know you haven't a moment, yet there you gawp. You'll be late again".

Bob bowed his head to the storm, and ate his meal. He was buoyed up with the thought of the afternoon, when he and Gregory and another would put a long-cherished plan to proof.

The bell on the shop door tinkled as someone came in from the street.

"There's another", Tryphena said. "Who is it this time"?

"Mrs. Calmamine", the baker said under his breath, as he tried to bolt the food then in his mouth.

"I'll go", Bob said, rising.

"You'll stay here", his mother said. "You get on with your dinner. You've got to deliver this afternoon, and you're late as it is. I'll take the next one".

"I'm not late, really, Mother", Bob said. Indeed, he had taken very special pains that day, that he should not be late.

"You're always late", his mother said. "You go read, read, read, read, read, till I wonder your eyes don't drop out of your head. What you expect to get from so much reading, I'm sure I can't think. You never see the gentry reading. Now, if you were like your father, you would read to purpose".

The bell on the street door rang again, and then a third time as the baker went out to the shop.

"Saturday is always our busiest day", Tryphena explained. "We have to bake double to last folk over Sunday; and then it's pay-day and shopping-day, too".

The baker was absent for several minutes, serving bread, buns and stick-jaw. Bob kept to his food; Engels talked about meetings in the past, where he had told them some home truths.

Presently the baker came back to the kitchen.

"Mrs. Calmamine would like a word with you", he said, and muttered under his breath, "Silly old hen".

The baker took his seat. Tryphena rose, dusted crumbs from her dress, dabbed her hair and went out into the shop. Mrs. Calmamine ran the hotel, the *Prince Rupert Arms*, a well-known sporting house always full of hunting men from November until April.

"Mrs. Mansell", she said, "I thought I'd better run over to speak with you about this meeting that is to be tonight. There's a good deal of feeling that the man, Mr. Engels, as they call him, is trying to stir up trouble here, and I thought it would be the act of a friend just to warn you in case he should involve your husband".

"Thank you, I'm sure", Tryphena said. "But my husband and I have both known Mr. Engels a long time, and the meeting is only a discussion. Speech is free, they say".

"Yes", Mrs. Calmamine said, "but you know that people say a good many more things than their prayers in this little place, and you know, now that it's harvest time, a lot of queer people are in the district. You see, I hear both sides, Mrs. Mansell, and what the magistrates and the farmers are afraid of is that these discussions may lead to things like rick-burning". She dropped her voice at this and said, "They're going to have someone at the meeting to take down the words used. I thought it would be the act of a friend just to come in to tell you".

At this Mrs. Calmamine nodded and bustled out, Tryphena muttering, "Thank you, I'm sure", but adding after she had gone, "Why can't she look after her own affairs"?

"What did she want"? the baker asked.

"Oh, she says that somebody is going to take down all that is said tonight".

"Why, yes", the baker said, "the reporter from the *Tatchester Times* is going to be there, that's all it is; but even if they send their police spies I say, 'Let them', and they'll hear some truths tonight. Won't they, Adolf"?

"They'll hear some news of their own property that they won't relish", Engels said. "They may learn what their pride is based on if they'll take the trouble to come to listen".

There came a call from the shop of "Telegram". Bob went to the shop for the envelope, and handed it to his father, who read it with shining eyes.

"See that, Tryph"? he said, handing it to her. "The Tatchester Comrades are sending a contingent".

"That will make nearly a hundred present", Tryphena said.

"Yes, indeed", the baker said. "This is a little place, but if a hundred gather in Condicote it means that a thousand will gather in Tatchester and tens of thousands, perhaps, in places like Leeds and Liverpool. We're straws maybe, but we show how the wind is blowing. Let the tyrants give heed, I say, if they've the sense in them to give heed".

"Now don't go woolgathering, Bob, looking at those pigeons", Tryphena said, "but listen to your father's earnest words. You've got a father to thank God for. Your father's meeting this evening may alter the course of English history. Remember what the martyr said when he was going to be burned, that he would light such a candle as would never be put out, and that's what your father's going to do this evening in Condicote".

"By the way", his father said, "you've got the afternoon off, Bob, from half-past-two. You're sure that Joe's boy knows all the places he's to deliver at"?

"Yes, Father", Bob said, "I'm absolutely sure".

"Because you go off, I don't want a lot of people complaining".

"That will be all right, Father; it will be delivered".

"Now, about tonight's meeting", Engels said. "I've been up and about, speaking as the occasion called, and I'm none too sure of what this meeting is to be about, nor what you want me to say. It's about your slums, I think you said".

The baker seemed a little perturbed at this.

"It's all in the file of the Yockford paper", he said. "It is to be about the slums. But what would be best, would be if you'd slip over to see them, when you've finished your dinner. We'll all slip over. It won't take ten minutes".

"I can't come", Tryphena said, "but it won't take you long".

"And Young Hopeful can come too", Engels said, watching to see Bob squirm at the suggestion. "He ought to begin to see these things with the people's eyes".

When they were in the street, Engels said,

"By the way, Rob, you've been very good in all you've subscribed to the *Banner of the Cause* and the other matters, but there's one thing I want to ask you to do, and that's to come down with some blunt to help defend old Olio, as we call him. His *Light of Freedom* has been doing a lot of useful work, and now it's charged, or he is, with a criminal libel, and unless we can raise the fifty quid or so the *Light* will have to stop printing. Could you be good for say fifteen or twenty quid? I would ask for thirty, but you've been so kind already".

Bob knew that any appeal for one connected in any way with the cause of radical reform would move his father. His heart sank at the size of the sum demanded. How could this drain on the purse go on in addition to all the other drains, the payments for the little halfpenny weekly sheet, the hiring of rooms for meetings, the charity which forebore to press for debts and the righteous but imprudent anger which ignored the coming of a dangerous competition?

"Why, times are none too good", the baker said, "but with the wife and her stocking, we can make it fifteen quid, I hope. Now, this is the place I want you to talk about. This is Fever Alley. The next court to it, just down the street there, is Muck Alley, which I'll talk of. I'll fire the first barrel. You fire the second barrel, and between us we'll bring some fine bird down, I don't doubt".

They were in the road which led from the market place to Tibb's Wharf. Just behind them was the public house, the *Drop of Dew*, where the meeting was to be held that night. The *Drop of Dew* somehow shewed that although it was in a bad neighbourhood, it was not the pub used by the people in the courts. It belonged to the main street, and kept its skirts about it to avoid contamination. Three low beer-shops further down, the *Four All Round*, the *Quart Pot* and the *King of Prussia*, were the houses used by the courts. All those were in full Saturday harvest at the moment.

"I don't see any alley", Engels said.

Indeed, the street opposite the *Drop of Dew* was

bordered by the ruins of a brew-house, long since out of use.

"It opens from this entrance", the baker said.

The entrance was under a part of the red brick brew-house. Looking through it, Engels saw a double row of red brick, tumble-down old houses with a good deal of black timber work in their fabrics. The alley between the houses sloped down to what had once been a brook but was now a kind of open drain into which four or five generations of alley dwellers had flung old kettles, worn-out pans, broken crockery, stones, ashes, fish bones and parts of cabbages, rags, old corsets and the remains of shoes. As the brew-house wall kept the south wind from breathing upon that bank of violets, those dwelling in the Alley got its full fragrance. There were seven houses on the one side and ten on the other.

"Why is it called Fever Alley"? Engels asked.

"They had the fever very bad there a long time ago", the baker said. "I don't know what fever; but a lot of people died. Gaol fever, someone thought. But come and see Muck Alley".

Muck Alley was much such another place, but smaller. It was a single row of seven little old houses which faced the backs of the western row in Fever Alley. It, too, led to the brook, which was used as an open drain. Both alleys swarmed with white-faced, vicious, swift, eager, rattish children, nearly all barefooted, all dirty and verminous, some half-clad, the others over-clad, in clothes sewn on so that the clothes should not be stripped and sold. These were shrieking as they darted about, some were fighting, some were weeping or being knocked about by parents goaded beyond endurance by the worries of being alive, or partly or wholly drunk. The place swarmed with people, and stank with the devastating stink of human poverty.

As they stood in the entrance to Muck Alley, two little boys came whining up for alms, saying that Father would beat them cruel if they got nothing, which was no doubt once true, but Father, at that moment, was in gaol for knocking the mother's ribs in. The baker gave them a penny.

"Why do you give them money"? Engels asked. "This place does not need peace but a sword".

The baker put a hand on Engels' arm and drew him to one side. A man with a swollen face who had come from one of the houses, was moving towards the entrance where they stood. He was muttering to himself; he was in drink and truculent with it. Behind him, one of his party, but keeping out of range, was a white-faced toothless man attended by a boy.

The purple-faced man went past them, muttering how he would bash them if they said anything to him, and so he would show them. He went out into the street, and on with his friends towards the *Four All Round*.

"I pulled you out of that chap's way", the baker said. "He's a man called Fight Rapp, and when he's drunk he's very dangerous".

"I'd have called the other man the dangerous one", Engels said. "Who was he"?

"A man they call Twister Cag".

"About these alleys: have they any water"?

"None laid on. They get their water from the town pump in the market place. They've two privies in Fever Alley and one in Muck, to serve the lot of them. They've three hundred people, mostly children, in the two courts. But come along out of it, now. I've got to get back. There are twenty-four houses in the two courts. They were built, I found, in the year 1795. The figures for the building I got, too. They cost £1900 to build in the money of that time, and they've been in demand and full ever since. There's no other place they could get for anything like the money. Now each room of those twenty-four houses will let for from two to even four shillings a week, and the smallest has four rooms. The property has brought in, I don't doubt, over £300 a year for pretty nigh eighty years, or twenty-four thousand quid, and that's allowing for repairs. They're always full. If you'll go in, you'll find sometimes six or seven people in one room, men, women and children, old, young, sick, dying and all sorts. Just up the street there, you'll see a brass plate with

'TOM'S CHARITIES'

on it. That's where the agent is. He's a pretty hard man and has need to be. He gets the rents out of them or turfs them out of the place. He gets a kind of living from it. The rest goes with the rest of the rents from Tom's Charities to the Church of this diocese. And in those dens you'll find incest, bastardy, theft, rape, drunkenness and violence of all sorts, with no child that isn't a thief or a beggar, and no woman who hasn't to be a whore when times are hard. Just now, its harvest, and they've all had harvest money; but in the winter, the good God alone knows how they manage; but what with theft and the rest they do, those that don't die. That's the Church's property. That filth whitens the surplices in all this diocese".

"Well, we'll see what we can do about it", Engels said, taking a final peep into Fever Alley. He was greeted with a volley of ends of cabbage stalk from a group of little boys, who fled, after firing, through the filthy gutter at the end of the row of houses.

As they walked back to the bakery, Engels said,

"You know, you used to be very keen on the cause in your young days. Then, when you came down here, we couldn't get you to do a thing. Now you're all keen again. What set you going again"?

"As to that", the baker said, "I don't believe you'd quite hold with it. But it sprang up between me and the wife from reading in the Bible. I know you are all for the new revelation, of Paine and that; but, in a way, all revelation brings folk to the truth. In our case, we got reading in Isaiah. There's a piece:

'Now, therefore, what have I here, saith the Lord, that my people is taken away for nought? They that rule over them make them to howl, saith the Lord; and my Name continually, every day, is blasphemed. Therefore my people shall know my Name: therefore they shall know in that day that I am He that doth speak; behold it is I.

'How beautiful upon the mountains are the feet of him that bringeth good tidings, that publisheth peace'.

"Well, we read that on a special evening; and suddenly we both felt, that it was meant for us. It had a light all round it, as we say; and indeed, Ad, I can't tell you the joy it has been since, to bring good tidings. Ah, it consoles one for everything to feel the Lord with one, and we two have felt Him".

Engels did not understand this, so said, "Ah, I'm sure".

"Now, Rob, that is too bad", Tryphena called. "You haven't had the plums I got specially for you and Mr. Engels. Sit down again and forget the alleys till tonight".

They sat again at the kitchen table.

"Will there be many of the gentry, as they call themselves, there tonight"? Engels asked.

"Ah, no; they won't trouble us".

"Oh", Bob cried, "I'm afraid I forgot. The Rector asked me to ask, that you would keep two seats, one for himself, and one for his wife, tonight".

"Where and when have you been seeing the Rector"? Tryphena asked.

"I went there after the mixing this morning", Bob said. "I always go for five minutes every Saturday. He told me I might".

"That's true", the baker said; "but I did not think that that still went on. D'you mean that you've been there every Saturday all this long time"?

"Yes. When he's been there".

"Well, you've kept very dark about it. And what do you do there in your five minutes"?

"He hears me my Latin", Bob said.

"Latin, eh"? Engels said. "Well, a dead tongue is a mark of the dead, if you ask me".

Nobody was asking him, but his position in that house made the remark a cruel thrust at Bob.

"There's Mrs. Pouncer for her tea-cakes", Tryphena said, seeing the shop door open. "Run up to the bake-house, Bob, and see if Joe has done them yet".

Bob was glad of the chance to avoid more questioning. He ran to the bake-house, where he found the tea-cakes just done, and breaking beautifully into their quadrants. He packed them on their edges into their wooden tray, brought them down to the house, where his father put them into paper bags for Mrs. Pouncer. As he went back to his place at table, something in his pocket caught Tryphena's eye. She rose from her seat as though to look at the fire, made a sudden pounce and pulled out the protruding volume. It was a school edition of the first two books of Virgil's Æneid, edited with notes and a vocabulary.

"What is this book, that you've got, Bob"? she asked.

"The Rector lent it to me", Bob said.

"Answer my question, Bob. What book is it"?

"It's a Roman poem", Bob said, "all about the founding of Rome".

"Let me see it", the baker said.

He took it, looked at it, and weighed it in his hand.

"I wonder the Rector can't find something more Christian to lend a boy", he said. "Can you read this, Bob? It's in Latin, isn't it"?

"Yes", Bob said. "I can make out some of it. The Rector explains the bits which stump me".

"That has always been the trick of the ruling classes", Engels said, "to try to bribe the clever ones away from the workers, with a little sop of learning or a coloured uniform. Latin, eh? while the workers are eight in an eight-foot room not a hundred yards from this door".

"How long have you been at this Latin"? the baker asked.

"He didn't learn it at Miss Cockfarthings, that I'll be bound", Tryphena said.

"Nor at the Academy", his father said. "Mr. Uley specially said he would have English boys taught none of that foreign nonsense".

"Please, Father, I did begin to learn it at the Academy", Bob said. "Mr. Owlpen used to give me half-hours at it sometimes on the half-holidays, when he found that I wanted to learn it".

"Mr. Owlpen"? The baker and his wife looked at each other. Mr. Owlpen was still talked of in that quiet town. "That dreadful man"?

"Yes", Bob said. "And then, a year ago, when I was going to be confirmed and went to preparation classes at the Rectory, the Rector saw me looking at his Latin books, and asked me if I knew any. And then he offered to lend me some; and last winter, he let me come in from time to time and taught me a lot, but his wife said he was too busy and I mustn't come there any more. I've read some Latin books right through, some Caesar and Ovid. That is, what are called books; they are really only sort of chapters".

"And what use do you expect Latin to be to you, Bob"? his father asked. "You will not find it of use to you in a bakery; I can tell you that beforehand; and you'll not find many in Condicote that will welcome you for it; quite the reverse".

"Perhaps Young Hopeful is aiming for the Church"? Engels said.

"It's very interesting", Bob said, "and I enjoy puzzling it out. And then, it is sometimes exciting; the words all mean such a lot. And then, it was the language here in England, for hundreds of years".

"Well, it hasn't been for hundreds of years", his father said, "and for the future, I hope we'll hear no more of it. Latin may be all very well for a man like the Rector, who has had to learn it, perhaps, for his Scripture reading, but you're going to be a working baker; and there's no doubt of its being the wrong thing for you. So no more five minuteses, please, at the Rector's back door. If you want to study, let it be something that you can make your blood boil for and give your life for, something with living men and women in it. I can give you a subject for study; so can Mr. Engels here. Go down by the *Drop of Dew* there, and turn to the right, and you'll smell a subject, Christian England, 1870, odd, with forty-seven people in one eight-roomed house, and one privy, shared with a hundred and fifty others. You'll find a man with six children living on six shillings a week; and a girl of sixteen keeping her bed-ridden mother by prostituting herself; and these are not the worst cases nor anything like the worst. That's what I call living subjects, my lad; study those, and don't muddle your head with a lot of idle gentry's knowledge. You're a working boy, not an idler living on the sweat of others while you stuff your brains with folly. Your subject is the life of your fellow workers, not a lot of dead stuff. You come to the meeting tonight, and you'll hear a trumpet blown, please God, that will rouse your dead nature".

He had spoken earnestly, and as usual in such cases, he had become carried beyond himself, into a quick excitement. He was a slender, active man, of more than the middle height. His hair, which had been black, was now grey. He wore short, mutton-chop whiskers. His eyes, which were very dark, had a good deal of fire in them. He was much bent; he stooped in his walk much more than most men. He had what was then called a baker's face, or flour face, the sort of pasty pallor caused by much inhaling of flour, stooping over mixing troughs and toiling by hot ovens. Excitement always made his white cheeks flush in bright red spots, and his breath to come pantingly, with some exhaustion. He seemed exhausted now.

"There, there", he said. "I must keep quiet for to-night, or I shan't be able to make my voice heard".

"Now, you see, Bob", Tryphena said, "you've tired your father, with your Latin and all. Do run off to deliver the bread, for goodness' sake. But, before you go off, Bob, I want to know what you're going to do this afternoon".

"I was going fishing", Bob said, "after I've delivered all the bread".

"Who are you going with"? the father asked.

"I was going with Gregory and Polly Collier".

"Who's Polly Collier"? Tryphena asked. "She's not go-ing to go fishing with you, I hope".

"No, it's Timothy Collier", Bob said. "We call him Polly because he imitates a parrot so well".

"Where are you going to fish"? the father asked.

Bob dreaded a question of this sort because Tryphena had a way of coming down to watch at any decided ren-dezvous. If she came to watch, she usually interfered. Bob had learned that it was not safe to tell the exact place.

"We haven't decided quite", he said. "There's a very good eel-place up above the mill".

Tryphena had no intention of walking far in that hot afternoon. She did not press the matter of the fishing-place, but she said,

"There's one thing I do insist, that you don't come in all plastered with mud. You've got to be neat for the meeting this evening, and your trowsers have to do you till Christmas.

"It's always the way with the young", Tryphena said,

"to wear their parents dizzy. If I didn't watch Robert day and night, he'd be worn to a ravelling with worrying after Bob. But there; I can keep Robert quiet this afternoon, that's one good thing".

"I'll be off up to the bake-house", the baker said. "I'll finish off there, and then I can deal with the counter".

"You'll deal with no counter", Tryphena said. "I'll deal with all that. You have to rest against tonight".

"Ah, rest", the baker said. "There's rest in the heavenly home, they say, but in an earthly home, it's wiser not to try it".

He rose from his place, with a nod to Engels, and the remark,

"You're for a walk in the woods, I think you said. You know your way. There'll be tea along about five, the same as at the Duchesses".

As he went out to the door and up the yard, it seemed to Bob that he had never seen his father so bent, nor so excited. Plainly the evening's meeting was more than usually important to him. He had always been a quick, impulsive man, prone to take things hard, and to work himself into a fever about the things which worried him. When a thing worried him, he was unable to judge between the thing, which might be trivial, and the worry, which might be intense. He seemed now to be in a fever which had made him exaggerate the importance of a little gathering in a back street in a tiny town in an unimportant county to the beginning of a new social philosophy.

Tryphena cleared away the baker's plate, and offered Engels another blue plum, (he took two). She was what people called "a fine figure of a woman". She had a fine figure, well-made and erect. She carried herself well. People often noticed her carriage, and looked after her. She had some good features, a strong nose, handsome dark eyes, and abundant, fine dark hair. Her skin was not clear; she had a tendency to pimples; and her mouth was not well-formed. Her ears were not shapely. The fashion of the time made it difficult for her to hide these behind her hair. The big, ebony cross which she wore as a brooch upon her chest was not worn in vain show: she was a deeply religious woman. She went much to church, forgave much, gave much in charity and consulted the Bible for guidance daily. She was a very good woman, quite without thought of self when misery was there to be relieved. For some years now, she had lived in great happiness, believing that the Lord was with both her and Robert, and that He was leading them in the way they should go. She was at one with her husband in the countless generosities of his present mood. She believed that the Lord had led them both to a sense of what their life should be, and that their duty in this life was two-fold, to find misery and relieve it, and to find evil and expose it. Having perceived their duty, they both did it.

It is fair to say, that their eyes had not long been opened to their duty. They had lived, as they put it, in darkness, till the Lord had opened their eyes on an unforgettable day by lighting up a text of Isaiah to them. Since then, they had followed the light, with the result, that many people in Condicote were asking if Tryphena were quite sane, and saying that the baker might make very good bread, but that he did not know which side it was buttered.

Though Tryphena was a good woman, and a devoted, if somewhat short-sighted and unworldly wife to the baker, she was not a good mother. She had an active conscience and strove to do the right, but she was not fond of Bob. All her motherly feelings were with her dead daughter, Tryphosa. Her first child, the boy, had been a sickly, puling little creature, who had died in the first six months of life. The daughter, Tryphosa, had lived to be three years old, and had died of measles when Bob was in his first week of life. Tryphena had been unable to bear a child and play the part of sicknurse, so Tryphosa had been left to the mid-wife and had died. "My darling little Osie" Tryphena called her.

This always sickly, and now dead child, remained in memory and in fantasy as an important figure in Tryphena's daily life. She was ever present in the mother's mind, now as a grown-up figure, to whom she could turn for companionship or counsel; now as a radiant, lovely being, who would sweep into the room, take her in her arms, and cry, "I have come back to you, Mother; you must have known that I would. The Prince, my husband, is in the coach without, and only waits your bidding, to come up to pay his respects to you"; and then again as the little child who had died, not dead, but recovering from measles, rising from bed, and coming to look at her little new brother, not yet christened Bob. Her day dreams about Osie varied daily, but these were the three main myths with which Tryphena's mind was filled. She had always deep down within her soul a grudge against Bob, as the real cause of darling Osie's death. Had Bob not been coming then, she could have nursed little Osie through it, but she had to bring this great clod-hopping boy into the world, and was looking after him while her heart's darling was being torn from her. It did not bear thinking of, but she indulged herself with a great deal of thought on these lines, and was often unjust to her son, and not very helpful to her husband because of it.

She was the daughter and sole child of a Yockford tailor. Her mother had died when she was little; her father had married again. As she did not get on very well with her step-mother, she had made a life for herself by helping in the parish work of one of the parishes. She visited the sick and did the altar on Saturdays. She also volunteered to attend a bleak room, every Saturday night, which a bold curate opened for political discussion. The room turned out to be a great success. As many as twenty would turn up to debate there. She, with her rather bold beauty, was a success as a hostess. She met her husband there.

When the baker had gone, Engels tapped out his pipe, filled it and lit it. It was a way that he had. He did it immediately after each meal without asking leave from Tryphena. Bob knew that Tryphena loathed the smell of tobacco, and loathed Engels yet the more.

"Rob is keen about this meeting tonight", Engels said. "I hope it will go well. The countryside needs stirring up. We haven't got the liberty or death boys that we had in the Chartist times when we first met. Folk have grown too fond of their own skins. I'd make it a question to be asked of every member, 'What have you done to get yourself hanged for the cause'? I wouldn't let anybody speak who hadn't risked prison for it. It isn't like it was. When I first met Rob, at my father's bakery in Red Lion Street, we'd thirty men in the bakery trade alone, not going out of Bloomsbury, who had done their month, and sometimes more. How Rob kept out of it, I can't think. Did he ever tell you how we smashed the Judge's windows that time, after the Lambeth meeting was dispersed, and Old Potts sentenced"?

"No, he doesn't tell many tales out of school", Tryphena said, "and I don't ask. He had to come back to Condicote just at that time, or he would have been in prison, the time you were there. Perhaps it's all for the best. If he'd been in prison, he wouldn't have come to the meetings at Yockford, and I might never have met him. You can't have prison, and a wife, they say".

"I'll be getting along", Engels said, "to stretch my legs".

"If you're going up the Stanchester road", Tryphena said, "Bob would give you a lift that way, in the bread van".

"Well, I'd like that, the first mile or two", Engels said.

"Well, run along then, Bob, and fetch the van", Tryphena said, "and take Mr. Engels with you as far as he wants to go".

Bob had not very much command of his face: few boys have. A momentary look of sea-sickness crossed his face. It was not missed by either Engels or Tryphena, who both put it away for future use. Bob had, by this time, finished his dinner.

"Will you come along, then, Mr. Engels"? he said.

"No, no", Tryphena said, "get the van ready and bring it to the door for Mr. Engels. Surely you know your manners better than that".

Bob went out to put Old Marrowbones to. He heard Engels say,

"Young Hopeful doesn't take very kindly to me", and Tryphena answered,

"He's all set on his books, his bathing and his fishing. Read, read, read, and bathe, bathe, bathe, and fish, fish, fish. I keep telling him that the one will give him water on the brain; another water in his blood; and the other the inward damp, as they call it; but it's no good talking to the young".

Bob brought along the van. Engels clambered up onto the driver's seat. They drove under the archway into the street, and away, Engels puffing at his pipe, Bob cursing his luck in having the beast.

"So you are going fishing, eh"? Engels said.

He looked round into the body of the van, where the bread and buns for delivery were stored. In a corner between loaves was a somewhat grimy towel. Engels reached behind for it, and pulled it out.

"What have we here"? he said. "Bathing towel, and bathing drawers, I suppose".

"I thought we might have a dip, if it keeps as hot as this", Bob said.

Engels unrolled the towel a little, expecting to find within it a catapult which he might either confiscate or report to the baker. Inside the towel there was no catapult, but a roll of turkey red.

"What's all this"? he said. "Very odd bathing drawers".

"Oh, that's not mine", Bob said.

"Well, what is it"? Engels asked. "You couldn't bathe in this, or you'd have all the bulls after you".

"Do bulls go after red"? Bob asked.

"So they say", Engels said. "Might I ask what you are doing with it"?

"Taking it to its owner", Bob said.

"Well, I wouldn't wrap it up in a bathing towel", Engels said, realising that there was something fishy about this red cloth. "You see, some of the red has come off on your towel already".

As they turned out of the street towards the country, they passed the corner house which bore the big blue sign with the gold letters,

WYE & SON
THE CONDICOTE STEAM BAKERY
BEST HOUSEHOLD AND CONFECTIONERY
WE MOVE WITH THE TIMES

At the door of the bake-house yard, a smart van was drawn up. It, too, bore the legend "WE MOVE WITH THE TIMES", and indeed, plainly had moved, for the van driver, Bert Leadon, looked derisively at Bob and called,

"What? Only just setting out? Why, we've finished delivering half-an-hour ago".

This was by no means true; he had only delivered along one of five roads, but it was a bitter job, because Bert had for a time been the driver for Bob's father, and had lost his job when Bob had become old enough to take it.

"So that's the rival firm"? Engels said.

"Yes, that is the steam bakery".

"How much is it a steam bakery"?

"It has a mixer which works by steam. They can do three men's work with the mixer easily".

"And it is a rival firm"? Engels said. "It has given you a bit of trouble"?

"Oh, I don't know", Bob said. "There's room for two. This is a little place, but it's a very big parish, and the farms aren't doing so much private baking as they used to do, not half as much. Twenty years ago all these farms did their own baking, but not now".

"What made Wye & Son settle here as bakers"? Engels asked.

"Oh", Bob said, "Old Wye owned the mill out towards Yockford there, and young Wye thought that he could run this as well".

"And it seems that he can", Engels said. "Why doesn't your father put in a steam mixer, and smarten up his van a bit"?

"I should think it's rather a costly matter, to put in a modern steam plant", Bob answered. "Then, you'd have to have somebody who understands engines, and Father doesn't, and I don't, and I'm sure Old Joe doesn't. Then, there's the question of the lease. I don't think we're allowed to run a steam engine. But you'd better ask Father about that; I really don't know".

He was not going to discuss his father's business, if he could help it, with this loathly creature, but the loathly creature kept on.

"I should have thought that a bright lad like you could have buckled to and learned how to run a simple engine", Engels said. "That would be more to the point than Latin with the Rector, I should have thought, and better fun, too, to the normal boy. But, of course, although I've been here forty years, I don't pretend to know the English; they're beyond me. I suppose your family has been a long time here, settled into the business, which has just gone on of itself".

"We've been here about a hundred and fifty years", Bob said. "Before that we lived up to the north of this. I don't know whether you know the walks round here, but there's a lovely foot-path up through the woods there, and from it you can get out onto the downland, as we call it".

"Oh, I've been that way", Engels said. "I don't think I'll go that way this afternoon".

Bob's heart sank. He had hoped to get rid of Engels at that point. He did not know that Tryphena had asked Engels to try to find out from Bob what he was thinking on various points. Unfortunately, both Tryphena and her husband looked on this man as an apostle of the Light, as a leader of thought, and one of the great men of his day. There would be no other foot-path into the country for three-quarters-of-a-mile. They drove on through the hot autumn afternoon.

"I suppose the fact of the matter is", Engels said, "that you're like the rest of the boys of this time, you're too big for your boots, and despise the lot you were born to. You want to learn Latin and be a gentleman, instead of being a baker first, and seeing that all bakers and their men shall have the right to learn Latin if they want to. Have you begun to think, by any chance, about what will happen if young Mr. Wye goes on absorbing your father's business"?

"Father hasn't talked of that to me", Bob said.

"No, but you've thought. What have you thought"?

"I haven't thought at all", Bob answered.

"I don't believe the English do think", Engels answered. "Whatever it is they do with their heads, it isn't thought. Both the nation and its individuals get tangled up in a kind of cobweb or sentiment and interests and God knows what, and they neither think nor do, till they must do one or the other, then God knows how, they get all the prizes. Well, the luck won't hold all the time. How'd you like it when young Mr. Wye offers your father a job as a pastry filler, and your mother a little charing once a fortnight"?

"You're taking a rather gloomy view of things, aren't you"? Bob asked. "We still supply the better gentry here. Father's still the best baker. Wye & Son have undersold us a bit with the poorer people".

"Well, that's what I call a real English answer", Engels said. " 'God give us still our old nobility'. A man whose pride it ought to be to make daily bread for his community, taking pride in only making for the Squire, a man who couldn't earn his bread in the open market in any way at all".

"There isn't a Squire", Bob answered, with a gleam of joy. "The Squire died years ago. It's only his widow, and she'd make a living in a city or on a desert island, or wherever you put her".

"She might make somebody make it for her", Engels growled.

At this point, Bob had to stop. Four small houses stood within two hundred yards of each other. Bob had to deliver bread at them.

At one of the four houses, the bread was taken by a charming young woman, for whom Bob had much admiration. She was dark, handsome, and only seven years older. As they exchanged greetings, a man's voice, within the house, asked,

"Who is that there"?

"It's Bob Mansell, with the bread, Father".

"Oh, well, tell Bob Mansell that I'm coming to speak to him".

In a minute, the father appeared. He was Captain Coln, R.N. He had given up the sea owing to a wound in the leg, and had since then lost nearly all his money, and lived there in his little cottage with his daughter and his books.

"Look here, Bob Mansell", the Captain said, "your father ought to give up this writing to the papers. You ought to see that he does. Look here at the stuff in this week's *Yockford Times*. I'll take a talk about my duty from my parson; but I'm damned if I'll take it from my baker. Will you just tell him that from me, in the most delicate manner in the world"?

Bob looked at the paper which the Captain held out for him. It was the *Yockford Times*, containing the last of his father's letters about the slums. He had not heeded the letter, nor any of its predecessors, but he had heard of them so often in the last few days, that he was beginning to loathe the thought of them.

"That's fine stuff, don't you think"? the Captain went on. "You just tell him from me, that he'd better leave all that to the deck department. I never saw such stuff, in all my born days".

Bob handed back the paper, saying that it was all true, as far as he could see.

"True"? the Captain said. "Very likely it is true; but how will stuff like that make it better? That's the good old English way, to go into hysterics about what does not concern you, and have your head in the mud all the time about what does. You persuade your father to make a better bread than he's been sending lately, or I'll be trying this new steam bakery by way of a reminder".

He went back to his inner room, growling about having

him up on the mat, by George. The charming daughter shook her head at Bob.

"You persuade your father to bake him some of those little hot penny loaves", she said.

Bob thought her an angel for those words; but they did not quite wipe away the pain of what the Captain had said. He went out to his van, hoping that Engels had tired of waiting and had gone; but no, there he still was, puffing his filthy pipe. They drove on.

"I suppose", Engels said, "that you don't care tuppence about these reforms that your father works for"?

"I don't know enough, yet, to be able to form an opinion", Bob said. "I ought to know more, first; that's why I'm so keen on learning".

"Yes; learning from the rich", Engels said, "taking bribes to hold your tongue. That's all that that is".

Bob pulled up at a cross-roads.

"I shall have to go along here", he said, "but quite the best bit of the woods is reached by that foot-path there; that is, if you want a walk in the woods".

"I suppose, if I walk in the woods, some flunkey or other will stop me for fear I might disturb the pheasants", Engels said.

"No, not over there", Bob said. "Those woods aren't preserved. You won't find any keepers there, nor any pheasants. All that side of the road belongs to Lady Crowmarsh; she doesn't shoot".

" 'O woman in your hour of ease' ", Engels growled. "Do you hear anything of your grand relatives, by any chance? Do you see the great Dixon family"?

"No", Bob said, "I never have seen any of them".

"No, I warrant not", Engels said, "but they are your kin. Your father's mother was a Dixon. He often told me about her. Did he never tell you"?

"No", Bob said, giving up all hope of getting rid of the beast for the present, "I just knew that she was a Dixon".

He drove on towards the gates of Sir Hassle Gassle, up a deep lane or gully, and then up a slope where once a gallows had stood; it was still called Stretch Neck Lane.

"Ah", Engels said, "your grandfather didn't like baking, and went into the sporting world. He began as a jockey, and rode some very good matches till he put on flesh and couldn't make the weights. Then he took a pack of hounds; oh, yes, he did; you could do that in those days; a subscription pack. He ran the hounds and got his sport out of the subscription. He was said at the time to be the best man on a bad horse in all England. It was there that he met Miss Dixon out in the northwest there.

"She was the beauty of the west, they say. She had had scores of offers; sirs, lords, and all sorts; but she scorned the lot and ran away with your grandfather.

"Well, that was the end of the subscription pack. They wouldn't have him any longer, and he could never get another. But he went a fair pace with a lot of other things.

"There wasn't much left of him when I met him, what with wine and women; but he once had been 'Handsome Frampton'. He told me that himself, so there couldn't be any doubt of it".

"When did you see him"? Bob asked.

"Oh", Engels said, "I saw him in London when I was a young fellow".

"And did you see the beautiful Miss Dixon"?

"No, she was dead by that time, and glad to be dead. Your grandfather was living then with a barmaid, a Welsh girl with a high colour. Ann her name was. They lived at *The Maypole,* up Seven Dials way. It was a flash pub, kept by a racing man, Jack Randle, or some such name. Your grandfather lived there till the place came to grief, and then he died in a livery stable. Your father was then a little boy.

"It was your great-uncle, who was then the baker here, who stepped in then. He took your father away to Condicote here, and presently sent him to my father's bakery in Red Lion Street, to learn the job. That's your family tree, and that's how I came to know your father".

All this was news to Bob. He had heard nothing of the kind from his father and mother. He was thrilled to hear that his grandmother had been the beauty of the west. He wondered if his father had any miniature or other portrait of her. He wondered why his parents had never mentioned his grandparents to him. Then he reflected that his father and mother were very strict Puritans. They would not approve of a beautiful lady who made a runaway match, nor of a sporting parent, jockey and huntsman, living in a pub, in sin, with a barmaid, and dying afterwards in a livery stable. No, they would not at all approve. No wonder they had not mentioned them. Still, he determined to ask his father about the family history later.

They drove on. Bob turned into the gateway to Sir Hassle's mansion. It had been built in the days of the Waverley novels, with an eye to romantic effect. The gate bore carven beasts of stone upon its pinnacles. Some people said that the beasts were hassles, others said that they were gassles, others that one was a hassle and the other a gassle, but nobody was quite sure. Some ill-meaning people had suggested that, perhaps, an ass had been the model for one and a goose for the other. A tiny Gothic lodge, with a turretted top, stood on each side of the gate, which now stood open; the lodge keepers were not visible.

At a little distance from the gates, the drive forked; the main sweep continued to the left, to the front door; the lesser way, which Bob took, led to the tradesmen's entrance, where he delivered the bread to a somewhat cross elderly woman, who said that she had been waiting ever so, and why couldn't he have come earlier, and she had a very good mind to complain.

At this, Engels suddenly interfered, by saying that it was like a flunkey to try to bully a tradesman. Let her pay for her bread herself, he said, before she took it on herself to speak like the mistress of the house. Let the mistress complain, and she might be listened to, if she spoke to the master, but that, for his part, he could not understand how it was that flunkies were allowed such insolence. A good mind to complain, indeed. A sour old frump, who lived by ministering to the idleness of the rich, to complain because the bread just out of the oven had not come sooner. Go and buy your own bread, and then you can complain, and be kicked out for your pains.

The attack was very brutal; it shocked Bob, for he knew that the old woman, though often crusty, was also often very kind, and this kind of attack, upon any woman, made him flush with distress and rage. The old woman trembled at the insults, and asked who was he to speak to her like that?

"Never you mind who I am", Engels said. "I'm a conscience, perhaps, coming back to this land that has lost it.

Another time you may not be quite so ready to get one of your own class into trouble".

The old woman said, that if the butler had been there he would never have dared to speak to her like that.

"The butler", Engels said. "Butler, bring me a clean glass; the under-housemaid looked at this one, and damned near poisoned it. I suppose you are the under-housemaid".

"I'll find out who you are, you may be sure", she promised, with her face twitching to keep back the tears.

Bob hurried to lay the loaves on the shelf appointed for them, and to be gone from the scene before the quarrel went further. He shook up Marrowbones, swung himself up into the driver's place, and then very politely took off his cap to the old woman and said,

"Good afternoon, Mrs. Skudgell".

He made haste to be away.

Engels said aloud, "The old trot, she may not be so uppish next time".

The next instant, they were round the great clump of laurels which hid the back door from the front. There on the grass border, looking at them, was Sir Hassle Gassle himself.

He was a spare, wiry, hatchet-faced man of about sixty-five or seventy. He had hard, pale eyes of a sort of steel colour, a face almost colourless, a mouth like a slit, which had certainly never kissed nor laughed, though it often sneered and sometimes snorted. He was a hard man to others in all dealings, but whether he was hard in himself, no one could tell; he had not been tested by life. There he stood, grim and erect, staring at Engels and at Bob.

A wave of terror swept through Bob; he took off his cap hurriedly, but received no answering salute from Sir

Hassle, who stood still, staring. Bob guessed at once, that he must have overheard some of what had passed. If he had been there when Engels had spoken, he might well have heard it all. The two doors, though centuries and miles apart in the social order, were very near in physics. The earlier Hassle, who had done very well in Army contracts in the Napoleonic war, had skimped his architect in the matter of the servants' quarters, and had trusted to the laurel to grow quickly and hide their nearness.

"He heard it, he must have heard it; now there'll be a row", Bob groaned to himself. He knew that Sir Hassle was his father's landlord, and by no means an easy one in case of any trouble. "Oh", he moaned to himself, "why couldn't this beast have got down at the woods, and not come up here at all"?

"I suppose that that's the robber baron", Engels said, "the great, broad-shouldered genial Englishman". He leaned back round the edge of the van, and called, "Good afternoon, Lord Livertwinge. Are the pheasants promising well this year"?

"Oh, hush", Bob said. "I shall be in a fearful row for this. He's our landlord. He'll get me skinned alive for this".

"Rats", Engels said, "he can't. Anyhow, he's not my landlord, and I'll say what I like. I'm not one of this race who never will be but always are slaves of some sort. A ramrod with a liver complaint isn't going to bridle my tongue, and if I may give you a bit of advice, I wouldn't let him bridle yours. Gods, I learned in youth what these fellows are. They don't impose on me. So he is your landlord, is he? What sort of rent does he charge you"?

"I don't know", Bob said, "A good deal, I think, for we

are right on the market place. Forty pounds a year, I expect. Sir Hassle owns all that side of our street, pretty
nearly".

"Yes, and the Church owns all the other side", Engels
said. "I know the game of property. And how long have
you Mansells been bakers in that house? Over a hundred
years, I suppose, and all paying twenty, thirty or forty
pounds a year to Livertwinge. You've toiled and sweated
all a century or more to give Livertwinge two or three or
four thousand pounds. And what have the Livertwinges
done for you in that time, except to put up your rent when
times are good, and distrain your goods when they aren't?
Why, they don't even give you common civility. Their
very flunkeys insult you, like that old trot at the door
there. And has Livertwinge ever tried to give you a modern
bake-house, with all the new equipments, patent mixers,
the new style oven, in return for all your thousands of
pounds; for it is thousands by this time? You know quite
well that he hasn't. Yet his rents have made it impossible
for you and yours to put them in for yourselves. And there
he stands and stares as though you ought to thank him for
letting you live, while the dog owes his butler to you and
a lot besides. Don't tell me about your Livertwinges".

"He sends all his tenants a brace each of pheasants,
every Christmas", Bob said, trying to stem the tide of contempt, in which he himself was involved.

"Pheasants"? Engels said. "A lot of tame birds, bred
to be shot. Why, they would perch on the guns, very
often, they are so tame. They have to be scared, or they
would never know they weren't domestic poultry. Then
the Livertwinges shoot them and send them as sops to all
the folk they rob, and then write to the papers to say what

manly fellows they are, all caring for Field Sports. You English want to clear your minds about essentials, my lad, or some other race will do it for you, in a way you won't relish. Now, I'm getting off here to walk a bit, to get the taste of Old Livertwinge off my mouth".

At this, he swung down from the van, and over a stile, which led to a field and small covert of Sir Hassle's. Bob drove on, thinking that it was all very well for Engels, who wasn't an Englishman, and didn't live in the district, to stir up these troubles, but for themselves, who had to live in the troubles after they were stirred, it might not be quite such fun. In any case, he would probably get the rough edge of Mrs. Skudgell's tongue for the next three months, even if Sir Hassle did not act.

"Why can't the beast keep to his own side of the fence"? Bob muttered. The warning of his friend Gregory came back into his mind. What if this fellow Engels were one of the dangerous men. What if he were sent to stir up troubles, and to drive desperate men into crimes like rick-burning? There had been rick-burning at odd times in those parts. It was still talked of with fear.

Times were bad in the countryside; the harvests had been poor for some years; the harder farmers, who ground their men, had had ricks burned, though people had hinted that the farmers had done the burning themselves, to get the insurance. Still, as Bob knew, the country gossips were always full of malice and uncharitableness. He had been brought up among people who had had the idea burned into them, that any loosing of any existing bond would let into England all the horrors of the French Revolution. He did not know what the horrors were, except that the guillotine cut off a lot of heads. What if Engels were really one of that kind of revolutionary, bent on getting a lot of heads cut off? What if his father were to join with such?

He drove on, worrying about what Sir Hassle would do. He knew, from Sir Hassle's face, that he would do something. What could Sir Hassle do? Could he prosecute Engels, for using language calculated to produce a breach of the peace? If he did, then he, Bob, would be called as a witness, and would have to tell in court exactly what had been said, and then all Condicote would say,

"What a dreadful thing that is about the baker; sending this revolutionary to insult people as he delivers the bread. I always did think Mr. M. queer; now, I know it. They say they have a plan all ready made, for killing the royal family and setting up a republic; and, of course, the bakers are in it, for they can stop supplies, or even poison them at the source", etc., etc.

He knew very well how the tongues of the ignorant old gossips wagged, over their tea and shrimps. Altogether, he was a much worried lad, so much worried that he had little pleasure as he drove in thinking, as he had thought for the last three days and nights, of the adventures planned for that very afternoon.

Somehow, the taste for that high adventure was spoiled by the image of Sir Livertwinge, with the ramrod figure, the bloodless face, and pale, inhuman eyes, standing on the grass border of his drive, staring at the critics of his power.

However, he was young: the job in hand needed some care and attention. His next delivery was up the road a few hundred yards, at the cottage of a dressmaker who lived with her mother. Here he received a welcome, a piece of cake, a cup of tea, and a copy of an old Chambers'

Journal. After this, he felt less troubled. His next stop was at a farm, a little beyond, then at a cottage, then at a little old mill, no longer in use as a mill, at the point where a lovely brook went over the road. After this, he took a turn which set him on the homeward journey, and now his heart felt lighter, and the prospects of the fun more alluring.

His task of delivering bread on each baking day gave him time for some of his studying. He had a habit of memorizing lists of Latin words while in bed, either at night, or before he rose in the mornings. At first, he had made himself learn five words a day, with their peculiarities and properties; then, as his memory grew stronger, he had risen to ten, and now made himself learn twenty. He was rigorous with himself, too; the twenty had to be known, and the work of the last week had to be gone over mentally. Then, in addition to the list of words, he had lately set himself to learn and translate five lines of Latin verse each night. As he drove on this occasion, he repeated his twenty words and five lines from Ovid which he had learned in bed the night before. The hot September day burned upon a world fast turning brown. Old Marrowbones switched at the flies. Whenever he stopped he heard a great drone of insects in the air, and the cooing of many wood-pigeons. Then, from time to time, the peace and quiet of the afternoon was rudely interrupted by the thought of Sir Hassle and of what might be happening even now at home.

"The worst of it is", he thought, "Sir Hassle will probably write to Father, and Father will get the letter on Monday morning. It will all be held over till then, and that is the kind of thing I loathe, waiting for the blow to fall".

At last, all the bread, rolls, buns, cakes and fancy work had been delivered. All the round which he had undertaken had been made: Jack would deliver the rest. He was driving home. In a few minutes he might be free for the long-planned adventure; but would he be free? Many times on Saturday afternoons, on his return from his rounds, he had been checked from freedom in the past. Often, as he drove into the yard to put away Old Marrowbones, one or other of his parents would cry,

"Oh, is that you, Bob? There's a basket made up in the bake-house to go out to so-and-so".

Many a good half-holiday had been spoiled thus in the past. As he drove down the village street, he thought that, quite possibly, he would find, on arrival, a stern message from Sir Hassle, insisting on an instant apology; or perhaps, what would be equally bad, a complaint from Sir Hassle as to the quality of the bread, as an excuse for bringing him up there once more for a real dressing down. Somehow, he knew that he would get the blame for what Engels had done. Such would be the worst that might happen: the next worst would be the one or other parent leaning out of the window with a message of what he was to do next.

The village street was still busy. There were many carts, traps and gigs standing by the pavement edges. Many people had come in to do their week-end shopping. He knew that the bakery would be busy, too. He turned into the archway to the bake-house yard.

As he drove in, he saw his mother busy in the shop and

waved to her. Joe came out of the bake-house to help
load the van. Jack, Joe's son, came out to take over the
van. Mr. Mansell was lying down, resting, they told him.
Bob, feeling that the Fates were now relenting, helped
to load up the van. Jack knew all the people on the beat,
but Bob went over their names in case he should have forgotten some. As Jack shook the reins and set Old Marrowbones out into the street, Bob knew that he was free. A
half-holiday was a rare thing to him nowadays; he meant
to enjoy this one to the full.

He might have gone into the shop, to say good-bye to
his mother, but he knew the danger of this. So often, his
mother would ask him to do some little thing and then
when that was done, perhaps another. He could not run
the risk of this. Instead, he walked swiftly to the low
brick wall at the back of the bake-house yard, over which
Gregory had escaped earlier that afternoon. In a moment,
he was over it, in the waste where the Abbey ruins
stood.

Although it was so close to the backs of the houses on
the main street, the Monastery close seemed in another
world. It was all thickly grown with grass, now matted
and tussocky. Somebody had driven a cow there to browse,
or the cow had contrived to get there. There was no other
living thing in sight, save jackdaws on the stumps of old
ruin. Bob ran across the waste, and clambered over another tumbled wall, which had for years been a quarry for
people wanting stone. Then, he was free to pursue his
adventure to the full and the thought of Latin grammar,
and of the angry Sir Hassle went utterly out of his mind.

On the other side of the swing bridge at Tibb's Wharf
he caught sight of the figure of Polly Collier, a pale-eyed,

rather dreamy-looking boy, who had been at the Academy with him, and was now back from a year at a school at Tatchester. He was going to begin in his father's iron-mongery at the beginning of October. Bob had not seen very much of him until the beginning of the summer holi-days, but now they were close friends.

"It should be lovely weather for it", Polly said. "You're in very good time".

They walked on, side by side. They were now well away from the little town, and heading for the country.

"I saw an old friend of yours yesterday", Polly said. "I've been up in London, stopping with my aunt. I saw Old Owley, selling matches in the Strand. He didn't rec-ognize me, but I recognized him all right. It was Owley, sure enough. So, as I went past, I said,

" 'Don't you know yet that you're a giddy goat, Pitch-combe? You must write it out another twenty times, I see'.

"He heard all right, but he didn't seem to notice. He was in a kind of daze; and when I went back and walked past him again, there was something very funny about his eyes; the pupils were all shrunk to nothing. That was a sign that he'd been taking opium. That's what you'll get, Bob, you know, if you go swatting your brains with books, the way you do. Brains weren't made for books: there never was a book yet that did a man any good".

"I expect that's the burglar's idea of laws", Bob an-swered. "But one man's poison is another man's meat. Was poor Old Owley very ragged"?

"Dressed off a scarecrow", Polly said, "but, of course, a lot of those chaps like to have holes in their clothes, for then people give them more. And I don't think you need pity him: he's probably happy; he's down where he'll stay. Now that he's fallen, he won't have to dread the fall. Golly, you used to make me sick, the two of you, sitting in that beastly little bedroom, with him spouting filthy poetry, and I nudging you to come away and have a run in the fields, and you there, with googly eyes, just lapping it all up. Caw, poetry! He was a balmy old bird, Owley, and I'd love to have seen that time when he took off all his clothes and said he was a pussy-cat, in the market place".

Owley was the master who had shewn Bob some of the delights of literature.

They walked on. At a little bridge over a brook, they found Gregory, lying prone on the bank, with a stick in his hand.

"Hullo, Greg, what are you up to"?

"There's a water-rat's hole just under here", Gregory said. "They're going in and coming out all the time".

"Well, we've other fish to fry this afternoon", Bob said. "We'll be off, so come along".

Although Bob had a taste for what Polly Collier called "filthy poetry", and spent quite a lot of his working day in repeating lists of Latin words with their meanings and peculiarities, he was still a boy and delighted in the adventure stories prepared for boys. Some of his scanty pocket-money went to the purchase of a monthly periodical called *Tom Goneaway's Adventures*. He had been following Tom Goneaway from his school days some years before to a stirring late boyhood passed in many parts of the world. In July, the monthly number had been "Tom Goneaway's Adventures in the Bull-ring". This had fired Bob's imagination. There in Condicote he could hardly hope to meet with Chinese pirates, or Comanche Indians on the Texan

Plain, but a bull-ring of a sort Condicote could provide, and he had taken great pains to work out the details for a Feast of Bulls, in which he and his two friends might play important parts. His heart had been beating for some days with excitement over the prospect.

He was not wholly moved by love of adventure. He had been prejudiced against Old Neakings at Nonesuch Farm. Two years before, when he and Gregory had been stalking antelope at Nonesuch with catapults, Old Neakings had chased them off the premises, cursing. They hadn't hurt any of the antelope, though Old Neakings had sworn that they had put them off their lay.

Silas Neakings owned a very fine bull, called by the cowman Roxer, but in the stud book, and by Neakings himself, he was called Condicote's Astounder. As a rule, Roxer, who was a dangerous beast, was kept closely shut up in a rather dark pen. Often, when they were in the district, and the coast was clear, the boys had crept to the pen, and had gazed, either through the slats on the bull-pen door, or within the door, if they were lucky, over the inner gateway, at the beast's bulk and gloomy turbulent eye. Nonesuch Farm was a haunt of theirs. They knew the ways of the farm's inhabitants on all week-days and holidays. They knew, that on Saturday morning the cowman went early with Old Neakings to Tatchester beast-market, from which they didn't return till late in the afternoon, or early in the evening. As a consequence, Roxer was never watered until late on Saturdays. Then, Saturday afternoon was a drowsy time at Nonesuch. People were not about the house; the maids would be doing their ironing, and Mrs. Neakings taking a nap before tea. The men would have had their short day, and gone off for their afternoon at the pub. Bob had suggested to his friends, that on the first fine Saturday afternoon they should let Roxer out into the field, and play him as Tom Goneaway had played the six terrible monsters from the Herd of Death.

"Did you hear, Gregory", Bob said, "that Polly here saw poor Old Owley selling matches in London"?

"Owley"? said Gregory. "Oh, that master who got drunk. Well, he always was a queer one. He'd some bats in his belfry, if anybody had. D'you know, I tried to get some fireworks for what you said, Bob, in case the bull's sleepy, but they'd only got a few Catharine Wheels from last year, and those were damp".

"It's just as well", Bob said. "All the English fireworks that I've ever seen have to be set off with matches. We'd never be able to light them in a ring with the bull charging about".

"Well, the Spaniards do", Gregory said.

"Well, they've probably got some sort of trigger that ignites them", Bob answered, "but our English sorts haven't. Besides, if you go letting off fireworks you'll have everybody in the farm running out to see who's poaching in their field".

"I half thought we could get a dog", Gregory said. "My brother, Diggory, has got a terrier".

"No, no, we want no dogs", Bob said. "They would yap and snap: they would be as bad as fireworks. You'll find that people running about with red banderas will excite the bull quite enough for anybody".

"Those big bulls like Roxer", Polly said, "they won't be like the real thing. He'll be heavy, like a great cart-horse. And then, the field won't be like the ring. The field down by the river's sure to be a bit heavy in the going: it won't be like a bull-ring, nice hard earth floor, just sprinkled with sand to keep you from slipping".

"Ah, you wait, Polly", Bob said. "I saw one of these big bulls going for a dog once. When he means business, a bull like this can go pretty fast; and he's got four legs, remember, while we've only got two".

"That doesn't make any difference", Gregory said. "That's a fallacy. We can go as fast on our two legs as any beast can on four".

"Well, I don't believe that's so", Bob answered. "It means that he's got four engines for travelling, where we've only got two".

"I think a great bull like this will be pretty dull to play", Polly said. "It won't be able to turn. He'll just make a blind lunge, and then go on to the end of the field".

"Well, we shall soon see", Bob said. "I expect he'll charge all right, as soon as he sees the banderas. You be very careful, you keep the banderas at arm's length. That's what the man told Tom Goneaway. Don't play the toro right onto your body".

They clambered into a narrow strip of ash and hazel spinney, which ran by the edge of the little river. In its covert they went cautiously forward, watching the trees ahead for any movement of bird or rabbit which might betray the presence of men. All was undisturbed till they themselves disturbed the quiet there. Soon, they crept to the spinney hedge, which was low but stout.

"This is the barrier of the arena", Bob said. "This is what we may have to run for".

"It isn't very high", Polly said. "Do you think Old Roxer would jump it after us"?

"I asked the cowman that very point", Bob said. "He said that a bull or a cow for that matter can very seldom jump. They haven't got the loins for it. And in the ring in Spain the barriers are quite low".

"They'd be higher than this", Polly said.

"Yes, of course", Bob said, "for they have spectators on the other side, and the bull might reach some of them with his horns if the barriers were as low as this. But this will be high enough for us, you'll find".

"It seems to me", Gregory said, "that he might charge right through it after us".

"Rats. It's a pretty strong fence".

"Yes, and the bull's a pretty strong thruster; he weighs a ton and more. A ton and more charging at twenty miles an hour comes with an impact of twenty tons. That would burst down a fence like this, like matchwood".

"If he does, then we shall have to dodge him, and play him back into the arena with our banderas. He'll go after the banderas anywhere".

From far away, on a waif of the summer wind, there came the blocking clop of a cricket bat upon the ball, and the faraway cheers of, "Well hit, sir", from spectators on the cricket pitch. Somehow, Bob thought that to be swiping a fast bowler to leg for six in the quiet of the cricket field might be better fun than being Tom Goneaway in the bull-ring of Sevilla, with the Terror of the Herd of Death about to come through the doors.

They were all crouched down close to the fence, peering through into the arena. No one was there to interrupt the Feast of Bulls. They saw a big rectangular field, not less than six acres in all: this was the arena. On its northern side, it was fenced with a tall, thick, thorn hedge, well-

ditched towards their side of it. They might, if sorely
pressed, fling themselves down into the ditch; it was a
deep ditch; the bull might not follow them down into it.
Opposite to them, on the western side, was a similar hedge,
very thick, tall and strong, with no possible escape for
them if the bull chased them that way. To the south, lay
the farm buildings, and yet another hedge which ran
down to the western hedge.

"Now you see", Bob said, "we must play the bull always
towards this side of the field, and never let him get any
of us to any of the other hedges. If he does get over or
through this fence after us, then we shall have to leap into
the river. He won't follow us there. But, I say, that he
won't come through the fence, and can't jump it".

They looked with emotion at the quiet arena. A few
rooks were pecking grubs down at the lower end of the
field. It seemed to Bob that he saw a mole heave up yet
another hillock of soil not twenty yards from him. The
place was quiet enough now, but in a few minutes, when
Tom Goneaway had pitched his cap into the ring, and had
advanced upon the bull, that quiet field might be noisy
enough, with the roar of Roxer, and the cries of all Sevilla;
the deep, coughing snarl of a bull fetching breath, and,
perhaps, the death cry of one of the cuadrilla.

It was no good waiting there till the cuadrilla's nerve
had gone; they were not looking too eager for the fray,
even now.

"Come on", he said, "we'll get nearer to the farm, and
see if the coast is clear". He saw that his cuadrilla would
have welcomed the appearance of anyone in that field, as
an excuse for postponing the fiesta. "Come on", he said
again.

He led the way cautiously along the spinney towards the farm. The place was deserted; now and then a bird went up before them. Now and then, in the little river beside them, a water-rat dived with a little plop, or some stone, loosened from the bank, collapsed with a tinkle of following soil. Bob, who was leading, held up his hand; the cuadrilla halted. Bob pointed to his left front.

From where they were, they could see the red brick wall of the byre which was Roxer's home, with the closed door which was soon to be opened. Near it a couple of bold rabbits from the spinney were humping about, grazing; plainly, the people of the farm were not about.

Beyond the byre, at some little distance, were the buildings of Nonesuch Farm, old even for farm buildings near Condicote. They seemed like the buildings of a place in a dream, asleep like the dreamer. The white fan-tailed pigeons on the roof were asleep in the sun; no noise of work could be heard; the only moving things there were the fox on the wind-vane above the barton, slowly swaying as a tiny gust caught it, and a thin, faint wisp of smoke going up from the twisted chimney.

"It is absolutely safe", Bob said. "You see; not a soul stirring".

He pointed to show the quiet scene, and at once at his gesture a blackbird went out of the spinney with a cackle, and the rabbits turned round and raced home to the spinney near them. The suddenness of the alarm brought the boys' hearts into their mouths; they waited on edge for Old Neakings to appear with his usual challenge,

"Now, out of that. I see you. I know who you are. Give yourselves up now; you're surrounded".

They counted ten, then twenty, yet no Neakings appeared; nor did anyone. The place slept on, as though it were high siesta, and no feast of bulls to be that week.

"It's all right", Bob said. "Neakings is at Tatchester, so is the cowman. I told you that they would be".

They waited yet for half a minute, but no alarm came; they had the place to themselves.

"Now then", he said, "we'll begin. We'll draw lots for which shall be which".

Bob had always felt that it was a mistake to leave this business till the last moment, but Polly had been away and the matter had not been settled. Each boy knew, that the chief man among the toreros is the espada, the man who delivers the sword thrust, and that it is to the espada that the hats, cigars, rings, fans, purses and flowers are flung. Their hero, Tom Goneaway, had been an espada, but he had also done something which thrilled the boys even more. They knew that the espada deals with the bull who has been wearied by vigorous, intensive playing up and down the ring. Another figure of the bull-ring seemed to them to be much more worthy of admiration. To them the most daring man among the toreros was he who pretends to be a statue, when the fresh bull first comes romping and roaring forth from the darkness of his pen into the excitement of the ring. The man, dressed in white, stands perfectly still; the bull, on seeing him, nearly always charges, or advances to the attack. If the man remains perfectly still, the bull, in ninety-nine cases out of a hundred, does not charge home, but pauses, stares, reflects that the figure is probably stone, or a tree-stump likely to hurt the head, and then moves away. In the hundredth case the man may flinch, the bull may see some movement of life, or a draught of wind may flutter the white robe; or perhaps the bull may be a bull of genius, very dangerous and unexpected; then the bull does charge home and the man is killed.

To each boy there this solitary figure seemed the hero of each Feast of Bulls, but now that they were coming to the ring there was not any great yearning in any of them to take that office. They were not so sure, that the bull would hesitate; they were not quite sure that they could remain motionless as the bull drew near; and they knew now that their companions were not so skilled in playing bulls away from a threatened comrade as these trained men in Spain might be.

"Now, look here", Bob said, plucking three blades of dead grass from a tussock, "here are three blades of grass. This long one is for the statue; this next one is for the sword; and the shortest is for the opener, who will let the bull out. You see these three pieces, long, middle and short. Now, we'll blindfold Polly, and he shall draw them from Gregory's hand. He shall draw first for himself, and then for Gregory. Are you agreed"?

"Yes, that seems fair", they said.

So they took one of the red banderas and blindfolded Polly.

"Wait a minute", Polly said. "We ought to say the fortune-teller's prayer first".

"All right", Bob said. "What is that"?

"Oh, it's what one always ought to say before casting lots of any sort. Take off your caps, now, and I'll say it".

They took off their caps, and Polly said,

"Direct us rightly as we draw,
According to Thy holy law".

It was plain from his voice, that he hoped that the holy law would not give him the long grass; but it did.

"Well, you're the statue, Polly", Bob said. "Now, will you draw for Gregory"?

If he had not been a little shaken by the blow of fate, Polly would have repeated his prayer, but he did not. He drew, and held up the blade.

"Well, Gregory, you're sword", Bob said. "That leaves me to be the pen-opener. Are you all content that the lots have been quite fair"?

Now that it came to the point both boys were perfectly content that it was not to fall to them to let the bull loose.

"Absolutely fair", they both said.

The statue looked out upon the field, and judged the easiest bit for a speedy rush to the little hedge of the spinney.

"Now, we'll get Polly ready", Bob said. "We'll dress you up in the bathing towels, Polly, and then you'll look just like a statue".

"Whereabouts would you like me to stand"? Polly said. "There's a good flat bit there which would be firm in case I have to run for it. Would that be too far from the bull-pen, d'you think"?

No, it seemed to the boys that that would suit very well.

"Remember, if you're absolutely pressed", Bob said, "you have to plunge into the river".

"He'll plunge after me", Polly objected.

"No, he won't", Bob said. "Bulls don't like getting their feet wet. Isn't that so, Greg"?

"Yes, I think I've always heard", Gregory said, "that bulls don't like getting their feet wet. Wild bulls used to get stuck in the mud, and then the wolves could eat them, and their fear of the mud has remained with them ever since".

"I expect you'll find one thing about this bull", Bob said, "that he won't have much staying power. He may be fast for a minute or two, but then he'll be blown. He'll be like that pig we chased of Old Callows'. He was blown in no time. You see, he's never really used his legs. He's not like a bull from the Herd of Death".

"I was reading in the paper", Gregory said, "of a thing they do to bulls on the plains in Texas. You dash alongside the wild bull on your pony, and swing onto the bull's back from your saddle, then you twist underneath the bull's neck, and catch his nose between your teeth. If you do that the bull is absolutely helpless".

"I should think you'd be, too", Bob said.

"No, you aren't", Gregory answered. "You take the bull in and brand him. It's called, 'bull-dozing' ".

"I should think it ought to be called, 'bull-nosing' ", Bob said. "But, we can't do that, we've got no pony, and I wouldn't trust my teeth. But you see, Greg, the bull would only have to put his head down, and there you would be, pinned to the ground. He would only have to turn his head sideways to gore you through and through. But, come on now; I think that makes Polly as like a statue as we can get him. Now, what do you say to going out into the arena"?

"All right", they said, and each one anxious that the other should not see his funk, advanced, clambered over the hedge and strode out into the ring.

"Now, the first thing we must do is the trumpets", Polly said.

The boys stood still, put their left hands to their lips and blew an almost silent fanfare, hoping that nobody would hear them from within the farm buildings. Then Gregory, as the espada, took off his cap and advanced to the imaginary president, and said,

"We have the honour to come before you and consecrate our lives to the playing of your bulls, in a manner worthy of this city, and of so noble a president".

In a falsetto voice which represented the president's wife, Polly Collier said,

"We expect no less from your valour", and pitched a key to him, which Gregory caught in his cap.

Gregory handed the key to Bob. Members of the cuadrilla bowed to the president, and with a gesture moved to their places, Gregory unfolding a bandera, Polly taking his place as near to the fence as honour would permit, and Bob walking slowly along the spinney hedge towards the farm buildings. He was telling himself as he went, that they were going to do a very crazy thing, and that it might not be such fun after all to be chased by a bull. To be caught by a bull would be no fun at all. He had known a little boy in the town caught by a bull. He had gone into the pen to tease the bull, and the bull had finished him. Then there was Old Sammy, only the year before, who had been used to bulls from childhood, and a bull had suddenly turned upon him, and crushed him by kneeling on him. However, the eyes of all Sevilla were on him at the moment. He left the shelter of the fence, and moved down the wall of the cow-byre to the door.

A swallow flew in to a late nest in the roof of the barton. There were little cries from the young ones, who would be deserted in a day or two, for they could hardly be

ready for the migration. Close to the door was Roxer's
watering-place, a big, iron cauldron under a pump fed from
the stream. It was full of water.

Bob stood at Roxer's outer door and looked about him.
There was no sign of life from the farm. In the field behind him, a rook rose, flopped, and then went on with his
grubbing. Roxer's door was not padlocked, just closed
with a hasp and staple secured with an old wooden peg;
but what, if when he opened the door, he should find
Roxer loose inside, not shut up, as usual, within an inner
pen? What if at the first half-opening of the door a furious
and thirsty Roxer should burst forth? It did sometimes
happen, that the cowman neglected to close the inner pen.
Thinking this, he dropped the peg from the hasp, and
opened the door a very, very little. It was dark within. He
had to open the door more widely. There was no cause for
fear. The inner pen was shut, and within it was Old Roxer,
who had been lying asleep, or chewing the cud. Roxer
rose up with a heavy lurch, and regarded him sullenly
out of an evil eye. Bob looked at him. He had been told
that the human eye had great power over animals. He
stared at Roxer: Roxer stared back, and then, presently,
lowered his eyes and tossed his head. The swallows flew
in and out. The little ones in the nest cried at each visit.
There in the corner of the pen, near the door, was the bull-
hook used by the cowman in taking Roxer to water. Bob
took it, thinking how grand it would be if he could hook
Roxer by the nose with it, and lead him, thus hooked, into
the presence of all Sevilla waiting there in the sunlight.
It was a temptation, for he had often envied the cowman
the power of leading a bull by the nose; but he put it
from him, being not quite sure that he would be able to

unhook it, and if Roxer were loose in the ring, dragging the bull-hook, he might very likely trip and break a leg. He was somewhat scared of Roxer, now that it came to the point. He seemed about as big as an elephant, and there was a gleam in his eye which showed that a valorous devil was burning under his ribs. Roxer tossed his head, and scraped with a fore-paw. Bob knew that in another instant Roxer would be pressing at the gate of his inner pen, and that then he would not be able to unhasp it. He swiftly unhasped it, and stepped back with it into the retreat prepared. He had feared, that at this point Roxer might go for him, but Roxer was thirsty, and paid no heed to him. He moved out directly to the watering-place, and greedily drank, then stopped, while Bob heard the water dropping from his muzzle back into the tank; then seemingly lowered his head again, and drank still more. This was not like the first bull which Tom Goneaway faced; that one came out romping and roaring, and charged within twenty seconds of his entrance into the ring. What if Roxer, from force of habit, or dislike of the flies, walked back into the pen after drinking? Such things happened even in Spain. Sometimes a bull, even from the Herd of Death, would refuse to fight, either from indisposition or genius or dislike of the crowd. Roxer seemed to finish drinking. Nothing happened. He did not move away from the tank, but seemed to have done with his drink. What was he doing? Supposing Roxer was just creeping on tip-toe back to the door to have a sudden stab at this unusual figure who had turned him loose? Animals could move silently when their enemies were near. Though he was scared lest Roxer should be creeping in just outside the door, the longing to know made him peep out. Roxer had moved from the water, and had dropped his head to some of the sparse grass not trodden out of life at the watering-place. He didn't look at Bob. He did lift his neck, and toss his head uneasily in the direction from which the light air was drifting. He lumbered out a few steps, put down his head and cropped the grass. There wasn't much good in it, but he cropped from force of habit and paid no attention whatever to Polly Collier, standing stock still in bathing towels less than a hundred yards away. Gregory leaned against the spinney fence, only fifty yards away. Bob waved to Gregory; Gregory waved back; Polly stood still, and the bull went on grazing. It was not thus in Spain.

Bob thought, "Of course, part of what excites the bull in Spain would be the thousands of people shouting. And then, of course, in Spain the picadors prod him up with lances. I wish we could stir him up a little".

He shook his hand at Gregory, as an indication that Gregory should waggle a bandera. Gregory took his flag and waved it, but Roxer paid no attention whatever.

Gregory had one gift which Bob had always envied. He could put two fingers into his mouth, and blow between them a very shrill whistle. Dropping his bandera, he now blew such a blast. Roxer lifted his head and stared fixedly, then turned to graze again. Gregory repeated the whistle, and as the bull looked up, Gregory seized the red flag, and waggled it vigorously. Unfortunately, it caught in a twig of the fence, and Gregory, with one eye on the bull, tried to clear it. The bull stared. Presently, his head dropped to the grass; he grazed, but with an eye towards the statue and Gregory. Gregory released his red flag, and waggled it, but Roxer, for some reason, paid no attention to the red flag. He had begun to perceive the statue. When he had come a few steps nearer to it, he ceased grazing, and looked fixedly at it. He stamped once or twice, thrust out his great head, tried to snuff its scent, whooffed at it, to attract its attention, and then stamped again.

"Now, it's beginning", Bob thought.

He left the byre door, crept out behind the bull, and edged a little nearer to the fence. The bull paid no attention to him. He was trying to think what that small white figure could be. It was something like the pump in the yard where he had been a bull calf, yet it wasn't quite like the pump. It was something like a tree-stump against which he had sometimes rubbed in the lower pasture, but it was not quite like the tree-stump. It was rather too like one of those little men in smock frocks who had helped to put the ring in his nose. It might be a good chance to get his own back. Very suspiciously he lowered his head to the grass. He would watch this thing, whatever it was. Bob felt that poor Polly Collier must be going through a pretty grim strain. Bob slid over to Gregory.

"What we really want is fire crackers", Bob said, "as we haven't got picadors. I think we'd better wait while we count thirty, and then we'll run out with our flags. But we must separate. We mustn't all be near the fence. I'll get round to his other side".

At this moment, there came an unexpected diversion.

There was, in Condicote, a broken-down sporting gentleman, known as Old Ratty. He had two dogs, Mungo and Pongo, both half-bred and very powerful, always together and very well-known. Ratty had taken these dogs for a walk; had gone into a near-by pub for a dram, and the dogs, growing tired of waiting had come out upon a roving cruise. They entered the arena through the fence exactly opposite Greg and Bob. At once they saw the bull, and agreed upon a plan of action. As they entered the arena, the bull saw them, and at once faced to them.

Mungo and Pongo came on together with their eyes bright and their tongues hanging out. Each knew exactly what the other would do, but both waited till the bull had declared himself. The bull quickened his steps, and advanced upon Pongo. Pongo darted in at him, as though to take his nose. The bull put down his head and charged him. Pongo, filled with joy, nimbly avoided him; Mungo rushed in, yapped at his hind legs and nipped him in the tail. The bull was pretty quick upon his feet. He swung round, put down his head, and charged at Mungo. Mungo avoided him, while Pongo leaped in, yapped at his hind legs and nipped him in the tail. The bull came round upon his heel, and charged at Pongo.

"I've had enough being a statue", Polly called.

He pitched his towels over the fence. He and the other two drew their banderas. The bull was fifty yards from them, facing round from dog to dog, with his horns weaving the air for the next charge.

"We'll give the dogs a breathing time", Bob said.

They waved their flags and advanced upon the bull. The dogs knew upon the instant, that the boys were on their side, and that now the boys were going to help to tire this quarry. They dropped down, and panted and watched. As Bob advanced, he could plainly see their tails wagging with delight.

"Call 'Dilly, dilly, dilly' ", Polly said. "It's said to infuriate a bull to have 'dilly' said".

"Dilly, dilly, dilly", they all called.

They waved their flags at arm's length, and repeated "Dilly, dilly, dilly. Come, good dilly". It may have been infuriating to the bull, but Roxer was now roused. He took a sudden decision, made up his mind that Bob was the danger, put down his head, and launched himself at him. Bob saw a ton of angry flesh hurtling towards him like a runaway traction engine, and Bob fled as he had never run in all his life. He flung away his bandera, and the next instant was over the fence into the spinney, scared out of his wits, and breathless; but the bull was romping fifty yards away, with his red bandera on one horn, and both the dogs hanging onto his tail, almost dragging him down.

He shook off the dogs, who scattered away as he turned upon them. Bob felt his terror drop from him; he scrambled back into the arena, waving a spray of hazel, which some nutter had wrenched off in the spinney and left. He seemed to remember that it was considered a great disgrace to lose the bandera in the ring. It was like the ancient soldier losing his shield.

"Stir him up again", Polly cried. "Hey, dilly, dilly, dilly".

All three boys advanced, waving and calling "Dilly". The bull was confused at the multitude of his enemies. He put down his head at Polly, but as it went down, both dogs rushed in, one on each side, snapped at his nose, then, skipping aside, nipped him in the quarter. He changed his purpose, swung round and charged at Pongo with Mungo yapping at his hind legs, sometimes nipping him in the shin or in the tail. Pongo raced towards the further fence, with the bull making good time behind him. At the critical moment, Pongo slid to one side, and the bull's head tossed nothing; but the head came up; he faced round much more quickly than the boys had expected from so big a beast. His breath came in a kind of coughing snarl. He looked magnificent as he wove with his head, and prepared for the next attack.

"Dilly, dilly, dilly", said the three, advancing in a line towards him, each waving a red flag.

The bull looked from one to the other, and from the swiftness with which he wove it was plain that he would be at one or other in an instant, but like lightning both dogs were at him, right under him, snapping at his nose before he could even duck, and then from under his horns, in again at his hind legs; and as he lashed round at Pongo, Mungo got him in the tail, and swung round upon it. All three boys were bent double with laughter, but they wanted to give the dogs a breather, and by this time they had a contempt for their enemy.

"Dilly, dilly, dilly", they cried. "Come along, dilly".

They had no fear, just a pleasurable dash of excitement, and a sense that, for the first time, they were really living. This was the top of life.

Suddenly, there came an incoherent, loud, angry roaring of swearing, from the direction of Nonesuch Farm. Oaths, new and old, were on the air. Looking up, they caught a distinct sentence.

"What the hell are you playing at, you little devils"?

Mr. Neakings had returned from Tatchester Market.

"Oh, God", said Gregory.

There was Old Neakings, in his Sunday waistcoat, gasping oaths at Roxer's door. The cowman was running to him from the farm. After the cowman came Patch, a strad-dle-legged man, who did odd jobs for Neakings.

"Call your damned dogs off", the farmer yelled.

"We're trying to, sir", Bob cried.

At this instant, Roxer went off after Mungo.

"Come along", Polly said, "hop it".

It was very good advice. The three farmers were run-ning into the field now. The boys hopped over the fence into the spinney, gathered up their gear, and fled. They heard Old Neakings' oaths fly after them, that he'd have the law on them. He knew who they were. They ran on to the spinney end, well out of sight, over the bridge, and along the river beyond it, then up-stream, dodging behind the alder clumps. They were quite safe.

"Just the last thing we were thinking of, Old Neak-ings", Polly said, "then, there he was, roaring like Old Roxer".

"Come on, it's absolutely safe here", Bob said. "This is a lovely place. We'll stop here".

They flung themselves down to gloat over the joy of the day. The afternoon had lost its burning light, for the sun was merging into haze in the lower quarters of the sky. A few fields from them, the hill, known as Arthur's Camp, rose up, crowned by a covert black with yew-trees. At their feet was a still pool of the river, where they had often bathed. It was a reach perhaps ten yards long by five broad, nearly six feet deep; a few yards down-stream it wimpled away in clear water over a pebbly shallow. At this point a wooden footbridge and a footpath led towards Condicote, which they could clearly see, as a few roofs, a church-tower with golden birds on its pinnacles, and three masts pointing delicately above the barquentine at Tibb's Wharf.

"I don't want to fish", Bob said. "What fishing could come up to what we've done this afternoon"?

"Gummy, it was perfect", Gregory said. "Who could have expected that the dogs would join in? We may not have had all that the Spaniards have, but no Spaniard could have enjoyed himself more".

"I understand now", Polly said, "why the Spaniards love it so. Who on earth would go fox-hunting, or playing cricket, when they could have a feast of bulls? But I vote we put some lines out, all the same, in case we're asked about our fishing".

This seemed politic, so they took out their lines, baited the hooks and set them in the bathing pool; they did not expect to catch much, there being little to catch except sticklebacks and minnows; still, the hope and the presence of water made it a joy to them. They sprawled on the grass, looked at the sunburnt, autumnal country, and from time to time, feeling the late afternoon to be a little cooler than they liked, sprang up, and were again in the arena, playing Roxer. Then they would fling themselves down on the grass and tell over all the afternoon.

"Did you notice old Roxer's eye when he first got going"?

"Yes, I could have sworn that he was laughing. He enjoyed it".

"I'll bet that he did. After being penned-in all day, it was just sheer joy to him to go for somebody".

"He didn't enjoy the dogs. He meant to hoist those dogs. He was real wicked, when he went for the dogs".

"I wonder, does it hurt much to be tossed by a bull".

"They say not. They say you have a sort of dreamy feeling, till some time afterwards".

"I'll bet you have".

They heard men approaching the little foot-bridge, just below the bathing pool. Craning his neck a little, from his easy stretch on the grass, Bob could see who it was. Half-a-dozen men were coming from Condicote to the bridge. As they came into sight through the gap in the alders, Bob recognized some of them, as well-known bad characters from the Condicote slums. They were walking in no sort of order, just straggling along, yet evidently going together. They were led by Fight Rapp, who swayed in his walk, and muttered to himself, (oaths and threats, it seemed). It was plain, that the others let him walk in front because they were afraid of him. With a little drink in him he was a dangerous man. Bob noticed with amazement that Fight was carrying a double-barrelled gun, with which he kept threatening to smash in some imaginary enemy's head.

After him, at a safe distance, came Twister Cag, who, although little, was also dangerous. It was said that a bite from the Twister always festered. Just behind the Twister came three men with pale faces, whom Bob judged to be men from a town. They wore town clothes and cloth caps; he did not recognize them. After these, at some little distance, came the Magpie, who from time to time strayed from the party to the blackberry brambles and then, having eaten of the fruit, ran after them to catch them up. He carried a long thumb-stick. Last of all came two others, one of whom Bob recognized as a seaman aboard the barquentine now at Tibb's Wharf.

Bob whispered to Gregory, "Did you ever see such

cheek: Fight Rapp showing his gun in broad daylight?
They're off for mischief. They're out to get pheasants at
Arthur's Camp".

The party passed behind some alder bushes out of sight
from the boys. Their footsteps clumped on the little
wooden bridge; in a minute, they reappeared again, this
time on the boys' side of the stream. They were keeping
in the same order and holding the course straight for
Arthur's Camp.

"Good-bye, King Arthur's pheasants", Bob said.

"Yes", Polly said, "that's what they're up to. It's getting near the first of October. Those fellows have the
word from some London poulterer to get pheasants on the
market for the First".

"That's where they're going", Gregory said, watching
them. "John Okle, the keeper at Arthur's Camp, is away
at present. His old mother is dying".

"Some of them are splitting away", Bob said.

They saw that Twister Cag and the seaman had edged
away from the party towards the left. The path on which
they were led towards a pub.

"They're off for the *Garden Path*", Gregory said.

The other six went on to the right towards the stile,
Rapp still leading, brandishing the gun.

"I'm sorry the Magpie has gone with that lot", Bob
said.

"He's as mad as a hatter, the Magpie", Gregory said.

"He's liker an animal than a man", Bob said. "But
then, one likes a lot of animals. There's no harm in the
Magpie".

"He bleats at people at full moon", Polly objected.

"Only if they're wearing blue", Bob said; "and if you

tell him to run home, he always goes. But he is said to be a wonder at setting wires and night lines and he can shoot with a catapult like Old Nick".

"D'you think we ought to warn anybody that they're going to Arthur's Camp? Mrs. Okle or somebody"?

"Oh, no", Polly said. "They'll have extra watchers, never fear, so near to the First. Catch them not having".

They lounged about, hoping for bites, but not getting any.

"It's a lot too clear a day, if you ask me", Gregory said, "for any fish to be biting. I vote we have a look at those blackberry brambles".

They had a look at the brambles. It was a fine year for berries of all sorts; even now there were good berries to be had.

"There used to be nuts in the hedge two fields on", Polly said presently. "I vote we chuck the fishing and see if we can't find some nuts".

They pulled in their lines and sauntered off to the hazels; a few nuts could still be had there.

"Nearer the river there used to be some spindle trees", Bob said. "Let's see if we can find some spindle berries".

They wandered on, in the last of the afternoon, but could not find the spindle trees.

"There was a hornets' nest in a dead willow along here", Polly said. "I saw it last year. It's sure to be there this year. We might give it a poke round".

"No poke round for me", Gregory said. "Three hornets' stings'll kill a man".

"Well, that's the tree, over there", Polly said.

The boys had no great eagerness to try the poke round. On the dead limb of the willow they saw a hornet feeding.

"They fear neither God nor man, hornets", Gregory said; "and I've seen them bite through a butterfly net, just as if it were butter".

Each of them had some tale of the prowess of hornets.

"How would it be", Bob said, "if we finished up with a steeplechase, from where we are to the mill, and then across, up into the woods, and back into town that way"?

This seemed a very good end to the afternoon. They rolled up the feet of their trowsers, and away they went, forgetting about the bull-ring in the excitement of being sharers in the Grand National Steeplechase. The sun went down behind Arthur's Camp, but it was still bright daylight. Presently, they stopped at the wood's edge.

"I say, Bob", Polly said, "you haven't half torn your trowsers".

Bob had been conscious of a draught coming through, but in the excitement of the race he hadn't looked. When he did look, he was aghast.

"You'll be arrested if the policeman sees you", Polly said. "However did you do that"?

"It was getting through that last thorn fence", Bob said. "But I didn't think cloth would go like that. Golly, I am covered with mud, too. That was that deep ditch we all went into".

"It's no good trying to brush it", Polly said. "That will only make it worse. You'll only smear it. Leave it till it's dry, and then it will brush off. Anyhow, you can't wear it again until it's mended".

"Ah", Bob said, "I shan't half catch it for this. I was an ass to propose that steeplechase. Everything had been perfect until then. I wonder what the time is".

"Oh, never mind the time", Polly said, "Who cares

about the time? The only trouble about it is that it's coming to the end of the day, and it has been a day".

"Gummy, it has", Gregory said, "a jolly good wind up, I call it".

"I say", Bob said, "this is a stunning view. I never saw a sky like that".

They were high up on the little bare top of a windy woodland. All the great expanse lay below them in a glow of light, as though earth, woodland, river and hill were exuding light, breathing it, as it were, into the sky's face, till the sky glowed and was rosy with it.

"Golly, it is a lovely evening", Bob said. "Who on earth wants to go to a beastly meeting"?

"Hold on a minute", Gregory said, "there's old Condicote church clock".

The three boys listened, while far below them the sweet bells of Condicote chimed the preliminary chime.

"Quarter-past-five, I suppose", Bob said.

He waited, but it was more than a quarter chime. It chimed the half-hour, the three-quarter-hour, then the hour. Then it struck six, and presently broke into the music of "Disposer Supreme".

"Six"! Bob said. "Ruin stares me in the face. I was to be at the meeting at half-past-five".

"Well, you won't be", Polly said. "It'll take you seven minutes to get home, and at least ten minutes to get tidy. You'll have to change all the things you've got on".

"I shall catch it", Bob said.

"Oh, you won't", Gregory answered. "Meetings never begin on time. Besides, if you ask me, you'll be well out of that meeting, by what I hear. People aren't too pleased with your father for the line he's been taking, and I've heard more than one of them say, that he'll get stopped if he goes much further. He's been writing letters about Muck Alley, and he's made all the owners of the property furious, and the people of the Alley simply mad. They want to be let alone. It's none of his business to come poking into their affairs".

"Well, I stick up for my father", Bob said. "Christians oughtn't to be asked to live, or allowed to live, in places like Muck Alley. Now, I'd better bolt home, and please the Lord it won't have begun by the time I get there".

He slipped through the monastery ruins to the bakehouse yard; here he found the kitchen door key tucked under the mat. He let himself in. When he saw himself in the looking-glass, he was aghast.

His face was filthy, his hands black; but as for his trowsers, the one pair that had to do him till Christmas, ruin stared him in the face:

"See what a rent the envious Casca made".

That unseen thorn in the hedge had caught it in the seat and torn a triangle in it. Two sides of the triangle were free, the base still held it to the fabric, but even if it were neatly darned it would show; it would be like the broad arrow, it would stamp him as a criminal for days. And that was not all; he was plastered with mud from down by the river and from the ditches of the steeplechase. He knew that mud. It did not brush off when wet. It took two days to dry, and then had to be cracked or scratched off.

"O golly", he moaned, "I shall jolly well cop it this time".

The trowsers had to come off. The alternative, his old,

dark, Sunday knickerbockers, seemed hateful and very conspicuous; he could hardly bear the thought of going in to a meeting of perhaps a hundred people, and seeing two hundred eyes slowly turning upon his old Sunday knicker-bockers. Still, it had to be. Then, he had to wash. Then, he had to find his other pair of boots. Where were they? He had had them the day before, and had taken them down to clean; but he had not cleaned them. He found them in the boot-hole outside the kitchen. They were not clean; they were filthy, and with no trowser flaps to cover them they would not pass. He had to find a knife, then to scrape, then to blacken and polish them; all this took pre-cious time. Then he had to wash his hands once more. He was not tidy; he knew that he would not pass muster; he was not at anything like the standard exacted by his par-ents on social occasions; and then, in addition, there was this shocking lateness. What was the time now, anyhow? It had been six, up there on the hill; he was half-an-hour late then. It had taken him from seven to ten minutes to get home from there; and everybody knew that the church clock was always wrong; then, there had been all the washing and changing and cleaning. O Heavens, there was the church chiming the three-quarters-of-an-hour; it was a quarter-to-seven already. Then, there came the mem-ory of Sir Hassle Gassle; he had been driven from mind by the joys of the bullfight, but he came back now. He would hear something more of that, he was very sure. Then, what excuse would he have for being late? What if Old Neakings had recognized them? He knew them, more or less, and, though an old man will not know a boy as clearly as the boy will know him, by sight or reputation, yet when an old man once does know a boy for any cause he remembers him with much shrewdness and sometimes vindictively.

The afternoon had been too great a joy. Tryphena had always told him, that people were always punished for joys. Why, she did not explain, but said that it was well known and that it was divinely appointed so.

He had meant to take a clean collar and handkerchief; but he was in too great a hurry; the old collar had to do; after all, it had been clean that morning. He forgot to take any handkerchief; did not think of it till he was in the street, running down the little slope towards the *Drop of Dew*. As he ran, he felt for the handkerchief, for it was a maxim of Tryphena's that he should display three or four inches of white handkerchief from his breast pocket whenever he appeared in any company.

"Now, I've forgotten my rag", he groaned as he ran on.

He had not far to go; just down the slope and turn to the left and there was the old *Drop of Dew*, by the two Cockfarthings brothers. The meeting was in the long room, up a twisting stair, where the two brothers held a farmer's ordinary on every market day. In the narrow passage which led to the stair, he was stopped by a man whom he did not recognize.

"No. You can't go up till he finishes speaking. He's on his legs now and will be done soon, I should think. He can't be much longer", the man said.

"Can I wait here, then"? Bob asked.

"Yes, wait round here; sit on the stair", the man said. "But I can't let you up, for fear of putting the speakers out. They've nearly done".

"Can you tell me, please, if Mr. Mansell has spoken yet"?

"Oh yes, long ago", the man said. "He was one of the first. It's Mr. Engels at it now. You'll hear him if you listen".

Bob's heart sank a degree lower. He had missed his father's speech, and he had not meant to miss it. He could hear the snarl of Engels lashing round with vehemence in the upper room.

"Yes", he was saying, "we give them our tithes, we give them our taxes, we give them our toil until we die, and what do they give us, but a slum to breed in and a pauper's grave to rot in? What you see here, in the Church-owned muck-heap of Muck Alley, just across the road, you will see in some Church- or State-owned muck-heap in every parish in England. The people are patient; they haven't the life to be impatient. How can they have, ground down as they are between such mill-stones? But sooner or later a cup like this will be brimmed, and when that happens, I tell the owners, whoever they are, that they will feel a people's vengeance".

Engels sat down at this point. There came a certain amount of stamping on the floor, or rather the poking of sticks and umbrellas on the floor. It is possible that many of those who were there were not too eager to show public approval of such doctrine. Bob had thought that the meeting would end at this point, but, to his astonishment, he heard his father say, that the Rector had asked him if he might speak a few words before the meeting dispersed. There was a hush in the room upstairs: the Rector began to speak.

He began by saying, that it was a maxim that one should hear the other side; that this was a free discussion, and the value of free discussion was that both sides could be presented; that they had heard a good deal lately about the badness of some of the dwellings in Condicote, and of the great numbers living in those dwellings; but, then, one of the great problems of modern times was to house the population. Who was going to build the houses? Where were they to be built? And how would the inhabitants pay the increased rents that would have to be asked for the new houses? Large areas of some of the English cities had been pulled down by the orders of their health authorities, no doubt deservedly pulled down. The multitudes made homeless by the demolition had flocked into other areas, and had made those overcrowded. In some cities, improved houses had been built for the poorest of the population. It had then been found, that the poorest either could not pay the rents demanded, or, by their habits, rapidly made those houses as repulsive as those destroyed. He mentioned these facts, not because he meant to dodge the issue, which was certainly a Christian one. You should do to your Christian brother what you would like him to do to yourself. You should try to give your Christian brother as fair a measure of quiet, cleanliness, happiness, hope and health, as you would like yourself, and those about you, to enjoy. But he did want that meeting to realise that the matter was not as simple as it seemed.

As to the administration of the charities supposed to benefit from the rents of Condicote, he had nothing to do with it, and could not speak of them without some enquiry, which he assured all there should be made. What he hoped would be the result of these discussions, (and he hoped, that the discussions now begun would continue), would be the formation of bodies within the church membership resolved to better such conditions as Mr. Mansell had described. He, himself, he said, had not been very long in Condicote, and was now about to go to a London living, but before he left them he hoped that some such body might be formed.

He paused at this point, and then almost immediately went on, so that Engels had no chance of interrupting.

"Let us pass the next few days", he said, "in investigation of the trouble, and then submit to the administrators of the charities involved a report of what we find".

There came a murmur of approval and dissent from the company. The radicals were angry at having their fighting speaker put on one side by what they judged to be compromise. Bob heard Engels call out excitedly,

"That's the Church's way, to dodge a plain issue".

There came cries of applause from his supporters.

"Give it to him, Adolf. Dot the black rook one in the eye".

Then, suddenly, a man whom Bob did not recognize, but who seemed to be a sort of groom, came hurriedly into the passage.

"Is the Rector here"? he said. "Someone said he might be".

"You can't go up. He's still busy talking", the watchman said. "You wait a few minutes, and he'll be done. They can't be much longer now".

"I can't wait. It's a matter of life and death", the man said. "Poor Mr. Okle, the keeper out at Arthur's Camp, has been murdered".

"Murdered"? the watchman said. "For God's sake, who went and did that"?

"God knows", the man said. "Poor John Okle. God, I drove him from the station in my trap, from the five train this very afternoon. Some damned murdering poachers. The Magpie was one of them, they say, and that man with the bloated face".

"I'll go up", the watchman said.

By this time, the radicals had set going their heckling. Bob heard cries of:

"Don't shirk the issue, Parson".

"Good old Church. Take the tithes and anything else you can get. You'll pay us back in the next world, won't you"?

The watchman hurried up the twisting stair. Bob heard him say,

"Excuse me a minute, gents".

The meeting hushed suddenly; then Bob heard the Rector say,

"Something very terrible has happened. I am called away".

He came out hurriedly, nodded to Bob, and said to the groom man,

"Ah, it's you, Richard. Have you any trap or conveyance"?

"Just in the market place, sir", the man said, "but I've had a job to find you".

"Well, please Heaven, he be not dead", the Rector said. "Has the doctor gone"?

"He's been sent for", Richard said, "but he's gone out Wicked Hill way, by what I hear".

They went out together hurriedly. The meeting had gone off like a damp squib. The Rector had turned the dispute into a channel of discussion, and now this much more thrilling matter of a murder at their own doors made everybody eager to be gone. A dozen men were down the stairs, and seeing Bob they said,

"Have they gone"?

"Yes, they've gone", Bob said. "The man had a trap in the market place".

"Were you down here, when he came"? the baker asked. "Did you hear about it"?

"Yes, he said he was murdered by poachers. But the Rector said, 'Please Heaven he be not dead'; so perhaps he may not be dead yet. He said, 'The Magpie was one of the murderers and that man with the bloated face'".

"Rapp", the baker said. "But the Magpie would never be in a thing like that. He wouldn't hurt a fly".

"Father", Bob said, "I just want to ask your advice".

The baker saw the distress in his son's face, and drew him out of the press into the street.

"What is it, Bob"? he asked.

"I saw a party going towards Arthur's Camp; about half-past-four it may have been. Rapp was leading, waving a gun; and the Magpie was following them".

"Following them; yes, but there's no harm in that".

"The last I saw of them was, they were all going towards the Camp, and then two of them, a sailor and Twister Cag, went off from them altogether. The rest went on, straight towards the Camp".

"In that case", the baker said, "I reckon that you'd better come to the police station and tell them just what and who you saw. That is your duty as a citizen. It won't be a bad thing to go there in any case, to ask the news; not that they're likely to tell us, though".

He pushed back towards the entrance to the *Drop of Dew*, where many of the audience still stood, discussing not the meeting, but the murder. The baker asked Engels to see Tryphena home. He led Bob to the police station, two hundred yards away. On the way, he said,

"You're sure it was the Magpie, who was with them"?

"Yes, absolutely certain, Father; there could be no doubt. He never wears a hat, and his hair is unmistakeable".

"I'm afraid that's true", the father said. "Well, please God, the poor crazy creature wasn't made a tool of by some of these wicked ones. You'll have to tell the Inspector about all those men. You say the Magpie was walking last"?

"Yes".

The baker had some confort from this. They passed up the road to the police station, where a small crowd had gathered in the hope of news. With some difficulty, the two reached the door. The policeman in charge said that the Inspector was out at Arthur's Camp, but that he would take any story the two had to tell. Bob told what he had seen, with the exactest truth. When the policeman asked him what he and his friends were doing by the river, he said that they had tried to fish, and were fishing when the party passed, but having had no bites they had moved on picking blackberries, not long after the party had broken up. He finished with an estimate of the time at which the party had passed. It must have been half-past four or a bit later, he said.

As he finished, there came a noise outside. He thought that it might be the Inspector, with news, but it was not; it was a re-inforcement of police from Yockford. They had been telegraphed for an hour and more ago, and had come in on the evening train. The baker knew one of them, and asked him if he had any news.

"Yes", the man said. "It's murder, all right. Poor Mr. Okle was shot dead, from within two yards, Dr. Gubbins thinks".

"Now, none of that", the Condicote man said. "It will all be public news soon, without your telling".

The police were not anxious for Bob and the baker to stay, now that their story was told. On pressing out into the street, they saw a sort of sea of faces all upturned to the station door, and lit by the gas lamp above it. From the faces, there came a gasp of,

"It's the baker. It's Mr. Mansell. What's happened, Rob. How is Mr. Okle"?

"Killed, they say", the baker said.

"Killed. Oh, for God's sake".

"Who did it"?

"Poachers, they say", the baker answered, as he thrust into the crowd, so as to get home.

At this moment, there came a movement in the crowd, like a swell running through a sea. Half the crowd was asking, "Who is it? What is it"? The other half was saying, "They've got him, the murderer". Above all this buzz came the voice of Chief Inspector Drew, bidding people to "make way there: let us pass".

Bob and his father climbed up to the top step of the Rector's door. In the glare of the gas, they saw the Inspector with two policemen clearing a passage to the station. The two men had the Magpie between them. The crowd was falling away, partly from respect for the police, partly from terror of the touch of a possible murderer. Somebody said,

"It's the Magpie. He's gone raving mad suddenly and killed John Okle".

Instantly, this was taken up and repeated and embroidered.

"He was foaming at the mouth".

"These madmen will kill anybody".

"He ought to have been locked up long ago".

It did not seem to Bob and the baker that the Magpie was foaming at the mouth. He did not understand what was happening, but he would have been madder than he was not to feel some alarm at that crowd, and the menace of the police, who spoke so without passion, yet held him so tight. He tried to smile, but he was scared, and kept licking his lips. The crowd made way. The Inspector thrust on ahead, and called out to all who were in the station. With these a lane was cleared and the Magpie brought into his cage.

The baker took Bob home. Somehow, that evening had not gone according to any plan. The meeting had had no climax. This news, coming when it did, had ruined the meeting; it was not possible to think of the meeting, when a murder had been done only a mile away and a murderer was under lock within two hundred yards.

In the kitchen of the bakery, Engels tried to bring the talk to the point. He could not understand the English paying all this attention to a man being killed.

"I must say", he said, "your Church is something I can't understand. There it was, proven to be in receipt of tainted money, yet daring to get up and say that all was for the best and the best possible. But for the news coming in just when it did, we'd have given old sky-pilot the order of the boot. How did you think I went"?

"You were at your very best", the baker said. "You were just yourself at your very best, and I don't think that Tryphena nor I would ask anything better, would we, Try"?

"No, indeed, we wouldn't", Tryphena said. "It was wonderful. And how did you think my Robert went"?

"Not bad, not bad at all", Engels said, with condescension. "You still drop your voice too much though at the ends of sentences, and that is always one of the tricks a speaker ought to try to avoid".

"Now, Ad", the baker said, "it's been a wonderful time to us having you here, and hearing you; but I do wish you could try to see as we see about the Church. It's the only thing that keeps men from savagery. And now, to-night, after all our excitement and joy, there comes a very terrible thing. The poor idiot, who was here this morning; you saw him in fact; is at the police station about this murder".

"What, Rob, the Magpie"? Tryphena cried.

"Yes; we saw him taken in there, with two policemen, just now, didn't we, Bob"?

"We did, indeed", Bob said. "And I saw him going towards the Camp, with a very shady-looking gang, just before the time of the crime".

"You mean to say, that the poor Magpie is in the station on a charge of murdering"?

"Yes", Bob said.

"No, no", the baker said, "that's jumping to conclusions. No. He was being taken to the station; but we don't know that he was being charged; come. He was being taken there, so that they might hear his story".

"A lot of good that'll do them. It'll take them three months before they know what it is he's trying to say.

"Tell me, Bob, when you saw the poachers in the field, just who did you see with him"? Tryphena asked.

Bob told his story again. Tryphena listened with excitement.

"Poachers", Engels said; "that is what you English call the poor who take the food that Nature gives".

"Poaching is only another kind of theft", the baker said. "It all comes from trying to get rich without working. It's the big shops in the cities, not the poor people wanting food, that cause the serious poaching".

"But, Rob, I'm troubled about the Magpie being questioned by the police who won't understand what he means", Tryphena said. "You know what a long while it was before we could understand him. Even now, we don't always understand. The police won't know one word".

"I was thinking, Try", the baker said, "that it would be kind to offer as an interpreter. But, of course, it's absurd to suppose that the poor creature could have harmed anybody. I'll go round to the station again and see if I can be of any service".

"Do, Rob; there's a dear", Tryphena said.

"Right, I'll go", the baker said. "Would you like to come, Ad"?

However, Adolf had no wish to enter an English police station unless pressed. The baker went up alone.

As soon as he had gone, Tryphena changed the subject from the murder of John Okle to the murder (accompanied with rape) of Bob's only pair of trowsers. She had noticed that he was in knickers and had from this leaped to the right conclusion. Bob came in for a severe scolding. However, he was feeling cheered, on the whole; the scolding was as nothing to what he would have received if the murder had not been there to engage most of Tryphena's faculties. He was now hoping that perhaps there would be no inquiry about how the bull got out from Neakings' bull-byre. Still, even if that did not get out, there would be trouble from Sir Hassle on Monday.

Presently, the baker returned. He was depressed.

"I couldn't do any good", he said. "They've arrested him on a warrant on a suspicion of complicity in a raid on the pheasants at the Camp, and they say that no charge will or can be made upon any other matter till after the inquest, which will be on Monday, they think".

"Did they say that they would charge him then"?

"No, no; they did not say that they would charge anybody. They just said, that they were prosecuting their enquiries. Whoever it was that did the murder, somebody or other made a sweep of the pheasants, it seems. You know what the police are. They told me nothing that I wanted to know; but it's all over the town now that the Magpie was with Rapp when Rapp shot the man".

"Yes, but he didn't shoot".

"No, I'm sure he didn't; but I'm uneasy about it".

"Did you see the Magpie"?

"Yes. They let me just see him and ask if he wanted anything. The Inspector was at the cell door with me. I only saw him a minute and asked if I could do anything. He said 'No' in his funny way, 'Num' as he calls it".

"But how is it known that Rapp shot the man"?

"Mrs. Okle and the daughter were both present it seems; they saw him".

"Have they caught Rapp"?

"No. But I gather that they've got their nets spread. Well, it is a sad end to a day that was to have been so bright to us".

"Now sit down, Rob", his wife said, "and we'll all have a cup of cocoa and be off to bed".

"I don't know that I can fancy any cocoa, thank you, Try", the baker said. "I'm upset by what the Basket, as they call her, was saying. She said, that the Magpie was the one who shot John Okle. She said that they got into a fight and the Magpie took John's gun and upped with it and shot him".

"But who would heed the Basket, Rob"? Tryphena asked.

"No one as a general rule. But she had been talking to Sallie who works at the Camp Farm; and Sallie was out at Okle's cottage half-an-hour after the shooting. She had the facts from John's daughter".

"I wouldn't trust her story. No, no; we know that the Magpie wouldn't get into a fight. Have a cup of hot cocoa; it will do you good, after your talk".

"Adolf", the baker said, "I know that you don't hold with the Church nor with prayer; but the two are good things, proven to be good to us. I wish we could persuade you to our way of thinking about them".

"Thank you; none of either for me", Engels answered. "The one is just an institution, deserving the fate of all institutions; the other seems to me to be a confession of the futility of the brain. I will use my brain in any emergency, not throw it over by taking to prayer. In a battle the captain is to see what is to be done and to do it; not to cover his head in a bag and consult an oracle which must be in his head all the time. If he prays, he must be appealing to his brain. There can be no doubt of that. Well, then; let him use his brain like a man, by process of reason or analysis, not like an old woman of the Stone Age, who happens to be afraid of the dark".

"That's just the one point I never can make him see, Try", the baker said, as he took the kettle from the fire and mixed the cocoa for his guest. "But for my part, I feel the need of prayer, and of very deep prayer tonight, for that poor crazy creature who has so often done work here for me. I hope that you will be mindful of him, too, Ad, when you go to bed. He needs the prayers of all of us".

"If he has murdered anybody connected with property", Adolf said, "I fancy a file, a rope ladder and a handsome bribe to the warder would be a lot more use to him than prayer. To tell the honest truth, when the law gets hold of anyone, in this or any land, prayer is only the oil that makes the mill wheels grind him without squeaks".

They went up to bed after this. The baker and Tryphena read the Bible together; and then prayed earnestly on their knees for a full quarter-of-an-hour for help to be vouchsafed to the poor Magpie in his terrible situation and for the truth of the crime to be made plain so that a poor innocent might not suffer. Usually, prayer cheered and illuminated them. Tonight, either they were weary or the Spirit was turned from them because of some sin of theirs. They rose from their knees uncomforted, and so to bed, wondering what they had done wrong. Tryphena felt that she had been too harsh to Bob, in that matter of his trowsers. The baker felt that he had perhaps received a first instalment of confirmation that he was on the right path, and would soon receive others.

"It may be, Try", he said, "that this is to be a persecution and a tribulation. If it be, we must endure".

As was their custom when in bed, they sang together a favourite hymn before turning to sleep. Bob, who was going through twenty Latin words, with their meanings and peculiarities, heard their voices; so did Adolf, who was trying to get to sleep. He wished, either that Nature would rob the English of this habit of hymn singing, or at least bring it about that they learned how to sing. Finding that Nature did not immediately grant his wish, he rapped on the wall, and the two singers, fearing lest they had been inhospitable, were silent.

Bob was up early on the Sunday morning, to make his mother a cup of tea, and to get the breakfast ready, so that she might enjoy a long lie in bed. He nipped round to the outside of the police station before he began to do these things. Several people were already there, staring, as people will, at the place where someone connected with a deed is supposed to be. He knew some of the men, and asked them, if they could tell him anything more about the crime. They said, that it was said that Rapp had done it; but it was thought that a lot of London men were in it, too, and that they had all had guns and had blown poor John Okle pretty near to bits. The station itself looked blank enough. The door was shut and the blinds were down. It fronted a lofty part of what had been the monastery wall. It stood in a still street where little happened. Inside it, somewhere, the Magpie lay, under lock and key. Bob stood and stared with the half-dozen others.

On the otner side of that brick wall was someone under suspicion of murder. They stared and stared, each with a heart full of feeling not easily to be put into words. Perhaps each one, if pressed, would have said, that he was there because murder is a frightful thing and the avenging law a frightful thing, and because now Chance or Fate had brought it about that these things were mixed with the destinies of one whom they had known. They were all, through the Magpie, linked to Tragic Destiny.

Bob stared his fill and then ran back to his work. He was troubled now lest he had been guilty in not trying to get the Magpie away from that very shady set of men. If he had called to the Magpie to go home, he might have gone. But in that case, the gang might have interfered. A scare rose up within him every few minutes, lest a question should be asked why he was late for the meeting, why he had kept them waiting and then turned up in such a state. He had admitted being by the river with two companions. What if Old Neakings went to the police with an account of three companions who had been baiting his bull by the river? He didn't feel happy about it.

"I must tell Polly and Greg what I've told the police", he thought.

He could catch them, perhaps, after Church.

Little was talked of in the baker's house that morning except the murder. The rumour now was that a large party of murderers had surrounded the keeper after netting all the pheasants in the covert. It was agreed now, that there were many murderers; nobody supposed that the Magpie had had much to do with it, but he had something to do with the netting, and was held till that could be cleared up. This seemed likely, so that the baker and Tryphena were cheered as they made ready to go to Church. Engels took it amiss that they let the crime interfere with the adulation due to him as the speaker at last night's meeting. However, it was the main event in life now. Last night's meeting was put out of mind. The baker hardly thought of it. Bob got away after breakfast, to warn Polly of what he had told the police. Polly had news for him.

"Old Neakings is swearing it was Old Ratty who let Roxer out", he said.

"No? I say, that's good news".

"It's a fact, and the funny thing is that Old Ratty can't be sure that he didn't. He was just a bit over his usual yesterday. I know this is true. I had it from Ratty's son".

This was good news. Bob went home. When he was there, he thought it wise to take his father aside and tell him something of the trouble to be expected from Sir Hassle.

"I'm sorry to hear of that, Bob", his father said, "for I did not much want trouble of that sort just now. Still, it is not anything for which you or I should be punished".

Soon after this it was time to get ready for Church.

"Will you come along"? the baker asked Engels.

"I? No fear", Adolf answered. "Why will you go? To see the nice fat clean clergyman who draws the rents from Muck Alley"?

"No, no, Ad", the baker said, "to join all our neighbours in spirit and go with them to God. That is what Church is to us".

"Well, I never shall understand the English", Adolf said. "I don't want to join all your neighbours. If I were living here I'd want to join battle with half of them; and as to going to God, I really don't understand what you mean".

"Well, you will, Adolf", the baker said, "and when you do, you'll be amazed at the way you've kept your doors locked".

Usually, as they went to Church, they were greeted by people, who walked some of the way with them discussing the week's affairs. On this Sunday, it seemed to Bob that all were rather curt and stand-offish. It is true, that they were all intent on the murder, standing in little groups, each with some crumb of news or rumour to add to the feast, but it was not wholly that. Bob saw that there was a feeling against them. He was sure of it, before he reached the Church.

"There is no doubt about it", he thought, "that meeting has roused things up".

After service, it was even more noticeable. Usually, after morning church people loitered and gossipped at the church-porch, and sauntered with them back to their door. They did not do so today. They nodded and held aloof.

"It is all that filthy Engels and the meeting", Bob thought. "It will be long before they forgive Father for last night".

He contrived to lag behind his parents; presently Gregory joined him; they slipped away, out of the stream of people, by the little track which led to the woods. In the covert, Gregory said,

"This will be the last time you and I will dodge out here after Church, Bob".

"Why"?

"Well, I've been thinking, ever since our time with old Roxer, that I've had enough of doing what I don't want to do, so I've decided to do what I want to do. I'm going to chuck all this and see a bit of the world. You won't split, if I tell you"?

"Of course not".

"Well, I'm going, the very first thing tomorrow".

"Going where"?

"To join the Tatshire Hussars. Coming with me"?

"No fear".

"Well, I'm going. I've had enough dragging old iron around for Old Tintacks all day long. Why should I stay? If I were to be with Old Tintacks another forty years, I should still be dragging the same old iron around, and getting no more for doing it. We've only got our lives. I'm going to have my fling while I'm young. I'll drag iron later, if I must. I've had enough of Mother and the rest ordering me around".

"You'll have a lot of others ordering you around in the Army", Bob said.

"Yes, and if I mind my tip I'll be doing some of the ordering myself, before I'm much older. If I get to be a sergeant, I shall be a sort of officer. In fact, the sergeants are officers and have batmen and a mess of their own".

"But suppose you hate it and then just have to stick it"?

"I can't hate it more than I hate Old Tintacks' shop. And there'll be the girls, who are always just crazy for a hussar in uniform, with spurs clinking; and then I shall have a horse to ride".

"Yes", Bob said, "and to groom and his harness to keep clean, before ever you start to clean your arms and uniform. You'll have three hours' cleaning every day, of one sort or another".

"That's all routine. You come along, Bob, and join the corps with me".

"I hate you to be going", Bob said, "but I couldn't be a soldier. It would never do for me; I'd hate it, worse than any life on this planet".

"Well, every man to his way, of course", Gregory said. "But I'm off. And if you change your mind and want to come along, why, I'll wait outside for five minutes at five-to-six tomorrow morning. Bill, the carrier, is taking me into Tatchester. I'll be there a little after eight, or so, and I'll be listed by nine. I'll be one of the Queen's Zebras, as they call us, from the blue and white stripes on our stocks. Next time you see me I'll be riding a horse and able to use a sword: three cuts, two points; one guard. When I've cut some of these foreign heads off, if they go getting uppish, I may get a medal from the Queen. 'Rise up, Sir Gregory' ".

"Your mother won't be best pleased, Greg".

"She isn't best pleased at present. Nor am I".

"She'll buy you out".

"She won't. If a fellow wants to serve the Queen he has a right to. And I'd recommend you come too, and join the corps with me".

"It wouldn't suit me", Bob said. He had seen some of the Tatshire Zebras in camp at Condicote the year before.

"Well, the corps is always open to a likely lad like you", Gregory said. "And now, as this is to be our last afternoon together, I vote we spend it down Old Neakings' way, to try to find out what happened to Roxer".

Sundays, in the 'seventies, though partially days of rest, were seldom days of ease. The mornings were made uneasy by the constraint of Sunday clothes and by the spiritual doubt if it were lawful to enjoy anything before church service. The service filled the forenoon, for in those days they gave full measure, the Litany and the Communion service, an anthem, and a twenty- or twenty-five-minute sermon. Then came the dinner, which was a real meal; and then a space during which it was certainly wicked to play, blasphemou͟ to seem happy, and everlasting damnation to work. For many years, Bob was not sure that he was not damned for having once cut his toenails on the Sabbath.

However, this Sunday afternoon was not so bad to Bob. His father slept; his mother, taking a Bible, settled to her chair, to study God's Word, as she said, and to fall asleep in the study. Engels went for a walk, with his pipe and his philosophy. Bob, in the quiet, slipped off to Tibb's Wharf, where he met his friends.

"We'll go down to Neakings'", he said, "and look up Mimby, the cowman's boy. He's generally mooning about in the fields. He'll tell us the news".

In the stubble fields, sure enough, they saw the melancholy little Mimby setting hazel springs for rats in the rat runs. He got a farthing a tail for rats; but he knew very well, that Sunday trapping would damn him to hell fire. Nevertheless, he had judged that it was worth it, like many a wiser sinner.

"Hello, Mimby. Are you getting many rats"?

Mimby produced a corpse from his pocket and handed it up for inspection. He was a lad of few words.

"How did you get this one, Mimby"?

"He hung hisself, click".

"Do you get many here"?

"Ah".

"Did you see two dogs around here, yesterday"?

"Ah. They got our bull".

"Did they kill the bull"?

"They bit his tail, proper".

"Will the bull die"?

"Master would have bowled their heads off, proper, for biting bull's tail: proper he would have".

"Did he shoot the dogs"?

"He got his gun, proper, and they got his tail, proper. Master said, 'I'll bowl their heads off'. But he couldn't bowl their heads off, for they'd got the bull's tail. He'd have bowled the bull's tail off if he'd fired off old Crackum with them hanging on the tail. Proper, he would have, if he'd done that. But Old Ratty came and call the dogs; then Master he go for Old Ratty, proper, for sicking they dogs at Roxer. Then we had a rare old time shooing the bull in".

"Whoever let the bull out"? Polly asked.

"Old Ratty done, so Master says, to give his dogs a run".

"Old Ratty"?

"Ah".

"But the bull's all right"?

"His old tail is all toothed up, proper toothed it is".

"But he's all right"?

"His tail is all toothed up, what the Lord Mayor has to eat. But now he won't get none, not off'n of ours".

This was as much as they were likely to get out of Mimby. It seemed almost too good to be true, that they should have had their day, that Ratty should be suspected of loosing the bull, and that the dogs should have escaped.

They turned for home, with all anxiety lifted from their chests. They could now talk of the murder without a sinking feeling. Gregory had a packet of five-a-penny cigarettes, which he smoked with a great air, but found difficult to light; he had a swagger stick of malacca cane and a flash blue necktie. With the cane as he went he made cuts and passes at these foreign heads supposedly gone uppish again. Bob knew what he meant, and was saddened.

As they slouched along, a noise of hoofs behind them made them look back. A two-horse van of peculiar make was approaching from the direction of Tatchester. A policeman was sitting beside the driver, who wore a kind of uniform. It was a black van. As it passed, Bob saw that it had a grille on the door at the back. Through the grille he could see the gleam on the helmet of a policeman.

"D'you see that"? Polly asked. "That's the Black Maria from Tatchester. As it's Sunday, I'll bet you any money it's got Fight Rapp inside it. They're taking him to the station, to charge him".

This put other matters out of their minds; they ran after the van, but could not keep up with it. They followed it all the way to the station; but were not near enough to see it unload. They came up panting just as the crowd was scattering from the station door. They had run nearly a mile and a quarter, and the van had been going at a good speed to check pursuers. However, even in Condicote on a Sunday afternoon a good many people caught sight of the van and guessed as Polly had guessed that Rapp was in it; they, too, had run, and had seen the police force of the station turn out to keep folk away from the station door, and then had seen the grilled door unlocked and a big policeman lead out the prisoner, no longer Fight Rapp, but a white-faced, scared man, hand-cuffed and shuffling, mortally sick still from his last night's drunkenness. Bob heard them say,

"It was Rapp, all right. They got him in Tatchester this morning in one of the low pubs down by the docks. He was drunk when they took him, or he'd have laid some of them low".

"What will be done to him, please"? Bob asked.

"Hang him", the man said, "he'll be hanged. He's looked his last on free air, and the Magpie, too".

"But they'd never hang the Magpie", Bob said.

"Ah. They will though", the man said. "He was an accessory to the fact. He was in it as much as the other chap; and they may get the rest of the party as well".

Nothing else was talked of that night in Condicote. All the story was known, more or less accurately, as always. Fight Rapp had gone from the scene of his murder straight towards Tineton, where he had hailed a van which was returning slowly towards Tatchester. The van driver had given him a lift for seven miles, then Rapp had climbed down at a pub and had drunken there, talking in a very wild way of what he meant to do to the police if they tried to put a hand on him. Then he had begged another lift from a car-man, and had come into Tatchester at midnight. He had gone to a haunt of his and had asked if he might lie low there for a while. Something of the truth had already reached Tatchester by means by which tales travel. His friend had given him a bottle of gin and had left him with it while he went to find out the facts of the case. On learning that it was a case of murder, this friend decided that it was not good enough, and therefore told the police, who found him so helplessly drunk that they removed him to the cells for the night and let him sleep it off.

But no man bothered about Rapp. He was a well-known, bullying, drunken scoundrel, with a power of blarney which sometimes deceived magistrates and often deluded women. He had murdered and now would hang. The main question in Condicote now was, would the gang of London murderers be caught too; and if they were caught, what would be done to them?

"Surely", Tryphena said, "only the actual murderer will be hanged".

"They'll hang Rapp and all they can prove to have been with him", Engels said. "This is a question of property, which is the dividing line between men and beasts in this land. I only wonder they can't burn him and his companions alive. But perhaps they will".

"But they could never hang that poor fellow, the Magpie", the baker said. "He is hardly sane. You may never have seen him, but he is well-known here. The boys call him Dafty Dick".

"They'll say that an example must be made", Engels said.

During that evening, "Old Tintacks", Gregory's master, the ironmonger, looked in. He came partly to talk about the murder, but partly also to say a word or two to the baker, whom he found in the bake-house, just beginning on the sponge.

"I've come in", he said, "because it has been represented to me, by one whom I need not specify, that there was someone, not a Condicote man, who was at your meeting last night, taking down every word that you said. I thought that as a neighbour I ought to warn you. Forewarned is forearmed".

"It was the Tatchester press man", the baker said. "I heard that he was coming".

"No, no, not this man", Old Tintacks said. "This was another man, not known here at all. My informant thinks that it was a Government Agent, watching for the Government. They have such men out, you know, now, ever since the rick-burning has broken out again. Anything that a man may say, may be taken down now and used against him. This man, whoever he was, took down your friend's words, too. You might like to tell him that. It's no light thing, to incite to violence. I know you and I know what is in your mind, but if someone who hears you then flies out and sets a rick on fire, why, you and those with you may be held responsible. Anyhow, remember, that the Government is watching now and taking special precautions".

"I don't fear", the baker said. "I said nothing but what I will avouch. Let them print it against me, I won't mind. Someone will read it who will be the better for it".

Bob was up before six the next morning, for it fell to him to take Engels to the station for what was called the Milk Train. As he looked out from the yard entrance at a few minutes before six, he saw Gregory in the market place looking for him. Greg came up to him.

"Are you coming along, Bob"?

"No fear".

"Well, so long, old man".

"Are you telling Old Tintacks"?

"No fear, nor anybody else. I don't want to be stopped. They'll all know soon enough. I daresay I'm making a mistake, but anyhow I'd rather make a mistake of my own than suffer from another's mistake which is what I'm doing at Tintacks'. I'll write and let you know how I get along".

They shook hands and parted. Bob knew within his heart that his chance of seeing or hearing from Gregory again was slight. The pen may, on occasion, be mightier than the sword, but in a recruit's room in barracks it is not.

In the house, Tryphena in curl papers was giving Engels an early breakfast, so that he might bear the Milk Train in resignation. It cut Bob's heart to see his parents' affection for this ugly fraud. They came out to the yard to say good-bye.

"Well, Ad", his father said, "you must come again soon to bring us a little London light and brush away the cobwebs".

"We feel all remade and uplifted by you", Tryphena said.

"Thanky, thanky", Engels said, as he tucked his rug about him. "You keep at them. They'll soon know the truth. Some of these Muck Alley people will bring the tiles about their ears. We shall live to see it. G'bye".

As he drove through the street, Bob saw his parents waving from the pavement.

"What are you looking back at"? Engels asked.

"They are waving after you", Bob said.

"Ah well", Engels said, "I won't turn. I'd get a crick in my neck. And you're damned glad I'm going, aren't you"?

"Yes, I am glad", Bob said. "You take all my father has to offer, and then mock at him, after doing your best to ruin him".

"It's lucky for you that the train's coming in", Engels said, "for it would be a pleasure as well as a duty to wring your young neck".

After this, Bob drove home. The post had just come. His father was reading a letter written on crested paper. He handed it to Bob.

"Sir A. Hassle Gassle requests that you will furnish your account by return of post. He will deal elsewhere in future".

"You were right, Bob", he said. "That little trouble has come, just as you said. Well, I'm surprised at Sir Hassle punishing anybody for another's offence, but he has the name of being hard. I don't like saying that of anybody. It may well be nothing but his disability; he suffers a great deal from his liver, I believe".

"It's a big account", Bob said.

"Yes, the house is a big and good customer, not only for bread but all sorts of fancy work for house parties and so forth".

"Don't you think, Rob, that you and Bob had better go up there this afternoon, and explain just how the trouble arose? You could show, that it wasn't your fault and certainly not Bob's".

"Engels speaks his mind to everyone", the baker said. "He isn't English. And I never could make him see, that the tongue is an unruly member. He sees a thing and then on the instant he says it".

"He's a brutal, bullying boor, if you ask me", Bob thought; but they were not asking him.

"It might be well, if I caught him at the inquest this

afternoon", the baker said. "If I go up to him and explain and apologize, he ought to let it pass. He shouldn't condemn me for what another did".

Somehow, Bob was sure that no good would come of an appeal to that cold face. Sir Hassle at that moment was reading in the *Tatchester Times* an account of revolutionary speeches in Condicote, in which the local baker had criticised some local property owners and had been followed by some inflammatory agitators among whom was the notorious Engels, or Muller as his name really was, who in spite of imprisonment still criticised the institutions of the land which had given shelter to his father and himself. The paper added that the Condicote baker had for some weeks been inveighing against the owners of the property in question, and had roused a very real resentment in the hearts of those he thought he was helping. Let the baker mind his oven, the writer advised, and let his foreign friends beware how they outraged British hospitality; we wanted no foreign agitators here, stirring up trouble; nor would the law tolerate such.

"So", Sir Hassle muttered as he read, "that fellow, who was offensive here, was the agitator, Muller or Engels. I thought his face was somehow familiar. Why, he has been in prison, more than once. And Mansell brought a man like that here, to talk in Condicote. He had better look out. I will not permit that kind of thing".

That afternoon, he walked down to the Coroner's Court, which was held for convenience close to the police station. On his way, he called for the owner of the Arthur's Camp covert, who went as John Okle's employer. The court was small, so that few save the witnesses and the jury could be present. The baker could not get in. He saw Sir Hassle enter, but could not reach him in the press. He waited outside, while the jury, nearly all of whom were farmers or cattle breeders, viewed the body and heard enough to convince them that John Okle had died as the result of a gunshot wound, wilfully inflicted by Rapp, with the help of his accomplice. The Coroner asked if this verdict was one of Wilful Murder? They said that it was. The Coroner therefore recorded it. The police asked for a delay of forty-eight hours before the holding of the magistrate's enquiry, in order "that they might prosecute their enquiries". This was granted. Great care was taken to spare the women witnesses from the annoyance of sightseers; the widow and daughter of the dead man were brought to and from the court in a closed carriage. A young lawyer from Tatchester, known as "Young Mr. Gallup", appeared on behalf of the accused men. He had his name to make. He wanted to have the conduct of a capital case. He, too, had his enquiries to make.

The baker waited outside the court, amid the crowd gathered there. Men talked of what they had seen, which was little enough: a glimpse of poor Mrs. Okle, a glimpse of Rapp and the Magpie, a glimpse of Okle's body in the mortuary. They talked of the chances and envied the jurors who would be hearing the whole case. Presently a man came out; he was the reporter from the *Tatchester Times*, about to race to the station for the train. He shoved through the crowd, saying, "Wilful Murder against both prisoners", and then broke into a run by the short cut. His word broke up the crowd, who loitered away talking of what would come next. The baker lingered, waiting for Sir Hassle to come out. He waited for some time, because Sir Hassle had enquiries to make of people who were there.

He came out presently side by side with General Minton-Price, the Chairman of the local bench, an elderly, but still upright and active soldier, who at the age of sixteen had been an ensign at Waterloo. The baker moved up to them and said,

"If you please, Sir Hassle, may I have a word"?

Perhaps he was wrong to interrupt, when Sir Hassle was deep in talk with another; still, the offence was not unpardonable. Sir Hassle passed him by, without acknowledging the baker's salute. He called over his shoulder,

"I can't discuss the matter. Furnish your account as you were told". He then passed on, saying to the General, and so that the baker could hear, "That fellow is heading for trouble".

The baker walked back to his shop with a bowed head. He was bitterly hurt. It was not that he minded losing the account; that had happened too often in the last two years to have much sting; what he felt was the rudeness, from one who was called a "gentle" man. He himself would never have talked to a dog like that. And he had been a tenant to Sir Hassle for twenty years.

"He ought not to have talked to me like that", he muttered. "He ought not to have refused me a hearing, even if he were the Chairman. I and mine have been with his property for over a hundred years. 'Can't discuss the matter. Furnish your account as you were told. That fellow . . .' " He was bitter at the rudeness and brutality of it. "Yes", he muttered, "Napoleon was right. The real cause of Revolution is Vanity. Injured Vanity. I must fight it down. I've no right to have vanity; it's the next bad thing to pride".

Unfortunately, he had vanity, although only a baker,

He went to his desk, made out the account, with great care, cutting from it the loaves delivered on the Saturday when there had been the dispute at the door.

"Sir Hassle shall have those, free", he muttered.

When the account had been drawn and checked, so that he knew it to be correct, save for that detail, he walked swiftly up to Sir Hassle's house and delivered it at the back door to a maid. After leaving the sculptured Hassle gate, he wiped his boots on the roadside grass, and walked home.

He was comforted as he walked by the thought that Sir Hassle's anger was a sign that he, the baker, was doing the Lord's work.

"I've made them feel the truth a bit", he said. "I only wonder now whether I can continue to the end".

He wondered, also, whether the verdict of Wilful Murder against the Magpie could be more than a matter of form. He was troubled by what he had overheard in the crowd. Men there had spoken as though the Magpie must be equally guilty with Rapp, which was absurd. He would find out as soon as possible what the evidence had been.

When he reached home, he judged that Tryphena had been recently in tears over some matter, which she had resolved to keep from him. He knew that they both had a way of keeping troubles to themselves in order to avoid speaking bitterly of people. He soon found out, that she had been weeping at what the Grey Mare, as she was called, had said about the Saturday evening speech.

"She was not there", Tryphena said. "She only read the account in the paper. Yet she came here, saying that she wanted her account, and that she would never eat our bread again. Now there was nothing in anything that you and Adolf said that was not true and trebly true. I told her so.

She said, that it did not become me to talk of what I could not understand. I laughed at her at that; and she went out fuming. No sooner had she gone, when in came Mrs. D. of the Calvage, in a fine taking about what she said was Red Revolution at her doors, and that you ought to be ashamed. I said, that we all should be ashamed at what was shameful, and that it was the being ashamed which had led to the meeting. So she asked for her account, too, and when she had gone, I felt a little exhausted".

"Well", the baker said, "it would be a bad thing, if we were to stop doing our duty because we lose a little custom. The Lord will give us wealth enough, in exchange for these few pennies, don't doubt that. Have you heard anything of the murder case? They found it Wilful Murder against the two men, but I've not talked yet with anybody who was in the court".

"I have", Tryphena said. "Mr. Callow, who was on the jury, looked in. He said that the police are quite clear now that it was not a gang of murderers down from London. There was a gang of poachers from London or somewhere; the police do not quite know where they came from; and Rapp and the Magpie went with them to take the pheasants. It was after they had done that the murder happened. The other poachers went away in a van. After they'd gone, John Okle came running up, and Rapp swore at him and shot him".

"Oh, Lord, oh, Lord", the baker said, "see what comes of drink and carrying a gun. But the Magpie wasn't in that".

"Ah, yes, but he was", Tryphena said. "Before Rapp fired, the Magpie tried to knock John Okle down with a stick".

"Yes, but how did they know that it was Rapp and the Magpie"?

"They saw them: it was daylight; and they found the gun, Mr. Callow says, with 'J. R.' burnt on the stock for 'James Rapp' ".

"I thought his name was Jabez", the baker said.

"Well it would be 'J. R.' "

"I don't like the sound of this at all", the baker said. "It's worse than I feared, a very great deal worse. I believe this makes the Magpie guilty of murder. He'll suffer for this".

"What d'you mean, Rob, by 'suffer' "?

"They'll hang him".

"Hang that poor innocent? But they couldn't".

"He was an accessory both before and at the time of the crime. He'll be in with Rapp, I'm pretty sure, in Rapp's condemnation. I don't know whether the evidence is enough to hang him. But if it is enough to condemn Rapp, it will do for him, too".

"But, Rob, my dearest, he is mad, or not sane; nobody here thinks of him as sane".

"He was sane enough to understand what Rapp said, to trip up John Okle. No, it will go hard with the poor creature".

"But do you really fear, Rob, that men would take that poor, afflicted thing and hang him on a gallows for that? We know the Magpie. Why, I've seen him a score of times playing tripstick with the boys in the market. He thought it was another game of tripstick. It is one of the things he does understand".

"Yes, but the jury won't understand".

"We'll tell them".

"That's my Try. We'll tell them. But it is a bad lookout, by all that I can see".

"But, Rob, it's impossible for them to hang the Magpie. He is almost one of us. He's been in and out of the yard here hundreds of times, and borne a hand at the mixing and had bits of new crust; and then those little buns that he loved. And he's as innocent as a child. Think how he used to hold out bits of sweet bun on his hand in the summer so that the wasps would settle on his hand. He used to love watching wasps. 'Ospies' he called them".

"There's one thing, Try", the baker said, "he hasn't been committed yet. He has to go before the Magistrates' Court. They are all local men who know something about him. They'll see that he is certified as not sane. I'll go round to see the Rector about it, straight away".

He went at once to the Rector, who assured the baker that the Magpie was in no danger, but would certainly be committed for trial.

"I have been to the cells", he said, "and spent some time with both men. They both feel their position keenly, the Magpie because he has not been under restraint, like this, for many years; and Rapp because he says, with tears in his eyes, that there has been some dreadful mistake of the poor overwrought women; that he was never near the coverts, and that they do not know what they are saying. Mr. Gallup, the young lawyer, who seems to be a clever and a good young man, is confident that they will get off. I pray so. By the way, Mansell, can you tell me the Magpie's name"?

"No, sir. I've known him better than most, but I don't know his name. He has no name; no rightful name".

"While you are here, Mansell, may I ask you not to

write any more of your articles about the slums here? I don't doubt the righteousness of your case, but I do see the unrighteousness of the results of your letters. They inflame a great many ignorant people and they do not have any weight, if I may say so, with those whose influence might better the conditions; rather the reverse. Will you think of this"?

It was not a pleasant remark to hear, though the Rector made it charmingly.

"As to that, sir", the baker said, "I feel that I must go on till the abuses which seem to me to be un-Christian are swept away".

"Well, suppose for one moment that you stir what authorities there are into pulling down those rookeries, where will the poor people go? There is no other place for them, nearer than one of the cities, where they would find even a roof to cover their heads. These slums may be bad, but they are better than nothing. Who will build them new homes, if these go"?

"I hope that a Christian conscience, when once roused, will both destroy the bad and build the good. That is to be the point of my next letters".

"I fear your next letters", the Rector said, "for the feelings you rouse may bear heavily on these poor men".

"Putting the letters aside for a moment", the baker said. "I've been wondering whether Dr. Gubbins ever attended the Magpie and could write about him".

"It would be worth going to the doctor to find out".

He went down to the doctor, who presently came in, looked shrewdly at him, heard the case of the Magpie patiently, and then said,

"I've been asked this already. The Magpie is not very

bright, but I am far from convinced that he is not pretty shrewd in some ways. Now about yourself, Mansell, I'm inclined to say that it is you who ought to be dealt with".

"Do you mean about my writings, Dr. Gubbins"?

"Your writings? No, I didn't know you did any. No. I meant your lungs. You ought to get out of the oven business: it's doing you no good. Think it over. A man's living ought not to be his dying, you know".

The baker turned back to his home. The day had been stormy for the business. All through the afternoon, people had been dropping in upon Tryphena, to say that they were surprised at Mr. Mansell's stirring up such bad feeling, and asking for their accounts. At tea-time, Mrs. Rawson came in, to say, that she had just had a telegram from her son, that he was now in the Hussars and that it was what she had always feared, since he had taken to smoking. She had seen her son Greg going off with Bob just after Church the day before, and she wanted now to know how much Bob had known of it, and whether he had had any hand in it. Bob had come in at that point, and Tryphena had said,

"Here he is. You'd better ask him".

Bob, who was always truthful, said that Greg had told him, and that he had done his best to dissuade him.

"Done your best", Mrs. Rawson broke in. "Did you come round and tell me? I could have stopped him and now it's too late".

Bob said, that he could not betray a confidence.

"A confidence", Mrs. Rawson said. "I always said that you were a bad influence on Gregory. I wish I'd put my foot down long ago, when people began to say such things of the Mansells, but now, it is too late. However, one thing

I can and will do; I'll go elsewhere for my bread. I'll thank Mr. Mansell for his account. Thank God, I still have two sons, even if my husband is with Jairus' daughter, who will give Bob what he deserves".

With this she flounced out.

In the evening, the two sons of Mrs. Rawson called to see Bob.

"Now I shall catch it", Bob thought. "They'll probably take me up the road and larrup me. That's something to liven up the evening. Or very likely they'll give me a black eye and lay me out".

The young men said they would like a word with him up by the ruins. They carried no sticks, but Diggory's pocket bulged a little, which Bob supposed would mean straps. In the Abbey ruins, Diggory asked Bob if he would have a weed.

"Mother's in a fair old taking", he said, "but to tell the truth, kid, it's a damn good thing Greg hopped it when he did. He's been sneaking bits of change from Old Tintacks and putting them on horses with the lads at the livery stable. He's sneaked a matter of two quid, Old Tintacks thinks. Greg was scared it would come out this week, so he hopped it. Don't you give a heed to what Mother says. Greg's a lot better off where he is. He'll have to toe the line where he is or get the toe, and that is what the young fool wants".

They talked a little more.

"You tell your father", Hickory said, "that he'd better watch what he's doing with that man Engels. That isn't his name, for one thing; it's Muller or Smijdt. The police have something against him. And what your father's doing is just giving away his business to the Steam Bakery up the road. Did you see the notice they put up this evening? Well, come and see it".

They went. In the Steam Bakery window was a notice:—

CONDICOTE STEAM BAKERY
WE DO NOT PREACH
WE PRACTICE

A small company was staring at it; a gas lamp had been left alight so that they might see it. Bob longed to smash the window and fling the paper into the gutter.

"You see"? Hickory said.

"Try", the baker said, "I've been troubling about the Magpie; and I am quite sure that he will be committed for trial tomorrow. He must be; there's no hope of his not being. As he has to be tried, he ought to be properly defended. Mr. Gallup, who has taken his case, says that he ought to have counsel, as good as can be had; and of course that costs money. How would it be, if I wrote a little paper about the Magpie, appealing for funds for his defence, and had the paper in the window here? Some of those who read might subscribe. But if they don't we both must do what we can. He has shared our life here so long and so often, we must share some of his trouble. Besides, from what I hear, he's in danger. Yes, Try, I know you don't believe it; but the danger's there. I put it to young Mr. Gallup. He wouldn't admit it. He said no advocate would ever admit for one moment the chance of defeat; but I could see what was in his mind".

"Rob, do write and do anything you can for the poor creature. What is money compared with human life"?

Tryphena said. "We have a little money left. Use it all. God will repay, never fear; we cannot let the boy suffer for want of it".

"I knew you would see it like that, Try", the baker said. "I'll write my paper now and get Jones to print it. Then, if he is committed, it can go up at once".

The baker set to work at once; when spurred by any anger he was prompt always. He wrote hard, not very easily nor very well, but with a sincerity which made his work moving. He headed the paper:—

"MUCK AND ITS CONSEQUENCES".

"A few days ago", (he began), "we spoke in Condicote about some Church property, which figures in the plans as Tom's Charities and St. Alpig's Chantry, but is better known and more rightly under the local nicknames of Muck and Fever Alleys. Come and see them. Come and smell them. Then tell us, if you dare, whether charity exists there, and chantry, or singing for souls, can be done there. They sleep eight in a room and six in a bed in these alleys; father, mother, brothers, sisters, young, old, sick, dying, well, sober and drunk. It is a wise son knows his father in these conditions. You will find daughters with children by their fathers, and mothers with children by their sons. It is snug, living all together thus, drunk, on a cold winter's night, when the rags and old papers have been thrust into the hole that was once a window, and the last bit of floor is smoking on the hearth. Oh, it is merry there on a Saturday night, in the end of the harvest, when the fleas have died down a bit and the lice of winter haven't really begun. Everybody in the alleys has money then. Even the women and children have done a bit of gleaning or a week of hopping. The men have had harvest

money, or at least some share of the bounty of the earth,
which not even English greed can quite rob them of. Kept
off the grass as they are, they still get a few ears of corn
here, a turnip there, an apple or a draught of cider in the
other place, with perhaps a rabbit or a partridge, which
they have carried home from the shoot. Then, indeed, you
can see the harvest thanksgiving. The pubs, which take one
quarter of all money earned in our towns, take here three
quarters and take it quick. Down go the quarts of ale, and
onto them the gin, so that the dazed fool of the one may
become the fighting savage of the mixture. Out of the pubs
they come screaming and raving, ripe for fight, for lust and
robbery: the men smash each others' faces, the women claw
each others' hats, the children shriek or fall senseless, or
are beaten into agony by a drunken parent who happens to
be able to reach the victim. Singing and shouting, they stag-
ger into the alleys which are their homes. The windows
have long since gone, but they can still tear the stuffings
from them and shout curses, bawdry and challenge, or
scraps of obscene song through the gap till someone smites
them from within. Then the battle is joined, house against
house, gang against gang, alley against alley, for these poor
drugged and darkened souls cannot know that their real
enemies are in the rectory or the manor, snug in evening
dress, by the fire with their port and their sherry, reading
of the dresses worn at the Duchess's ball. No, they think
that their enemies are Bill's lot, up the row, or Jake's set
over in No. 7; so to it they go, with fist and tooth and
boot, and men are maimed and children darkened and done
for, while the diseased harpy welcomes the victor and picks
his pocket as she loves. Often of a Saturday night, the folk
within three hundred yards will get no sleep till three of a
Sunday morning. The bells will chime for midnight, and
usher in the day of God, and then Mother Midden will

sally out, screaming to have Mother Vixen's back hair down. In the middle of the filthy court the two half-naked savages will bite and tear, while the little boys fling filth from the upper rooms, and drunken girls will dance, taking off their clothes. The police know better than to venture near on such occasions. Then at two, perhaps, the young heroes, the poachers, will return from their affrays, having robbed a covert and smashed up its watchers; they come in flushed with joy to find their doxies and light up the spree with burning brandy.

In such a sweet scene of harvest festival, some thirty years ago, a half-witted woman, who had already borne seven bastards, to the lustful of the local hopyards, begat yet an eighth to the man known as Dogga, who was shot a few years later in the fray with the Godsdown keepers. Dogga is said by some to have paid ninepence for the joys attending fatherhood. Others say that he paid nothing, but only promised. In any case, the said sum of ninepence was the father's sole contribution to the maintenance, nurture and education of his son, who was born, (as he had heard tell), at the back of the workhouse, in the shed provided for female vagrants not accompanied by men. After seven years of life in and out of the workhouse with his mother, the child got away with some tinkers who needed a boy to beg with, and lived for perhaps the next eight years on the road, when he was not in gaol or in a workhouse. As far as can be learned he never learned to read or write, perhaps not from want of teaching so much as want of proper nourishment which made his brain incapable of learning. Of God and His worship he knew nothing, except that he must have heard Him mentioned in oaths. At the age of fifteen a charitable institution tried to improve him, by giving him six weeks of misery in a Home (as it was called), of which he kept a lively memory and terror. The words, "Tell

Master. Stick" would make him quake, even years later, as many often saw.

As the master whose stick brought about this result was rewarded for each boy for whom he found employment, he soon contrived to find work that even so poor a creature could perform. He got him a job on a bee farm, where he worked at many mean mechanical jobs in the fitting of frames, wiring in foundation, etc., etc., but found relaxations of his own in the coverts which border the farm. From this place it was that his father's companion, the Cosher, as he was called, got hold of him for use with his friends.

These facts can be learned, if they are not already known to my readers, by enquiry in the Alley, where he has often lodged. He has not been a burden to the rates, he has not been in gaol, but has contrived to exist, partly upon the charity of those almost as poor as himself, partly on the birds and mice which he was expert in trapping. In the spring, he lived much on birds' eggs, on young plants, and the young of rabbits. He would be much in the fields, the further from men the better for him, lying low, in hiding places, during the daytime, changing his den nightly, and eating, often raw, the creatures he had snared. He was expert, as I have often seen, in the catching of bees and taking of wild honey, of which he was very fond. In the autumn, when it became too cold for him to lie abroad, he would be more in the alleys than at other times. He was not minded there; he was harmless, even when the boys tormented him. Sometimes he would be given odd jobs, of a mechanical kind, which needed no intelligence; these he could be trusted to do. He had no vices. He never smoked nor drank. The full moon excited him, or frightened him, it would be hard to say which; perhaps something of the two. He had a fondness for the night; he was certainly more nearly sane at night-time than by daylight.

Within the last few days, this poor creature, by an accident of association, for which he can but be pitied, has been involved in calamity and sent to take his trial on a capital charge. We ask all those who saw the poor creature in Condicote and know how ill-fitted he is to understand the gravity of his situation, to help him in his distress by subscribing to A DEFENCE FUND now being opened for him". . . .

At this point, the baker broke off to consult Tryphena about a possible treasurer for the Defence Fund. Tryphena said, that the Rector was the best person to be treasurer, but that he was going to leave the parish in a few days, and would, therefore, not be the man in this case. Besides, the beginning of the article, she said, would make it impossible for the clergyman to be linked with the appeal.

"But, Try", the baker said, "it's all true. It's necessary that people should understand how the Magpie came to be born".

They debated this together, then prayed for guidance upon it, and at last consulted the Bible, by opening the Book with closed eyes, after praying that their hands might touch a helping text. The baker opened at Isaiah 62 verse 9.

"But they that have gathered it shall eat it and praise the Lord; and they that have brought it together shall drink it in the courts of my holiness.

"Go through, go through the gates; prepare ye the way of the people; cast up, cast up the highway; gather out the stones; lift up a standard for the people".

In the next verse were the wonderful words:—

"Behold, the salvation cometh; behold, his reward is with him, and his work before him".

Tryphena wept as her husband read.

"Oh, Rob", she said, "it is as if the Lord Himself had laid His very hand upon you. There can be no doubt. You must do this work yourself. You must be the manager of the Defence Fund. And we will give fifty pounds ourselves as a beginning. You can say, that the fund has already received a gift of fifty pounds from one who does not wish his name to be known. The only thing I would recommend is, that you send it to be printed at Yockford, where they would do it so much quicker, and where it would not be talked of if the need for it should never come".

The baker, therefore, ended his article with the announcement, that he would receive all subscriptions offered for the Magpie's defence, and that an anonymous donor had opened the fund with the gift of fifty pounds.

He telegraphed to the printer at Yockford that an important package was going to him by passenger train that afternoon, for instant printing; and then sent off the article, with full directions that it should be set up and printed as a double leaflet on four sides of paper. He asked for no proofs. The printer was to correct from the manuscript and send two hundred copies by passenger train the next morning.

It was possible that the leaflet might never be needed. Both he and Tryphena felt, that night, that the Lord was so much upon their side, that very likely the Magistrates would not commit the Magpie, but dismiss him, or at worst cause his mental condition to be looked to.

By the twelve-forty-five train from Yockford the package arrived for him from the printer, all clammy from the press. Bob, who had gone to fetch it from the train, brought it to the bakery, and the family read it through with intense interest.

The Magistrates were to meet at two-thirty. The baker and Tryphena arranged copies of the leaflet upon two cardboards, so that it could be displayed both within and without the window as soon as the worst was known. When all was ready, the baker went round to the police station to see Mr. Gallup, who was there with his client. He was admitted to the cell of the Magpie, who was delighted, as ever, at seeing a familiar face. The baker told him to cheer up.

"We get Magpie out", he said, as he would have spoken to a baby. "We get Magpie home. Nice buns for Magpie".

He had brought some buns, of the sort with sticky tops and candied peel which the Magpie most loved. Mr. Gallup received the news of the fifty pounds for defence with pleasure, but pointed out that the defence would have to include Rapp, too. The baker had not thought of that. He had no wish to defend Rapp; but a moment's thought showed him that Rapp was a fellow mortal, for whom Christ had died, and that his need at the moment was dire.

"Of course", he said, "the money must be for the two of them; but specially for the urging that the Magpie is not sane".

Mr. Gallup said that the best possible should be done. He promised to get the baker into court. He said, that little would be attempted, in the way of defence there; that would all be done at the Sessions. As to the chances, he said, he thought that there were women in the case, all weeping and wailing, and that, worse luck, they were both very good looking.

"That tells", he said, "tells a lot with a jury. Still, I always hope for a verdict. The point is always to say you will get the verdict, always, always, always, and never flinch from that. It's astonishing how that will turn people in Court the way you wish. ALWAYS HOPE is my motto . . ."

Presently, the baker was in court, facing the Magistrates' bench. The prisoners were brought in; the Magistrates entered; the police gave evidence; Mrs. Okle and her daughter gave evidence; other evidence was called; and Mr. Gallup reserved his defence. The Magistrates were General Minton-Price in the Chair, old Mr. Colway, Sir Hassle, Mr. Hankerton and Sir Peter Bynd. Their grey heads turned towards the Chairman while they talked a little together in low voices. They looked up from their papers and glanced now at the two poor Okle women, in black, in the shiny pew, now at the prisoners waiting for their fate in the shiny dock. Presently, they said, that there was certainly a case to go to a jury and that the prisoners were, therefore, committed to take their trial. The Sessions would be on a week later at Tatchester. The police helped the two women away; other police removed the two prisoners. A minute later, the officers of the court had called the next case, which was more genial hearing, being a bastardy case.

Leaving the court, as he had much to do, the baker met a friend.

"They're both committed, you've probably heard".

"Yes", the man said, "so Joe was saying. And they'll swing before Christmas, as sure as Tom's in Tatshire".

"Not the Magpie", the baker said, "not that poor creature".

"Ha, won't he, though", the man said, "the two together. It will be a case of the Staffordshire Knot, for they'll hang that child murder case, along with the pair of them all at the same time".

A pang went through the baker's soul that perhaps they would. "Ah, but, they shan't", he muttered to himself. "Hope always. They shan't. The Lord is on my side. He won't let them".

As he passed the back of the police station, he saw a little knot of men waiting about the black van. He knew the van to be a Black Maria. As he came up to it, the back door of the station opened, and policemen led out the two prisoners, the Magpie first, smiling and chattering at the light of day and the company, then Rapp, sullen, but for all his ferocity cowed and scared now. His face was twitching. It occurred to the baker, that he was expecting to be set upon by the crowd. Both prisoners were helped into the van. As Rapp was being helped in, a man called to him,

"Cheeroh, Fightie. Keep your pecker up".

His face flushed at this. He replied, "I'll peck some of them over this, you'll see".

At this, a policeman climbed into the van behind him; the black, grated door was closed on them and locked; then the van drove away.

The baker walked home.

"Mr. Gallup was quite right, Try", he said. "They're both committed. Now, with the blessing of God, we will launch our appeal and may God grant that it will prosper".

Outside his shop window there was a wooden frame

on which he often hung announcements, that he was prepared to do family bakings, for Sunday dinners, etc. On
this frame he now tacked the outspread leaves of his paper.
In his window, against the imitation wedding cake, which
was the permanent decoration there, he placed the board
on which the leaflet had been already arranged. On the
counter in his shop, he laid the pile of leaflets for sale at
a penny apiece. Before the leaflets were in place there,
three men had stopped to read what was on the card-
board, and displayed in the window. In a few minutes, the
news had spread. The windows were darkened by the
craning heads. The rudeness of the comment could be
plainly heard. A woman said in a fierce voice, that Mr.
Mansell ought to be ashamed of himself, writing such
things in a public thoroughfare. She pushed into the shop
and demanded her account. It was a scandal that a married
man should display such filthy reading for all to see, she
said, and that for her part she hadn't believed what had
been said about Mr. Mansell, but that now she would
see what the law could do. The baker told her, that she
should have her account; but that perhaps she might like
to give some part of the money to the Defence Fund.

"No", she said, "I give no money to defend the killers
of a fine man. The sooner the dirty murderers and their
defenders are hanged, the better I shall be pleased".

Several people came into the shop to hear the row.
After the woman had gone, the rush of people coming into
the shop for copies of the leaflet continued till after dark.
When the lamps were lit, he had to go to the post office,
to telegraph to the printer to run off a second two hundred
copies and send them by the night mail. He felt the glow
of fame. From within the den of his kitchen, he or Try-

phena had seen the best of all Condicote pausing to read his writing, and coming in to buy it. Old Mr. Colway had bought a copy. Young Mr. Cothill had bought a copy. The Rector's maid had been sent down for a copy, and had only brought a halfpenny instead of a penny. The tradesmen had bought a good many copies; but dozens of folk had read without buying; the piece was well known now. The comment and criticism was bitter. He heard a good deal of it, as he sat in his kitchen.

"Look here; did you ever? See what this baker's been writing? That's pretty dirty talk. Of all the filthy writing I've ever seen, it's about the dirtiest. He could be had up for that. He jolly well shan't bake for me nor mine again. Suppose one of my girls was to read that".

Before the clock chimed for seven o'clock, all the leaflets for sale had been sold. Those who knocked at the door for them now had to be told, that no copies were left, but that there might be more first thing in the morning. Two, who came in too late thus, were plainly enemies wanting copies for no good purpose. By eight o'clock, Bob who was coming in from delivering some cakes, reported that the pages had been torn from the notice-board outside.

When they went to bed that night, the baker and his wife knew that they had raised up a pretty storm, and had received no single penny piece towards the Defence Fund.

"I didn't expect any answer at once", Tryphena said. "It will take some little time for the writing to sink in; but it will bring in friends, you will see, Rob".

Rob thought that it would. He was puzzled that people should have found the writing "coarse", "filthy" and "disgusting". He had written in a mood of strong emotion which had in itself justified the strength of any language

used. "But why should people call it coarse"? he asked
himself. "They know that what I have written is really
a soft, faint understatement of what goes on in those dens
night after night. Why have they been shocked by the
language and not shocked by the fact"?

E pur si muove. They *had* been moved. By the next
morning's post came what was for him a large pile of
letters. Seven of these were angry or curt notes asking
for accounts to be closed, and saying that the writers would
deal elsewhere in future. Three were from friends who
told him, that if he wanted, as he said, to help the Magpie, he was going the very worst possible way about it,
and two were anonymous, unstamped letters on which
he had to pay double postage. The first of these two letters said, that if he came down Muck Alley any night he
would get what was coming to him; the other told him to,

"Mine yur busness baikur, cus people in Muk aley giv
their children the bes they cood lik others done. soe go
rid to Putny on a Pigg".

No subscription came to the Defence Fund; there was,
however, a note from Mr. Gallup asking for the promised fifty pounds, and asking him to make it guineas, as
being more usual, so that counsel might be fed. The
baker had no banking account, save in an old stocking.
He sent off the money, having made it guineas, and felt
the happier for having done it.

"We won't flinch, my Try", he said.

"Flinch, Rob, no; you'll never do that. We'll save the
poor creature, never fear. People are afraid that we're

defending Rapp, but presently they'll see the truth. The new package of leaflets came, while you were at the post office, so I opened it, and some have gone already".

"Good", said the baker, "I'll put out a leaflet on the notice-board again".

He did so. As on the day before, a small crowd gathered to read and to comment. Some people came in to buy, but fewer than had come the day before.

At about eleven that morning, when the baker was busy in the shop, he saw through the window, a certain respectful drawing away of people who were reading the notice propped against the cake. He saw, then, that Sir Hassle was about to pass. The heads, which had been craned there, now sheepishly uncovered. Sir Hassle cocked his finger upwards, in recognition of their salute. He put his eyeglass to his eye, moved stiffly for a few seconds to the window and glanced at the pages spread before him. He was there for perhaps five seconds; the baker, who was watching him, saw no change upon his face. At the end of the five seconds, his eyeglass dropped from his eye; he turned stiffly and walked on.

"That was Sir Hassle, Rob", Tryphena said. "He didn't seem to like it. He always drops his glass like that when he doesn't like a thing".

"He isn't meant to like Muck Alley", the baker said. "He's meant to hate it and all it stands for. The sooner he learns to hate it the better".

"He will learn to hate it", Tryphena said, "but he'll hate you first and worse for making him aware of it".

Meanwhile, Sir Hassle, who had to speak to the saddler, passed on. He met with his lawyer, who was walking to speak with a man at Mrs. Calmamine's. The two talked together for a moment about the chances of a horse in one of the autumn meetings. Then Sir Hassle said,

"Have you seen that newspaper cutting in the baker's window? You ought to step down that way".

He nodded and passed on. The lawyer, who knew that Sir Hassle had a prejudice against the baker, thought that he had better see what the matter was. He walked down to the bakery, read the article, thought for an instant, and then, being a kindly man, stepped into the shop, and drew the baker into the yard for a few words.

"I do just want to ask you", he said, "to think again before you keep your pamphlet exposed there. I thoroughly approve your trying to help the poor man, and here is my guinea towards your fund. But all the first part of your paper is an appeal to prejudice and class feeling. It won't help your man; it won't help your appeal. It must damage both. And remember that the law is a very strange thing. Comment on a case sub judice is what is called a Contempt of Court. I won't say for a moment that your paper as it stands constitutes a Contempt, but your enemies, if you have any, might wrest it into seeming so".

"Thank you", the baker said. "I know you mean kindly. But all that I say there is true, and I can feel nothing but Contempt for a Court that will try a poor lunatic like the Magpie".

"But he has to be tried", the lawyer said. "That fact cannot be altered, by any amount of contempt of the system. He has to be tried, at the Tatchester Assizes next week. Surely your position should be to help him through the ordeal. Go to him in his cell, cheer him up, see that he gets little comforts and what counsel you can command. Give evidence on his behalf, tell the jury all these facts about him, which you write there. Frankly, to write them and publish them thus can only harm his cause; and may even make it difficult for you to give evidence on his behalf. Believe me, he needs all the help he can get. May I ask if you have received much for the defence fund"?

"No", the baker said, "the original gift and your guinea".

"Well, does not that a little bear out my point, that you ought to modify your methods? Think it over, won't you, Mr. Mansell, as a point that ought to be thought over? And forgive my interfering".

He left the baker thinking it over.

"The lawyer wants me to haul my colours down and think it over, Try", he said. "He thinks I may be causing prejudice and making it impossible for me to give evidence. He says I ought to give what I have written there as evidence, in court, and not display it here".

"Give evidence in court, Rob, before the Judge"?

"He thinks so".

"It might well be the saving of the poor Magpie, if you did that".

"Let us ask the Lord about it", the baker said.

They knelt down and opened the Bible. The text under the baker's thumb as he opened it was the first verse of the Thirty-fifth Psalm:

"Plead my cause, O Lord, with them that strive with me".

"There now, my darling", he said, "is not that a direct

answer? I will take down the notices and burn the leaflets, and I will write by this night's post to Mr. Gallup, to ask if I may give evidence".

His heart shrank from giving evidence, for he had not been feeling very well for some months. At times he felt his head all clouded and wretched. When he had to speak in public, he liked to lie down to rest in a darkened room for an hour or more. He could not expect to be able to do that at Tatchester. Still, he would do all that he could, to the limit of his strength, knowing very well that at that point the Lord would step in to give him His strength. He went outside and removed the notice-board, while Tryphena, leaning over the show cake, removed the copy from the window. One or two lads who were gathered there said,

"Baker's going to cop it now, for using such language. It's two months for you, Baker".

The baker grinned at them; going indoors, he destroyed all the leaflets, except one file copy. For the rest of the day, men and women, who had been told of the leaflets, came to the shop to see them. They asked for copies. From their requests, the baker learned that odd reports had gone abroad concerning them. One man asked to see "The attack upon the Queen"; another said, that he'd been told, that the baker had said the Church ought to be abolished.

The baker wrote to Mr. Gallup, asking if he might give evidence on the Magpie's behalf. Remembering what the lawyer had said, he asked if he might visit the prisoners in their cells.

"If that's allowed, Try", he said, "we must do that, at all costs, more than once".

"Oh, Rob, I don't think I could visit Rapp", Tryphena said.

"I don't like the thought of it myself", the baker said, "but I blush that I had to be reminded of a Christian's duty by a chance comer, like the lawyer. It's our duty to visit the Magpie, for he has been one of our workmen here; and it's our duty to visit Rapp, as he is in an extreme of peril, as well as without earthly friends".

Meanwhile, the leaflet produced its effects, as writings will. There was in Condicote a widow who disliked the baker for what she styled his insolence in having political views. She had sent her maid to the bakery for a copy of the leaflet on the day of its appearance. Having read it, she sent it to the editor of the *Tatchester Times,* with a letter asking if the writer of such things could not be prosecuted. The editor, in a leading article in his next number, said that he was sorry to find that there were in Condicote men so dead to a sense of rightness and decency as to try to make political capital out of the late deplorable crime. That the article sent to him was in the very worst radical taste, and that he, therefore, strongly advised its writer to stick to his oven and his peel before the anger of his fellow citizens, if not the Law of the Land, was severely visited upon him. For his part, he concluded, after quoting some of the leaflet, he could not understand why the law had not already been invoked.

This reached Mr. Gallup in his office as he sat at work upon the case. He had received the baker's money and offer to give evidence; a friend had sent him a copy of the leaflet; now here, in the *Tatchester Times* just brought in by his clerk, was editorial comment on it. He rose up swearing, and at once called in the clerk.

"Take this letter", he said, "and let it go at once . . .

" 'Mr. Gallup begs to acknowledge the receipt of fifty guineas from Mr. Mansell for the use of the defendants in the case Crown v Rapp and anor. He notes that Mr. Mansell wishes to give evidence on behalf of the younger defendant. He begs that Mr. Mansell will at once suppress the enclosed document and cease from publishing further papers likely to prejudice the defendants' case'.

"Oh Lord", he said to his clerk as he finished, "Lord save an accused man from his friends. Here are two men up for murder. It's a poaching case. All the prejudice of the haves in all these parts is dead against the prisoners. Yet up steps the only friend they have and lets fly a blast like this. Lord, I wish I could only have the punching of him".

While this letter was being dictated in Tatchester, Sir Hassle was sitting in the office of his lawyer in Condicote. As he owned most of one side of the little town, he had much legal business. He went into three or four questions, of tenancies, sales and repairs; then said,

"About that man, Mansell, the baker, and his tenure of the bake-house. I've been displeased with the way he has been behaving, bringing down radical speakers and setting up inflammatory leaflets and so forth. You may remember we had complaints before about this, as well as a good many complaints, from the people on both sides of the bake-house, of the noise and inconvenience of the workers in the yard late at night. I've made up my mind, that I'll have no more of it . . . He's got to go".

As the lawyer looked a little blank at this, Sir Hassle said,

"I take it, that he holds the bake-house on the usual short agreement. But I know he does".

"Yes, yes, Sir Hassle", the lawyer said. "All your property in the town is held on short agreement; it has often given you great advantage. But the Mansell family have been tenants to you and to your forebears for a hundred and fifty years, which is a long time. Might it not be possible to consider giving them a somewhat longer time of grace than the strict letter of agreement entitles you to"?

"I do not think so", Sir Hassle said.

"There might be real difficulty in his getting any other place that would serve him as a bakery", the lawyer went on. "It is not easy to get such premises. As you know, the neighbours complain of the noise of the night workers moving about and so forth".

"Not nearly so much as they complain of the kind of stuff he's been writing and speaking. I suppose twenty people have complained to me of his rubbish. As a matter of fact, he will have more than the three months. You can give him notice at once, now in October, that he is to be out of it on Lady Day; that will give him five months in which to look about him and perhaps to consider his position. Between ourselves, I'm not sure that his latest paper is not tantamount to a Contempt of Court, which will certainly not be overlooked. If I'm right about that, he will be out of business, I should imagine, for some time".

"Very good, Sir Hassle", the lawyer said, "I will see that he has notice to quit. It shall be sent tonight".

"No", Sir Hassle said, "let it go by hand today".

"Very good, Sir Hassle; it shall go by hand at once".
After Sir Hassle had gone, the lawyer had several mat-

ters to attend to, so that the notice to quit was not sent
at once. At noon, the lawyer rang for a clerk, and gave him
instructions to prepare the usual form of notice and bring
it for signature. The clerk did as he was bid, but while
the letter was preparing a client came in, to see the lawyer
on business. He remained to gossip about horses likely
to do well at Stanchester. They talked a long time, so
long that the clerk laid aside the letter and slipped out
to lunch. He always took his lunch, a pint of bitter and a
portion of bread and cheese, at the *Black Joke*, a pub with
a skittle alley attached to it, just up the road from his
office. At lunch there, he met young Mr. Wye, of the
Steam Bakery, who often took him on at skittles after
lunch, and sometimes gave him a useful tip for him to
pass on to his master.

"What is good for the Downland Stakes, Dick"? he
asked.

"Ah, I'll talk about that later", young Wye said, "not
in here".

They lunched at the bar, sitting on high stools; the
barmaid, who was a blonde with a high colour, looked at
them as she would have looked at two cockroaches. Presently, they knocked the crumbs off their waistcoats, wiped
the beer from their lips, lit their pipes and went out to the
skittle alley, where their predecessors were ending their
game.

"Now, you want a real good thing for the Downland"?
young Mr. Wye said. "I can give you one, and that's what
few would do. It's Curator, the fastest thing in the race.
I had it from the stable. It comes from right inside. He
could fall down twice and win. You can use it and you

can pass it on to your boss, but you'd best be quick to get on".

"Ah, Curator is it"? the clerk said. "Thanks. I'll have a quid on with Tom. Now I can give you a quiet tip. One of your rivals in the bun and bread line is getting the knock, to get out of it by Lady Day".

The two looked at each other.

"Notice to quit"? Mr. Wye said.

The clerk nodded.

"Too much red revolution"?

The clerk nodded.

Young Mr. Wye looked at the clerk, then looked at the pigeons tumbling in the sky above the roofs.

"Has he got it yet"? he asked.

"This afternoon he will".

"Good-oh, thanky; that's news. I'll be getting along then", Mr. Wye said. "This'll be worth Curator and something more. Thanky".

He went off in a hurry, leaving the clerk to finish his skittles alone.

He went straight down the street, to Mrs. Binding, who owned an empty house in what was called the Gate. It had in its basement an excellent vaulted oven; it was the only place in Condicote which was so equipped. Many years before there had been a school for young gentlemen, (that is an expensive army crammer's), in the big manor, now partly ruinous, just beyond the Gate. The oven had done the school cooking as well as outside work, but the school had failed owing to the riotous behaviour of the young gentry, and the Gate was too far from the street for the bakery to compete with the Mansells, whose customers passed their door daily. No one had used the oven for years, but the house in which it lay was now empty, and in good repair. Mr. Wye knew that if the Mansells were thrown out of their present home, they would try to take the Gate House, which could be used as a bakery without any alteration or expense. There were points about the Gate House which might suit them very well. Mr. Wye was determined that he would be before-hand with them. He saw Mrs. Binding, went with her to the property there and then, saw what could be done there, and determined to take it for a short term, which Mrs. Binding agreed to. After leaving Mrs. Binding, he called upon the lawyer who acted for her and made the bargain sure.

"Not too sure", he thought, knowing what slips may come in the taking of premises, "but the chances are that I've spiked that gun for them".

Meanwhile, the lawyer took the written notice to the Mansells, and signed it with a heavy heart. It seemed to him to be a dirty piece of work, to get rid of an old tenant and a very old association for an error of head due to too much righteous feeling; however, his not to reason why . . . He had his instructions, and presently despatched the office boy with the letter. It was delivered there just as the baker came in to his tea, at the end of the drawing of the batches, when the van had gone off with its load.

"Here's a letter from the lawyers", Tryphena said.

"Let them all come", the baker said. "I can't think of anyone going to law with me. Just wait one moment till I get this flour off, then we'll have tea".

"Perhaps someone has left you a legacy", Tryphena said, as she poured the water into the teapot.

"Not much of that", the baker said, as he washed his hands under the tap above the sink. "No, rather the other way about. The word has gone about that I'm not to have a long date for things. I'm to pay on the nail, henceforth, for eggs and flour and all the rest. Never mind.

> " 'O, Mother, I'll marry the baker,
>   Who bakes me the sweet penny buns.' "

He was in very good spirits, for during his work that afternoon he had felt again, for the first time for some weeks, that quickening in his soul which assured him that he was right in the course of action he had set forth upon. A Puritan would have said, that he had the blessing of the Lord upon him. He used to call the feeling "a guidance" and had never yet failed to regret going against the guidance. He had described it once to Engels, who had laughed at him, as "a kind of light which springs up inside me, and shows me this way or that".

He dried his hands on the roller towel and went to the table, with an eye at the shop, through the glass of the door.

"Now let us see what these men of law say", he said. "What have I been doing now, I wonder".

"Read it, my dear", Tryphena said. "I expect it's to do with the paper in the window".

He opened the oblong envelope, which had upon its flap an embossed imitation seal.

"Read it aloud; do let me hear", Tryphena said.

The baker read.

"Dear Sir,
   We are instructed to inform you that under the terms

of your agreement with Sir Hassle Gassle your tenancy
and occupation of the premises at No. 27, The High Street,
Condicote, are to cease and determine as from next Lady
Day, the 25th. of March next, when the entire property
will be reconditioned.

> Yours faithfully,
>
> etc., etc."

"Just read me that", he said, handing the letter to her,
"and tell me if you ever met the match of it".

Tryphena read it and turned white. "It means that we're
to be turned out".

"That's the idea. It's the order of the Front Door".

"But, surely, Rob, they can never turn you out without
showing some just cause? What have we done that we
should be turned out"?

"Any stick will do to beat a dog with. But out we have
to go, you may be sure".

"What does he mean by the property being reconditioned"?

"That he's going to put in ten pennorth of new plumb-
ing and raise the rent fifteen pounds", he answered. "I
don't know what he means. He's been wanting to get rid
of me for some time".

"But, Rob, the Mansells have been his tenants for ages.
We have been here more than a hundred years. Surely
he would see that and let that weigh with him".

"If he hasn't weighed that already, he won't now. No,
it's this revolutionary baker, who won't leave well alone.
He's got to go".

"But not without cause shown, Rob".

"His will is the cause. I've known Sir Hassle for a
long time, and whatever he might do for others, he will

do nothing for me. I've never yet got anything from him, and in this case I'm not going to ask. He and his hardness of heart are my enemies. I am glad to be quit of any touch and truck with him".

"I am glad, too, then, if you are glad", Tryphena said. "Let him turn us out. Let him ruin us".

"He won't ruin us, my dear; the righteous is not forsaken and hasn't to beg his bread. Come now; we're young, and Condicote isn't the only place in the world. I know my job, and the world will always need its daily bread. It can't do without that, can it? We will just kneel down here and ask the Lord's guidance".

They knelt and asked and received comfort from the asking. On rising from her knees, Tryphena said,

"Don't you think, Rob, that it would be a good thing to go round to Mrs. Binding? You know the Gate is still to let. It is not expensive, and you said once, if you remember, that the furnace there is very good".

"Yes, that's the only place in Condicote", he said. "We could do very well there; except that it's out of the way. People don't pass the door there as they do here. I'd be inclined to say, get up out of here and try again somewhere else: at Yockford, say".

"Oh, no, Rob; think of the expense of moving all that way. And then, there'd be all the getting known in the new place, and the old-established businesses to fight against. We are known here, and besides, it would never do to own defeat".

"We may have to own defeat", he said. "We've lost a lot of our business to those chaps just up the road there, and we are losing more daily. This leaving here will lose a lot more. But I'll go round to Mrs. Binding. I'll have a look at the place again. It used to be a pleasant place when it was all humming with the school. But you cheer up about the leaving here. I'm cheered. If I'm on the side Sir Hassle isn't, then I know I'm on the side of God. We'll tell the truth and shame him and the devil, too, if he's not too much of brass for shame".

He saw to one or two things in the bake-house, and then went up to speak to Mrs. Binding about the Gate. She told him, that she was very sorry, but the premises which had been vacant for two years had now been let, but she was not at liberty to say to whom, as she had been asked not to. She did not know what was to be done with them; but the fact was that they were let, subject to all being in order, and then, if it should fall through, why, she would let him know. She had already removed the notice, "To Let", from the front gate.

The baker walked back in some anxiety, for he did not want to have to go to the expense of putting in a furnace in the new home. It was an expensive matter. He was feeling that the word had gone abroad about him, that he was to be put out of business. He was to be pressed, (so he could see), for any monies due, and to have short shrift if he failed. It would cost a good deal, to get out of his present premises and establish himself elsewhere. If he had to borrow money from the bank, to put in a furnace somewhere, he would be handicapped from the start. He wondered who could have taken the Gate.

"It wasn't let yesterday", he thought, "for I was along by there in the afternoon, and the notice was still up".

"The Gate is let, Try", he said. "It is just possible that it will fall through, but as far as Mrs. Binding can see, it is let".

"Who has taken it"?

"She could not tell; but she'll let us know if it comes to nothing".

"Is it anyone we know, I wonder", Tryphena wondered. "We might be able to arrange with him".

The baker was not prone to believe evil of men of his own rank. He did not suspect the rival firm. He judged, that God had meant to try him, and resolved, that he would not be tried beyond his strength. He debated with Tryphena and later with Bob, what could and should be done. Tryphena thought that she had heard, that one of the houses further up the street had a bake-house attached to it, which was not in use. The baker felt that she was mistaken, as he would have heard of it. Bob was all for getting away from Condicote and trying elsewhere, in a place such as Tatchester, where there might be public libraries and other delights.

"Well, come along, Bob", his father said, "you and I will just go up the road a piece, and find out if your mother is right about the bake-house. It is in the Cat and Fiddle Alley. I can't believe she can be right".

He had trouble in finding anyone who knew about any such place, but at last met an old woman who said, that "Yes, in old Mr. Harker's time they had a brew-house there; no, not a bake-house, a brew-house, by the spring, for brewing beer". He judged, that Tryphena had confused the two things.

"I thought she must be wrong", he said. "I don't think anyone but ourselves baked bread here in Condicote except just the private baking, which has been going out ever since I was a child. Now you are all for Tatchester, Bob. Well, you are young, you want to see the world;

but a city, after this, is a sad place, Bob, full of degrada-
tion of life. Why do you want the city, Bob? You have
had a glimpse of it now and then".

"Well, Father", Bob said, "it is full of life, and more
is going on in it than goes on here. You get a chance to
know what is being thought and done. You have more
choice of friends. You have more chance of getting somewhere. You have a wider field and more fun. You yourself had a time in London, and often say you wouldn't
have missed it".

"There's something in that", the baker said, "but I'm
afraid that if I were to go to Tatchester, it would be
as your mother foretold just now, a great expense, a lot
of old-established firms against you, and a world of trouble
to build up a business. Here we're known, Bob".

"I'd like to say, Father", Bob said, "that if you stay
here you'll have a great expense, anyhow, putting in the
plant; and you'll have a lot of trouble from the Steam
Bakery. They're going ahead; and now that we are losing
business and being turned out of the shop, they'll go ahead
quicker. If we were in Tatchester, you could belong to
debating clubs and political fellowships and no one would
mind or be able to punish you for it. It would be the
other way about; they would rally round you. Here, as
far as I can make out, the minute you say what you feel
and know to be true, someone gets up and says you shan't
bake for them. You can be a man in a city, and here you
can only be a parasite, as far as I can see. It is like living
under a microscope; the instant there's a wriggle from
you, the observer says, 'A germ. Put him in the disin-
fectant'. Then, I want to say this. I'm getting to be able

to work, and to think of what I'm to do with my life. I don't want to be a baker all my days. I don't know quite what I do want to be, but I know I don't want to be that".

"Why, Bob, what is there in baking that you don't like"?

"There's nothing in it that I do like, really, and if I stick to it too long, I shan't be able to take up anything else. It will be too late".

"It's bread and butter, Bob: a man ought not to quarrel with his bread and butter".

"I think he ought to, Father, if it isn't agreeing with him".

"It is agreeing with you. It has agreed with me, until just the last few months".

"I don't mean in health, Father", Bob said. "I mean in the way he looks at it. Ought a man to hate his daily work"?

"No, certainly not. That is failing in our duty. We have to do our duty in that state of life to which it has pleased God to call us".

"But if someone were a genius, able to invent wonderful engines or paint pictures or build cathedrals, and he had been born a crossing-sweeper, would it be his duty to sweep crossings all his life for people who didn't want to get their shoes dirty"?

"You're considering an extraordinary case. I'm speaking of the usual rule for everyday people like you and me, old fellow. In an extraordinary case, you'll generally find that God has His way of bringing the genius to light. But for plain you and me, it is the rule for a cobbler to stick to his last, and not to presume".

"But is he bound to stay on at work he loathes and

does badly just because he happens to be born to it, when the world is full of things he wants to do and might do well"?

"It is the general finding of the world that it's better in the long run, Bob. The world has been at it a long time, and that is its general verdict of the case".

"It surely is right to try to do better things, whatever one is doing. The world would never have got anywhere, Father, if people hadn't tried".

"I'm speaking of plain people, like you and me, Bob. But go on and talk it out, old fellow. I want to hear you. We need not turn in home for just a minute; the fresh air may do me good. You say you don't quite know what you do want to be. What do you think of most. What would you be, if you had your chance"?

"I suppose I'd like to be a learned man, and know all sorts of things; and be able to help on knowledge. The Rector once said to me, that every bit of knowledge is good, because it is an attribute of God, and every bit of it lessens ignorance, which is a blindness to God and the things of God. I used not to think of getting knowledge much, till he said that; and some people say it is only punk, but I think of it all the time, and it seems to make all the world so different".

"Yes, but, Bob, getting knowledge is all very well; but men have to live; they cannot live by books alone. You will have to earn your living, as it is called; you will have to toil at something in order not to starve. You say you hate baking. You may find that you will hate other things even more; and then where would you be? One of these thoroughly unsettled men you meet everywhere who cannot stick at anything, but drift from one job to another.

When I was a young chap, like you, I remember thinking how much better I could preach than the parson of
those days, who didn't seem to me to have the gift at all;
and then what a pity and shame it was that a fine eloquent
chap, like yours truly, should be shifting buns with a peel.
Then I went to London, to have the run of my teeth,
as it was called, and also to learn the business in a flash
London shop. There I found, that I wasn't such a preacher
after all, but made a poor show at it when I tried. And I
learned, too, that God has his design in putting each one of
us where he is, and that He wants us, certainly wants us,
to put our talents to use; but at the same time, He does
want us to prove, that we can put them to use; He wants
us to be faithful in small things before He trusts us with
the greater. So, when I had wrestled that much clear to
myself, I made up my mind that I was to be a baker,
not one of these swayers of the crowd, like Mark An-
tony or Bradlaugh, but a baker of daily bread; and it
was a bitter pill, for I'd had a fair old opinion of myself.
Well, a lot of bitter pills make good medicine. But although I was a baker I didn't quite neglect what my heart
told me was right. I read a certain amount and thought
of the problems of the working man and did all I could
for those who could help that cause better than I. Then
I met your mother, and, of course, when a man sets up
house he has to give up a whole lot of things and ideas
that he once thought the world of. When you have children coming, you have to fend for them and let the world
fend for itself. Still, we both had our hearts in the cause;
and, of course, lately, with you growing up, and no other
child to prepare for or do for, we have been able to do
something for the cause again. But now we can do it,

Bob, don't you see, by having this work of baking to fall back on. We could not have done, even what we have done, unless we'd had this behind us. No, what I would suggest your doing is to go as I did up to Town to put in, say, a year in some flash modern bakery, where everything is up-to-date and the men the very pick; it should be quite possible to work you in somewhere.

"Probably what is the matter with you, Bob, though you may not put it into words, is a wanting to break with the old birds in the nest, and try your own wings a bit. You probably feel that young wings are strong wings and can fly better without brakes. All young folk feel that way, and it is better not to try to keep them at home. When you have been on your own a bit, you'll feel like the rest of us, that the nest is the important thing, and that one has to come back to it sooner or later, and that, in any case, it is the rallying place where all fall back in case of need.

"But the way things seem to be shaping, there may not be much nest for you to come back to. Still, God won't desert us, you may be sure of that, and you may be sure, too, that He'll give you a direction when the time comes, and then your way will be made quite clear. But I do ask, as your father, and as one who has been through this for himself, years ago, not to quarrel with a job before you've settled to it. A lad always kicks against the restraint of a job at first. He has had fun at school, and been perhaps a sort of leader there and then has to give up friends and games and that and buckle to at a job, getting up at five every morning and worse, and not getting any praise from anybody but rather a lot of kicks and curses. Small wonder he doesn't want to stick at it. But he has only to wait a while, and then there comes the wife and the babes, and the galling task becomes sacred for their sakes. Or that's how I've come to look at it, old man".

"Father", Bob said, "would you tell me something about your father and mother"?

"Why, Bob"? his father said. "They make rather an unhappy story, on both sides. Mother ran away from home to marry Father, and presently Father ran away from Mother to live with a barmaid. Poor souls, they were all three to be pitied".

"Did you ever see the Dixons, Father, your mother's people"?

"Why, yes, Bob", his father said. "You know, Bob, I may be unfeeling in my judgment, but I have often thought that some rich people care more for property than for persons. You see, I am half a Dixon. My mother was a Dixon; but that did not weigh at all with any of them. What I was in myself, or what the half of me as a Dixon was, did not matter. They never enquired; they never so much as asked if I were a boy or girl; I had no truck nor dealings with any one of them, till there was a question of some house property in South London. Some of it had been left to my mother's branch of the family, and my mother's share of it, such as it was, came to me. It was a very little matter, but they had to discuss with me about the disposal of the property. Some of them came here to see me about it. Now, Bob, the last thing the Lord will ask, when He judges a soul, will be what property he has, or has had. I was young and very proud at the time, and I was quite bitterly hurt at being ignored for twenty-five years as a human being, and then suddenly consulted as an owner of property. I made over all the property to them, and bade them get out of it. I said bitter things, and I've been bitterly sad about it since.

"And now, Bob, old fellow, you think of what I have said. I'll show you Mother's picture one of these days; I've got it put away. And do be sure, old boy, that it's a man's daily work that gives him his happiness, if he'd only have the sense to see it".

Bob had heard all this before, most young people have, but his father spoke with a greater tenderness than usual, owing to the seriousness of the times for him.

"Well, Try", the baker said on his return home, "the place in the court there is no longer to be had; we must just make up our minds to the fact that we shall have to put in a furnace in any place we decide to take. We can probably afford it, and if we can't, why, then, perhaps the banker will give us a little credit, and let us pay it back gradually. But the bakery can wait for a little. The thing that can't wait is the poor Magpie, whose case is coming on.

"Now, it seems to me, that there are two things that should be done at this point, or rather three. I'm going over tomorrow, to see the poor prisoners in the prison; that's the first. The second is: I want to bring old Adolf in to be interested in the case. As it springs out of poaching, which he has always been strong on, I've written to him, asking him if he can't come down or send someone. They wouldn't mind squelching me, if I said anything; but they'd be afraid to try to squelch *The Banner*. That's the last resource, of course, if everything else comes to nothing. The third thing is, that perhaps we ought to get up a petition here in Condicote on behalf of the Magpie.

We might get the magistrates who committed him to sign it, and a whole lot of others would, even if they refused".

"I'm sure *The Banner* will take up the case", Tryphena said. "As to the petition; I don't think there'll be any need for that. I was talking to Mrs. Calmamine today. She said, that no jury would dream of convicting the Magpie. She is in her bar, every night, and knows all that's said. That's the bar's opinion. It might be best to hear what Mr. Gallup says tomorrow".

The baker sent off his letter to Adolf. He went to Tatchester as he had planned. Mr. Gallup received him with bitterness.

"You're the man who wrote that mad pamphlet at Condicote. Well, I always say, God save an accused man from his friends. Your precious paper has just about ended them".

"I meant it for the best", the baker said.

"Well, for God's sake, try your worst, next time. It will do less harm, perhaps. Anyhow, it can't do more. You say you want to give evidence on behalf of the younger prisoner. How can you, after writing that pamphlet? You'd be pounced on at once and blown sky high, and jolly well would you deserve it. Are you aware, man, that that rotten rag of yours is tantamount to a Contempt"?

"No".

"Well, let me tell you, that it probably is. Besides, I'm in charge of the Defence and that plea of insanity is a rotten plea, let me tell you".

"It is not", the baker said, "how can it be? The poor man is not fit to plead. I've known him for years, and know that to be the fact".

"Well, I am to judge of what course to take to save my clients, and I tell you frankly that your courses are likely to be fatal to them. May I ask you, therefore, for God's sake, to stand clear and give me half a dog's chance"?

"Have you half a dog's chance"? the baker asked.

"Yes, if men like you will give us the field. I've got Slaughter for them. Upper Slaughter's worth half the jury in any case he puts his back into. Now, if you want to see the prisoners, come on; but no more pamphlets, mind".

He took the baker with him in a four-wheeled cab. The baker thought that it was hard to be so bitterly abused, when he had just paid fifty guineas into this man's hand. However, he was going to visit two poor prisoners. Soon after this, the cab reached the prison gate; the steel locks clicked; the baker, for the first time in his life, entered a world where men were not free.

He returned home, full of misery at what he had seen. He was cheered on his arrival by the news, that *The Banner* was following the case, and would send somebody to follow the trial; Adolf himself might be free to do it. A letter came from Adolf, the next morning, to say, that he had followed the case from the first, and that he would attend to it in person.

"Good old Ad", the baker said. "That's like Ad, all over, to put his back into a movement. He will bring the poor Magpie out of it, if any man can".

Meanwhile, his own affairs were heading for ruin. His customers closed their accounts daily. Nearly a quarter of his remaining custom was lost to him through the pamphlet alone. Word spread abroad at once, that he had been turned out of his premises, and serve him right. All those to whom he owed small sums, for fuel, flour, eggs and other matters used in his trade, sent in their bills and asked for early settlement. The Steam Bakery took all the custom which he lost. Mr. Wye junior was a happy man; his very bright eyes grew brighter.

In the excitement of preparing for the trial, the baker and Tryphena did not heed the passing of the business. They worked hard. Tryphena bore a hand at the mixing; Joe and his son came in to help; Bob always was a tower of strength when there was need. Tryphena cut down the household expenses, and looked ahead to see what could be saved in the months to come.

The baker and his friends had often talked of "the Law's delays". Now that the law had taken hold of Rapp and his companion it moved fast, too fast. In a few days the Assizes were on; the Grand Jury met to decide whether there were a True Bill against them.

It was before the Grand Jury that the point was raised, whether the younger prisoner, known as the Magpie, were sufficiently sane to be allowed to plead. The prison doctor gave evidence on this point. Dr. Gubbins from Condicote also spoke. Their evidence agreed. The younger prisoner was not very bright in some ways, but was by no means wanting in intelligence. The Grand Jury, without much delay, found a True Bill against both prisoners.

The Judge, in thanking the Grand Jury for the manner in which they had discharged their arduous, unpleasant, but necessary duties, said that it was in his power to reward them, by giving to such of them as cared, an order to view the local prison, where they might see something of the kind of thing to which their findings might, in certain circumstances, in some cases, ultimately lead. While those who chose to accept were giving in their names, the press men sent off their telegrams. The editors of all the local papers brought out special editions, to say, that a True Bill had been found against both prisoners in the Arthur's Camp case.

At this time, it became known, that the case would come on in the forenoon of Thursday. It was not thought likely that it would last more than the one day, though Mr. Gallup still vowed that it would go till Friday night.

Tryphena said that she could not possibly go to the trial. The baker was glad of this. Women, then, were "not supposed" to go to trials.

"I'll bring you all the news of it", he said, "when I come back. Old Ad will sit next me; and if things go badly, though I don't think the Lord will permit that, we'll have a petition out next morning, and something else as well".

They talked together far into the night, often stopping talk to pray, as their custom was, ex tempore, now for the Magpie, now for his defenders, now for the Judge to be enlightened, now for the prosecution to be darkened; they tried to their utmost power, to bring some fence or barrier of light and tenderness about the two prisoners in the cells fifteen miles away, who needed such help, if ever wretched men did.

The first morning of the trial happened to be the day of Tatchester Hiring Fair, which was always a time of much rejoicing in the countryside. When Tryphena walked with the baker to see him away by the early train, she found that the station was crowded with people going to Tatchester. There were many farmers, some with their wives, some with carter's cattlemen or shepherds. These were all going to the Fair. The baker had no quarrel with them. But many others were going out of idle or vicious interest in the murder trial; they meant to be in the court, if it could be managed, and to gloat over every incident and every misery.

Among the company were some of the professional and trades people of the little town; the doctor, who had to give evidence, the Rector, who brought his wife in the hope of being some comfort to the two Okle women after the ordeal of cross-examination; the lawyer, who had some business in the case called for later in the session; and a fair show of the shop-keepers, who meant to see the trial and to do some necessary business also. Presently two carriages drove up; one with the owner of the Arthur's Camp coverts, the other with Sir Hassle Gassle, who greeted each other on the platform and at once stood aside and talked to each other, as members of another world, removed from the common man. A kind of unseen fence sprang up round them at once, as though their presence sowed spikes and prickles. All kept their distance from them and even dropped their voices within hearing of them, or stood away, as the two, deep in talk, walked slowly up and down the platform. They were going to lunch together at the County Club, so the baker heard. He had planned not to salute his landlord if he chanced to meet. Now that he met him face to face, he saw Sir Hassle take off his hat (though stiffly) to Tryphena; it was a way that Sir Hassle had with the wives of tenants; so the baker took off his hat (though stiffly) in return, and looked at, and was looked at by, the hard steel gimlets which served Sir Hassle instead of eyes. No sort of recognition showed in the eyes, so the baker hardened his own to match, and so the two passed, nearer than they were ever to pass again.

Now, with a good deal of shouting from the station officials, the train drew in, and halted; some people got out and were able to get through the press; then in the rush, the two magnates were escorted to a first-class carriage by the station master, the professionals entered the second-class carriages on each side of the first; the rest stormed the carriages at the end of the train, and forced themselves in with a lot of good humour and a certain amount of fun, as well as some not very seemly jokes about parts of their bodies. The baker kissed his wife and climbed into a carriage full of people.

"Expect me when you see me", he cried, "but I expect I'll be back by the eight-fifteen tonight: so you can meet that unless you hear or unless you see me before".

A porter came along the train, shutting the doors of the carriages and crying out, "All for Tatchester; all for Tineton and Tatchester. Take your seats, please". Somebody blew a whistle, while the guard, at the end of the train, waved his green flag. The train started. The baker, leaning out of the window, waved to Tryphena; then the train drew away from the station, round the curve of the line, into the autumnal orchard land, where the trees had dropped most of their leaves yet still kept odd gnarled and withered apples on their twigs. It was a fair October morning, with a good deal of haze, which would presently clear away, and leave a soft and warmthless sunlight to put a sparkle on all the wet and faded earth.

The baker turned from the window, and surveyed the fellow travellers. They were the two brothers Pyx of Pyx Court, the last of a family which had held Pyx Court since the reign of Henry the Second; their cowman, Bill, and Tom Carter, their carter; also Mrs. Carter; all going doubtless, at the Pyx' expense, to the Tatchester Fair; there was Tom Sot, as he was called, who kept a pub down in Tatchester Parade, and smelt already of his stock in trade; there were also two women, whose names he did not know, but he knew that they came from out Battler's Down way, and a girl of fourteen, the daughter of one of them. This girl, who had never been in, nor very close to a train before, was already overcome by the experience and white to sickness point.

"Pore little thing, then", her mother was saying, "it does go to the liver, they say, travelling in a train the first time; but after you've been sick once or twice, you'll enjoy it ever so. Why, your father was sicker than you are, and he's a man".

John Pyx began the conversation, by saying that it was a nice day for the Fair. His brother, pointing out to Arthur's Camp, which the train was then passing, said,

"You can see the neck of the hill, there; that's where poor Okle was shot; just the other side of the rise. Well, that case will be settled today, one way or the other, but it won't bring poor Okle to life again".

John replied, that the case was on in the morning and could not take long, for he did not see what defence they could make; it ought not to take more than an hour or two. His brother said, that, "Very likely Mr. Gallup would plead Guilty and then appeal for mercy for the men, as there must have been some provocation; he might plead that". The feeling in the carriage was against this. The women were urgent, that there should be no mercy.

"The great murdering brute came along and shot poor

John Okle, and left his poor wife a widow and his daughter defenceless; why should he have mercy? Did he give any mercy? No, let him swing for it; the rope is too good an end. The only pity is that there were others in it besides those two that were got, some of the flash London lot, who were up to every deviltry; the only pity is that they were not there to swing, too, for they'd been in it, up to the hilt, and had planned it all".

Here the baker put in to say, that he had no word hard enough for Rapp, who had done the shooting, but that the case of the Magpie was different. He had known the Magpie, and could speak for him as one not mentally alert, certainly not alert enough to know what Rapp was doing when he lifted his gun at the keeper. He ought not to suffer from being unfortunately present when the shooting was done. This roused a storm of opposition. The Pyxes had had some experience of the Magpie.

"Don't you tell me that the Magpie is not all there", John Pyx said. "I had a lot of young turkeys out in the orchard the year before last, twenty-seven of them; my Bessie had reared them and they were getting along to be nice birds. Then one fine night they all disappeared, all the lot of them, and, of course, we never saw them again. Well, along about last month, a man in Yockford came up to me and said, 'You might like to know who it was boned your turkeys that time. It was Gipsy Toe, the Gowker, as they call him, worked you that quiff; him and the Magpie. The Magpie stole 'em. He could go anywhere on tiptoe as silent as a ghost; he charmed your dog; he could charm any dog; and the Gowker had a mare all ready the other end of the field. They got the mare quietly on the grass to a cart they had, and the turkeys were sold that morning in

Yockford Market. I tell you this', he said, 'as I was in with them then, but I've got religion since, and here's eighteen shillings', he said, 'to help pay you what I owe, and all the rest shall follow', and he's sent me a shilling since then. I won't tell you the fellow's name for some of you might know him, but I believe all he said. So don't you tell me that the Magpie is not all there. He'd a deal of cunning in him, and let people think him dafter than he was. He may not have been a very bright scholar or anything of that sort, but he's been clever enough to go about with a shady lot of poachers for a great many years and keep himself somehow out of prison. There's no more artful lad in the county, if you ask me".

"I don't know anything about him", the other Pyx brother said, "but it seems to me that he's got what has been a long time coming to him. Sooner or later, a man who goes about with that Muck Alley lot will end up in the dock on a serious count".

That was the general verdict of the carriage, that he had been very clever, in dodging justice so long.

"You can't do it all the time", they said. "You may get a run for a long time, and he has had one, but they get you in the end, and make you pay for it all".

The baker said, that they had all been going on the assumption that the two men were guilty. "What right have you to assume on hearsay that he stole your turkeys, and what right have we to assume that Rapp shot the keeper"?

"What right"? John Pyx asked, "why, the right any man has to believe the truth when he hears it. The man who told me about the turkeys was telling the truth; I could see it; besides I've seen the Gowker since and he confirmed it. He's in gaol now, the Gowker, himself, poor

chap, for Old Dick's crop of damsons that he swiped. As to
Rapp shooting the keeper, I heard poor Mrs. Okle give
her evidence, and I know that she was telling the truth. I
don't assume on either point. But while we're on the topic,
I might say that you, Mr. Baker, have been assuming that
they are innocent, and saying so, which seems to me to be
going a bit far".

"Well, well", his brother said, "they'll get at the truth
of it this morning, sanity and guilt and everything".

The train stopped at Tineton, where a crowd was waiting to get in. The door was opened, and in came two stout
elderly women with baskets. Room was squeezed for them
on the unpadded wooden seats; the baskets were piled on
the racks overhead. Two men and three boys pushed in
after them, to jam the space between the sitters' knees. The
train moved on with a jerk, which sent them off their feet
into the laps of the sitters; there were squeals and cheers,
good-humoured cries of, "Here we come round the mul-
berry bush", "Look out for the Zagazias", "Oh the rail-
roads of Old England", etc., etc.

One of the new comers was full of old Captain Dixon's
funeral, which had taken place the day before.

" 'Lay me between my two wives', the Captain had said,
in his last days, 'and let 'em fight me out between 'em'. So
they'd done their best to humour him; but when they
brought un to grave, her wouldn't go in; there wasn't room
for un, not between 'em, so they had to widen up the grave.
Parson was in a rare taking. Old Captain forgot the brick-
work; his bit isn't like a grave, not really; it's more like
what you might call a vault".

The man was cheered by the success of his anecdote
among the company; he went on from strength to strength.

"There was Old Dick, the other day, dug Dr. Gubbins' grave; old Dr. Gubbins, not this young fellow. Mrs. Gubbins said to un, 'How much shall I pay you for the digging, Dick'? 'Ah', Dick says, 'I can't bring myself to charge anything for the Doctor: he's brought me a rare lot of custom in his time' ".

Somebody produced a mouth organ from an inner pocket, and, after asking if folk would mind, began to play upon it "I dreamt that I dwelt", and followed this up with "And thou wert the cause of this anguish, my mother". Touched by these sweet melodies, the company began to sing, and so with song and merriment came into Tatchester station, where they crawled from the fugg of the crowded carriage into the crisp October, and found that the city had turned into a sour-smelling fog the mist which had lain like lawn on the meadows by the river. The baker knew Tatchester well. On reaching the platform, he saw Engels, who was waiting for him. They went off together to the Court House.

Presently, as the fog began to clear away a little, they saw the open space, which had for centuries served Tatchester as a market square. It was now a broad part of the main thoroughfare, four times the breadth of any other street in the city, and receiving into the lake of its wideness the traffic from four roads which here mingled for a while. It had once been an important point in the Roman legionary camp. A good many people had gathered in the square and on the pavements adjoining, to see the arrival of the Judge, who always drove to Court from the Judge's lodgings in the coach kept for the purpose.

There came a sudden waft of pleasant wind which took the fog away. The sun stole and then strode out of the dimness in heaven; he shone in glory. All the wet and rime-frosted roofs sparkled suddenly. The pigeons, which had been moping on the roofs and in the scroll-work about the windows, came to life, took wing and tumbled in the light above the town. Tatchester was famous for its pigeons; there were many hundreds of them at that time, in the old buildings of the city, the seven Gothic churches and the great cathedral; they were of all sorts, but most of them tumbled or half-tumbled, from a strain of tumblers which had escaped not long before and brought that faculty to a race or company of birds which had before been staid. The baker had been coughing ever since his arrival in the town, for the bitter fog, which irritated his nostrils, burnt, as it seemed, into his throat and lungs. Now, for the first time since he had left the train, he breathed a breath or two which did not hurt.

"This way for the monkey show", Engels said, taking the baker by the arm. "The comrades are keeping seats for us: we shan't have to fight for them".

The baker was glad of this, for he was feeling upset by the foul air of the train and the fog, by the excitement of the occasion and his coughing. He followed his friend across the square, up a few steps and along a paved alley, then into a dark passage, and up some stairs to Tatchester Court House, known sometimes as the Sessions House.

They pushed past a group of policemen who were blocking the gangway. Some friends of Engels waved to them from the seats allotted to the public. The two edged past those in their way to reach these friends, who gave up their seats to them.

"We've got seats with the Press", they said. "Now you sit here, and perhaps after it's all over, we'll meet across the way for a bite of dinner and a drop at the *Blue and White*".

The baker and Engels took the seats, the two friends nodded and moved away.

"That's Pitchfork of *The Banner*, the short one", Engels said. "The other is the one they call 'T Square of the Workers' Hopes' ".

When he was seated, the baker looked about him at the court. Though he knew Tatchester, he had never before been in the building. It was a show place, well-proportioned, with a barrel roof and much dignity of line. The roof had been painted by an eighteenth century Tatchester man, named Brownlow, who had contrived to fill the centre of the barrel of the roof with a figure of Justice, blindfolded and bearing a sword, while about her skirts a swirl of smoke or cloud came out in bulges with a fat cherub in each bulge. The walls were panelled as far as the wall-pieces, with good solid panels of the time of George the Second. The panelling had darkened from age, dirt and soot; the Justice above it had gone grimy, but neither was to be cleaned for another forty years.

At the western end of the room, which ran east and west, there was a raised platform or stage, arranged in tiers of seats. In the middle of these tiers, raised above them by two little flights of three stairs each, (one on each side of it), was the Judge's throne, which resembled a big eighteenth century pulpit. It was made of walnut, nearly black from age and dirt. Instead of a sounding board, it had above it a dirty red canopy. The chair of Justice, also of walnut, had upon its tall back a panel painted with the Royal Arms. The back of this chair of Justice was carven or turned with much elaboration. On the ledge in the front of the Judge's pulpit, facing the congregation, was a writing slab with pen, ink and papers for the Judge's notes. Beside this on each side was a pewter pot stuck full of dried lavender, fresh rosemary, and sprigs of bay. In the midst of these herbs, in each pot, was a pomander or orange decked with cloves. These things had been place on the Judge's slab at every session for some hundreds of years, to save the Judge from that infection of gaol fever, which in 1579 had killed the Judge, the counsel, the officers of the court and most of the witnesses and accused. A stone with verses on it marks their common grave in Saint Alpig's burial ground, near the Cathedral.

"That's where his royal Nibs will sit", Engels said. "And the counsel for and against will be on the sides right and left of him. Then the big table below the Judge's seat is for the clerks and other officers of the court. Those seats on the right are for the jury, all honest and true. Those seats on the left are for the witnesses, and that place on the right is where the witnesses stand when they give evidence".

Between these things and the space of tiered seats where the baker and his friend were sitting, was a large wooden enclosure of about breast height. It was made of walnut, like the other fittings. Peering over this, the baker could see that it contained four plain oaken chairs, and that a flight of stone steps led down from it to a darkness into which he could not see.

"That's the prisoner's dock", Engels said. "They'll bring the prisoners up those steps, and set them on those chairs between policemen. We shall have a good view from here. We're Press and in the very front row. You look as if you'd never seen a place like it. Were you never in a court before"?

"Never one like this before. I was on a coroner's jury once".

"Well, a little goes a very long way, if you ask me", Engels said. "It may not seem much, to look at, but when you have all this against you, as I have had and may have again, it can squeeze you pretty damned small".

Though the walls and roof of the building were dirty and the Judge's canopy grimy and subject to moth, the windows had been cleaned. They were, however, of old glass, rather thick and greenish, so that the room was not as light as it might have been. The windows had not been made to open. Modern taste had contrived cords by which a small square in each window might be opened at the bidding of the Judge. As it was now brisk October weather, they had not been opened that session. There was a heavy weight, rather than a smell, upon the air, as though all that weight of justice had pressed it flat; pressed it to death, perhaps, for refusing to plead. The flavour of the place was unpleasant. Little mirth had been known there, little joy, no love and no beauty. It had seen in its hundred and fifty years a great deal of human misery, and a weight of anxiety not easy to reckon. It had seen and heard sentence of death passed upon some hundreds of men, women and children, who had stood in that dock, and had hoped till the jury had returned; and had then known despair, never again to be lifted from them. Some shadow of the horror which had lain on those humble and erring and violent hearts was about the place forever. The baker felt it, and thought that it was horrible.

But now the policemen in the gangways took on a more bustling air; they put on their helmets and took position in the aisles; the sergeant passed the word, that no more were to be admitted; the seats were full. A little man, trying to push in, was told to get back. He said that he was evidence, and at last caught the sergeant's eye.

"Here", said the sergeant, "what are you? Are you Evidence"?

"Yes".

"Well, you ought not to come in this way, if you're Evidence. You ought to have come in by the Witnesses' Door, down the stairs there, first to the right and then along the corridor. You know that as well as I do; but since you *are* here, why, you'd better go across the floor. But look sharp, because His Lordship will be in in a minute and it's not really allowed".

From without at the door of the Court House, there came the wail of a trumpet and a roll of kettle drums. It was the custom of Tatchester to play the Judge into Court, with trumpet and drum, both of whom wore a mayoral livery and received an allowance of bread and beer for doing it. At the sound of the trumpet, the sergeant and other policemen stiffened to attention. An old, frowsy man, in a dirty robe and much dirtier wig, called out,

"The QUEEN'S JUSTICE is in the Precincts".

For an instant, his interruption checked the jabber that was going on all over the Court. It died down. People looked up, expecting the Judge to be entering; then, seeing that it was not the Judge, but only the Jury and Counsel, the chatter broke out again, louder than before.

The Jury filed into their seats; they filled two rows. The baker was disturbed by noticing, that Counsel were talking together. The fierce, bullet-headed man, with a red face, bushy eyebrows and coarse mouth, was Slaughter; but was not the other barrister, the lean man, of sixty-five or more, with a hatchet-shaped, colourless face, the counsel for the Crown? He could not understand how the two could come in together, apparently on terms of friendship, when in the next five minutes they would be inevitably on opposite sides, fighting against each other for two men's lives.

"Surely", the baker thought, "this must be yet another iniquity of the law. What is to prevent these two men, if they're friends, from arranging from time to time which of them is to win? But perhaps", he muttered, "perhaps the Crown Counsel will come in with the Judge. That man may be what the lawyers call Mr. Slaughter's Junior".

Mr. Gallup, who was at the table below the Counsel, came from his place, and handed something to Mr. Slaughter, who made some evidently coarse remark, for two or three of the Clerks at the big lower table guffawed, and the big sergeant hid a grin. And the baker took an even deeper dislike to the bullet-headed man. He wore a frowsy old gown, and his wig was none too clean.

They took their seats and chatted a minute, till presently the cathedral bells, only a hundred yards from them in the great tower, chimed for the hour; and at the first stroke of the clock the man in the dirty robe cried out,

"Pray rise, for the Queen's Justice".

There was a sudden hushing of all talk, and a shuffle and thump as the people rose. Silence followed, so that the baker was suddenly conscious of the great beauty of the volume and tone of the clock bell, booming out the strokes of the hour. In that brief interval, somehow, two policemen appeared in the dock with the two prisoners, and stood to attention there against the dock bar, facing the Judge's seat. The clock ceased striking. There was a little pause, then the bells broke into the chime of "Holy, holy, holy". To this music, slowly, and with something of a limp, for he had had a fall from a horse lately, the Judge entered, coming through the side door used by the Counsel. He passed the central table, bowing right and left. He passed the great table, bowing right and left to the officers of the court assembled there and ascended his throne, bowed to the Counsel on his left, took his seat, took a keen look at the two prisoners, glanced at the paper before him, and allowed the noise of the audience re-seating itself to die away. Presently, when there was absolute silence, the indictments were read: then, when all forms had been observed, he stated that they were met together to try the case of the Crown versus Rapp and another on the charge of the wilful murder of John Okle at Arthur's Camp in the parish of Condicote in that County.

"Who is appearing for the prisoners"?

The red-faced, bullet-headed man rose, bowed and said, "I am for the prisoners, m'lud".

The Judge said, "Ah. Mr. Slaughter, I believe. And the prosecution"?

The hatchet-faced man rose, bowed and said,

"I am for the Crown, m'lud".

The Judge bowed and said, "Ah yes, Mr. Friezewell Knipton, I believe".

Mr. Knipton began his case, telling how the Arthur's Camp cover was used for the breeding and preservation of pheasants, who were left in the care of the naval-pensioner, John Okle; that John Okle had been called away owing to the illness of his mother, and that in his absence a gang

had been organized to raid the preserves so as to obtain a
large number of pheasants for some firm of city poulterers,
not yet traced, who wished to store their shop for the first
day of October. Unfortunately, it was a fact that the big
poulterers like to have pheasants for their customers even
in the morning of the first day on which pheasant shooting became lawful. He described again the organization as
far as it was known of the gang to which the prisoners belonged, and of their procedure at Arthur's Camp, and
stated that he could call evidence to show that the two
prisoners remained on the scene of the raid after the others
had gone, and were interrupted by John Okle, his wife and
daughter, whose story will presently be given to you by
themselves. That since the Coroner's enquiry, and the first
proceedings before the Magistrates, the Crown had received most valuable help in the person of another eye-
witness, whose evidence, though peculiar, could not be
doubted. He proposed to call scientific evidence to show
that the shot which killed the deceased had been fired from
the gun used by the prisoner, Rapp. The gun was in court
at that moment. It was one of the exhibits in the case. It
was much as it had been when the prisoner had placed it in
a hiding-place not far from the scene of the crime. He proposed to call evidence to show that he had been secreting
the weapon. The cowman who had seen him would swear
to his identity. With regard to the other prisoner, though
he had not participated in the actual killing, yet the evidence was conclusive as to his being an accessory. Not only
so, it was to be proved that his actions had contributed ma-
terially to the fatal issue.

He went on with a clipping, precise speech, without any
feeling. He gave the baker the feeling that he had filled

his mind with nails, instead of facts, or that each fact had become a nail within his mind, and that now each nail was being driven into the coffins of the two poor men.

The baker had a good view of the prisoners in the dock. Rapp, who was ever sullen, was now cowed and scared. The days in prison, without much drink, had taken the flush from his face. The baker thought that he looked ill and evil. The Magpie, who had no doubt suffered a good deal from being in prison after a life in the woods, looked paler than usual. He seemed to be pleased and excited by the bustle of the court, and the appearance of the Judge in his scarlet. His eyes wandered about the court. The baker thought that they were following the flight of the few flies which still moved to and fro there. They were the things the likest to birds that he had seen in these last weeks; but though his eyes wandered, they always came back to that scarlet figure, whose handsome, clear-cut face watched Mr. Knipton as he drove in the nails. Now and then, the Magpie touched Rapp upon the sleeve, and pointed out the Judge to him. Rapp, with a kind of snarl, shook him off.

Presently, Mr. Knipton had no more nails to drive. He stopped, bowed to the Judge, and said,

"I cannot doubt, that when the jury has heard the evidence which the Crown will call in this case, they will find both prisoners guilty of the atrocious crime with which they stand charged".

The first witness called was Inspector Drew, of the Condicote Police Station, who swore that on the evening of the crime, at eighteen minutes to seven, he had been called to the keeper's cottage at Arthur's Camp; that he had driven there at once, and had arrived at seven minutes to seven, where he found John Okle dead. He had been followed, three minutes later by Dr. Gubbins. He left the doctor to make his examination and went out with Mr. Jones. On being taken to the scene of the crime, he was able to rope off the area pointed out to him as the place where the body had been found, to place a police constable on guard there and to make an examination by lantern light. Guided by Mr. Jones, who had been the first neighbour to come to the cries of the bereaved women, he had marked out with pegs the exact position of the body in which it had fallen at the instant of death.

By Mr. Slaughter: "You mean the position in which it was when Mr. Jones found it".

"The exact position in which Mr. Jones found the body. I mean, the exact position of the body as Mr. Jones found it".

He added that he had made an exhaustive search for footprints on the spot as soon as there was daylight. The deceased at the moment of death must have been facing very nearly southwest and must have been fired at from a point about nine feet from him, by a person standing to the south of him. Unfortunately, the ground was very dry after the hot September weather, and the footprints of the shooter were not well marked; but he must have stood there, fidgeting about, for some twenty or thirty seconds, he judged, before firing. Okle's footprints were better defined, as he happened to be on a patch of grassless earth, at the instant of the shot. He wished that he could have made more of the prints; he had been in Australia in his young days and knew what could be done with tracks. On examining the covert rides and the runs of the pheasants at the end of the Camp, he found evidence that at least five men had taken part in the raid, but could give few helpful hints about them, the ground was too dry.

On being told that the court was not concerned with the raid on the pheasant run, which must have preceded the murder, the Inspector went on to give evidence of the arrest of the younger prisoner, known as the Magpie. He had known the Magpie by sight for many years. Acting on information received, he had gone to a place known as The Old Tan-pit in Condicote, that same evening, and had there found the younger prisoner in a sort of nest or shelter that he had. He had taken him into custody, and had found in his possession a long stick, now in court, and three small russet apples, such as grew on the tree at the Okles' cottage, and on no other tree in the district, as far as was at present known.

On his standing down, another police officer described the arrest of Rapp, in the outhouse of a public house at Tatchester. Neither prisoner had made an intelligible remark on being charged, the younger because he did not seem to know what was meant, and Rapp because he was recovering from drunkenness.

Dr. Gubbins, who followed, gave evidence of the wound that had caused John Okle's death. He said that he had had a good deal of experience first and last with gun-shot wounds, as a country practitioner, in a district where guns were used by many. He had also been for a time an assistant surgeon in an Austrian Army Hospital, during the Austro-Prussian War. He had no doubt, that the death had been caused by a charge of Number Five shot fired from a distance of from eight to ten feet. It could scarcely have been a self-inflicted wound, in fact, that was quite impossible; the nature of the wound and the absence of scorching made that impossible. He had examined the keeper's gun, and was certain that the fatal wound had not been inflicted by it. He was certain that the keeper's gun had not been discharged for some days. He had examined the cartridges used by the keeper in his work. They were not of the kind that had caused the death. Their pellets were altogether different. He said that death must have been absolutely instantaneous, and that a body receiving such a wound would have crumpled, as it were, and then fallen (probably) forward.

He was followed by a government gun expert, who said that the keeper's gun had not been loaded for at least five days before the fatal event. He had discovered beyond all possible doubt that the cartridge found in one of the barrels of the gun now before them was the one that had contained the fatal charge: he gave his scientific reasons, and added that the undischarged cartridge in the other barrel was exactly identical with the cartridge which had caused the death. He differed from Dr. Gubbins in one point, because he felt confident that he knew the precise distance; he was convinced, that the shot had been fired from a distance of eight feet six inches from its objective. He had tried the gun, with identical cartridges at models and also at the heads of animals freshly slaughtered, and was certain that his distance was exact. At any other distance, he had found, either a scattering of pellets or a greater shattering of tissue as the distance was increased or diminished.

Another government expert gave evidence, that the boots of both prisoners showed that they had been in red earth similar to the Arthur's Camp earth within a few hours of their arrest. The elder prisoner's boot exactly fitted a print in a patch of boggy earth in the pheasant run.

Unfortunately, a great many people had been all over the place within a few hours of the crime, and the local police had not been able to keep the ground clear. Many footprints, which might have been of the greatest help to Justice had been obliterated or over-trodden.

The owner of the Arthur's Camp preserve came next. He said that he had lately purchased the estate and had determined to raise a head of game for the amusement of himself and his friends. He had employed John Okle, as gamekeeper, and had not thought it necessary to call in an assistant watcher when the illness of Okle's mother called him away. Okle had asked him if he should call in somebody, but he had not thought it necessary. The poachers had not been much of a bother at Arthur's Camp, and he had judged that Okle would be back by daylight on the Saturday evening. He was very much upset by Okle's death; especially by the thought that there in Condicote was someone watching for even such a chance as this, to come down on two defenceless women and rob in the absence of their protector. He was taking what steps he could to prevent any recurrence of such a raid. He stated, that about one hundred pheasants had been taken, and that they had not been traced. The two-horsed van, in which it was supposed the booty had been removed, had not been seen beyond the Pillers Oak. It was thought that the game was taken here to Tatchester and there put upon the night express for London and removed on arrival. The police were still making active enquiries.

After this, Mr. Timothy Tineton was called.

Timothy, a draper's assistant in Condicote, came into the witness box, and was sworn to tell the truth. He was a timid young man, conscious that being a witness was next worst to being charged. He testified that on the Saturday afternoon of the crime, he had been walking with a companion in the direction of Arthur's Camp, and, hearing the church clock strike five, which showed them that it was later than they had thought, had just turned for home when they came upon the company of six men, some of them carrying guns.

Mr. Knipton asked, "What impression did the party make upon you"?

"A very unpleasant impression, sir. They were coming with guns, where I knew they could have no right whatever to be with guns, and they looked guilty or evil, as though surprised in doing something wrong".

"My lord, I protest", Mr. Slaughter said. "Looks are not evidence".

"I think, Mr. Slaughter, we must permit the witness to tell his tale".

"Certainly, my lord", Mr. Slaughter said. "I only feel it right to state that the imputation of guilt thus early may weigh against the prisoners. After all, many people might be startled by suddenly and unexpectedly meeting with strangers".

"I will deal with the point, Mr. Slaughter", the Judge said.

He made a note on the paper before him. The witness went on.

"Where exactly was your meeting-place with this party"? Mr. Knipton asked.

"At the stile through a big thorn hedge which leads from the field near the river into the pasture".

"How high was the hedge"?

"It must be eleven or twelve feet high", the witness answered. "Too thick to see through then, for the ditches were very blind, and many of the shrubs and thorns in the hedge had not yet shed their leaves".

"So that you on the one side and the party, whoever they were on the other side, came upon each other unexpectedly, suddenly. You had not seen them, nor they you"?

"No".

"Will you show the jury on this six-inch map the exact spot on which you met this party"? Mr. Knipton asked.

The witness pointed the exact spot on the map.

"And you can give the exact time of your meeting with this party"?

"It must have been about five minutes past five, sir. We had heard the church clock strike five a few minutes before, and we said, 'We must turn, or we may be late for our tea'. We have tea at half-past five, sir".

There was a titter in court at this. The poor young man blushed and became exceedingly uncomfortable.

"To continue, then", Mr. Knipton said. "You saw six men. Tell the court, do you see any of those six men in the dock"?

"Yes, sir, the two prisoners were among the six. The elder prisoner was leading".

"Had you seen him before"?

"Yes, sir, frequently. He was often to be seen standing at the street corner".

"You say you saw the younger prisoner. Are you quite sure of that"?

"Quite, quite, sir. He came last. He was bareheaded, and the white patches in his hair were very conspicuous".

"You had seen him before"?

"Yes, sir, very frequently".

"You say, that the elder prisoner, Rapp, carried a gun"?

"Yes, sir".

Mr. Slaughter interfered here. "He said nothing of the kind. He said that *they* (meaning the party or gathering) *were coming with guns*".

The Judge turned to Mr. Knipton, and said, "That is my note, also, Mr. Knipton".

Mr. Knipton bowed his head and continued.

"Will you please tell the court which of these six men carried guns. Did the elder prisoner carry a gun"?

"Yes, sir, he carried a double-barrelled gun openly. As he was the leader of the party, we came almost into him at the stile. He swore at us and threatened us with the gun".

"In what way did he threaten you"?

"He almost upped with his gun as though to shoot, and snarled at us".

"Will you show the court with this stick the movement which you try to describe"? The witness, blushing and sweating took the stick and showed the movement. "You say that the prisoner snarled at you. Can you indicate to the court what you mean by snarling"?

"He snarled, 'Err, out of the light, there, or I'll something your something heads in'".

"And you got out of the way"?

"Yes, sir; he had been drinking and was quarrelsome, and I knew him to be a dangerous man".

"In what way did you know him"?

"By hearsay, sir".

"And did the younger prisoner carry a gun"?

"No, sir, he carried a thumbstick".

"What is that"?

"A long walking staff, sir, forked at the end, for the thumb to rest in".

"Do you see such a staff among the exhibits"?

"Yes, sir; the staff on the table is much such another".

"What was he doing with the staff"?

"He was twirling it, sir, like the drum major does, between his fingers".

"Which of the others carried guns"?

"Three of the others, sir; and the fourth was turned to the hedge snapping his gun together. It was one of those which take to pieces".

"And on meeting with these armed men, you were frightened, were you"?

"Yes, sir, because we could see that they were furious at being met there. We looked back, after we had got clear, and saw them looking after us, as though they had half a mind to do us injury".

"But they did, in effect, let you proceed, without any molestation"?

"Yes, sir".

"As you proceeded towards Condicote, did you notice any other people in the fields near Arthur's Camp"?

"Yes, sir; two men strolling away from the Camp, in the direction of the *Garden Path* public house; and then a few moments later some boys who had been bathing in the stream; nobody else".

"And after this you proceeded home with your companion. How soon afterwards did you hear of the tragical event at Arthur's Camp"?

"Shortly after seven, sir".

"Where were you then"?

"I was in the reading-room at the curate's house, when someone brought the news. The friend who was with me in the field was with me then, playing chess. I said, 'That may have been done by those men we saw. We must go round at once and tell the Inspector all we know'. So we went round at once and described them. It was only a walk of a hundred yards to the police office".

"Thank you, Mr. Tineton", Mr. Knipton said.

He sat, and Slaughter rose and said that he would like to ask the witness one or two questions.

He snorted a little, cleared his throat, twitched his robes and fixed his bullying leer on the unhappy Timothy.

"I would be relieved to know, and I am sure that the court would like to know, what you and your companion were doing so close to the scene of the crime at the time of the crime. Hey"?

Timothy felt that he was accused of murder and gave up hope of leaving the court alive.

"I was out for a Saturday afternoon stroll", he stammered.

"I put it to you, that you and your companion, who will presently follow you to the witness box, were trespassing in pursuit of game. That when you met the party of which you speak, you naturally were terrified that you had been discovered and would reap the reward of your wrong-doing. That it was that that made you fly from the covert, and that in your terror you imagined guns and other horrors which had no existence save in your own guilty imagination. Hey? Come, sir, answer me. Was not that the reason? What? Is your guilt so confusing you that you cannot give the court a plain answer"?

Mr. Knipton was on his feet with, "Really, my Lord", but the Judge let the question stand.

"I was out for a Saturday afternoon stroll, sir", Timothy repeated.

"And why, when you were interrupted, did you fly with such guilty consciences"?

"Because we were afraid we might be late for tea, sir".

There was a titter in the court at this.

"Afraid that unless you hurried to your alibi the evidence of this party of which you speak might fix your crime upon you"?

"No, sir".

"But I say yes, sir. For what other reason did you hurry"?

"Miss Grimshaw doesn't like anyone to be late, sir; especially on a Saturday".

"I thought when I saw you", Mr. Slaughter said savagely, "that we should find there was a lady in the case".

The court laughed outright. The Judge bent to his notes. Poor Timothy blushed scarlet and his eyes filled with tears.

"She has to get out, sir", he said, "as soon as she has washed up, to do her Saturday shopping".

After this, the baiting of Timothy relented; his companion was called and swore to the presence of Rapp and the Magpie with four others in the pasture below the Arthur's Camp less than one hour before the killing of John Okle. He added that on looking back he had seen one of the party moving towards Okle's cottage, while the others held on straight to the covert. Then a farm labourer, who had been at the Okles' cottage with some sacks of chicken feed, swore to seeing four men, one of whom was Rapp, coming in to the covert, through a gap made for shooters, just as he turned his cart into the lane. He said that he knew it was Rapp, because he had seen Rapp fighting on the previous Saturday in the *Four All Round* public house. He had not seen the Magpie, whom he had often seen in Condicote. When asked if any of the party carried guns, he replied that he was pretty sure that they did, but that Rapp certainly did, because he saw him break his gun in the middle and put in cartridges. On being asked what he thought of this he said, that he had supposed they had had leave to do a bit of rabbitting, as the rabbits was eating all the young trees.

After him, there came the evidence of a porter from the station, that John Okle had come in by the five-thirty train, and had chatted an instant, before going off. He had been offered a lift in old Mr. Callow's dog-cart. Old Callow, who was somewhat deaf, gave evidence that he had taken John Okle with him from the station to the white gate. From this gate there was a cart track which led from the road near the river to the farm house below the Camp and thence onwards into the covert to the keeper's cottage. He gave the time of dropping John at the gate at about twenty minutes to six. It would be a matter of seven minutes' walk, being mostly uphill, from there to the cottage in the wood. Callow's groom confirmed this.

Though these witnesses had not brought the case very far, it was now lunch time. The morning had slipped by, as though it were only a few moments long. The preliminaries had taken some time; all the police evidence had been given slowly; and many questions had been asked by

Counsel. Now the Judge rose, amid a general rising of the audience. The baker was wakened from a dream by Adolf's arm upon his shoulder.

"Come on out, now, Rob; we'll get a breath of air and a sup of purl or so".

"I think I'll stay", the baker said.

"You'd much better not".

"Well", the baker said, "I'll try to clear my head".

He went out with Adolf. Outside he met the two journalists from London. The party went across to the *Blue and White*, where Adolf and his friends had some purl, to warm the cockles as they said. He who wanted a clear head left them there and ate a bun and drank a mug of coffee in a little shop near St. Alpig's. He was in a state of high excitement. His blood was throbbing in his veins; he was conscious of a red mist across his eyes. He had always believed that the theatre was a gateway to the pit; now he realised for the first time the power that simulated action might have on people, if the reality were this. He mopped the sweat from his brow. He noticed that his hand was shaking. This was a gladiatorial show, that he had watched. He felt ashamed that he had been present at such a thing, yet at the same time he was held by it; he was in it, he had to play a part in it. He prayed, as he crumbled and tried to swallow the stale currant bun,

"O Lord, give me strength and wit to help them".

He knew, he could not help knowing from the feeling in court, that all were hostile to the two accused; all the temper of the audience was against them; a brute and a fool together had snuffed out a fine man; every man there, almost, was sending out a kind of hate against the two, which must in the end destroy them. Somebody asked him if he had been in the court. He said yes, and that he thought that the prisoners were not guilty.

"There aren't many", the man said, "who can think that".

"It is a terrible thing", the baker said, "to think that sometimes innocent men have been condemned in courts like that".

"Not in British Justice", the man said stoutly. "In France, and foreign lands like that, they might".

The baker drank a second mug of coffee, thinking that it would clear his brain.

When he returned to court, a few people were loitering back to their places. In a few minutes, the sightseers and officers of the court came flooding back. The curtain was about to rise on a thrilling act. Word had somehow gone abroad, that Mrs. Okle and Gertie were to give evidence. A young man, moving to his seat among the sightseers, said to a friend,

"They say the murdered man's daughter is simply a stunner to look at".

As at the morning sitting, there were the usual ceremonies at the Judge's entrance. A late-comer, trying to squeeze in quietly, after the Judge had taken his seat, was rebuked by the Judge, and told to leave the room. After this, there was a hush. Mrs. Okle was called.

She came into the witness box, supported by her daughter and a married sister. She was a rather short, comely, matronly woman, with good features. She had abundant dark brown hair, and looked not more than forty, though really nearly fifty. Her daughter was a very lovely young

woman, having her mother's beautiful hair and an ex-
quisite complexion. All three women were good-looking
and bowed in grief.

They were sworn. The voice of Mr. Knipton was heard
assuring them that the entire sympathy of the court was
with them in their late cruel bereavement. That all there
knew how painful and indeed frightful an ordeal it must
be to them to have to stand there to answer questions; but
that, unfortunately, there was no alternative. It fell to
him to have the unhappiness to question them on the late
tragical occurrences. He wished them to understand, that
he felt acutely for them and would do all in his power,
consistent with his duty in that court, to make the ordeal
as little painful as it might be made. He felt that he might
assure them from his brother engaged for the Defence,
that they would be spared all that might be spared. His
brother, engaged for the Defence, assured them that that
went without saying. The questioning then began.

Many of those present had been present at other hearings of the story, at the inquest, the Magistrates' court and
the Grand Jury. They now felt that they were watching
the real performance, after the rehearsals. There was a
depth and reality about this hearing; they gloated over it.
They told themselves that they were there to see justice
done on the killers of poor John Okle; but perhaps most
of them were there to see some souls in great misery dis-
playing their misery. They would have gone to a public
execution for the same reason and with the same excuse.

Though the stories were familiar, this way of telling it
was new. Mrs. Okle said that she had been busy, after
feeding the birds, in that late afternoon, in preparing a
pasty for her husband, when suddenly, her daughter, who

was with her in the kitchen, said, "Whoever is this, coming up the path"? At that instant, she herself was bent over the fire, while her daughter, who had been at the table, had gone to the door to see who was there. She knew that someone was coming, because she had heard the click of the latch in the gate which led to the garden. Almost at once, before she could get to the door beside her daughter, a man, wearing a black mask and holding a double-barrelled gun at their heads, cried to them, "Don't you move. Don't stir. Keep just quiet where you are, and nothing will harm you". She said, that after the first instant of terror, she thought that it must be young Mr. Cothill, or one of his friends, having their fun, as college men will; but then she realised that this was not one of the gentry, but a bad man who meant evil. "Just you stay quiet", he said, "or I'll blow your heads off, and I'd be sorry to have to do that".

She did not recognize the man. He was certainly not from those parts. He did not speak like a countryman, but like a townsman, from one of the cities; she could not say which. He was not a countryman, because his head and hands were pale and sickly-coloured; what the men called "Skilly-coloured", or "gaol-bird coloured". After the first, he lowered his gun from the shoulder, but kept it at the ready. He had mouse-coloured hair and a sore place on the side of his left thumb, as if it had had the skin rubbed off. She noticed this as it was on the gun-barrel quite close to her. The man wore a dirty brown overall suit, such as any mechanic might wear to protect his clothes. It was much smeared with dark stains, as though it had been used for pig-killing, and this made her feel that he would kill her and her daughter just as though they were pigs. She asked him what he meant by coming in that way, to frighten people? He said that he didn't mean to do them any harm, and they had best keep quiet.

She realised that it was useless to scream. "We are right out of the world there, in the covert. It is more than a quarter-of-a-mile to the farm, and if I'd screamed nobody would have heard me, and then he might have shot me and there would have been Gertie with no one. The next nearest house is half-a-mile away". She heard men outside, and prayed that it might be Okle coming back, with perhaps a friend; but the time was still too early; he couldn't possibly be back sooner than he had said. She knew that it must be city men, as her husband called them; that is, a gang of men come specially to get a lot of pheasants for the First of October. It had never happened to them before, but it was what Okle had often talked of as possible. She knew that the men would drive the pheasants into nets and carry them off; she knew that there would be half-a-dozen of them, all armed; she began to fear that Okle would return, find them there and be shot dead.

She noticed that the man had a wart with thick hairs in it on the left side of his chin. He was quite a youngish man, less than thirty she would say. From time to time, he would say, "You can sit down on the floor, if you've a mind to, but any movement and I shoot. If you, mother, run away, I shoot your daughter. If daughter runs away, I shoot mother. Now you know it. And don't talk. I don't like it".

Yes, she had thought of trying to dash out, to get to the farm. To do that, as the man stood in the doorway, she would have to get back into the inner room of the cottage, and she knew that she had pushed the bolt of the back door that morning. Then, if she ran, she knew that that would leave Gertie alone, and she knew that Gertie was much more timid than herself.

After a long, long time, Gertie said, "Mother, I'm going to faint", and did faint. "Sit down on the floor and prop her up", the man said, "but don't you try moving or I'll shoot your heads off, the both of you". She sat there, holding up Gertie. She noticed that the man had low walking shoes, burst at the outer bend and only one sock. Presently, someone whistled "Half a pint of mild and bitter", which was a signal, for the man said, "You can get some water for your daughter now, but don't you try to follow, or you'll be shot". He backed out, up the path to the gate and out. She saw there were several men; but had to look to her daughter first. Among the men were the two prisoners, pulling apples from her tree. She had no idea how many men altogether. She saw three near the gate. There must have been several in it, as they had made quite a lot of noise in the near-by covert and at the feed pens; the pheasants had made a lot of noise, too, but not one that could be heard by anybody at that time of the evening. No, she did not follow, nor try to follow; she had her girl to look to, and was afraid one of them might come back to molest Gertie, or be waiting there to shoot them. She heard her clock strike six, and knew that Okle would be in in a minute, but the clock was ten minutes fast, and it must have been four or five minutes before Okle came up at the back door. She heard his step on the brick path and ran out all weeping and crying to tell him; and he said, "Only just gone, you say? I'll stop them yet". At that he snatched his gun from the wall, where it hung. It wasn't loaded; it had not been loaded since he went away; and ran out after the gang.

He knew that if they were carrying a great net-load of pheasants, they would have to go slowly, and that their cart would have to be in the lane. There was a chance of stopping them before they got away. She ran after him, with an arm round Gertie, who had had a sup of brandy and was all right, now that Okle was there. Almost at once, when they got across the neck of the covert to the rough bit, they came upon the two prisoners. Rapp was carrying a gun; the Magpie had a long stick. "They were coming back from the lane towards us. I saw no other of the men, but I saw a van being driven along the lane going very fast. I only saw the tilt of the van, nothing more, and I could hear the noise of two horses going very fast. Okle was well in front of me. I heard him say, 'What are you doing here, Fighter'? And Rapp said, 'No concern of yours. This isn't your covert, but Mr. Jones's field'. Then Okle said, 'You'll have to answer for all this. You just put up that gun and come along and see the police at the station'.

"Then Rapp said, 'You've got a fair cheek to come and order me about. I've as much right as you have in this field. Go and crow on your master's dunghill, flunkey'.

"Then Okle said, 'You were in with the gang that has just been driving the birds here. Now you'll come along and answer for it. You'd best not try fighting with me, my lad'.

"Then Rapp said to the Magpie, 'Tripstick un, Maggie, tripstick un. Twiddle him over, there's a lad'. And at that the Magpie poked his long stick at Okle's legs and flung him down almost. However, he did not quite fall, but jumped back and recovered, and then pointed his gun low down at the Magpie's feet and said, 'Now you walk in front of me'. He'd no sooner said it, than Rapp fired at him and killed him".

"And what happened then"?

"I don't know".

"You don't know where the two men went"?

"No. They were gone when I could see to Okle".

After her evidence, Gertrude Okle gave similar evidence, and added that after the fatal shot, she who had been hanging back at the fence clambered over it and ran to her father's body, and that she saw the two prisoners turn and run away. She did not know much what happened next, except that it was almost ten-past six, as others had told her, when somebody with a cart saw or heard them crying. These people, the Joneses, husband and wife, were driving home from Condicote. They stopped in the lane, ran to them and gave every help in their power.

Mr. Slaughter began his cross-examination with the assurance that like all those in court, he felt deeply for them in their affliction. It was one of the sad duties which sometimes fell to members of his profession, to have to question the sorely tried and deeply suffering. The questions which he had to ask were dictated by the duty which had fallen to him. He would ask them to believe that they should not be brow-beaten nor bullied.

He asked that mother and daughter might be together in the witness box while he questioned them. However unusual it might be, it would give them comfort to which sorrowing ladies were entitled. After all, they experienced the tragedy together, they had both suffered and seen together the horrors which had destroyed their home; it would help if he were able to question the joint, rather than the particular memory of the event of the fatal Saturday.

Adolf nudged the baker, with the whispered remark, "A neat stroke that. He got on the soft side of both the women and all the court".

Mr. Slaughter began with the gentlest, most fatherly of all bedside manners to ask about their eyesights. He noticed that they were wearing glasses; they were shortsighted, as he had been led to believe? They could not see well without glasses, and had to wear glasses continually? They were, in fact, very short-sighted. From this beginning he led them to declare, that they did not know whether they were wearing glasses at the moment of the murder. Neither Gertie nor her mother knew whether they had had their glasses or not. But both were sure that they had not needed glasses. Every sense in them was awake and tense. They knew what was going on. They had seen and known the whole dreadful happening. "It was all one great glare of light", Mrs. Okle said. "I saw it all lit up". "It was like the Judgment Day", Gertie said. She said no more, because at this point she fainted. Mr. Slaughter said that he grieved indeed to have added to their pain. He would trouble them no more, and begged that no other in that court would inflict that agony upon them.

Merioneth Jones, who came next, testified to having heard cries as of women in distress, as he drove slowly home from his Saturday marketings; he had found the two Okle women at the dead body of Okle, and being a very masterful man had sent his wife on with the cart to fetch the Shepherds, father and son, from Battler's Down, further along the road. They were with them in ten minutes. With their help, he carried the body to the cottage of the Okles, and went off for doctor and police. He was confirmed by the elder of the two shepherds, a strange, silent man, little used to human society.

After he had spoken, all thought that the case for the prosecution would be closed; but Mr. Knipton rose and said, that a remarkable piece of evidence had just been brought to his notice, and that though it had never been offered at any of the previous hearings, at inquest or before the Magistrates, he felt that it was of the utmost importance, and he, therefore, proposed to call Thomas Zine.

Zine was called, and moved, in a sort of scarlet trance into the witness box. He was a bull-necked, powerful young man, a bit of a dandy in his rough way; he had a zinnia in his button-hole, and wore a white stiff collar. He was naturally red in the face, with pop eyes. Emotion had sent all the blood in his body into his face and made his eyes protrude even more than usual.

He took his oath in a whisper. Some friend of his somewhere in a back seat, cried, "To 'em, Tom". There was a loud cry of "Silence in the court", and his solitary backer said no more. Mr. Knipton helped his unwilling, resty steed into the arena.

"You are a blacksmith's assistant, are you not? Living near Battler's Down, a hamlet close to the Arthur's Camp cover"?

"Yes, sir".

"Will you tell the court what you were doing on the afternoon of the murder of John Okle".

"Yes, sir. I went to the funeral of old Mr. Haizey, the father of the present blacksmith. After the funeral, I was

asked in to Mr. Haizey's, (Mr. Haizey lives in Condicote, longside the forge), to eat and drink as the custom is,
as I'd been one of the bearers, and I stayed talking there
till along about half-past five, or a quarter-to-six, maybe;
then I set out for home. I took the short cut across that
end of the cover, for although it's preserved I knew John
Okle wouldn't mind me. It's a path runs across just behind the Okles' cottage. I was in the footpath in the wood,
when I heard voices which sounded like a quarrel between
somebody, and looking down through the trees, I saw two
men disputing with another man, so I stopped a minute.
I said to myself, 'One of those is John Okle. He's having
a bit of a row with some rabbitters'. I stood and watched a
minute: I saw that one of the men was Okle, and the
others were as like those two prisoners as two peas, and
this one of the two seemed to encourage the other to strike
Okle with a stick, and he poked the stick between Okle's
legs and gave him a trip".

"Did Okle fall"?

"No, he didn't fall down. He almost fell. He stumbled
and went forward and then recovered".

"Wait one moment, will you please"? Mr. Knipton
said. "You say that the man who was the more like the
elder prisoner encouraged the other to strike Okle. How
did he encourage him"?

"Why, I mean, he sicked him at him, as you'd sick a
dog at a cat. He called out something, like 'Stick him,
Maggie' ".

Mr. Slaughter was on his feet. "M'lud, I must protest.
'Something' and 'Something like' is not evidence".

"You shall question later, Mr. Slaughter".

"M'lud, I must challenge the remark. It might be wrested as a positive identification of the prisoner".

"The witness makes no such suggestion, if I understand him, Mr. Slaughter. He is telling the tale of something not clearly seen and not very clearly heard. His words were, (I am certain that I have them correctly noted), 'He called out something like, "Stick him, Maggie" '. That is, the words sounded something like that. Was not that your meaning, Mr. Zine"?

"Yes, sir".

"You are not certain of the words"?

"It was either sick him or stick him".

"Are you certain of the name? Was the last word Maggie"?

"It was Maggie or Aggie".

"You are certain of the speech, except for those two letters? It was 'sick him, or stick him, Aggie or Maggie' "?

"Yes".

"And this was called by the one of the two, who held a gun, to the other who held a stick"?

"Yes".

"Can you describe the one who held the gun"?

"Yes; he was shortish and thick, and you could see he'd been drinking".

"And the other"?

"He was mimby-looking and had a shog of hair".

"When the one with the gun called out this 'Sick him or stick him, Maggie' in what way did he call it"?

"With his voice".

"Yes, yes; but did he do it as if he were joking, or as if the words were, shall we say, a bit of a song"?

"No".

"I wish you would shew the court exactly how those words were spoken. Try to imitate what you heard".

Mr. Slaughter did not protest; the court grinned. The Judge did not at the instant see Mr. Knipton's scheme. Thomas Zine gulped in a few deep breaths and braced himself for an effort. He swallowed once or twice, each time as it were swallowing down an attempt which would not have succeeded. Then he let fly with a violent, "Stick him, Maggie", which made everybody jump. It had an unfortunate effect on the Magpie in the dock. He leaped up and thrust with his hands, saying, "Stickee, stickee, Maggie". Mr. Knipton looked at him, with a smile, and gazed at Mr. Slaughter with an eye of triumph. The look said, "I think, my learned friend, I got you there".

"Now, Mr. Zine", Mr. Knipton said, "to go back a little. When those words were called or shouted by the man who held the gun, what did the other man do"?

"He leaped towards John Okle, prodded his stick between his legs and gave him a twist, so as he almost fell. He stumbled down, but recovered".

"Do you recognize the stick among the exhibits on the table there"?

"No; but it was a long stick, like the thumb stick there. It wasn't a walking stick".

"And what happened after Okle had recovered, as you say"?

"He upped with his gun and pointed it at the young fellow's feet, the young fellow who'd poked the stick at him. He called out something, 'Now you just march in front of me', it sounded like. And the next instant, there came a bang and John Okle had fallen forward".

"What had happened"?

"Well, I didn't know what had happened. I thought his gun had gone off, and perhaps blown back and hit him on the head and stunned him, but I couldn't see very well, and there was a lot of smoke, for it was black powder".

"You did not think that Mr. Okle had been murdered"?

"No".

"Did you not wait for him to get up? When he did not get up did you not feel sure that he had been injured? Did you not run at once to pick him up"?

"No, I thought the other two would do that".

"And did you look to see if they did".

"No, I couldn't see them again. They ran off down the hill. And then I saw two women running up".

"But when you saw this, surely you realised that a crime had been committed, and that Okle had been hurt, perhaps murdered, by one of these two men. Why didn't you run up then"?

"Well, I didn't want to be mixed up in it. I had on my Sunday clothes from the funeral. I went on away home".

"And why did you not come forward sooner, when you knew that a crime had been committed, and that Okle had been killed"?

"I was afraid they might say it was me".

"But why; you have no gun".

"No, but one never knows in a place like this what the law won't do".

Mr. Slaughter rose to question the witness.

"How far were you from this dispute, or whatever it was you saw, or say you saw"?

"A matter of about half-a-cable".

"What d'you mean by half-a-cable"?

"Well, what my brother calls half-a-cable".

"Never mind about what your brother calls it, or doesn't call it. That's a sailor's measurement. I suppose your brother's a sailor. What do you, who are a landsman, call it?"

"I call it same as he does, about half-a-cable".

Mr. Knipton intervened.

"It may save the time of the court if I assure you that the distance has been measured, and will be between a hundred and five and a hundred and ten yards. If you say a hundred and seven yards, you would probably be within a foot or two".

"And at that distance", Mr. Slaughter said, "you claim to have seen and heard, or at least seen, everything that happened late in a September evening, after sunset, when the mists were closing in"?

"Yes. Like what I said".

"And you will stand there, facing the jury, and declare a thing like that"?

"Yes".

"Did you mention this, that you saw or say you saw, to anyone whatsoever"?

"No".

"Only within the last few hours, you began to feel that it was too important to keep quite quiet"?

"Ah".

"What do you mean by 'Ah'? Answer me, yes or no".

"Yes or no, then".

"You saw all this that you have described. You are sure that you did not dream it. Did you dream it? Did you make it up, or imagine it from what you had heard or read about the crime"?

"No, I saw it".

"You are absolutely certain of that? You saw it clearly, and could have no doubt of it"?

"Yes, I saw it all; clear as I see you".

"Yet you told the court, not two minutes ago, that you 'didn't know what had happened', that you 'couldn't see very well' and that 'there was a lot of smoke'. So you didn't see it clearly"?

"Not if you come to that".

"Never mind where I come to, as long as it is the truth. Now, I ask you: did you see all this clearly"?

"I don't know what you mean by all this".

"This shooting which I put it to you you have imagined or dreamed. You saw it clearly, or didn't you"?

"No".

"You didn't see it clearly? There was smoke or evening mist"?

"Yes, like what I said".

"And you admit, that as you didn't see it clearly, you may have been mistaken about some material points or parts of what really happened".

"I seed it clearly and yet I didn't see it clearly, if you understand what I mean".

"I do not understand what you mean, nor, I am sure, will the jury. You say that you watched a crime and took no steps to interfere or help because you were wearing your Sunday clothes. You say you saw it clearly and didn't see it clearly. I put it to you that you didn't see anything at all; but have so racked your brains over the case that you cannot distinguish what you have heard or read of the case from reality. It comes to this, then, that you saw something obscurely, and since then have been told what it was that you may have seen. People have told you what you saw".

"Not more'n what I've told them".

"But you said just now, that you had not mentioned this to anyone whatsoever".

"Nor I done".

"Where were you, before the funeral, that afternoon"?

"Some of the time, at the *Four All Round*".

"A public house"?

"Yes".

"Drinking"?

"I only had a quart".

"Did you go anywhere else"?

"I called in at the *Quart Pot,* 'cos it was on my way".

"You had some drinks there"?

"No; only a quart".

"And another quart after the funeral at Mr. Haizey's"?

"No".

"Two quarts"?

"No. We only drank port wine after the funeral".

"No sherry"?

"Yes".

"Nothing else"?

"No, except a spot of gin to settle it".

"Now I see why you were so clear in your unclearness. That will do, Mr. Zine".

After this, there came another witness, a cowman from the Rectory Farm at Tineton, who swore to going across by the church at a little after eight o'clock on the evening of the crime, carrying a lantern, to look at a sick cow in the byre below the Ash. Hearing someone, or something, grubbing in the ditch there, he had called out; and going towards the noise had seen the elder prisoner, who had given a natural explanation of his presence there. He had no hesitation in swearing that the prisoner was the man.

After he had spent about an hour with the cow, he had returned home, but had turned aside to the ditch where he had seen the prisoner; he had not liked the man's looks, and wished to be sure of him. He had found the gun now in court, half-hidden in the dead grass over the ditch.

On his return home, he met the Rector, who told him that the keeper at Arthur's Camp had been murdered. On his showing the gun, the Rector had urged him to come in to Condicote to tell his story, and to bring the gun. The Rector had then driven him in to town, and the gun had been left with the police. He had seen both prisoners before, in the street at Condicote, and had recognized Rapp at once when he held the lantern over him. No, he hadn't seen him putting the gun into the ditch; he had heard someone moving or grubbing there and on looking to see who it was had seen the elder prisoner, who had seemed both startled and angry at being seen. It might have been more than an hour later that he found the gun; he had had a bad job with the cow.

No, when he had seen the prisoner, he hadn't seen the gun at all; but then, he hadn't looked at the ground; he had looked at the man. He supposed that the man was setting wires and might well not want to be seen doing it. But the gun had been in the very bit of the ditch where the man had been grubbing. Yes, it might be that someone else had put the gun in that place, but there were only the two sets of footprints in the moist earth there, Rapp's and his own; that had been very plain. They had proved that with science and that.

A police officer swore to having been taken to a ditch near Tineton Ash, where he had taken plaster casts of certain footprints, some of which exactly fitted the boots worn by the elder prisoner when he was taken at Tatchester on the morning following the crime.

After a brief pause, the usher called for Gwilym Bacchus, whom the baker knew as one of the drivers employed by the Steam Bakery to deliver bread. He was a lad of about twenty years of age, short, thick-set, bright-eyed and active-looking, a first-rate football player and long-distance runner. He was much sunburned. He said, that on the evening of the crime, he was delivering bread on the roads leading from Condicote to Yockford. At about five o'clock he was in the lane running under Arthur's Camp covert towards the *Garden Path Inn*. He was near the *Garden Path Inn* at a quarter-past-five, delivering bread at the farm at two cottages and at the inn itself. He saw a good many people altogether in and near that district, and finally crossed the little bridge to Condicote a few minutes after half-past-five by his watch. He always kept exactly the times of his rounds, for Mr. Wye insisted on that.

He was certainly on and near the road there from five-fifteen to five-thirty that evening; he only left the road to go to doors with his loaves; he did not enter any house there; only tapped at the doors and left the bread; sometimes he chatted a little. He would have noticed the two prisoners, if they had been on that road then, but he had not seen them. He gave a list of all he had seen. He had not seen Mr. Dabbytott.

Zachary Mouldwarp and Ebenezer Hordystraw gave similar evidence.

Mr. Bert Sexton of Condicote gave evidence that on the day of the crime, the church clock of Condicote was five minutes slow by post-office time. There had been complaints of it. He had put it right the day following the crime. He always wound and righted the clock on Sunday mornings, before the ringers came.

Captain King-Dimmock of Condicote swore, that he had for years kept a record of weather there. The weather at the time of the crime had been fine, owing to the presence of a large anti-cyclone centred over Dublin. The winds had been light and northerly. The evening of the crime had been especially beautiful, with an unusual afterglow, which had caused a great deal of comment.

After Captain King-Dimmock had stood down, there came a slackening in the stream; it reminded the baker of "slack water" in a tideway. Mr. Knipton was on his feet again.

"That closes my case, m'lud".

Mr. Slaughter rose to say that he had listened, as all must have listened, with admiration of the talents of the learned Counsel for the Crown; that to one who was constantly in the courts, it was always a matter of surprise that forensic genius should have such power to make the worse appear the better cause. To those who had listened, as he had, to the terrible and damning indictment brought by Mr. Knipton, it must have seemed impossible that men so charged with such an array of damning facts should escape the meshes of the law. If they were guilty it would be, of course, a scandal that they should escape. He hoped presently to lay before this impartial jury facts which would convince them that gross errors and mistakes had been permitted, and that the case against the two prisoners rested

upon mistaken identifications made by persons in such states
of emotional upheaval that they were unable to observe
accurately or to describe with truth.

From this prelude he passed to a survey of the circumstances attending the death of John Okle. The case against
his clients rested primarily upon the evidence of the widow
and daughter of the deceased man. He would deal with
that when the time came. At the moment, he wished all
there to remember that a great deal of bitterness had been
roused against the elder prisoner by the statement that the
murder had been committed by his gun, that his initials
were burned upon it, and much more of the same sort. He
would demolish that false statement at once. The gun was
not the prisoner's gun and never had been. He would like
to remind the court, that in a country society, in which
sport is a prevailing passion, much bitter feeling is ever
manifested against poachers. That feeling had been present here. He was very much afraid, that his clients had
suffered much, not only from that feeling, but from the
prejudice so easily aroused in a commercial country, which
attached undue importance to questions of property,
against persons who had no property, and few visible means
of support. However, let them, as impartial jurymen, put
from their hearts any prejudice of the kind, and weigh, as
they surely would, the evidence which he would shortly
bring forward to impugn, to shake, and finally, he had no
doubt, to destroy the evidence produced by the prosecution. He would not longer delay the hearing of the witnesses, but stated that he would call evidence to show that
Rapp and the Magpie were not those who had taken part
in the raid or in the killing subsequent to the raid. He
would bring evidence of an unimpeachable kind to prove

that both prisoners at the moment of the crime were engaged in innocent amusement in a respectable house of
refreshment near Condicote.

He was a big, coarse, bullying sort of man, whose rough-
ness of manner had checked his advancement. He had
agreed with Gallup in the recess, that things were not looking too rosy for their two birds; but he had dash and
daring; he did not readily lose heart; he meant to give
his clients a run for their money. The Crown had the
widow in tears; that had meant a lot to the jury; well,
he was no mean actor, he would give them a show, too,
presently; he could cause tears too, when he was in form.
They should see.

He said, that from the first, he had been amazed at the
readiness with which the Crown had accepted the identifications of some of the material witnesses. He, for his
part, meant to put forward at once certain evidence which
he hoped would demolish the Crown case from its foundation of mistake.

"By God, the man's a wonder", Adolf whispered to the
baker. "He'll save him yet".

The baker passed from his state of dream to one of
growing excitement. Could it possibly be that after all
the two victims would escape from the net and be set free?
All through the day Knipton had drawn mesh after mesh
round the poor fellows. The baker had felt the verdict
already formed in the minds of the jury. They were all
plainly convinced of the prisoners' guilt, and eager to come
to an end, give their verdict and be dismissed. And now,
after all this weaving of the toils, here was Slaughter
with hope, speaking with confidence, as though it were
quite impossible for any clear-headed man to believe for

one instant that the two prisoners were other than model churchmen, excellent citizens, good fathers, patriots, philanthropists. No man can fail to be impressed by courage or cheered by hope, if someone carrying those blessed banners do but come by. The baker bowed his head between his knees and prayed with all his might, that the Lord might strengthen Slaughter and continue him in his God-like task of trying to save these two unhappy ones. He was a great believer in the efficacy of prayer. There was a text always in his mind, that the fervent prayer of a righteous man availeth much. In his private prayings he was accustomed to pass into a state of exaltation in which he judged that this prayer had been heard. He was very conscious of this exaltation now.

"The Lord is with us", he muttered. "The Lord is with us. We'll get those poor fellows off, after all".

The usher called a name. As no one answered, he called a second time.

"Thomas Silverbitch. Is Silverbitch there"?

A man rose in some confusion from the waiting witnesses, and said,

"I am Josiah Slimbridge. Perhaps you mean me"?

"Yes, of course, Silverbitch", the usher said testily. "You know your own name, I hope. Come on, now, and don't keep the court waiting".

The man came hurriedly to the box, apologized to the Judge, and took the oath, while a titter about "Silverbitch" went round the court. He was an elderly, red-faced, honest-looking man, well-known by sight and repute to the baker as a watch and clock maker of Condicote, who said, that he had for many years advised the people of Condicote as to the glasses they should use. He had studied the question, as a young man, and held certificates. He had fitted, in his time, many hundreds of people with spectacles, eye-glasses and lorgnettes. He had first fitted Mrs. Okle with glasses in the year 1854, the year of the Crimea. She had before that time worn glasses habitually for ten years. She had poor sight. She was short-sighted, naturally. From time to time, since then, he had fitted her and refitted her with somewhat stronger glasses. The last time he had fitted her had been eighteen months before. She could not see well without glasses; she would be lost without them. He had noticed this time and time again. If she had come from her cottage without glasses on the evening of the crime, he felt sure that she would not have recognized anybody at the distance of a few yards.

"But, of course", he added, "one recognizes by many things, shape, voice and so forth. Still, in recognition, sight is all important. The proverb is true, 'seeing is believing' ". Mrs. Okle's eyes were certainly poor guides to her, poor woman, and would be still poorer guides to anybody else. He had glasses similar to hers here in the court. He had some printed cards also, shewing black capital letters of different sizes. The eyes of those with good sight could read even the smallest of these letters from across the room. Mrs. Okle could read only the biggest of them from that distance when wearing his glasses. He was sure, that her sight was such as to make accurate identification almost impossible for her on a September evening, when the light was already gone. Her daughter had slightly better sight, but still was very short-sighted. She always went about with glasses. He had specimens of the glasses usually worn by her. Still, in cases of identification, other things did undoubtedly help.

For his part, he felt, that neither woman could quite certainly have told who it was who stood by the bramble-thicket when her husband had been shot.

The Judge at this point asked the witness if he could state in a few words why he held this conclusion.

He answered, "Yes, my lord; it is a case of distance and light and bad sight. Like many others in Condicote, I walked out to the scene of the crime the day after it had happened, to satisfy myself on this very point. Your Lordship may like to know that we were having then the same exceptional, fine bright autumn weather that we are enjoying now. The day after the crime was just such a day as the day before. The conditions of light were the same. Now, in late September the sun sets before the supposed time of the crime; it falls into haze, the evening closes in and darkens. And this is especially so at the scene of the crime. By a little after five-thirty, the sun is gone behind Battler's Down; it is off the scene of the crime, anyway. Then consider, my lord, the place of the crime. The covert, all dark with many yew trees, is on two sides of it; a hill with more covert, behind which the sun has dropped, is on a third side. A still, hazy autumn evening is over all. The poor women (and, my lord, I do want you to know, that I feel the deepest pity for their situation), came running up, both very short-sighted, both wildly excited, to a fence eleven yards from the scene of the killing. They, on their side of it, must have been more than eleven yards from it. The murderers, whoever they were, must have had their backs to the women, or partly so. Anyhow, their faces must have been in shadow, and to sight such as that of the two poor bereaved women, invisible, or almost invisible, I do truly believe".

Mr. Knipton rose to examine, but with the politeness of one who knew that that type of witness is not to be shaken nor set aside. Mr. Slaughter felt that he had scored all the points in that first round.

After the optician had gone, there came an oculist from London, who had examined the sight of both the Okle women, with the full consent of the prosecution and solely in the interests of justice. He agreed with the watch-maker, that the women had bad sight, and that if they had been without glasses at the scene of the crime they could scarcely have identified the persons present.

When he had finished, Mr. Knipton asked him, if he had not known of cases in which deep and overwhelming emotion had so clarified all the faculties that perception, recognition and mental power had been increased tenfold.

He answered, that he had known of such cases, but that no evidence had appeared to show that this was one of them. Mr. Knipton said, that everything in the present case seemed to make it just such a case. Two good and gentle women had been exposed to terror in its grimmest shape and had then seen their dearest possession brutally murdered. Surely, in such a case, the soul takes to itself faculties beyond the senses and perceives and utters with powers normally in abeyance. The witness said it might be, but that in most cases a great shock nullified all the faculties; it blunted and blinded. The usual result of a great shock was to cause not super-consciousness but un-consciousness. The two fought it out for some time "on this line", till Mr. Knipton retired. Mr. Slaughter looked cheerful as he sat down.

The day was over now. Darkness had been settling in upon the court for the last half-hour. The Judge rang a

little bell that was on the ledge in front of him. One of
the ushers hurried to him; the Judge spoke, but the baker
could not hear the words. An usher went to each side
of the court house, and with some trouble pulled-to the
squares which had been opened in the windows. The haze
of the October evening was darkening again to fog. The
case stopped for a few moments. All there watched the
old, fumbling ushers tugging to shut the filth-stiffened
window-squares, yet not daring to tug too hard, lest they
should snap the rotten cords. At last the squares were
closed. Then the two old men shuffled out for lights.

They returned presently, each bearing a long white
burning wax match twisted into a long thin iron linstock.
With these, they turned on, and then lit, the gas jets along
the rows of seats and above the Judge's canopy. Each jet,
on lighting, gave a little sound like *pob*, and shot up in
a blue mist (at first) like the wraith of a gentian. When
all the gas jets had been lit, the baker saw the scene
through a kind of fog; here an evil flame, there a face
or two, or part of a face; there the Judge, between two
flames, there the shadow, or darkness of Rapp and his
guards.

The ushers seemed to take an eternity of time in lighting the last jets and going to their places. A woman stood
up suddenly and cried in a loud voice,

"Oh, I wish the kind God would end my sorrows for
me".

A loud titter followed the cry. The woman collapsed
in a faint. The Judge said something to the attendants.
A policeman and one of the ushers, with some trouble, got
to her and removed her, moaning and clutching. Her collapse was as it were a trigger which released some of the

gathered hysteria in the court. As she was borne out, three other women felt come over of a sudden, said so and hurried out. The last of the three, a little old woman in a black dress, was swaying on her feet as she neared the door. Engels called out to her, "Hold up, Ma". There was a loud cry of "Order", and a rebuke from the Judge, that anyone who thought to make his court a beer-garden would find his mistake forthwith. He asked who cried out then? The officers were unable to shew the culprit. After this, the case went on.

Mr. Slaughter said, that Rumour had made much of the theory that the gun found at Tineton, which had been proved, scientifically, to have been the gun which shot Mr. Okle, was the property of the elder prisoner. He said that it was now established that it was not and never had been the prisoner's gun; that it was the property of Mr. Hill, and had been taken from Mr. Hill's home in some unexplained way, by some unidentified person, on the day of the crime.

The baker came out of his exaltation of prayer. All that Mr. Slaughter did and said seemed to come as direct answers to the appeals his heart was always making to God to save the two. Now here was another witness come to save them.

Old Baldy Hill, one of the hardest-headed old knaves that even Condicote could produce, was in the box, to do what he could for his friends, but also to put himself right with the world: it was his gun.

His appearance was in his favour. He was a very fine old man to look at, with delicate silver hair, and a clear blue eye. He wore a smock frock, as most of the old men did at that time. It was clean. He himself was spotless;

and he had a great bunch of spindleberry pinned upon his chest. He leaned upon his staff. A close observer, looking at Baldy Hill's mouth, and noting the leer and puffiness of its line, might have doubted whether the rest of the exterior told absolute truth. But there he was, being questioned by Slaughter.

"About the gun lying on the table, Mr. Hill. You recognize it as your property"?

Baldy was a slow witness. He took his time in answering. Before he replied to a question, he wanted to go round it in his mind, and see where it might lead.

"Yes, sir, she's my property".

"How do you recognize it"?

"Because of the initials J. R. burnt on the stock, for John Rudge, my dead son-in-law, and because of two marks you'll find, one on the under piece where there's a three-cornered nick; the other on the barrel on the right, like a flaw in the metal, corkscrew shape".

"When was it last in your possession"?

"The morning of the day Mr. Okle was killed. I had it out at Nova Scotia Wood that morning with Mr. Harold, getting a few rabbits. I came home with it, if you understand me aright, having had the morning's rabbitting, and just put un down on the table. I went along with the rabbits, after, to Mr. Harold's, and when I come back, he was gone, and four Number Five cartridges, what I'd left with un. Yes. I've a license for the gun. I'm employed by Mr. Harold, to keep down the vermin and mind the dogs and that. No, he'd never been Rapp's gun. John Rudge's and then mine. What did I do, when I found her gone? I called my daughter. I thought she'd took it, to clean for me. No, she hadn't seen him. She said, someone must have crept in and stole it. It's a serious thing for me, not having a gun. I went round at once to the police station. About one o'clock that would be. I gave all about it. Mr. Marcle, the policeman, come and look at my cottage. 'Ah', he says, 'they must have come in by the open door and took her'. 'Yes', I says, 'that's what I say'. 'Well', he says, 'he'll turn up, you'll find'.

"Yes, I've missed the gun. I'll be very glad to have un again. The vermin have to be kept down, autumn and all times. Do I know the prisoners? Yes, by sight. Yes, and spoke to both of them, but not so as to know them. Did I never lend the gun to either of them? No, I never did. I don't believe in lending guns, wives nor horses. I never lent the gun to anybody, except once to young Mr. Harold".

After he stepped down, his daughter, Keren Happuk, swore that the gun on the table was her father's gun, that she had seen him bring it in and leave it on the table on the morning of the crime. Their cottage near Tibb's Wharf was never locked, during the day, as someone was always about in it and would hear any thief come in. But on that Saturday morning she was very busy getting up her dress for church next day, and being busy and that someone could have crept up and taken it. Anybody could have done that, watching his time.

Mr. Harold gave evidence, that Hill had had the gun that morning, and had reported its loss to him, immediately, so as to be able to borrow a gun, in case of need.

Marcle, the policeman, gave evidence, that Hill had reported the theft at the police station at seven minutes to one in the afternoon of the crime. Both Mr. Harold and a local gunsmith, who had repaired the piece, identified the gun as Hill's.

Another man had started to come towards the box, at the usher's summons, when the Judge checked him and said that the court would adjourn for three-quarters-of-an-hour. It might be necessary to sit late.

There came a sigh of relief from the strained audience. The Judge rose, twitching his robe; all rose in deference to him. In the silence of the court, the baker was much struck by the swish of the Judge's robe against the panelling of the seats as he passed out. It was a curious noise of dry silk. It set the baker's teeth on edge, and gave him what he called "goose flesh". The door presently closed upon him. Instantly, a babble of talk burst out. The doors were opened; a draught, smelling of fog, swept in upon them; the gas jets wavered; the noise of the street could suddenly be heard: horses' hooves, wheels, the cries of boys selling the football papers, and then, among all these sounds, a waft of bells from the cathedral tower.

"Here's a bit of a rest from eloquence, anyway", Engels said.

"I don't mind the eloquence", the baker said. "The thing I can't abide is the cross-examining".

"These fellows would make a man say black is white, after a two minutes' badgering. It's a game they play. Those who don't know the dodges are lost at it at first", Engels said.

"It's not the way to get at the truth", the baker said.

A lady, who had been sitting in front of them, and from time to time looking round at them with great dislike, now tartly spoke.

"It's the way to upset a liar", she said, as she rose and thrust out of court.

"Go home and nurse the baby, Ma", Engels called after her.

Somebody behind them said, "Shame". Engels looked round, but could not be sure which of three young men had spoken. They sat in a row together, two rows behind them. All the three were now staring with blank faces across the court. No man could say which had spoken. The incident was dead in an instant, for an usher turned out some of the gas jets, for thrift's sake. People laughed; there came a great buzz of talk and a drift to the doors.

"I want something hot after all this", Engels said. "I'm going over to the *Cygnet*. Won't you come along and have a bowl of broth and a brandy? You'll be dead without it. Besides in the *Cygnet* you will learn how the case is going. We'll meet all the comrades and hear all the news".

"You go", the baker said. "I want to stay here and think things out".

"If you can think things out in this fugg", Engels said, "you ought to get called to the bar at once".

"What I can't understand", the baker said, "is that no one so far, has said a word about the Magpie's being daft. I suppose it will be done"?

"But that wouldn't defend Rapp", Engels said. "Slaughter has Rapp to think of. I'm longing to see what line he'll take. Well, we shall very soon know. Now I'm going to cut. If you're wise you'll come too, for the Lord knows when you'll have another chance. They'll be hours at it yet".

"You go", the baker said. "I can't eat, while those two lives are in the balance".

A good many of the people who had been there from the start now took themselves off. The baker heard them saying that they would miss the last train if they stayed. Three men, who were busy writing at the table, covered with green baize, below the Judge's throne, made jokes among themselves. The baker wondered what they were.

"They must be used to this kind of thing", he thought, "to be able to joke when men's lives are at stake".

They were well-fed, cheery-looking men, full of good nature, he thought; yet they didn't seem to mind what was going on at all.

"Have you heard this one"? one of them asked.

A tale was told, in a low voice, and welcomed with shakings of smothered laughter.

Presently, the usher who had turned out some of the gas jets, brought in a long-headed broom and swept up a few odds and ends of paper and pencil shavings which had been dropped on the floor during the day. He made a lot of noise, by knocking his broom head on the legs of the fittings, and gathered little of the mess that was to be gathered. His real reason in sweeping was perhaps to make it unpleasant for those who had remained in court, but he kept repeating to each person whom he neared,

"I want to have the court tidy for the Judge's summing".

Presently, he went so far as to open the small ventilating square in one of the windows and to let in the fog from without. This roused one of the writers at the table to cry,

"Here, I say, we don't want to die of quinsy exactly", and at this, he shut the pane, but imperfectly, because the rotten cord which pulled it, snapped at its eye, so that it would not draw-to. The baker was aware of a raw draught and of the smell of fog. He was sensitive to these things; they touched up his throat and gave him what he had latterly often felt, a sense that he was in a fever; it was not altogether an unpleasant feeling; it had something in it of the unreality of intoxication, time became unimportant, as though he were partly released from it. The fever gave him also a sense of the importance of what was being enacted there, in that evil old house. He was deep in his thoughts, when another usher entered, saying, "Now, outside everybody, please. The court's adjourned".

"What? Go on with you. What d'ye mean, adjourned"? the three writers at the table cried.

"The court is adjourned till tomorrow", the usher repeated. "Mr. Slaughter's been with his Lordship. It's acos of the Defence it's adjourned. So, outside everybody, if you please. Tomorrow at ten you can be here again, and ask him yourselves. I'm only an officer of the court, doing my duty. *If* you please, everybody. I don't want to be here all night. I've got my likings for my evenings, same as everybody, *though* I'm only an officer of the court".

The baker went out with the others. In the street, the fog struck rank on his nostrils and made him sneeze. A policeman told him that the *Cygnet* was just across the way. In the *Cygnet* bar, he found Adolf and his friends having a snug time over rum-hot.

"I was just coming over to fetch you", Adolf said. "The case is adjourned, because the Defence wants a rested jury before he puts in his hot shots. Now come along, and have something. They've very good steak and kidney in the ordinary here".

However, the ordinary was almost at an end now; the

steak and kidney, which Adolf had enjoyed, was not "off". The baker ate a mess of cold meat with a cold potato, thinking that it was not now possible to reach Condicote that night, and wondering what he should do about a bed. From where he sat, he heard the talk in the bar. Adolf and his friends were enjoying themselves. All the usual frequenters of the *Cygnet* were spellbound by these brilliant London men, come down to watch the trial. Someone with a banjo began to sing an imitation of Mr. Knipton cross-examining a lady, to discover to what point she would live with him and be his love. He could not make one in that company. He was sick at heart and stupid in the head from that day of excitement and strain in that poisoned air. He asked Adolf, how he thought things were going.

"Pretty fair", Adolf said; "but we shan't know what guns he's got until tomorrow. Of course, from what has been done today, you can see that he's going to try to prove it a case of mistaken identity".

"If you were taking the case, Adolf, what course would you take"?

"I"? Engels said, "I'd get both prisoners out of the land, and across to the far side of the world. They've got prejudice against them, which is a lot worse than evidence, if you ask me. Two tickets to the Poles is what they need".

"Mistaken identity", the baker said. "Well, it may prove to be the case".

"A lot can be said for it".

"Hey, Ad", a man called. "Come along in and hear this one".

"Well, see you later, Rob", Adolf said, and left him there.

The baker sat on over his unpleasant meal, thinking of the defence.

"Mistaken identity", he muttered. "How could the Okle women be mistaken"?

It seemed to him that the course the defence should have taken would have been to plead Guilty, and to plead, in extenuation for Rapp, that the gun went off by accident; and that, in the Magpie's case, the prisoner was not sane.

After his meal, he asked about a bed, and was told, that there was a little room not yet taken upstairs, which he could have. He wrote a note to Tryphena, to say that the defence had hardly begun, but that he ought to be back at home by the last train on the morrow. He asked her to pray for the two poor chaps, for some of the evidence had been crushing. He posted this at the General Post Office, so that his wife might have it by the first post; after this, he crept back to his room in the *Cygnet*. It was a horrible little room, seven feet by six, with a leprosy on one wall where the paper was coming off, and a kind of necrosis on the other where it had already come. He could not sleep. The people downstairs made a din till closing time. After that, they kept coming along the passage beside his door till after midnight. By this time, he was wide awake and listening to the quarter-hour chimes of the cathedral and all the lesser churches. Late in the morning he slept, but woke unrefreshed, to wash and tidy up and come to a foul inn-breakfast in the frowsy coffee room. He was glad to pay his bill and get away from the *Cygnet*. Adolf was not yet down, so he went out alone, and walked to the cathedral, where he dodged the vergers who wished to shew him the sights. To escape them, he had to fall upon his knees on a hassock; they left him alone when they saw that he was praying. He prayed for the two prisoners, that they might be found Not Guilty, so that they might live good lives of repentance and amendment thence forward.

On his way to the court house, he thought, that he had better not go to the *Cygnet* again. The *Cygnet* was expensive, and he had very little money with him.

The court looked brighter on this second day. A lady had sent a large glass jar, full of yellow and white chrysanthemums, to stand on the ledge of the Judge's desk. An usher was putting the jar in place, but saying aloud,

"I don't know what His Ludship'll say about this lot, I reely don't".

Presently, after the usual ceremonies, His Ludship let him know. He looked at the flowers and said,

"These seem a little out of place here. Remove them".

After they had been removed, the defence continued. Mr. Slaughter said that he wished to remind the court, that the crime must have been committed between ten minutes and five minutes to six o'clock. He wished them to bear this in mind, because he proposed to call witnesses to prove that the two prisoners were at least a mile from Arthur's Camp at the time of the murder, and were peacefully and pleasantly employed there from long before until at least an hour after the murder had been committed. The court had heard how the witnesses for the prosecution had seen the two prisoners at Arthur's Camp at five minutes past five on the afternoon of the murder.

They had deposed to the elder prisoner carrying a gun.
He hoped to shew them to their complete satisfaction,
that he was not carrying a gun, but something much more
peaceable, a flail. Some of the party with, or near whom
he was walking, may have had guns, he did not know;
that was not the point. The prisoner had carried a flail,
as should be very soon established.

Another man entered the box. He was a big, slow,
beery man, who kept the *Four All Round* public house at
Condicote. He looked round the court with a smile which
assured everybody that now they should have some fun.
Yes, he knew the prisoners. Yes, he had seen them on
the day of the crime. A lot of folk had seen them. He
had had a match that afternoon at the *Four*. The prisoner,
Rapp, had backed himself to thrash a bushel of wheat
with a flail sooner than Pursy Grainger, a sailor in the
barquentine. What was the match? Why a contest or trial
of strength. What was it for? Why, five shillings and a
gallon. Gallon of what? Why, of beer. B.E.E.R. He
wished he'd some of it there.

Yes, Rapp had fancied himself; but the fact was Rapp
hadn't taken care of himself, or had taken too good care
of himself, whichever way you looked at it, and to thrash
with a flail was real work. He himself had backed the
sailor, who had won hands down. Rapp had had a quart
or so of the gallon, and had then gone out with his flail
with all the party, out into the fields for a walk.

What time had they started on their walk? Why, about
four. Yes, four. Yes, he was in a proper taking at being
beaten, but Pursy had offered him his revenge on Monday. What did he mean by being in a proper taking. Why,
nothing. He was vexed, that was all; the same as you

would be at making such a mucker of it. He'd gone out, growling, and swiping at the thistles with the flail, but that was nothing. No, Rapp never had had a gun; he never had seen him with a gun. He'd known him on and off for years, and was sure that he never had used a gun. He was not carrying a gun that Saturday, but the flail he'd thrashed the match with. He was a thorough gentleman, Rapp. He knew he would never hurt a fly. Why was he called Fight Rapp? He didn't know that he was. No, they'd got it all wrong. He was called Fly Trap because of his big mouth.

There was a general laugh at this, and the big, beery man stood down.

The usher called, "Hezekiah Dabbytott", and a voice answered, "That's me". There was a stir in the court as Dabbytott entered the box and took the oath. He was a little, bent, wizened man, bow-legged and like a man of another world. He might have come out of the Old Stone Age. He was a familiar figure on the roads near Condicote, where he cracked stones for a living.

"Will you tell the Court, Mr. Dabbytott, what you saw of the two prisoners and did with them on the afternoon of the crime"?

"The afternoon of that Black Saturday, I was at Tibbses Wharf, a bit after five. How do I know it was a bit after five? It was Saturday, and on Saturday at five I'm paid. I'm a stone cracker, what cracks road metal.

"I'd been paid and I'd had my pint. And I was going out of the town to try for a rabbit down *Garden Path* way. Yes, I take rabbits when I can, same as anybody. I'm here to tell the truth. I'll tell it, please God.

"It would a been then along about twenty-past-five, as

near as touch. Then, as I come to the bridge, the town side of the *Garden Path*, I see Rapp and the Magpie on the road, just in front of me".

"They were just in front of you? In which direction were they going"?

"As I come round the curve of the road, there they were walking towards the *Garden Path*, same as I was. Rapp was swinging a flail, so I says, 'I hear the sailor got the verdict', I says, meaning about the thrashing. So he says, 'Ah, but I'll lay him low on Monday'. So I says, 'Fly, what if we try for a rabbit in the old skintles opposite the *Garden Path*'? So he says, 'Come on, then, we'll come along. Nothing like a bit of sport', he says.

"So we crept into the skintles, where the old brick works was in Mr. Tollingses time; but we failed of any rabbit. Then we tried the whinny on the *Garden Path* side. Then we tried the skintles again; but we couldn't get a rabbit either side. They are artful things, rabbits; come to look at it. They'd had boys past 'em, that's what was what. So along about half-past five, I says to Rapp, 'Come on', I says, 'they're all quiet here. Let's go off to Arthur's, ther's usually rabbits there, outside the cover'. Had I a gun? No, I didn't need no gun. A catapult is what I use. Makes no noise. I'd kill a rabbit at thirty yards with one of my catties. Had Rapp a gun? No, he had a flail, I tell you.

"But to go on. 'Let's go off to Arthur's', I says. But Rapp looks at Arthur's from where we were. You can see across the fields to it from there. 'No', he says to me, 'no, it's no good going to Arthur's, cos, look, there's a party there now, a lot of 'em; they will have scared every rabbit and every jack sparrow'. So I look across to Arthur's. Yes, I mean Arthur's Camp, where poor Mr. Okle was killed.

I looked across to Arthur's and there, just as Rapp says,
I see a party of men, five or six of 'em. I see them all by
the covert end, just where poor Mr. Okle was found. No,
I couldn't see what they were doing. I thought they'd be
Okle's watchers, or these Saturdayers, after blackberries
and nuts and that. So I says, 'No, no good trying there
after all those have been there. What do you say', I says,
'to trying out to Tineton Great Oak'? 'No', Rapp says,
'I'm weary of my thrashing against that sailor on a day
all hot like this. I'll turn in here to the *Garden Path* for
a pint. Will you have a pint"? he says. I says, 'No', I says,
'no, for I've had my pint for the week: one pint in the
week I never exceed. You can ask anybody, the fact is
known'.

"It was along about half-past five, not earlier, not later.
Why wasn't it? Cos it was just gone half-past five by
Christ's clock in the belfry. So at that very hour Rapp
turns into the back door of the *Garden Path*, him and the
Magpie, together, and I went on to Tineton Greak Oak
alone".

The mind of Mr. Knipton now shewed another kind
of tool. In prosecution, he had shewn his skill in driving
in a succession of nails; now, in cross-examination, he
shewed a power of corkscrew, which gyred down into the
cork of promising bottles, gave a slight tug, and shewed
the uncorked vessel to be empty of the water of life. He
rose to his feet, and with great gentleness enquired,

"May I ask about the remainder of the hunting, Mr.
Dabbytott? Was there better fortune at the Tineton Great
Oak? Did you find a rabbit there"?

"No, I got no rabbit that day".

"They were too artful"?

"They'd had boys and that past 'em".

"Have you known the prisoners long"?

"Yes".

"You have been a friend to them"?

"I've known 'em".

"Precisely. They are men you have known".

"One of them, the Magpie, isn't a man; he's mimby".

"You've found no harm in Rapp"?

"I never found any harm in him".

"You know him to be incapable of hurting a game-keeper"?

"Yes".

"When you overtook the two prisoners on the road to the *Garden Path*, were they walking fast"?

"No".

"Just sauntering"?

"Yes".

"Like two men out for a stroll"?

"Yes".

"Were they all hot and panting"?

"No".

"Did a van come past you, while you were on the road, near the *Garden Path Inn*"?

"I don't remember".

"Try to remember".

"A many vans pass at different times".

"You do not remember the blue van of the Steam Bakery going by"?

"No".

"Did you pass or were you passed by anybody or thing while you were on the road with the two prisoners"?

"I don't remember".

Mr. Slaughter was on his feet. "Perhaps I may explain, that from the bridge where the witness overtook the prisoners to the place where they all left the road is well under a quarter-of-a-mile. At tea-time on a Saturday they would be unlikely to meet with many; but as a matter of fact, they did meet with one who will be presently called".

Mr. Knipton dropped or seemed to drop the line on which he was working. He looked at the ceiling, and then asked,

"When you looked across at Arthur's Camp and saw the five or six men outside the covert end, where exactly were you"?

"Near the *Garden Path Inn*".

"Can you say exactly where"?

"Yes, in the whinny bit, the *Garden Path* side of the road".

Mr. Knipton turned to the Jury. "I have here a map of that part of the road. This is the inn, here. This is the ancient brickworks, still known as the Skintles. This here, I take it, this field marked as the Roughs, is the whinny bit where you were standing? Can you follow this map, Mr. Dabbytott? That is the field you had in mind"?

"Yes, the whinny bit".

"You and the prisoner looked from that point across at Arthur's Camp, and saw five or six men, but not what they were doing"?

"Yes".

"How far from the road were you, when you stood on the whinny bit, and saw these men"?

"A matter of thirty yards. Along about thirty".

Mr. Knipton seemed to forget the matter of the whinny

bit just as it promised a bit of sport. He turned to Mr. Dabbytott and said,

"Do you go much about with the prisoner, Rapp"?

"I don't know what you mean. Go much about with".

"Be his companion: go with him on parties of sport and pleasure. Do you, or did you in the past when he was at liberty"?

"Not over and above".

"Did you not go once to Yockford Races with him"?

"I don't know what that's got to do with it".

"You did go with him? Yes or no"?

"I may have done once".

"I will try to refresh your memory. It was three years ago. Surely you remember"?

"Maybe it was my brother went".

"Oh, no, it wasn't. Perhaps you may have forgotten the Races. Perhaps you may remember what happened after the Races. You and the elder prisoner, Rapp, were charged with assaulting a gipsy, breaking his nose and robbing him of his waistcoat with spade guinea buttons. Come, sir, do you remember that"?

"Any man may have his misfortunes".

"And the Judge gave you both six months hard labour, to make you both less capable of hurting for a time. I put it to you, that you have made up this story of going to the *Garden Path*, to save an old accomplice from punishment".

"If you was to come outside . . ."

"Well, sir, what of it? What then"?

The witness gulped and said, "I could show you the very spots we stood on when we saw the men over at Arthur's. But you aren't paid to believe. You're paid to say white is black".

"How much have you been paid to say what you have told the Court"?

Mr. Slaughter was on his feet, with "Really, my lord, I protest. The suggestion of my learned brother cannot be allowed to pass".

"I'm sure that Mr. Knipton will admit that a word spoken under provocation was one that he would prefer to recall".

There was a brief passage of arms, then Mr. Dabbytott retired. There came a call for Richard Cowarne.

A little, dapper, bright-eyed man stepped into the box and took the oath. He was very neat in his dress and in his movements. The baker did not know him. He was clean-shaven, and smiled upon the court.

Mr. Slaughter began. "You are a retired market-gardener, Mr. Cowarne, from Chester Hills, I believe".

"That is so".

"Will you tell the court what you did and saw at the time of the crime now being investigated"?

Mr. Cowarne said, that he and his friend, Mr. Tarrington, of London, had been spending a quiet week of holiday at the *Garden Path* at the end of September. In the late afternoon of the Saturday of the crime, they were sitting smoking over a cup of tea, the time being well after five o'clock, but not later than half-past. They were saying how nice it would be if someone would come in and make a party of skittles. They had no sooner said the words than they heard footsteps on the flagged path to the door. The two prisoners appeared; one of them, the elder prisoner, carried an old-fashioned flail; the other had a walking stick or staff. The elder prisoner was very hot and weary; he said he had been thrashing a match at the *Four All Round*

with his flail, and had come out for a cooler. He had had
some refreshment and had then accepted an invitation to a
game of skittles. They had played together for two hours,
pretty nearly, and had played on by lamp-light long after
the alley was too dark for daylight playing. They had
played until seven-thirty, or later. They had certainly been
playing at the time of the crime. No, the elder prisoner
was not the worse for drink, only hot and tired from his
match. The skittles had resulted in a win for Mr. Cowarne
and his friend, a win of sixpence, which they had refused
to take seeing that one of the players, the younger prisoner, was not quite all there.

Mr. Knipton's manner suggested, that he knew that Mr.
Cowarne was incapable of inaccuracy of statement.

"Will you tell the Court, Mr. Cowarne, how you had
passed the afternoon of that day"?

"Certainly. My friend and I walked round Condicote,
starting from the inn, going north across the fields, turning
east over Duke's Down through the wood; then south
along the high ground to Ghost Heath and so back to the
inn—eight miles or so; a very pleasant walk".

"And then had tea"?

"Yes".

"Were you tired"?

"Pleasantly tired".

"Pleasantly careless of the passage of time"?

"Yes".

"And you did not notice the time"?

"No".

"Had you a watch"?

"It was being mended by the gentleman who gave evidence".

"Yet you can be sure of the exact time of the appearance of the two prisoners? You say it was not later than half-past five o'clock. How do you know that it was not later"?

"The accused man told us the time, as he came in".

"You asked him"?

"Yes. He looked at his watch and told me".

"I see. Tell me, was the prisoner breathing hard"?

"Yes, panting and dripping with sweat. He was complaining of the heat. He'd been thrashing a match, he said, and wanted a cooler".

"And the other accused man; was he hot and panting"?

"No, cool as a squirrel".

"After the skittles, when it was seven-thirty or later, was it the prisoner who told you the time"?

"Yes".

"In what words"?

"He said, 'How time's flown. We've been playing two hours. It's gone seven-thirty' ".

"Did you think that the time had flown"?

"Yes".

"When you had begun your game, had you light enough"?

"For some time. It was a lovely sunset glow".

"Did the prisoner talk much during the game"?

"No".

"Was he drunk"?

"He'd had a good deal, we thought, but he played well. We could not make out all that he said. He talked about forgiving somebody who had most cruelly wronged him, and that he had done it".

"Done what"?

"The forgiveness".

Mr. Tarrington, who followed, corroborated Mr. Cowarne's evidence.

"When we heard the footsteps coming to the door, we went out to meet the new-comers. Cowarne asked the elder prisoner what the time was. The man looked at his watch and said, 'Five-thirty'.

"Yes, it was bright at that time, bright daylight. The elder prisoner came into the house, saying that he was hot and wanted a drink. He was breathing hard and said he had been thrashing a match. I told him, that he would find the landlady in the yard at the back, if he wanted a drink. He went out there and called for a drink. After that we played skittles. I didn't much like the man, nor his looks, but he was the sort one meets in these country inns. He seemed rather drunk and confused; still, he was civil enough to us.

"Yes, after we had played some time, we had to have a light in the skittle alley. The elder accused man had said that they'd been playing two hours when he went. No, it hadn't seemed like two hours".

After him, Philip Woolhope, the landlord of the *Garden Path*, gave evidence, that he had been to Mr. Haizey's funeral on the afternoon of the crime, and had stayed on with young Mr. Haizey after the burial. He had not been back at the inn till near eight, when the two prisoners had been gone some time.

Mrs. Woolhope, his wife, swore that she had served the elder prisoner with beer on the evening of the crime. She had not seen him properly, at the time, as he had kept in the dark of the passage. She did not know him; but had seen the Magpie once or twice. Later, she brought them more beer to the skittle alley, but it was dark then, and again, she had not seen him properly. She could not pretend to say what time it was when the two first came in. She supposed about six. She had had a very busy time with the cider all that day, and had not been bothered about time. After all, the work has to be done, she added, whatever the time is.

No, they had no clock at present at the *Garden Path*. It had stopped, and was not back from the menders yet. They went by the church, which they could always hear, when the wind was northerly. Being busy, she had not noticed the time, but it might have been five-thirty or six when the two men first had the beer. It was always dark at the back of the *Garden Path* because of the privet hedge. Besides, if it had been later, the lamps would have had to be lit, and she had not lit them when she first served the beer.

Mr. Knipton asked her what drinks the two prisoners had had.

"The older man had a quart when he come, in; but he give the boy one of our penny gingers, what we make ourselves. Later he had another quart. Gentlemen usually had a quart at a time. It wasn't hardly worth having less".

"Was that all that he had, just the two quarts"?

"No, sir. Just as he was leaving, he asked for some gin. He seemed upset about something. He asked for sixpennorth of gin and then another and another, the three goes, just before he went out".

"Did that strike you as unusual"?

"No, sir. Gentlemen usually take gin to settle what went before. But the three goes is unusual".

The baker nudged Engels, as she stood down, and said,

"Those last witnesses have done the job. That's an alibi. That's safety".

"Don't you be too sure", Engels said. "I've had an alibi, too, in my time, but when the hounds want blood, it takes more than alibi to whip them clear".

There was a short delay, then the usher called for one Susan Gurney. Presently, a little old, trembling woman was in the box. She was dressed in a black dress on which there were many little black beads or "bugles". As her shrunken body trembled continually, these adornments trembled too. She was a seamstress in Condicote, she said. She had seen Hezekiah Dabbytott and the two prisoners on the road near the *Garden Path Inn* on the evening of the crime. She had been coming from the *Poltings,* a new house further along the road, where she had been hanging curtains and fitting chair covers for the couple just moved in to live there. She had left the *Poltings* at twenty-past five, and had met the three on the road a few minutes later, twenty-five or twenty-seven past perhaps. How did she remember? She was always terrified of men on a Saturday, and had to pass the three of them close to. She passed them just twenty yards from the *Garden Path* gate. No, not any of them had spoken to her nor molested her; but men had in the past; you never could tell of a Saturday. She knew all three by sight well. Rapp had a flail, the Magpie a long stick: no gun.

Mr. Knipton rose. He said, "I would like to ask you one or two questions, Mrs. Gurney. Is your sight good"?

"Yes, thank God, sir; or I could never do my work".

"When you passed the three men, was the light good"?

"Yes, sir, it was all a bright glow".

"Did you notice the prisoners"?

"Yes, sir".

"You looked at them particularly, to be sure whether you would be in danger from them"?

"Yes, sir".

"Did you notice anything peculiar about them"?

"Yes, sir. The prisoner, Rapp, was all swaying and dripping hot and panting".

"Not the others"?

"No, sir".

"Was he talking"?

"He was breathing very hard and dragging his feet, and dragging the flail. He was growling".

"But he did not speak, either to you or to his companions"?

"No, sir; he never spoke to me".

"Did you see the blue van of the Bakery on the road there, as you passed"?

"No, sir".

"Tell me, Mrs. Gurney, how did you know what time it was"?

"I heard the church clock go the quarter, sir".

"Had you heard it strike the hour"?

"No, sir".

"How long had you been working at the *Poltings*"?

"Ever since two, sir, to try to get all done before Sunday for them".

"And you had no clock to guide you"?

"No, sir. I had the work to finish".

"You are sure that it was twenty-past-five, when you left? Might it not have been a good deal later? Half-an-hour later"?

"I think it was twenty-past-five, sir".

"You think it was, no doubt. Please don't think for one moment, Mrs. Gurney, that anyone here doubts you. But you say you had no clock to guide you and had not heard the clock of the church strike the hour. Tell me, did the people at the *Poltings* see you when you left"?

"No, sir. I'd been paid for my work. When I finished I called to Tutu, the maid, that I was going, but she didn't answer and I could not see her; so I came away".

"You left because you had finished your work, not because of the time"?

"Yes, sir".

"Did the people at the *Poltings* give you any tea while you were at your work"?

"Yes, sir. Tutu brought me in a cup as I was working, as I wanted to finish".

"Was this cup of tea brought to you long before you left"?

"Yes, sir. I did the two chairs after it".

"This Tutu is a girl of fifteen, I understand"?

"Yes, sir".

"I want to fix the time of your meeting with the prisoners. Do you know the time at which the family at the *Poltings* usually takes tea"?

"At half-past-four, sir".

"And Tutu and the cook have tea, then"?

"No, sir, after the family has finished".

"About five, perhaps"?

"Yes, sir".

"Was the cook not present on this afternoon"?

"No, sir; she has the Saturday afternoon off".

"When did you have your cup of tea? When the family took theirs, or when Tutu took hers"?

"I was so pressed, sir, to be finished if I could, that I really couldn't tell".

"But if you did the two chairs after you had had the tea it must have been early, must it not, or you could not have been away by twenty-past-five? Come; it takes a long time to do a chair"?

"I was doing my best to be finished, sir".

"I am sure you were. Was it light enough for you to see to do your work until you had finished"?

"It was a very light room, sir, all facing the evening light, and a lovely evening. I could see to do my work. One reason I hurried so, was to have the light".

"Tell me, Mrs. Gurney, after passing the prisoners that evening, did you go straight to your home"?

"Yes, sir".

"Did you hear the church clock strike six or chime the hour, as you walked home"?

"No, sir".

"Are you quite sure of that"?

"I don't remember hearing it, sir. I may have done".

"Was it light, when you reached home"?

The old woman hesitated and seemed to fumble in her memory.

"I can't remember, sir".

"Can you remember whether the street lamps were lit? Were the lamps at Tibb's Wharf lit"?

"Yes, sir; I am sure they were, sir. I saw the reflections in the water".

"Then it must have been after six"?

"I don't know, sir".

"But the lamps on Tibb's Wharf are not lit till six at this time of year. On the evening of the crime they were

lit at a few minutes past six; so that it must have been
after that time when you saw them. Mustn't it, now"?

"Yes, sir; I suppose it must".

"Now it could not take you an hour to walk to your
home from the *Poltings*. It is less than one mile. If you left
the *Poltings* at twenty-past-five, you would have been at
home at twenty-to-six, wouldn't you"?

"Yes, sir".

"The lamps would not have been lit then; you could not
have seen their reflections"?

"I suppose not, sir".

"But of course you could not. Therefore, you must have
mistaken the time at which you left the *Poltings* and the
time at which you met the prisoners? You must have, must
you not"?

The old woman was fatigued and terrified; she was very
near collapse. She did not answer, though her lips moved.

"Thank you, Mrs. Gurney," Mr. Knipton said. "I will
not bother you with any more questions".

She did not understand what he meant. An usher
nudged her and told her that she could stand down now.

As the usher did not call any other name, the baker
looked up to see what was delaying the case. Mr. Slaughter was on his feet, saying,

"That is my case, me lud".

There was a shuffling and fidgetting in court; the Judge
bent over his notes and wrote busily for several minutes.
Presently, he said, that the court would adjourn so that
Mr. Knipton's address might not be interrupted by the interval. He rose and passed out, while all present rose out
of respect.

The baker felt himself shaken by the arm.

"Coming out, Rob"?

"Yes, I'll come out, but I feel dead beat. I want to walk in the air a bit".

He went out with Adolf, and then left him, so that he might walk alone in a deserted street somewhere at the back of the court house. He kept thinking of a walk into the fields in the April before all this. He had been in a grass pasture near the farmhouse known as the Roughs. He had seen and heard the Magpie witching, (as the country people called it), the farm horses to him. He had held his head back, uttering a strange penetrating cry; all the seven horses in the field had ceased grazing and had presently moved over to him and had thrust against each other for the privilege of being near him. When he and Tryphena had come nearer, they had seen him surrounded by all the horses, who were thrusting their heads to him to be fondled and handled; he was laughing at them and talking to them in the madman's jargon which he kept for most people. He and Tryphena had thought it a very beautiful thing.

"Talk of St. Francis and the Birds", he said. "Some painter ought to paint the Magpie and the horses".

He prayed as he walked, that somehow that day's evidence might prevail. People called this a Court of Justice, he reflected, but how was it just to submit two such souls to this?

It was not now only the Magpie that he thought of. Rapp, that terrible fierce creature, was now to him no worse than the penitent thief upon the cross, involved in a condemnation utterly unjust. What chance had two poor, untaught, uncouth souls against all this enormous accumulated power of custom, intellect and order, which had neglected them for forty years, and now rose to crush them flat?

"Now I see what it was that Christ meant by the kingdoms of this earth. They are the iniquity and the devil".

He came out of his exaltation of prayer. It was almost time to be going back to the court. He could not taste food, but feeling his mouth parched, he went into a little tearoom and drank a twopenny mug of sweet tea. Then he went back to his seat, to listen to the comment of the crowd, and the bets that were being offered and taken. For a few minutes, he heard nothing but voices saying,

"Guilty. There can be no possible doubt about Guilty: of course they're guilty".

Then a young man from somewhere behind them said, "These people are going on rank rumour and prejudice. Why, they were saying in Condicote as soon as the murder was known, that these two were the ones who had done it. Yet Slaughter comes with a little cold sense and now you'll see them change their tune. I said from the first they were charging the poor chaps unjustly. So they are. It's a damned iniquity, the way they've hounded them down".

The baker looked round at this man, with gratitude. He was a young gentleman just down from a university, "doing the court" with a friend. Usually, the baker thought that such young men were not enlightened, but here was one worth hearing, a wise one, who would come to something.

Presently, he heard his name called. Adolf was there, urging him to give the law a rest. "This is going to be a real break in the proceedings", he said. "They'll be an hour yet, they say. What say you, to a real good dinner"?

"I couldn't eat", the baker said.

"Well, I'm for a chop and tater", Adolf said, as they

left the court. "And if you'll take a fool's advice, Rob, you'll have some of the same".

"How do you think it's going"? the baker asked.

"Not too well, if you ask me", Adolf said. "This chap Knipton has got the case, and the witnesses and the feeling of the court, as well as twice the wits of the defence".

The young man, who had praised Slaughter, passed out of court with his friend. He was saying,

"All the same, it will mean rope for the two of them by the look of things".

The friend agreed, and so they passed out.

Outside in the world, it was foggy and raw. The baker was wondering whether he had not better make for home, all sick, tired and almost penniless as he was.

"No", he thought, "I'll see it to the end. I've still three shillings, and can get a bed and food enough for that".

He was glad to be able to move about. Even the fog of outside was better breathing than the fog of the court. He went briskly up and down the street outside the court house, trying to settle in his mind what the truth of the case was, and what the importance of those days of Trial was. He knew that it was an important event. God is Just. Any act of Justice must, therefore, partake of the very Nature of God. But could the mind of God, the Divine Spirit, all glory, beauty, wisdom and power, need the sour old ushers and these blood-thirsty barristers in wigs and the torturing of witness after witness?

"Oh, this is an evil thing", he muttered. "It may be the best man can do; but oh, how it needs amending and improving".

He came to the doors of the *Cygnet*. Going in, he drank a cup of soup and then a big bowl of hot, very sweet coffee, for which he paid a shilling. His hand so shook that he could hardly drink.

"Lor'", Adolf said, "you're in a taking. What's the matter"?

"Nothing", he said, "only to tell the truth I'm so excited, I can hardly bear it. How do you think it's going"?

"Not too badly, they think here"

"Thank God for that".

"What you want", Adolf said, "is a big hot brandy and then another of the same. I've had one and I'm going to have another. We've got the two Counsel and then all the Judge's summing still to come. He'll go on till midnight, very like. You'll want something to keep you going all that time".

"I shall keep going", the baker said. "I'm not going to stay in here. I must be in the fresh air a bit, or I shall drop dead, I think".

"Well, see you later".

The baker walked round the court again. He kept thinking now, that in Jerusalem something of this sort must have gone on, from midnight till mid-day, now at the High Priest's house, now in Pilate's court, then at Herod's court, then back again at Pilate's, everybody eager for all the forms to be observed. Is this your prisoner? No, not mine, the other fellow's, but he must be tried before the holiday, or he can't be tried at all. Had the jury there been sworn to "well and truly try, according to the evidence"?

The baker found himself suddenly weeping for the poor beset Christ, seized in the midnight, without sleep, jostled and manhandled, mocked, bully-ragged, cross-examined, scourged, (apparently because a good scourging would be on the safe side anyway), and then condemned, by somebody perplexed and trying to help, yet having after all to apply the code.

"Ye are doing it unto me", he sobbed. The day in court had shaken his nerves all to pieces. "Something of the Spirit of Christ is in the dock there in Rapp and the Magpie", he exclaimed. "It was that little something that Christ died to save. Oh, I've been a proud and wicked sinner to let my fear of Rapp keep me from being by him in his woe. Oh, if they'll let me I'll be by him from this time till it's over. I don't care if he shot fifty keepers. Would Christ have cared? Somewhere in his dark passionate heart is Christ's own brother, if I were only Christ enough to find it; but O God, I'm only a dark, damned sinner".

Something in Cowarne's evidence struck him. He had said that the Magpie had been as "cool as a squirrel". It struck strangely home now. Why, the Magpie was just like a squirrel, with bright eyes and quick movements and frequent gibber. Poor old Magpie, with no more harm in him than a squirrel. He knew that Rapp was guilty. The boys of Condicote had long played a game called Tripstick. Two boys, each having a four-foot stick, would face each other in any open space and then by adroit moves and thrusts try to trip each other up with the stick. The Magpie had been clever at it. Why, he had seen him playing it a score of times, sending even bigger lads headlong, amid roars of laughter. Of course, Rapp had called to him, "Tripstick him, Magpie", and the Magpie, thinking it a game, had thrust his stick between Okle's legs, and nearly had him over.

He still hoped. But if the verdict went the wrong way

. . . and it might . . . why then, if he wrote that to the Judge, the Judge would see, and go to see the Queen about it.

"I must get the Magpie some sweet stuff", the baker said. "He has always been fond of sweet stuff. I'll get him some sticks of that stuff they call Sambo".

It was a confection of pink sugar, done up in bars, so made that at each end the image of Sambo appeared in white sugar. No matter how much you bit off from either end, there was always a Sambo there. The Magpie loved this stuff, both as a dainty and as a work of art.

It was not easy to find a shop open in that part of the city. The baker had to go far from the court house, among many little streets. On his way, a girl of sixteen offered herself to him for ninepence. He told her to give up that life.

"I've very little money with me", he said, "but here's sixpence. Only promise me to go to your lodging now; and in the morning go back to your home".

The girl took the sixpence and laughed. "Gah", she said, "sky pilot". She plucked her old skirts about her and moved to the door of a pub. Not far from this place, the baker came upon the shop for which he had sought. It was a tiny sweet and eating house, licensed to sell tobacco.

He went in. It was much like a hundred others in Tatchester and the neighbouring cities. It had two little tables, a counter, and a few shelves, with glass jars containing sweets of different sorts. There was a case containing papers of tobacco. An elderly woman served him with three pennyworth of Sambo. He would have bought him sixpennorth, but noticed suddenly among the tobacco, some rolls of sailors' plug, done up in twine. He thought, "That would be just the stuff for Rapp. I must have something for Rapp, too."

He bought sixpennorth of it for Rapp. The woman thought that it would be rather strong; it was said to be very strong.

"It isn't for myself", he explained, "but for a friend, who likes it strong".

He thought that very likely the Judge would sum up till nearly midnight and that then the jury would have to discuss the verdict. Very likely he would have no food till next morning. He had better buy something here and eat it while the jury found their verdict.

"Could you put me up a sandwich, ma'am"? he asked.

"Why", she said, "I'd rather not cut any more from that ham. It's not like a Marcham ham; there's something got into it. I won't have any more ham until tomorrow; but I could boil you up some hard eggs, if you wanted to take something with you".

"I do, please. Have you a few raisins"?

"No, I never stock raisins. You're the first person ever asked me for them".

"Well, I'd be glad if you boiled me up a couple of eggs then, but not hard because I can't digest them; just so as to be set. You won't be long, will you? I ought to be gone now."

She was not long, because the kettle was boiling. He put the eggs, done up in a paper bag with a twist of salt, into his inner pocket. He had had two shillings: now the girl had had sixpence, Sambo threepence, tobacco sixpence and the eggs fourpence. He had fivepence and his return ticket left. He would have to spend the night in the station waiting-room.

He hurried back to the court house, knowing that he had stayed too long and fearing to be late. He was late.

A big policeman stopped him at the door.

"You can't go in", he said, "the court is sitting. It's been sitting a long time. Mr. Slaughter is addressing the jury".

"But, please, can't I go in"?

"No one passes this door while the court's sitting. Those are the orders".

"But I'm helping in the defence and I've got some things for the prisoners".

"What sort of things"? the policeman asked suspiciously.

"Tobacco and sweets", the baker said, holding out his packets. The policeman turned them over with his hand.

"Well, I can't pass you in, that's not allowed", he said. "But as long as you rest quiet, you can stay by the door here. You'll catch a word or two, now and then. If anybody was to come out, I'll keep the door ajar. But no one comes out when the court's sitting, least of all in an Address".

They stayed there together while Mr. Slaughter within surpassed himself. Slaughter had not been easy in his mind, when he rose to address the Court. During the interval, Rapp had begged to see him, and had then told him, that he was guilty. He had not told him this in order to withdraw his plea of Not Guilty, no, but to beg that his Counsel would do all in his power to get him off, so that he might amend, be a good man, make his peace with God and perhaps help poor Mrs. Okle. All his life, if spared, would be devoted to good deeds. "Oh, Mr. Slaughter, I do beg you to use your every power for me and the pore

Magpie". It had been a shrewd blow to him. He had tried to believe in his client's innocence. He wished that the man had kept quiet, till after sentence at any rate. Yet, what if the confession were the result of nerves? What if it were not true? He would have to ignore it, and proceed as if it had not been made. But it had been made, and it was a great handicap, now that the real struggle began.

The feeling of the court was dead against both prisoners, he could feel that; the mass of the evidence was against them, too. Still, he had fought against odds as great and carried the day. He was not going to surrender: he was going to show them what advocacy is.

He was what actors used to call "a fifth act actor", that is, he always had strength left for his big scenes at the very end of the play. He was really an actor. He had a fine and well-trained voice, with a great range; he had a power of emotional appeal. Now he summoned up all his powers and trusted to them to demolish the nails and wire nets of Knipton.

Men had said that old Upper Slaughter was getting to be Lower Slaughter, but in the case of Crown v. Rapp & anor, he was in the top of his performance. The baker, who had set him going, could very seldom catch a word or two, but he knew from the hush in court that everybody there was held breathless. The policeman now and then said a kind word. He was a big kindly man, very fond of dahlias.

"It's what I call the perfection of a flower, a dahlia. Wonderful colour and every petal a miracle, and all put together in a way that beggars description".

Suddenly, after a long, long time, the door was smitten hurriedly from within. The policeman was swift to undo the catch and to let the door open. A wild-eyed, white-faced man reeled out of court, and was promptly very sick. His friend, who followed, bearing his hat, led him away.

"The court's gone to his stomach", the policeman said. "It often goes to people that way; especially if they're wearing new clothes. It's the smell of the new cloth".

He was mindful of his promise; he had left the door slightly ajar, so that the baker heard Mr. Slaughter's peroration.

"Weigh carefully", he was saying, "the evidence put before you. Much of what has been sworn on behalf of the accused comes from the lips of men in humble walks of life, from rude, untutored men, not accustomed to give evidence, not used to the arts and ways of counsel, but pitting their truth, under every disadvantage, against skill of no mean order, amid all the splendour with which law, in this country, is invested.

"Thank God, gentlemen, Truth can be known as Truth, even from the humblest lips. I am sure that you could not but have been profoundly impressed, by the sight and by the truth of those nervous but undaunted witnesses, trembling in the unaccustomed glory of a great building, fearful, perhaps, of offending in some way that mysterious and dread power of Justice, yet resolved to endure all these things to save two innocent men from doom. Truth sustained them, gentlemen, and the Truth that sustained them shone through them.

"Gentlemen, I know that you who listened, as I listened, with tears to the anguish of a bereaved wife, will hesitate to send to the gallows two fellow-Christians, identified only, if at all, through eyes blinded by those tears.

"Let it be your boast tonight, Gentlemen of the Jury, that impressed and swayed as you were, (and who can fail to be impressed and swayed by the talents of my learned brother) let it be your boast, I repeat, that impressed and swayed as you were you yet followed Truth, clear-eyed, and by your verdict returned the elder prisoner to his friends and the younger to that charity, which has never yet failed in a Christian land".

He felt, when he sat down, that he had touched them home, but that he was still many hours from the deliberation of the jury. They would have a long time to forget his warmth; they would be stone-cold before the Judge dismissed them to find their verdict.

There was a pause in the trial at this point. The Judge was busy writing. Many people rose to go, lest they should be kept there till after midnight. In the press of people leaving, the baker was not able to get in for a minute or two. When he had taken his seat and the Judge had finished what he was writing, Mr. Friezewell Knipton rose to his feet, bowed to the Judge, and began his address to the jury. He said, that they had heard witnesses to prove that those who claimed to have seen, could not have seen the crime; that awakened and alarmed intelligences in instants of crisis could not observe, or, if observing, remember; and that people sworn to have been in one place, were quite certainly, at the times vouched for, elsewhere, and otherwise engaged. Such discrepancies of evidence were familiar to those engaged in courts of justice. He proposed to deal with the evidence brought forward by the defence.

The baker listened, while the gimlet-like mind of Knipton bored its neat holes in what the defence had built up as a bulwark round the accused. He listened in horror.

"Surely", he thought, "he must realise that he is trying to have two men hanged".

The question of their possible guilt did not matter to the baker. He, himself, usually forgave all who wronged him within a few days. He tried to think how it would have been had he been shot instead of poor John Okle. He would have forgiven his murderers at once in that new life, which, in his belief, began as soon as the soul left the body. Tryphena would have forgiven, too. John Okle would have scorned to prosecute his murderers; he would have flamed out with indignation at the very thought of it.

"When I come to think of it", the baker muttered, "no man known to me, not Rapp nor Sir Hassle, would put any human soul through an ordeal like this, no matter what he had done. God forgive me for thinking it", he muttered, "but I've always thought Rapp was guilty. Well, guilty or not, he hasn't deserved this".

Well, what then did he deserve? If you told Rapp to go and sin no more, he would go and sin a good deal more. What sort of a world would you get, if you had brutes like Rapp loose killing with brutality or cunning at their own evil pleasure men much finer than themselves? The text floated up into his mind, "Father, forgive them". How could you forgive them? And if you didn't forgive them, then you had a scene like this court. How would Father forgive that?

Long before Mr. Knipton had finished, the autumn evening closed in. The ushers came in, as on the evening before, with their matches and linstocks; the blue jets shot up from the gas standards, with the same *Pobbing* noise. After the gas had been lighted, the court looked even less real than by daylight. Mr. Knipton's white face looked liker a mask than ever. He had two dark smears for eyes and brows, and a slit for a mouth, out of which proceeded a bloodless appeal for blood.

After a long time, it seemed to the baker, that he had proved that the two Okle women had clearly seen the killer, that they had recognized the Magpie, a man marked by Nature, anyhow, for immediate recognition anywhere; and that the other witnesses for the defence should be dealt with one by one.

"As to the witness, Dabbytott", Mr. Knipton said, they had heard him for themselves. They had heard from his own lips that he was a violent man, an ancient partner of Rapp's in crime, and confessedly breaking the law with him on the day of the crime. The evidence that he had given had been quite patently designed to benefit his friend in adversity, but he hoped to shew that it would have a material effect in establishing the case for the Crown. He would return to that later.

"Gentlemen, the defence centres on the arrival of the two accused men at the *Garden Path Inn*. If they were at that inn, as is alleged, at half-past five, and remained there, playing skittles, till half-past seven, they could have had no hand in the killing of John Okle.

"Various witnesses for the defence have testified to the vital acts and times of the accused during that afternoon. Now, Gentlemen of the Jury, I ask your very earnest attention to various points in the evidence of these witnesses, especially to those points which relate to the time of the prisoners' arrival at the *Garden Path Inn* and to the condition of the elder prisoner when he reached the inn.

"You heard the landlord of the *Four All Round* public house say that the prisoner Rapp left the inn, after his thrashing match, at four o'clock. The quantity thrashed at the match, only one bushel, is not large, but it was done at speed, and all who know anything of country work will know, that thrashing with a flail is harder work even than mowing with a scythe or reaping with a sickle. No doubt the one bushel to a man not in condition was exhausting work. It was done in the heat of the hot September day. No doubt that when it was done the prisoner needed a drink and fresh air. He had the drink, a quart of beer, and went out into the fresh air. No doubt, he was both hot and weary then, at four o'clock.

"I do not know, nor do I enquire, how he passed the next hour; but he is next seen at five minutes past five close to the Arthur's Camp coverts. He was not hot nor weary then; no; but cool, resolute, leading a party with very evil intent and plainly determined to brook no interference. What was it that he planned to do there at that time? Something less peaceable than thrashing wheat, for he had exchanged his flail for a gun, with which he threatened two harmless passers-by. That was at five minutes past five; the time was clearly noted, by two very good, sober witnesses. Please mark this point, clearly, gentlemen. He was seen, not hot, not weary, not going towards the *Garden Path*, but going directly from it, in the opposite direction, with a party of associates. Where the witnesses saw him, it is about ten minutes from the *Garden Path* by the footpaths in the fields. As it is a thousand yards, mixed going, few men could walk it in less. It is quite clear that he was not then going towards the *Garden Path*, but away from it with a purpose which brooked no interference. Who can doubt, that he was going to commit the crime of raiding the coverts in the known absence of the keeper?

"That appearance of the prisoners at five minutes past five we may accept as certainly proven. How and when do they re-appear? You have heard the testimony of the bereaved women. You know from various witnesses that the murdered man must have reached home about twelve minutes before six, and must have been killed within ten minutes of that time. He must have been shot, as I think, between ten and five minutes before six. Shall we say at five-fifty-three? Both women clearly recognized both prisoners. It has been urged, that they are short-sighted, and that the scene of the murder is dark, overhung with yew trees, and certain to have been dark on that evening and at that time. Gentlemen, you are all familiar with the phenomenon of the afterglow. You all know with what glory the autumn sun goes down. You all know how, on certain nights, after he has sunk below the horizon, a glow or radiance suffuses heaven and earth for some time after his sinking. The night of the crime was such a night. All over this quarter of England such an afterglow illumined earth and heaven as many of you cannot fail to remember. It was by such a light that the two poor women at Arthur's Camp recognized the slayer of John Okle. And how could they not have recognized the prisoners? Both are conspicuous men, the one with hair which cannot but be recognized, the other with a build and a manner not easily to be disguised. Both are well known in the town and district, conspicuously known, notorious, in a community where all are known without disguise. And you will remember, too, that they did not depend on sight alone.

They heard the voice of the one prisoner calling to the other by name. They could not be mistaken, short-sighted though they may be. Therefore, we may be certain, that at about seven minutes before six both prisoners were just outside the Camp coverts in their deed of blood.

"I say nothing of Zine.

"Now, you have heard the witnesses for the defence assuring us, that during all this time the prisoners were at or near the *Garden Path Inn*, indulging in innocent pastime. Let us a little examine their evidence.

"First, we have the witness, Dabbytott, an old companion of Rapp's, who swears that he met both prisoners sauntering out from Condicote towards the *Garden Path Inn* at twenty minutes past five.

"He came up with them, he says, at the bridge on the town side of the *Garden Path*. It is a little bridge over the stream. If you will look at the map of the district you will see, (and I ask you to remember), that at that bridge there is a stile and from that stile a footpath leads across the fields to Arthur's Camp coverts and the scene of the crime. Please remember that.

"Mr. Dabbytott says, that the prisoner was not hot nor weary, not panting, but walking quietly, swinging a flail. Being otherwise disengaged, he at once assented to trespassing in pursuit of game, and for a few minutes crept about in search of rabbits. Not finding what they sought, they adjourned to the *Garden Path Inn*. But before they so adjourned, a very remarkable thing occurred. They looked across to Arthur's Camp, from where they were near the *Garden Path*, and saw a party of five or six men just where poor Mr. Okle was found. Mr. Dabbytott was very certain, that he saw all this from the rough piece to the west from the inn. But gentlemen, Arthur's Camp and all the scene of the crime is invisible from that point. A glance at the contour map will show you that, beyond all doubt. You will say, that a map is not evidence. But go there and see, as I have. A jut of high ground, shooting eastward there, shuts the fatal covert from view. Mr. Dabbytott did not and could not see any part of the covert from that point. The covert cannot be seen from anywhere very near to the *Garden Path*. The nearest point to the inn from which it can be seen is the stile near which Mr. Dabbytott first overtook his friend.

"Mr. Dabbytott says that he does not remember being passed by any person or van, while on the road near the *Garden Path Inn*. The van of the Steam Bakery, as it is called, was on that particular bit of the road delivering bread at the inn and at the houses nearby, between twenty and thirty minutes past five that evening. The driver of the van denies that he saw him or the two prisoners there. Mr. Dabbytott does not remember passing Mrs. Gurney though she clearly remembers passing him and his companions. These two facts seem to me very significant. Perhaps I may make them appear so to yourselves.

"To go back to Mr. Dabbytott. He says that he left the prisoners at the *Garden Path Inn* at about half-past five. And here we have two witnesses, exact enough as to the prisoners' presence but not exact about the time at which they appeared. You have the very good witnesses, Mr. Cowarne and his friend. They had been for a long walk together and were happily tired, after the walk, not wanting to know the time, not observing it; but feeling that a quiet game of skittles might be good fun. To these two, appear suddenly the two prisoners. The elder prisoner, very hot and panting and giving as an excuse for his heat that he had been thrashing a match with his flail. All this, remember, just ten minutes after Mr. Dabbytott found him not hot and panting.

"Now, it is a very interesting point. Mr. Cowarne, no doubt eager for a game of skittles, and wishing to enter into conversation with the new-comer, asks him if he can tell him the time. The elder prisoner, looked at his watch and said, that it was half-past five. The man was breathing hard, panting and dripping with sweat, because as he said, he'd been thrashing a match.

"But, Gentlemen of the Jury, he had finished the thrashing match at a few minutes before four, and had recovered from the heat of thrashing, as we have proved, by five minutes past five. What had put him into this sweat and panting, at half-past five (if it were half-past five)? It could not have been the thrashing. Something else had exhausted him. The younger prisoner was not hot and panting, or was less noticed, perhaps, keeping always in the background.

"Then, gentlemen, I ask you to notice Mrs. Woolhope's evidence. On his arrival at the inn, when he called for beer, 'he kept in the dark of the passage'. Why did he do that? Why did he shrink from observation? Why, having proclaimed the time, did he keep in the shadow and in the dark seclusion of the skittle alley? Why, when he finished the game, did he again call attention to the time? And especially to the fact that he had arrived there at half-past five? 'We've been playing two hours'. Do not those words seem to point to an eagerness that he wished it to be believed that he had arrived there at half-past five?

"Gentlemen, we now come to a very important witness;

Mrs. Gurney. You have seen and heard her. I do not doubt that you are satisfied that that humble, God-fearing woman spoke the absolute truth. What did you gather from her, as to the time at which she saw the prisoners? She, too, like so many country witnesses, was more concerned with the getting of work done, or done in time, than to enquire the exact hour. It is not remarkable. To most country dwellers, the church clock, in the absence of the sun, is sufficient reminder of the passage of Time; but to all the getting of the daily task accomplished is more important. Can any of you who listened to her doubt that she had not heeded and was not heeding the hour, but was all intent on finishing her engagement at the *Poltings?*

"She gives her evidence as to the time. But what is the evidence? That she had heard the church clock go the quarter. She had not heard it strike the hour fifteen minutes before. She could not therefore tell whether it was a quarter-past five or an hour later. But I want you to consider yet another thing. She was depending on the quarterly chimes of Condicote church. You all know the sound of quarterly chimes, four bells for each quarter, eight for each half hour, twelve for each three quarter and sixteen for the hour before the hour strikes. The sound has suggested the verse of a poet:—

> *ALL MEN MUST DIE*
> *ALL LIFE MUST END*
> *O CHRIST ON HIGH*
> *BE THOU OUR FRIEND.*

Now, gentlemen, the *Poltings* is rather more than one mile and two hundred yards southward and westward from Condicote church. On the day of the crime, the wind was northerly, and so likely to convey the sound of the chimes in that direction; but like many northerly, fine weather winds, it was a light wind, coming in gentle gusts. The sound carried by such winds comes capriciously, as is well known; parts of the message are dropped, for parts of the air currents have not strength to carry them. I am myself certain, that Mrs. Gurney, intent upon her work and not too heedful of the hour, caught only a part of the message of those bells. What she heard was the first portion of the chime for five-forty-five. The rest, the wind failed to bring to her. A little reflection will show you, that this must have been the case. She was working in good daylight until she left. She was near the *Garden Path Inn* in the midst of the bright glow, which was one of the features of that evening, but which at that moment must have been beginning to lose its glory. She did not see the blue, conspicuous van of the Steam Bakery, which was on that bit of road between five-twenty and five-thirty. She walked straight home from that point, yet found the lamps lit at Tibb's Wharf when she reached the bridge near her home. The church clock, as you may remember, was at that time five minutes slower than it should have been. Gentlemen, she could not have been near the *Garden Path Inn* between five-twenty and five-thirty; the van lad would have seen her. She must have been there between five-fifty and six o'clock, and as I think at almost six o'clock. God sent her there, that her presence might confound the wrong-doers.

"For what did she see at that time, in that great blaze of the expiring light? She saw 'The prisoner Rapp, all swaying and dripping hot and panting; breathing very hard, dragging his feet, dragging the flail, and growling'.

"Gentleman, did you ever hear a more complete description of a man in bad condition after a great exertion?

"Consider, gentlemen: six or seven minutes before she met them the two prisoners had been outside the Arthur's Camp covert in their deed of blood. When once that deed had been done, when the fatal shot had sped, and the poor gallant victim had fallen, it was a matter of the utmost urgency to the slayers to get away, and if possible to establish an alibi. Leave the widow and child desolate, but fly, fly, to what safety can still be found.

"Put yourselves for one instant in the prisoners' place. They were there in that lonely, rough, red-earthed field beside the thicket, between the two arms of the covert. They could fly west, north, east or south. Rapp was the killer, Rapp was the brain and will of the confederacy; to the savagery of the wolf he now added the cunning of the fox. He decided on the instant, taking the right course, as a savage or wild beast so often will.

"What did he do? If he went north, he would have run into the witness Zine; he may even have seen the witness Zine. If he went west, he would infallibly have met some of the other witnesses—Mr. Jones or one of the shepherds: he may even have seen or heard them. If he went east, he ran the risk of meeting with the workers on the farm. But to the south were the open fields, deserted at that time of day, without witnesses now, without loiterers or lovers. By running at full speed across those fields, he and his associate could reach the road from Condicote at a stile where they would be unlikely to meet with anybody; they could then walk slowly, as though coming from Condicote, and enter the lonely, not much frequented inn of the *Garden Path* at their ease, to establish, if possible, the alibi, for which the criminal heart longs.

"As the crow flies, it is not a long run. I said, a little while back, that it is a thousand yards of mixed going, by the footpaths, to the stile where Mr. Dabbytott overtook them. But if the alibi were to be established, this space had to be covered at top speed. No clothes could be cast away. They had to run as they were, in their thick country clothes and heavy boots, and Rapp carrying his incriminating gun, a gun weighing nine or ten pounds of penalty weight. On the way, I do not doubt, he thrust the gun into some ditch where he had before left his flail. Or did Mr. Dabbytott wait at the stile for him, carrying that flail? Was that alibi at the *Garden Path* already arranged with that trusty henchman?

"We cannot know these points at present, but we know that the prisoners ran. They had to run. Behind them were the gathering spirits whose task it is to avenge the shedding of blood. Run? They had to run. Seven-leagued boots would have been too slow for them. They ran that thousand yard course as though their lives depended on it. You have heard, that the elder prisoner was in bad condition at the time of the crime. His exertions at the thrashing match were as nothing to his exertions now. He ran that thousand yards, and reached the stile, gasping, broken, panting, dripping with sweat, gurgling incoherent noises. The faithful Dabbytott was there; they went on to the inn of their salvation.

"Why did not Dabbytott see the widow Gurney? He passed her. Was it because Rapp had contrived to tell him that they were all in for a hanging matter, since he had killed the keeper? They went to the inn. The younger prisoner, hanging back from the other two as an inferior, was not much noticed. But Rapp, the leader, was at once seen, in spite of his anxiety to screen himself, to be hot and weary. But Fortune favoured him. As he entered, Mr. Cowarne asked him just that question he longed to be asked. What time was it? He answered, altering the time to suit his case, half-past five. Later, with much effrontery, he tried, and with success, to persuade his temporary companions that they had been playing for two hours instead of for an hour and a half.

"Up to this point, he had succeeded, or must have thought that he had succeeded, beyond his wildest hopes. He had established an alibi. He had persuaded two good witnesses and a possible third, that he had entered the *Garden Path* before the time of the crime, and had been there for two hours together. Why, at that point, did he go back to get the gun? It was a stolen gun; it was a gun which held within it the overwhelming evidence of guilt. He must have flung it or thrust it away in his mad rush from the scene of the crime. Now that it had been cast away, why on earth should he have wished to retrieve it?

"Gentlemen, he had been drinking hard for some days and alcohol had confused him. It is plain, that when he left the inn, he had planned to go to an old haunt of his here in Tatchester. I do not doubt, that he needed the gun as a weapon or as property always easily sold in case of need. But, gentlemen, the gun lay in the fields out towards the scene of the crime. To retrieve the gun, he had to face the innocent blood which he had shed. Out there in the fields, now that it was dark, the ghost of his victim walked. How could he face that ghost, all guilty as he was? He could not. Callous as he is, he could not. He drank, in desperation, noggin after noggin of gin, and then, only, could dare the shed blood crying from the ground.

"Gentlemen, can you doubt that at this point all the alcohol which he had that day drunken, capped by the gin taken before he left the *Garden Path*, confused and unsettled the astucity which had guided him hitherto? From that point, his actions are those of a guilty and drunken man, wandering in confusion to his own undoing.

"Gentlemen, I do not doubt, that your good sense and clear-sightedness will decide that a verdict of Guilty is the only possible verdict to be pronounced in this case. I doubt not, that you will decide that both prisoners are to receive in full measure the punishment that all laws, both Human and Divine, prescribe for the wilful shedding of Man's blood. I await that verdict with tranquillity".

"There's a fine, human bloodhound for you", Adolf said, as Mr. Knipton sat. "That's the kind of fine, trained intellect who keeps the haven'ts bitted. Yes, my fine vampire, the *Banner* and the *Cry* and a few others will have their pins into you by Saturday night. 'How they deal with poachers in Tatshire'".

"I wonder how tranquilly he would await the verdict, if it had just been all twisted in that way against himself"? the baker asked.

"Gods", Adolf said, "I wish Judge, Jury, Counsel, Ushers and all might be in the dock suddenly, to see Justice for themselves a little. They'd think it was a pretty blindfold figure, if they did".

The Judge finished writing at his notes, and told the Court, that he would begin his summing-up in five minutes' time. It was now pitch dark outside. A good many people, who had watched the case to this point, rose from their seats, when the Judge rose, and then left Court for home. When the baker could get from his seat in the tier, he found, that the two prisoners had been removed.

"Where are the prisoners"? he asked a policeman.

"They've been taken down".

"Could I speak with them"?

"You're not Counsel nor Law, are you"?

"No".

"No one not Counsel nor Law can speak to them".

The baker looked blank. At that instant, Mr. Gallup came by.

"Mr. Gallup", the baker called, "please may I see the prisoners? Only for a minute. I'd be so grateful".

"See them? Yes. This man's all right, officer. He's concerned for the defence. You can only stay a minute, though".

He was glad to have the baker there. He wanted to have Slaughter to himself for a moment. He led the way down the steps in the dock to a stone corridor. In a bare room, hung with a varnished map of Tatchester, were three policemen. In a chair by the fire, Rapp sat, sweating, beside the Magpie, who had fallen asleep.

Slaughter was saying something to Rapp.

Gallup caught his eye and whisked him away. The baker came to the policemen and handed over the packages, which they turned over, with shrewd looks at him and them.

"I've brought them some sweets and tobacco", the baker said. "The man at the door saw them. It's only sweets and tobacco".

"I suppose it's all right", a policeman said. "Here's a friend brought some tobacco, Rapp".

"It's me, the baker", Rob said. "I thought you'd like some tobacco. I just came to say that I'm wishing you well. Good luck".

Rapp was not very sure of what he was saying.

"The gent's brought you some baccy", the policeman said.

Rapp came out of his dream, whatever it was.

"I've been praying for a bit of just that", he said. He unrolled the twine, turned back the linen cover and bit a piece from the roll of pressed leaf within. He turned it over in his mouth and chewed upon it. "God, I could do a go of rum", he said, "three goes of rum'd buy all the women in the world, as far as I'm concerned".

"I'd like to shake hands, Rapp, and wish you all possible good happy luck tonight", the baker said.

"There's a lot of luck in a shop like this", Rapp answered. "But these Judges ought to remember that there's another Judge elsewhere than them what will call to account later".

"Indeed, indeed there is, Rapp", the baker said. "You trust in Him".

"I do always put my trust in Him", Rapp answered.

"Give me your hand", the baker said.

Rapp held out a hand; the baker took it, and then caught at the other and shook them both.

"God bless and guard you, Rapp, and send you free tonight".

Rapp leaned suddenly forward and whispered fiercely, "How's it going"?

"It's going well, please God", the baker said.

"Ah, please God. There's a lot of 'em says that at the end. I don't want no 'please Gods'. I've had too many of 'em".

He hunched himself together and huddled over the fire, sweating, shivering and growling. Then he glared at the baker.

"Yah, you", he said. "You and your Gods and your Pleases. Lots of 'em come in and say, 'Oh, it's going fine', and put a ray of hope in a pore fellow. 'Is it', I says, 'is it going fine'? 'Yes', they says, 'please God'. It's the rope is what they mean. God, I'd like to smash your mealy face in. By God, I'll do it, too".

He rose up, but the policemen closed in.

"Here now, none of that, my lad", they said.

In their closing-in on Rapp, they woke the Magpie. The baker went to him.

"Mag", he said, "I've brought you a bit of Sambo. You 'member Sambo? You like Sambo"?

"Ha, goody, goody, goody", the Magpie said, taking the bars, biting the end off each bar in turn, and then gazing at the face of Sambo.

A policeman opened the door and said, "Stand by, all. His Lordship will be up in a tick".

"You'd better hop it", a policeman told the baker.

"Could I possibly sit just below the dock"? the baker asked. "I've known this poor lad for years. I'd like to be near him".

"What do you think, Joe? Could this chap sit near the dock"?

"Why should he"?

"I've known the Magpie".

"You don't look dangerous. I should think it's all right. Yes, if there's a seat, you could. But cut upstairs at once, or the court'll be set".

The baker did cut upstairs and found the house reassembling. There was a seat just under the dock; he took it. The jury were being shepherded back to their seats; the baker looked at them. Each of them had hoped for a real rest between the address and the summing-up, but they were not to have one. The baker thought that each one of them looked much the worse for their two days in court. How could twelve deadly weary men give a fair verdict? Eleven of them would be so fagged and sick, that they would take anything that the one less weary might propose. But then, the baker was not sure that that was not a wise arrangement. The one with life would decide, not the eleven with death.

With the usual ceremony, amid the silence of the court, the swish of the dry silk upon the panels gave the baker goose flesh as the Judge limped to his throne. He lapsed to his seat, and looked through his notes as the court fell silent and settled to seats. When all were still, he surveyed the assembly with a shrewd eye, and then, with a clear and very beautiful voice, began to marshal the case in its entirety, detaching what he saw to be vital. The baker was at once hushed by the beauty of the voice, to which so many had succumbed. It was not beauty of voice alone, with it went an extraordinary clarity of mind. The two qualities together gave to the hearer an impression of a most upright, most generous, but yet formal nature.

The gas jets were now full on again. The baker could see the Judge's noble head, all precise and clear-cut, with the features made all the more remarkable by the strange setting of the wig behind it. For a while, the baker listened with admiration, as to a new instrument being played by a master. Then, as the Judge drew mesh after mesh about the two who were there before him, still hoping against hope, the baker felt sick at heart.

"Father, forgive him", he prayed, "for he knows not what he does".

He was not clear in his mind how men would get along in a world which refused to punish murder. If pressed on the point, he would probably have said that men would not commit murder, if society had not murdered their human souls; but he could listen and trouble no longer. He had taken in all of the case that he could absorb. He was now incapable of more. He fell asleep. Waking with a start, he heard the clear voice going on and on, shewing that such an one had impressed him and that such another had brought light upon a dark point.

"Certain comments have been made", he said, "upon the state of mind, or degree of sanity, of the younger prisoner. You have heard the comments; you have been able to study his sanity for yourselves. You have seen him. You have heard his ejaculations from the dock. But you are to remember, that sanity is a matter usually pronounced upon, in modern life, by qualified medical men. You have heard that the prison doctor, who has had him under close medical supervision during his committal here, has refused to declare that he is not accountable for his actions. As I came into this court this morning, I heard a man say that the jury would give the younger prisoner the benefit of the doubt. I have to warn you that you are not here to do any such thing. You are here to find a verdict according to the evidence. If, on weighing the evidence, you think him insane, or not responsible for his actions, you must declare it. But you must bear in mind the further important fact, that the younger prisoner has never been incapable. He has maintained himself for a good many years.

"I must remind you, too, that he understands and obeys those to whom he is accustomed. With those who know him he is, and has been, a useful ally. So much has been made clear".

He spoke for some time upon the meaning of "accessory", and on the guilt of accessories. So much he made very clear.

He said, that there had been comment upon the case, much talk about it, much gossip, some prejudice and many false rumours. The jury must put from them prejudice of any sort, either for or against, and cast their verdict impartially, according to the evidence which had been put before them.

Finally, he told them that the law put upon them as citizens a very terrible responsibility. They had to decide whether the lives of two fellow beings were to be forfeited for causing the death of John Okle, a man of whom all had spoken good things. "The doing of justice", he told them, "is perhaps the finest attribute of wisdom. It is so rare and so difficult a thing, that all religions unite in making it the chief attribute of Deity. Knowing this, I ask you to bring to your deliberations hearts and minds opened to the enlightenment from on high which alone can make our decisions wise. Thus lit, thus helped, you need have no fear. You will speak the truth from a certainty of the truth. May the good God attend you in your task".

He rose, and all there rose as he left the court. The officers took charge of the jury, who filed out to their discussion. The baker turned to have a glimpse of the prisoners. They were just behind him.

"God be your guard", he said. "All will go well, boys".

The Magpie was pointing out the last glimpse of the Judge's scarlet robe, perhaps still thinking that it had something to do with hunting, and that presently the hounds would be there. Rapp was swaying from side to side, like a man drunk. His face was working; he looked like a man about to have a stroke. The policemen turned them at this point and led them away.

The looks on the two faces were too much for the baker, who had to cover his eyes. Somebody near him cried, "Ten to one, guilty". Another cried, "Anybody here for not guilty"? The verdict of the court was clear enough to anybody.

"The doing of justice", the baker repeated, "is, perhaps, the finest attribute of wisdom".

He had no quarrel with the statement. It seemed truer the longer he examined it. But when you made justice a big thing, it became somehow so big, that it dwarfed all other things. When it was still only a little thing, you could take an eye for an eye and a tooth for a tooth, and be accounted a wise judge. But when it became a big thing it dwarfed all the human instruments concerned with it. Law, then, became a part of the wisdom of the universe, a passionless, limitless ecstasy and excellence, which seemed to have the power to annihilate whatever flawed it. How could men continue to judge and punish as men when they could perceive in some measure as God perceives?

Justice was about to be done here. The finer kind of wisdom was to be applied to Rapp and the Magpie for the first time in their lives. Wisdom had not had much chance with them hitherto. Rapp was the son of Basher Rapp, who had broken gaol from Stanchester in the 'forties, maiming one of the warders in the process. He had been given a lifer and had died in prison. Rapp's mother was a well-known slut, who had brought up her son to the race-course gang, the kosh and the garotte. Father and mother alike had died in prison after lives of violence and savagery. Who had taken the young Rapp and tried to turn that violence to good? Who had bothered about him one way or the other till he had taken to the ways of death?

Then the Magpie. How had wisdom touched the Magpie? He had been begotten by some chance drunkard upon a drab in a ditch, in harvest time, and born in a workhouse ward, or in some other ditch in the following year; then all had neglected him, allowed him to grow up and maintain himself as best he could, without help, without guidance, without training or suggestion of any sort likely to be helpful or to bring out any seeds of good which might be in even such a creature so nurtured. Then, after thirty or thirty-five years of such neglect, suddenly all this pomp and pageantry of the State, the scarlet, the wigs, the powdered and shiny counsel, the ushers who yelled, yet could not make their words heard, even after all the practice, and the big, well-fed, rosy-cheeked, cheery policemen, were arrayed against the two creatures of their neglect to bring them to a shameful and shocking end.

"Oh God", the baker muttered, "it is an infamy, oh God. I'll tell them that it is, no matter what they do to me".

He remembered the two boiled eggs which he had bought in some other life, years before. He pulled out the bag in which they were, and spelled the name printed on it: "Martha Spuddock. Refreshments". He could not think of refreshments, but kept the bag on his knees.

Presently, he heard his name called; a young man, with a pleasant face, was leaning across to him from the barrier to speak to him.

"Mr. Mansell, please"?

"Yes", the baker said.

"Oh, Mr. Mansell, I'm from the *Tatchester Times*. I've been asked to try to get a word from you. You know the younger prisoner, I believe? You think that he's not quite all there"?

"He's a poor lunatic, who ought to be in a home", the baker said. "He has lived all his days in a den of infamy, belonging to the church, and now they want to kill him in a den of infamy belonging to the law. There is not one soul in Condicote would not say that he's incapable of understanding his position".

"Ah, thank you, Mr. Mansell", the man said and passed out of the court. Someone behind the baker said,

"That's the famous Condicote baker, who gets up all the agitations and that".

He did not turn to see who had called him this. He was thinking that he would soon be getting up a bigger agitation than he had yet roused. He wished that Engels were there; but Engels no doubt was with the comrades arranging something that might be done.

One of the ushers, who had had an evil eye upon the baker since the trial began, now felt convinced that as he was sitting near the dock, he must have some kind of privilege, or be in some way attached to the law. He came over to him and said, that the jury wouldn't be long now. The baker asked what he thought the verdict would be.

"Oh", the man said, "I never follow the cases much. One case is very like another to me".

A man joined them as they chatted. He said that there wasn't much doubt of how the verdict would go; but that he expected that the barmy one would be recommended.

"As for Rapp", he said, "he'll get the necktie and deserve it. He's a damned wicked man".

"I've known many wicked men", the baker said, "but I've never known anyone wickeder than myself".

"You don't believe in the rope, then"? the man said.

"I do not".

"Well, say what you like", the man said, "the rope's the only thing that keeps folk safe at night. There's nothing like it. Abolish the rope and you establish anarchy, straight away".

People were coming back to court now; most of them with jokes and gaiety; they brought the smell of fog with them, also the smells of tobacco and of spirits.

Presently, the usher and the stranger moved well away, satisfied that the baker was one of these crazy-headed men who are all for upsetting things. Soon the ushers broke out into their unintelligible yells; the counsel sauntered to their places, brushing crumbs from their waistcoats; spectators hurried back, pushing to place; the bustle and stir of the court began; clerks coming and going with papers. There was a sudden hasty rising as the Judge entered. He came in with dignity, moved to his throne, surveyed the court for an instant, settled his robe about him and lapsed into his seat. The audience settled after him like a congregation settling to the sermon. There was a little noise below the prisoners' dock as the police brought the two men up the stairs from the cells. They took their places in the dock, on each side a big policeman in blue; on the right a rosy-faced policeman, with a look of genial good nature; on the left the other type, a white-faced, hard, keen policeman, with a look of ruthless, unlovely virtue. Between them were the two victims; Rapp sullen and trying to be defiant, with his jaws bulging and working on a wad of the baker's tobacco; the Magpie twisting the twine from the packets into one of his famous snares. When the Magpie saw the Judge, he seemed to connect him again with the hunting field: he cried,

"Ha, Yoicks".

He was sternly nudged by both policemen; many people tittered, even then. The jury slowly edged into their two rows after their foreman; they sat, the foreman stood.

There was a hush for a few seconds; the foreman of the jury had never before had such a task to perform. He was an undertaker in Tatchester, with a very good eye for a horse and an old engraving.

He was asked the usual questions: they had considered their verdict and had agreed among themselves, that both prisoners were guilty, the prisoner Rapp as the killer, and the younger prisoner as his accessory. It seemed to the baker, that the foreman paused at this point as though he were about to recommend the younger prisoner to mercy. However, he said nothing more, but presently sat down, mopping his brow. The Judge asked Rapp if he had anything to say, why sentence of death should not be passed upon him. Rapp replied that his counsel had said everything, but that it was all a mistake; he was innocent and the Magpie too.

The Judge now asked the Magpie if he had anything to say. The question had to be repeated by Mr. Gallup, who was close beside him. He said,

"Yes, he had a lot to say; the old huntsman ought to have brought his hounds".

He laughed as he said this, and though the words made the baker shudder, he felt that they might well lead to his being found insane. The Judge put on the black cap and sentenced both men to be hanged. Rapp said Amen at the Judge's prayer for mercy on their souls, then leaning forward asked,

"May I speak a few words, my lord"?

On being told that he might not make a speech, but that if he had anything pertinent to his case to say he might say it, he said, that on behalf of his fellow sufferer he would like to thank everybody. That they were two innocent men, victims of mistakes and false accusations; but that they forgave everybody, as that was a Christian's duty, to forgive. He forgave everybody and hoped that they might all meet in a better place; and the Judge was not to mind his duty, however unpleasant. He (Rapp) forgave him and would pray for him that night, aye, and every night until the end.

Several, who heard this, remembered it afterwards as a very moving speech. It did not move the Judge, who looked fixedly at Rapp as he spoke and after he had finished with the same look of clear, upright, narrow intelligence which had been upon his face all day. It was now late at night; after fifteen hours he had arrived at the truth about Rapp. He looked shrewdly at him, and in his heart said something like, "You are a rogue and a knave, my man", he then rose and took up the notes from which he had spoken.

"God, he's going to hang the poor creature", the baker gasped. "He's not recommended him nor anything. The Magpie's going to be hanged".

The policemen had already removed the two prisoners to the cells; there was a noise and upheaval of people preparing to go. The Judge had left his throne. In an instant more he would be gone. The court stilled suddenly. The swish of the dry silk upon the panel gave the baker goose flesh.

"No, my God, I must protest", he muttered.

He saw red. He had the eggs in his hands now; he had dropped Mrs. Spuddock's bag.

"Stop", he cried to the Judge, "stop. How can you sentence a poor lunatic like that to death"?

As his cry came on a stilled court, the audience was thrilled. The Judge, who was quite near him, not ten feet from him, turned on him with a look of amazement, touched with indignation. The baker spoke again.

"If no one else will protest, I will", he cried. "The sentence is an infamy, and this court a disgrace, and there's for you, you red-coated abomination"; and at that he flung his egg straight at the Judge, and hit him full on the chest. The egg had not been quite hard-boiled. It burst on the lapel of the scarlet robe, and sent its golden blood slowly lacing down the hem of the garment. The second egg went wide. The Judge's look of indignation deepened. A policeman leaped at the baker.

"I don't care", the baker cried. "Do what you like with me. I say you shan't hang a poor madman without some-one saying it's murder".

"Now no more of that", the policeman said, taking him by the arm, "you know better than to behave like that in here. Now out you come".

"I won't", the baker cried.

Another policeman closed-in and took him by the other arm. "Go easy now", he said.

"We've got you. Go quiet now, Joe", the first man said. "It's Contempt. Hold still, will you".

"We'd better hold him below".

"No, no. There comes the Judge's officer".

The Judge's officer attached the baker for Contempt. In a few minutes, the baker was in the Judge's presence, within a few feet of him, so that he could see close to the fine face which had presided all day long in the court. He had not yet taken off his wig and robe. An usher had brought some hot water in a small pudding bowl and was trying to remove the egg stain with a wet rag. The Judge stood at a table while this was doing. A clerk was there. Two or three nondescript people seemed to have some right to be there. They had the withered looks of people in some way connected with public offices. The officer reported that he had the Contempt.

The baker had long believed that the law was slow to move. The law's delay had been a proverb with him. It dealt swiftly with him now.

The Judge gently drew his robe from the usher's hand. He had had some twenty hours of unremitting attention, and for nearly three hours had been speaking to the court on points of great importance. He now began again, without hesitation, to say that no court could permit its dignity to be violated and its officers insulted. Courts and officers of the law had, therefore, been given special powers to support the dignity of their important office. A very little thought would convince anybody not resolute in foolish opinion that these powers were for the good of the people. He himself was determined that no court over which he had the honour to preside should be used with contempt. A contempt was both an insult to the Majesty of the Law, which derived from the Majesty of the Sovereign, and an attempt to interfere with the administration of justice.

In former times, a Judge could have caused the offender's right hand to be stricken off in open court. Those times were over, but a rigorous punishment would still be exacted for such an offence. The prisoner would purge his contempt by going to prison. The officers charged with the removal of such prisoners were there at court. The baker had no time to say more than that he was glad to go to prison as long as he could feel that he had said something for a poor lunatic. He was led away out of the dingy room, down the dark and dirty stairs from the stink of fug into the stench of fog, and so, into a four-wheeled cab to the prison.

In the cab there was one of the policemen with whom he had struggled in the court house. The baker held out his hand and said,

"I hope we may shake hands. I hope I didn't hurt you in there".

The policeman weighed some sixty pounds more than the baker. He did not like to shake hands in the presence of the officer in charge. He grinned at the baker.

"Hurt me"? he said. "No, bless you, that was nothing. You didn't hurt me".

It must by this time have been one in the morning. The dingy, old, dirty, ruinous streets of Tatchester passed slowly by, half lit by a few dirty gas lamps. The baker knew the town well, and recognized the turnings, the South Gate, the Lamperns, the Grass Market, the turning for the railway station. He saw the line, with its signal lights of red, and lighted signal box. Then the cab trotted under a railway arch where the fog was very thick, and then out to the gardens and wastes of the suburbs, where a wind came suddenly to blow away the fog, and to show a dark and awful block of building before them, heaped up against the sky. This, he knew, was the prison or gaol, where now Rapp and the Magpie would be in condemned cells, waiting for death to set them free. Presently, the cab stopped at a gateway which had been built by someone who had been reading *Ivanhoe*. It was meant to represent the gateway of a mediaeval castle, yet it was all skimped and niggardly, with mean little useless turrets, into which not even a cat could enter, and imitation loop-holes through which not even light could pass. At this gate, there being no trumpet for the wayfarer to blow, the officer had some trouble in making himself heard. Not many wayfarers asked to be admitted there at one in the morning. However, somebody opened at last. A very efficient bright, clean set of steel locks and bolts let open a little part of the big door, and a lamp shone out onto the cobbles of the yard, so that the baker could see the steaming, bony horse, drooped between the shafts, and the many capes of the driver's coat.

The policeman helped the baker out. The flush of his anger had long since gone from him, leaving him white and sick and faint. He had had time to consider that he had done for himself now, probably for ever, and that he had not helped the Magpie, only done his cause harm, probably; and that his wife and son would suffer more than himself for this protest which had failed. The officer seemed to bear him a grudge, for bringing him out so far, so late at night. The policeman was kinder.

"You ought to keep out of this sort of thing", the policeman said. "You haven't got the physique for it; by physique I mean the avoirdupois. But I'll pass the word along, if you understand me".

He didn't in the least understand, but the officer was growling,

"Now come along here, Contempt, or do you want to keep us here *all* night"?

He, therefore, came along, entered the wicket gate, and so "Child Roland to the Dark Tower came".

Meanwhile, Tryphena and Bob, having finished work, walked to the station to meet the last train from Tatchester. As the baker was not on it, they knew that the case had not finished.

"He won't be back till breakfast, then", Tryphena said. "I do hope he won't get overheated in that closed court, and then get a chill rushing out into the night air. His chest isn't as strong as it should be".

"He's not a good one for taking advice", Bob said.

They talked about the Magpie's chances. It was a less pleasant night than usual, the fine weather was breaking. A drizzle was setting in from the west, with hot moist air.

"Rain coming", Tryphena said.

"It seems like it", Bob said. "I wonder, Mother, if you could shew me the miniature of Father's mother".

"Yes, he said he was going to shew it to you. I'll fetch it".

She brought it down. It had been painted in the year 1820. It was a delicate thing, framed in a rim set with seed pearls.

"She was supposed to be a great beauty, wasn't she"? Bob asked.

"So your Father says".

"Did you ever meet any of the Dixon people"?

"Yes, Bob, I did. They are very proud people. And

when they are touched, poor people can be even prouder than the proud. Your father and I had to meet the Dixons once over some property. I'm not happy when I think of the meeting. I was very rude to them, and your father very proud. We walked out of the house".

"Are they still at that place"?

"No, the brother, your great-uncle, is dead. Your great-aunt is alive; but she does not live in the great house. I believe she lives near Chollingdon".

"I suppose she's almost the only relative I have alive".

"Yes. It sometimes happens that one has few relatives. But do not talk of the Dixons. You are related to them, God has seen to that; but between us and them are the two prides: pride of place and pride of hope. They have a kingdom; we long for one and try to bring it to be".

"Well, I'd have liked to have seen the beauty of the west", Bob said. "It is odd to think of a grandmother being a beauty, though".

He boiled up some water for Tryphena, who wanted to wash her hair. When he had made up the fire, so that she might dry it, he saw that the shutters were secure, had a look at Old Marrowbones in the stable, heard the crickets chirping in the bake-house, came in, barred the door and went upstairs to his Latin words and bed.

It was about half-past three the next morning that he was conscious that something was happening. Someone was in the yard, shaking the kitchen door. He looked out of his little window, which was just over that door, and saw that somebody was there. It was raining briskly, and the wind had risen.

"Who's there"? he called.

"Oh, it's you, young shaver. Don't make a noise. You

know me. I'm Engels. Just call your mother, and then let me in, will you"?

"Is my father there"? Bob answered.

"No, he's not here", Engels said. "But don't make a noise and wake everybody up. Call your mother, like what I said".

Bob was conscious that there was somebody with Engels, someone who had brought him, probably. He lit his candle, and slipped across to his mother's door. The old clock on the stairs said that it was half-past three; in fact, the bells gave the half-hour almost immediately.

"Is it your father"? Tryphena asked.

"No, it's Mr. Engels", Bob said. "He wants you to go down".

"Whatever for"? Tryphena asked in some agitation. "I do trust nothing's happened to your father".

Bob lit her candle, and saw that she was in a great state of agitation, unable to find her dressing-gown. Her hair was done up in a most peculiar way, but then, he had always heard that women's hair was a very odd matter. He found a pair of bedroom-slippers, and helped her with her dressing-gown; then they went down together and opened the door.

"Ah, thank you", Engels said, coming in. "Thank you. I seem to have been driving half the night. We went astray somewhere or other. Don't know where we haven't been".

He diffused about him a warm flavour of brandy. He was more than half drunk.

"Has anything happened to Rob"? Tryphena asked.

"Yes, it's a dirty scandal", Engels said, dropping his

voice. "He flung an egg at the Judge and hit him. He's been put into prison for contempt".

"Into prison"? Tryphena cried. "Where"?

"Oh, Tatchester. It was after sentence; but it was contempt. I was out of court, or I might have stopped it".

"But how long will he be in prison"?

"Till he's purged his contempt. But I had to come to tell you. I couldn't let you not know. So I got a jarvey. We've been driving half the night. I don't know where we didn't get to. I'm dead beat. If you could raise a spot of brandy now, with a blue ribbon round it. Gosh, I don't know as I've ever felt deader beat".

"I've got a little brandy, in case of sickness", Tryphena said. "Run to fetch it, Bob, will you? It's in the box on my dressing-table".

When Bob had gone for it, she stared blankly at Engels.

"But how long do they usually keep people in prison for contempt"? she asked.

"Oh, a goodish long time", Engels said. "It's no joke, contempt. It's a penally fence or a fenally pence, I'm told. He'll have to pay a swindging fine, too. The worst about Robert is that he's so impulsive. But he got the Judge all right. Copped him fair on the boko".

Tryphena tried to tell herself what had happened. Rob was in prison, she understood. But what was this contempt? He had flung an egg at the Judge. That meant that he would be in prison for "a goodish long time". Did that mean that her darling Rob would be shut away from her, so that she could not brew him a posset or look after his cough or consult him in prayer? Her world swam all about her.

"But I don't understand", she said. "Why did he fling at the Judge"?

"He disapproved of the lunatic being sentussed, I mean santissed, I mean nuntissed; you know what I mean".

"D'you mean sentenced"? Bob asked, as he rejoined them.

"The very word I mean".

"Did you bring the brandy, Bob"? Tryphena asked.

Bob had in his hand a small bottle of eau de Cologne, which he now held to her.

"I'm awfully sorry, Mother", he began, "but I can't find any other bottle than this on your dressing-table. Will this do"?

"Bless the boy, no", she said. "That is scent. It's the brandy in the wooden box; there, I'll go get it".

She ran upstairs, not suspecting that Bob, who hated Engels and knew that he had had enough to drink, had determined that his enemy should have no more to drink, and had therefore hidden the flask. Engels sat on a kitchen chair.

"It's a bad business, this", he said. "It will just about do for your father, you'll find. He'll be a marked man from this out. And so silly, too; after sentence; nothing could do any good, then. He ought to have known better. Gosh, boy, I do want a spot of that brandy to pull myself together with".

"Mother's looking for it", Bob said quietly.

Engels swung his arms about as he sat.

"I'll get you to make me up a shakedown somewhere", he said. "I'll never get anyone to take me in at this hour. A sofa or anything will do for me".

Tryphena came down. "It's very funny", she was saying, "I can't find that flask, though I can be sworn I saw it only yesterday".

"Well", Engels said, "a spot of gin or a bottle of beer would be better than nothing. You could hardly expect a man who has been all over this county, looking for the road, to go to bed without a drop of cheer".

"We've neither gin nor beer", Tryphena said, "I'm sorry".

"You always had them when I stayed", Engels said.

"We always had them in specially", Tryphena said.

"I suppose you've no objection to my staying the rest of the night", Engels said.

"But that would never do", Tryphena said. She knew enough of the scandal-mongers of the town to know that that would never do.

"Why wouldn't it do"? Engels asked. "I've come all these miles to tell the news. You surely don't mean to turn me out"?

At this moment, footsteps sounded on the flagging of the yard, and someone shook the kitchen door.

"It's the driver", a voice said. "Do you want me to stay, or shall I be getting back"?

"You can get back", Engels said.

"That will be seventeen-and-sixpence", the man said, "the drive from Tatchester; and the same back, thirty-five shilling".

"Thirty-five bunkum".

"I'd ought to charge you more", the driver said. "It's no weather and no journey for an old horse and man, like us two. But thirty-five is my due, and if you'll give it, I'll be getting along".

"If I'll give it. Where's your book of legal charges"?

"We don't go by any book of charges. We go by what is usual, and always five shilling extra for a journey after midnight".

Engels put his hand into his pocket, and then said,

"You told me the charge would be one pound, the round trip".

"That is not so, sir", the driver answered. "Come, sir, don't keep me and my horse waiting any longer. We've a long way to go to get to bed".

"I never heard such a bare-faced swizzle in my life", Engels said. "You told me one pound, there and back".

"Very well, sir, if you refuse the charge, I shall drive round to the police station; it's only round the corner; and see what they can do".

Engels turned to Tryphena.

"Did you ever hear such cheek"? he said.

"But it must be thirty shillings there and back to Tatchester", Tryphena said. "And they always charge five shillings after midnight. You'd better give it. He is only asking the proper fare".

"Proper fare be damned".

"It is the proper fare", Bob said.

"How often have you driven it, my shaver", Engels said. "You keep your remarks for the Latin class. As a matter of fact", he added, dropping his voice, so that the driver might not hear, "I'll be shot if I've got the fare. I'll have to borrow it of you for a day or two, if you will kindly oblige me".

"Oh, dear", Tryphena said, "I don't believe I've anything like so much in the house. How much can you make up out of what you have"?

"I"? Engels said. "I've nothing, not a tosser".

"I'll see what I can find", Tryphena said, "and perhaps we could break open your money-box, Bob".

"I like that", Bob said.

"It'll do you good to go without some of those lolly-pops you set your heart on", Engels said.

"Well, am I to have my money or go to the police"? the driver asked.

They heard him stamp and splash the rain from his hat.

"You shall have your money", Tryphena said. "But wait for just a moment".

"All right, lady", the driver replied.

They heard his steps move from the yard, to the street, where the horse was standing.

Tryphena had upstairs a little private store of her own, saved out of her housekeeping money; it had nothing to do with the family savings; it amounted to a few pence more than three pounds. She moved upstairs to this.

"I'll see what money I can find", she said.

"No, no, Tryphie", Adolf said. "Let me come too. I can't bear to give you trouble. I'll help you look. My dearish Tryphie, my heart bleeds for you in your trouble".

He was close behind her and she was a comely woman, but he was a little drunk. She reached her room and was able to turn the key in the lock in time to keep him out. Her heart beat pit-a-pat. What a night: Rob in prison, shut from her perhaps for years, a shaven convict ruined for life; this drunken amorous man in the house with her; the neighbours wakened by the dispute with the driver, and now all bent at windows with their ears cocked for more.

"Now, Tryphie, let me in to help look," Adolf cooed.

"Now none of this", came the voice of Bob on the land-ing. "Down you come, Mr. Engels. You're not going to torment my mother".

"Who's tormenting, Latin-class"?

"You are. And you'll just get downstairs out of this, or I'll call the driver and have you round to the police station; then you can pay your own fare".

"Anything to oblige", Engels said.

Tryphena heard him move downstairs. He slipped on the bottom stairs and fell. He hurt himself a little; just enough to make him less amorous.

Tryphena opened her store, took out a pound, then thirty shillings. Then she reflected that he must have money, that if he had a room in Tatchester he would have some little store there, with the means of paying for his keep. The pretence of having no money might well spring from his drunkenness. What an unexpected side to the Saint and Apostle; and what a new unexpected manly Bob.

"Outside is your place", she heard Bob saying. "You don't come in here while I'm the master".

She moved downstairs. The yard door was open; the rain was splashing everywhere. The candle flame, which lit the scene, was blowing about and casting leaping shadows. Adolf was in the doorway, ruefully rubbing his elbow.

"Where is the driver"? she asked.

"No, don't you, Mother", Bob cried. "You'll get sopped with rain. I'll call him. He's only just round the corner. I'll call him. Ho, driver".

He was as eager as his mother to have a sober man as a possible friend, if Adolf should be impossible. The cabman was standing a few feet away from the door, with one of the capes of his coat tossed up to screen his hat from the weather.

"Where are you, driver"? she called.

He came forward at once; he was a little, old, sad-faced man, with drooping moustaches on which the rain gleamed. She gave him the money.

"This is thirty-five shillings", she said. "You will go back to Tatchester and take the gentleman with you". She turned to Engels. "I've paid the driver", she said. "He will take you back to Tatchester. Thank you for bringing the news".

"Well, I didn't think", Adolf said in a loud voice, "that when I came here at three in the morning to tell you that your husband's in prison you'd kick me out into the rain like a dog, without a bite or a sup; nor so much as a little teeny kiss".

"Now will you come along, sir"? the driver asked.

"I'll come along when it suits my fancy. She gave you thirty-five shillings, she said. Well, your fare's a pound. You told me the round fare was a pound. Hand over the extra fifteen shillings".

"We'll talk of that after a drink, sir", the driver said. "Come on, now; you will be wet through, standing in this rain".

"Come on", he called. "I'll leave this baker's wife, who won't even give a friend a crust nor a sup nor a corner of the yard to sleep in. Good-bye".

He moved off with the driver after this. Bob closed and bolted the yard door, so that the guttering candle, which looked like an icicle hanging from a burst water pipe, burned steadily. The last remark of Adolf smote Tryphena's heart. She had turned Rob's friend from the door.

"Oh Bob", she said, "I can't bear to turn them away without anything".

"Without anything; I like that", Bob said. "You've paid his cab fare. What more do you want to give him"?

"I must give him something to eat and drink".

"He's had more than enough to drink, as it is", Bob said. "I'd give the driver something perhaps, but not that fraud".

At this point, they heard voices raised from somewhere in the street. Going into the shop they heard plainly that the two were disputing about the fare. Adolf was lifting his voice.

"I tell you, as you know quite well, you agreed with me for one pound the round trip".

He was as the storm beating on a rock, long since so worn by tempest as to show no new mark, no matter how grim the gale. Windows were being opened along the street. A man from across the road told them to shut up and let folk get to sleep. Adolf walked towards the interferer and called to him,

"Who are you to tell me to shut up"?

But at this point there came the measured, slow, heavy, resolute tread of a policeman and his question,

"Now, what's all this"?

"Nothing, officer", Adolf answered. "A man across the street tried to be funny, and I just asked him what he meant. I always insist on knowing what a man meant. It saves mishunderstaddle".

"You'd best take this gentleman home, driver", the policeman said. "Now, sir, if you'll step in, the driver'll soon have you home".

To the great relief of Tryphena and Bob, the cab door

slammed; the driver called to the horse, and the cab started. Here and there the windows of the neighbours closed: the little town settled again to sleep.

"Now, Mother", the new Bob said, "you're not to worry. You get back to bed. What that drunken fraud said may not be true. It won't be all true, anyway. So you run back to bed and rest. Even if it were all true, it wouldn't be too bad to bear".

They went back to their beds. Presently the morning came and soon after the morning the truth.

Ill news travels fast; the news of the baker's trouble was soon in Condicote. The first trusty account of the case came from a Tatchester clergyman, who made the journey specially, to break the news to Tryphena and her son. It was true that the baker had been sent to prison; he would be there for several months. It was probably false, that he would have to pay a fine of fifty pounds as well, though fines were sometimes inflicted. For the first six weeks of his imprisonment he would not be allowed to write nor to receive visits. Soon after this first announcement it was made known that there would be no fine.

When the news was some three hours old in Condicote, at half-past ten in the morning, young Mr. Wye, thinking the moment propitious, went round to Tryphena, said that he was sorry to hear the news, which he plainly wasn't, and that he was prepared to offer her ten pounds for the baker's business as it stood. "Of course", he said, "it's more than it's worth, but I'm always prepared to give a little too much, when people are in trouble".

"Thank you", Tryphena said, "but Mr. Mansell's business is not for sale".

"Isn't it"? he asked. "I understood it was".

"You understand wrong then", Tryphena said.

"Well, of course, you know your own advantage best".

"There's a lot of difference", Tryphena said, "between knowing advantage and trying to take advantage".

"Good morning, then", Mr. Wye said.

"Good morning". He went out whistling, but resolved to do that haughty dame down a peg, and seeing his way both clearly and cheaply.

Saturday was their busy day; there was no escape for them; the world came for its bread (and to see how they took it) and had to be faced. It was a day of anguish to them both, for many came, with mean motives, which were not disguised. Early on Sunday morning, when the full weight of the blow came home to Tryphena, and no work occupied the mind, she could not rise from bed, but lay, shedding tears. "Now, Mother", Bob said, "I want you to think what Father would have had you do. This isn't being a good wife to him. You must get up, you've plenty of time, and come with me to Early Service. You can bring all your troubles there, and leave them there".

"Oh, Bob, I couldn't face the people's eyes".

"Oh, yes, you can, Mother. Come on, now. It's what Father would have you do. And you'll find yourself strengthened by it. Now my dear Mother, you must do as I bid for once. Here's your stockings and I'll have the shoes blacked in a jiffey". She said she couldn't, but Bob knew better, and got her there in time.

He thought that it might be well not to take her to the Morning Service; he read the Bible to her, instead. In the afternoon, as it rained, they stayed indoors. Bob read the *Pickwick Papers* to her. "O, Bob, it isn't a book for Sunday. It·isn't right to read such books on the Lord's Day".

"Mother", Bob said, "if the Lord thinks cheerfulness wrong, I'll turn Mohammedan".

"O, Bob, what a sinful thing to say".

"Mother, get some of your puritanism out of you. Sit you down now and listen".

She sat and listened. Presently, a boy crept into the yard, and cried out, "Who flung eggs at the Judge? Yah!", and fled. Bob had not read much further, when a little company appeared. They crept into the yard, not knowing that they were watched through the curtain. They disposed themselves like the Waits, and began to sing, to the tune (more or less) of "Hark, the herald angels sing". The song was as follows:

> *"If with eggs*
> *A Judge you chriss-un*
> *When you're copped*
> *You're sent to Pris'n".*

They did not sing it well, from laughter, which kept exploding. It was all of the poem; when they had sung it once they repeated it. Then, with bursts of laughter, they began it a third time. One of the boys was young Mr. Wye's brother, a pale and pimply lad of sixteen. "Mother", Bob whispered, "I'm not going to have that. That's Scab Wye, the one we call Foot & Mouth Disease; I'll soon scatter those herald angels".

The song improved in quality; the singers thought themselves immune. Bob crept downstairs, out into the shuttered shop, where he very cautiously undid the door. If he entered the yard suddenly from the street, he would take them by surprise in the rear. "If with eggs" the voices recommenced.

"Now I've got you", Bob shouted. He went straight at the Scab and collared him, while the others, screaming "O it wasn't me, sir. It wasn't me", fled to the street and away. "It wasn't me", the Scab moaned.

"O yes it was", Bob said, "I saw you and heard you. Take off your trowsers".

"O please let me go, Bob".

"Don't you Bob me. Take off your trowsers. Right off. And give them here".

The Scab took off and handed over the trowsers. "Empty the pockets", Bob said. The Scab trembled and did so. "Take all the contents", Bob said. "Have you got them all"?

"Yes".

"Now cut out of here", Bob said.

"I can't, not with no trowsies".

"You've no business in this yard. Get out of it".

Out he went, "ther nis namore to say". Bob packed the trowsers in brown paper and wrote a note to Mr. Wye, senior.

Dear Sir—Enclosed, please find a pair of trowsers left in the yard here by your son. Will you please keep your refuse henceforth in your own yard?—Yours sincerely, R. Mansell, jr.

He delivered the package at Mr. Wye's door two minutes later.

"Now", Bob thought, "the herald angels will not be quite in such voice".

In the evening, Bob took his mother over to Tineton Church to the service. It had been a dreadful day to them, but he was resolved to hold the house together.

Next morning, however, their world fell all about their ears.

Mr. Wye had passed the Sunday afternoon and evening in suborning the Mansell workers. Joe, Mrs. Joe and their sons, were all bought off and given better jobs at the Steam Bakery. They were all ashamed of their treachery, but they were desperately poor, with their hordes of children to feed, and though they shed tears in telling Tryphena what they had done, they ceased to work for the Mansells. On the Monday morning Bob had no one to help him. Baking is skilled work, not to be learned in an hour or two. There were no workers to be had in Condicote. Bob and Tryphena had to do as best they could, with an odd hand brought in from Mr. Cockfarthings. By telegraph, they contrived to hire a journeyman from Yockford; and did get the bread both made and delivered; but knew from that day's experience that they were ruined.

Each post brought them bills from money owing, or letters closing old accounts.

"Now, Mother", Bob said, "we must face the facts. We're ruined here. We cannot discuss with Father till we see him, but it's plain that we shall only lose money by paying these imported journeymen week after week, till Father comes".

"We ought to try to keep your Father's business going, Bob".

"I agree; but we can't; the business is done for. We need two men and an occasional boy here, in addition to myself. We just can't pay them".

"Then what do you think we ought to do"?

"Close our doors".

"Shut up shop"?

"Yes. End it and begin again somewhere else, and in another way".

"Where, and in what sort of way, Bob"?

"Some city. Why not Yockford or Stanchester? or London for that matter"?

"I couldn't go back to Yockford", Tryphena said. "Stanchester might do, but I know nothing of it. But what sort of life do you suggest our trying"?

"I say, not a baker's life", Bob said. "It's too hard for Father: it's got onto his lungs. Why not something without all this mixing and night work and breathing flour and furnace all the time? Why not a dining house, a sort of refreshment room? We're booked here till March. I daresay Sir Hassle would let us out before March. I'm sure he would, for Mr. Wye wants our bake-house, and would probably pay to have us out in January. We shan't be quite penniless. We've got enough to start in a quiet way. Then, with the sale of some of the things here; the horse and van, and so forth; we'd have quite a fair nest-egg to fall back upon".

"It's a dreadful plunge to take, Bob", Tryphena said.

"Well, it's like diving", Bob said. "You don't like the look of it, but you get an awful chill standing shivering and not taking the plunge".

"I do wish we had your father here to discuss with", Tryphena said, bursting into tears.

"It's Father I'm thinking of", Bob said. "If we get out of here, and settle in Stanchester or some place, it will be an absolutely new beginning for Father when he comes. All the past will be wiped away: he'll be starting quite fresh; there'll be a new lot of people; and what is more important, a new kind of work, which might give him a lot more leisure for the things he really wants to do".

"Yes, but, Bob", Tryphena said, "my dear boy, we don't know anything about the refreshment business. It may take years to make one. And suppose we were not to succeed. There we should be with hardly any money, tied to new premises without any friends".

"We shan't be much worse off than we are now", Bob said. "In a place like Stanchester there must be lots of people who would rather eat meals elsewhere and pay a little more for them, than cook themselves or go home for them. I believe one can make anything go, if one means to make it go. And if the worst comes to the worst, we'll be no worse off there than here. I'm young and strong. I can get something to do. Three people eager to live can always get a living somehow".

"Your father will miss the country walks here", Tryphena said.

"There'll be new walks", Bob answered. "But I don't want to urge Stanchester specially. There are other places. There's London. What about going to London? But I don't think Father would like that, nor you very much".

"O, your father could never live in London", she said.

It was decided between them that the bakery had better close. They dismissed the hired man, and put up a notice, that the long-established business was now closed.

For some nights after the baking ceased, Bob heard the crickets chirping in the bake-house. Presently, they seemed to know that it was no good staying there, where the ovens would not be hot again; their pleasant song ceased. The little domestic fairies moved elsewhere.

One of the bitternesses of the first week, was the discovery that Adolf and his radical friends did nothing to protest against the sentence on the Magpie. Their articles were attacks upon the Game Laws. They said that the food created by Nature for all had been shut by the greed of the rich from the starving poor, and that at Tatchester, the seat of a holy Bishop, two poor, starving men had just been sentenced to death, for trying to snatch food for their families from the armed guards of the village tyrants: They said nothing about the poor crazy Magpie, who so often had come gibbering about their yard. "He is to be hanged", Tryphena said. "Well, thank God, Bob, your father stood up for him. He did his best".

"He stood up like a Christian", Bob said. He remained in thought for a while. "It's a cruel thing", he said, "but it is possible that his counsel would petition".

He knew that Mr. Gallup was in Condicote on that day. He waylaid him, and asked him about it. "You're the son of the baker, are you"? Mr. Gallup said. "Well, first and last, your father has done just about all he could to blast any chance those two poor devils ever had. As for a petition, Mr. Slaughter tried it. He has had no sort of support from here, whatsoever. A few from the Alleys have put their marks to it. The magistrates who committed won't stir. Everybody else is delighted that the men who shot the keeper will get their deserts. The two will be hanged. They know that now. It's no good raising false hopes. They're done". He spoke angrily, because he was vexed. He had been spoken of as "hand in glove with the radical baker", whose silly head he would have liked to punch. Bob went home, knowing that the Magpie was "done".

They waited for long days till the day came for their visit to the prison. To avoid being much eyed, and perhaps questioned, they left Condicote by an early train, which reached Tatchester before nine in the morning.

As they were not to see the baker until two precisely, they had five hours to wait. They stayed for a long time in the station waiting room, sitting upon a hard horsehair settle beside a grate heaped with slack which smelt and smoked but gave forth no heat. After being chilled to the bone here, Bob said that perhaps the Cathedral might be warmer. In the Cathedral porch, a verger wanted to shew them where the martyr was murdered. They said that they did not wish to see the site. Inside the nave, another verger came down on them to shew them where the blood had run. To avoid the two men, they had to sit in chairs and pretend to be absorbed in prayer. There was a small service at ten-thirty, through which they sat. After it, they walked into the northern aisle. Here the two harpies, who had been watching them, told them that people were not supposed to wander in the Cathedral without an official guide. So they went out into the cold and presently found the little church of St. Alpig's, which was in a drowsy state of fugg from a stove, not untouched with incense, for the Rector liked things high. For many years afterwards, Bob felt grateful to St. Alpig's for sending his mother to sleep for a long time. When she woke, much refreshed, they found a little eating place, where they had two meat pies and a pot of tea for sixpence for the two of them. They talked as they ate of whether they could not run the eating house better. Then with their hearts crushed within them, feeling that all there were saying, "There go the Mansells. Mr. Mansell's got six

months in quod", they walked out of the city to the grim
building in the Fields. As they drew near it they saw
that though all the windows were barred with iron, they
were glazed with ground glass, so that no one within might
even look on the free outside world, the light and colour
and moving men.

They went under the sham portcullis of the gateway to
a paved yard in which two damaged Russian cannon from
Sebastopol stood one on each side of the door. A policeman directed them to a side door, marked "Visitors Only",
where three women in shawls and a man with a cold in
his head were standing abjectly, waiting for the clock to
strike two. When it struck, their hearts which were already low, sank lower, for they met, for the first time
with the bright, steel, clicking efficiency of the system
which then made men inhuman and brutes devils.

They were shewn into a long room divided into little
cubby holes. Each visitor was shewn by a warder into a
cubby hole. When inside his cubby hole, Bob found that
it had a window or opening closed by a wooden shutter. A
little bell rang near-by. Instantly, the wooden shutter rose.
Bob found that he could see through the opening into a
passage, ten feet long by four feet broad, where a warder
sat on a raised chair, so as to look straight down the entire
passage. In the stone wall across the passage, just opposite
Bob, were other windows or cubby holes, from all of which
the wooden shutters had risen. Bob could just see that in
the cubby hole opposite Tryphena his father, dressed in a
grey prison dress, had appeared.

The warder on duty in the chair called in a harsh voice,
"No whispering, now. No trying to pass objects. Anyone
whispering, anyone trying to pass anything, the privilege

will stop. Say anything you got to say so that I can hear. Out loud now, mind, in English".

Bob called, "Hullo, Father, how are you"?

"Ha, Bob, old man", the baker said, craning to see his son, "I'm fine". He did not look it. He looked sick and broken, and had a cough. His eyes burned in his head like two sparks. The half-hour, for which they had so longed, began.

They were shy at first. But one of the prisoners in the row asked how Annie was, and the man with the cold in his head said that they'd killed the Berkshire boar on Tuesday, a beauty he was, over eight score. After this the ice was broken. The baker said that he was very well and enjoying thinking things out. Lots of things had come much clearer. Tryphena wept though she tried hard not to weep. Bob had to do the talking. He asked, what about going to live at Stanchester, presently, and opening a little eating place. The baker, who was in that state of nerves and misery in which the prison food becomes loathsome, spoke with joy of the scheme; but doubted if there would be money enough. Bob said that there would be, never fear. "Well", the baker said, "I've been told by the doctor here that I must get out of the furnace trade. It's getting to my lungs. He says there's no great harm as yet, but that if I go on at it I'll get a ticket to the cemetery".

Bob said that he had heard that there might be a good opening for an eating place near the Pipe Works. The baker said that he knew the place, and that there would always be a lot of men coming out of the works twice a day, to eat something hot and tasty, if it could be had on the spot. It was such a joy to him to see a familiar face, a free face, and to talk of freedom; and to think of not having to face the eyes of the people in Condicote, that he even laughed and was merry. "You go to Stanchester tomorrow and see about it", he said. They went into ways and means. Somehow, it did not matter that what they said was being overheard by the other people there. In that grim place, all who were not gaolers were in the brotherhood of misery. They were so happy to be together, and to be able to discuss the things vital to themselves, that they forgot the prison gaoler sitting at the passage end, not five feet from them. They reckoned together that when all had been paid off, and when about half of what was owed to them had been paid in, they would have perhaps thirty-seven pounds to begin the world with. "And then there's the good will of the business", the baker said. "That's worth sixty pounds of any man's money".

This staggered them both; for they knew now what other men thought on this point. They talked on, discussing what things could be sold by auction before they left. They had some furniture as well as all the bake-house gear, the horse and van and harness. All these things might double their capital. The baker in his hopefulness was nearly hysterical. The warder in the passage, who had had his eye upon a clock, now cried: "Closing time, please, please, gents".

The baker said "Good-bye, all", and instantly a wooden shutter fell across the windows of all the cubby holes. "Outside, now, please, all visitors", the warder said. They were in the cold passage again, shut away by the system from the man they loved. "Now you come with me, Missus", the warder said, taking Tryphena's arm. "What you want is a good cup of tea". He gave them both hot tea in a little snuggery he had. "Don't you worry about your man", he said. "He's getting on fine". After tea, he played them a tune upon his flute. He said that the tune was called "Trees while you walk". Presently, as they rose to go, he became suddenly very grave; his eyes filled with tears. "There's one thing I'd like to say, Missus" he said. "Perhaps, as you're from Condicote, you might like to see their graves".

"Whose graves are those"? Tryphena asked.

"Those two necktie cases", he said. "The two who went out of it on Monday".

Tryphena shuddered and blanched, but the warder took her by the arm and led them from the snuggery to a small gravel yard, which contained a row of eleven small white-washed headstones. The two at the end had only just gone up. The ground near them had plainly been newly disturbed.

"You see", he said, pointing, "J. R. is there. And M. we didn't know the second name of, so we put him in M. W. We always take a great pride in our little graveyard. It's always the neatest kept of all our places".

Bob stared at the two stones, marked J. R. and M. W.

After this they returned to wait for an hour at Tatchester Station, where the fire, after smoking for seven hours without giving any warmth, had ceased to smoke and gave out cold.

The cold changed that night to a mizzling rain, in which they set forth to Stanchester city, to look for a new home.

Stanchester was then a small walled city, remarkable for its tan-pits and the pipe works. The tan-pits were falling into disuse when the Mansells went there; the pipe works were the chief industry. Stanchester drain pipes of earthenware and porcelain are still known all over the world. They were then famous. No other nation used anything of the kind.

Mother and son spent some hours on the wrong side of the city, looking for some place which might serve them. They found nothing there. The city was ill-built, with narrow, winding lanes. The Cathedral close and one broad street in the centre of what had been the Roman town were the only spacious parts of it. They were scared by what they saw. The spacious parts seemed too grand and the narrow lanes too mean for them. "We'd better go down to look at the streets near the Pipe Works, Mother", Bob said.

The main street in which they were, dwindled down into a lane called Goldworkers Lane, which seemed to have been designed by a rivulet on a rainy day. It curled about upon itself till it reached a narrow pass, where all the traffic trying to get out of the city met all the traffic trying to get in. The foot passengers were able to avoid the traffic jam by going through a stile at the side. A short walk brought them within sight of the Works.

The first sight of them showed an array of chimneys, most of them smoking. Below the forest of these were many shorter squat buildings, like oast-houses, which Bob knew to be kilns. A road led down towards these buildings. A placard on its wall said TYLER'S ROAD.

On the left of the Tyler's Road was the wreck of a tan-yard, still stinking although the new process had put it into bankruptcy ten years before. Near this lay what remained of a brewery. Bob could see in its yard a lot of black rotting casks falling out of their hoops. Like the tan-yard these things were as corpses waiting the resurrection when they would be swept up into the prosperity of the Pipe Works. In the dark of a winter day, with a mizzling rain falling, they looked forlorn enough.

Beyond the brewery was a long line of trim red brick building topped with blue slate. This was the main wall and entrance to the Pipe Works. The offices were there. There was a big green double door for the workers and two smaller doors for clerks and managers. All the rest of the left hand side of Tyler's Road was trim, ugly, red brick wall.

"So those are the famous Pipe Works"? Tryphena said.

"Yes", Bob said, "and there on the right is the very sort of place we want".

On the right of Tyler's Road, the pavement or sidewalk was raised three feet above the road. It ran (with a footrail at its side) along a row of dingy red brick houses of irregular heights, all of which had an air of having come down in the world. From the windows of three of these, placards hung with the legend

THIS HOUSE TO LET
ENQUIRE WITHIN

There were eleven houses in the row. At the end of the row there was a sort of open disused space, into which people had flung old iron, parts of packing crates, newspapers, tins and broken pots. Beyond this, was another trim red brick building, where the Pipe Works had put out a tentacle.

The place was looking its worst, but Bob was cheered by the sight of the houses to let.

"See, Mother", Bob said, "here are some houses to

let and these are certainly near the Pipe Works. Let's try here".

He knocked at the first door, and having no answer, knocked again; after what seemed a long time an old woman who had been watching them from behind a curtain came to the door of the next house and said, "They've gone away. Oh, they've been gone away a long time". No, she didn't know whose house it was really; nor where they could ask about it.

They walked down the street to the second house which was to let; the old woman watched them curiously. The second house to let was one of the bigger ones. It was a shop with odds and ends in the window. There was a chipped inlaid tea-caddy, a lacquer tray with some of the mother-of-pearl gone, some red glass vases, some blue and white mugs and plates, an old pistol with its lock gone, and a chair so draped with a Paisley shawl that the struts missing from the chair and the places worn threadbare in the shawl were alike hidden. There was also an old globe of the world, but some of the plaster had fallen from Australia. Bob thought that the place might be the shop of a receiver of stolen goods or a pawnbroker's; but if it had .been a receiver's shop the people would have been bolder, and if it had been a pawnbroker's the window would have held a concertina. A frightened-looking woman was just inside the door. Bob wondered what on earth it was that was frightening her. He said, "Is this house to let, please"? and she said, "Won't you come in"? and led them to an inner room, where a frightened-looking man stood.

The inner room was full, like the outer shop, with odds and ends of furniture and china. There were chests of drawers, two or three tables, a large blue and white basin with a jug of the same pattern, both cracked, some cyclamen in the pots in the window, a little fire, very hot, two or three clocks, none of them going, two grandfather clocks pointing to different hours and ticking still, a stuffed dotterel in a case, much moth-eaten, two sanderlings in a case, also moth-eaten, a sheldrake in a case, and the poor thing's head had twisted awry and was coming off the neck. But what interested Bob was the strange look of scare on the man's face.

"They have come about the house", the woman said, and Bob, who was noticing the man's face particularly, saw a look of joy flash across it.

"Could we see the house, please"? Tryphena asked.

"You'll show them the house", the man said to her.

"Will you come this way"? the woman said. "This, of course, is our living-room and there is a cellar-basement down here. I'll light a candle, but it is light when you get there".

She led the way down steep stone steps to a well-lit cellar-basement. There was a little area there with a coal cellar and a sink with water. Above the living-room was one bedroom, and above that, reached by a ladder from the bedroom, was an attic. Bob saw that his lot would either be the cellar-basement or the attic. The rooms had been well kept. The windows were clean. There was a good deal of light. The walls of the attic had been lime-washed; so had the basement. The rent was twenty pounds a year and the tenancy, yearly. It appeared that the couple had still six months of tenancy, that they wanted to get out of it, and that if they could let it for the six months it would mean much to themselves. The agents would quite certainly continue the lease at the end of the six months to anyone who took it. Of course, if they were going to make a little lunch place for the workers at the Pipe Works they would have to make some small alterations, but it was perfectly placed for their purpose. The main entrance to the Pipe Works was not a hundred yards from them down the road on the other side. Tryphena asked about the range. Oh, the range was very good for all that they had to do. The woman showed it. Then, were there bugs in the plaster?

"Not a bug in the house", the man said.

Bob went to the window of the living-room and stared out at the array of dreary chimneys, kilns and other buildings of the Pipe Works.

"Ah, you don't want to look too much at those", the man said, drawing him away. "They aren't good".

"You come from the country"? the woman said. "This isn't much like the country on this side, but at the back you'd be surprised the green we can see, and the birds sing in the close just like in a woodland".

"Tell me", the man said, drawing Bob away into the shop, while Tryphena talked with the woman, "tell me; you just look and tell me. There's a big kiln down there on the right. Do you see it"?

"Yes".

"Did you see it nod"?

"No, it didn't nod", Bob said.

"Ah, he didn't nod at me at the first", the man said, with a look of anguish on his face. "But now he shuts his eyes and nods. Didn't you see it"?

"He didn't. Really, he didn't", Bob said.

"Ah, then; it IS me he wants", the man said.

Tryphena came in, at this point; she was saying: "We

have other houses to see, and then we can let you know". The woman, who had evidently heard that phrase, after similar interviews, more than once, opened the door for them. It seemed that her eyes were begging them to take the place.

The next house to let was five doors further down. The bell did not ring, so they knocked: on the third knock a sinister-looking man of about forty, short, compact and with evil eyes, asked what they wanted. He was in his shirt sleeves and was chewing a short straw. On hearing that they wanted to see the house, he called, "Channaria", which seemed to be short for Joanna Maria. Channaria was not easily roused. She, too, had to be called three times. She did not come then but asked what it was, and the man called,

"Somebody to see the house".

They heard Channaria curse and then come down. She was in no hurry to come down. When she came, she was smoking a cigarette, which was then so unusual among women that it stamped the smoker as a hardened baggage on whom lightning from Heaven might at any moment descend. She was a slatternly, bold creature with some rouge and make-up from the night before still on her. She was frowsy, uncombed and wrapped in a dirty wrapper.

"Well, there is this room", she said to Tryphena. "There is the basement and the room above. I can't take you in the basement; the steps are dangerous. You can see the room above".

She showed the living-room on the floor in which they were. It contained a table and a few chairs. Three or four sets of old boxing gloves were tossed in a corner; on the wall there was a photograph of the pugilist, Heenan, wearing boxing shorts made out of the Stars and Stripes flag. The room was dirty; the windows uncleaned. The woman led the way upstairs to the bedroom above, where there was an enormous double bed with a strange canopy above it of very dirty old pink muslin. Sitting up in one half of the bed was a second slatternly woman, evidently the first woman's sister. She had a patch over one eye which somebody had blackened in some dispute. She, too, was smoking a cigarette and had a bottle of beer beside her. Tryphena was scared at the women. Bob, being an impressionable boy and realising that these were women who had seen something of life, was in some ways attracted. They did not feel their welcome so warm as to linger long there. They got out. Channaria said that they would excuse her showing them out: Bill would show them out; which Bill did. The air of Tyler's Road was not particularly fresh, but it was fresh after that house. Tryphena, as soon as they were out of ear-shot, said she wondered how the Lord let such people prosper. Bob thought that they had not prospered much.

They came out of the house, to the rain which was now increasing. At the door of the curio-shop, the woman asked them to come in for shelter and to have a cup of tea. Tryphena seemed not eager to go, but Bob, who for some weeks now had been assuming mastery, urged her to go in. The woman had made them some tea and cut them some bread and butter. "Will you tell me", Bob asked, "why this house is No. 27"?

"There used to be houses on both sides of the road", the woman said, "but the Pipe Works took them in one by one, and now only Twenty to Thirty remain".

At this instant from just over the way a great steam whistle blew. Instantly, from the big double doors nearly opposite, a crowd of lads came charging; some of them raced, others caught the caps of the racers as they passed and pitched them into the mud; there were yells and jokes; some young women came running, with pattens on their feet and shawls clutched round their heads; the young men caught them round the waist and tried to kiss them, or pretended to. After the runners came the older men and women, who walked fast to get out of the rain.

"Dinner hour", the woman said. "A lot of them bring their dinners with them and eat in the Works, but those who live near, go home".

"Is there no eating place where they could buy dinner"? Bob asked.

"No", the woman said. "Now you mention it, it seems odd that there isn't. But at dinner time and closing time twice a day you'll see that crowd pass".

"Aren't they very disorderly"? Tryphena asked. "No, a lot of them are young".

"It is kind of you to let us shelter like this", Tryphena said. "And then to take such trouble for us".

"O, you're welcome; and perhaps you have no shelter to go to".

"No, we're strangers in Stanchester".

"We were thinking", Bob said, "of perhaps starting a little eating house for the workers here. Do you think it would be the kind of thing they'd come to"?

"The better sort would be glad of it, I'm sure", she said, "but there'd be not much profit. There's the pie-works, that makes meat-pies so cheap, in the Glove Walk".

"I think, all the same", Tryphena said, touched by this

honesty, "that I'd like to see the house again, if you wouldn't mind".

"Certainly; come upstairs".

The two women went upstairs. The man drew Bob towards the window; but was careful to keep behind him.

"It was just here", he said, "I was standing just here, when he first shut his eyes and nodded at me. Nod. Then again, nod. And you see, all these nods mount up".

"They don't mean anything", Bob said. "It's only just his fun".

"Ah, no; but that's where people mistake. It isn't fun. For lately, he's taken to showing his teeth. That isn't fun; don't you tell me".

"O, but all people show their teeth when they laugh".

"Ah, it's easy for you to say that. But you look, now. Look carefully. That big kiln on the right. Didn't he nod? Didn't he show his teeth"?

"No, not the least little bit, I do assure you".

"O God", the man said, "I knew it. It's only ME he wants, nobody else. Next week, he'll start to gnash, and the week after he'll start to call me. O boy, life's a horrible thing, when a kiln like that determines to have a man".

Bob was beginning to find that life held much variety, but at this instant his mother returned, they made their farewells and left.

When they were in the rain again, Tryphena said, "I did not like that woman the first time; I thought she was keeping something back from me; but now I feel that the hand of the Lord has been upon me and on you, too, Bob, in bringing us here. He means us to be here. I talked with the woman, Miss Lypiatt, in the bedroom. She is afraid that her brother is going mad and wants to have him into the country. She thinks that we might do well with an eating place, there; but she thought we should need a bigger range; and certainly a bigger sink, for washing up. She thought that some would come in for breakfasts, too. She says that there's an old watchman at the Works, who was in the eating-house business once, who could tell you the sort of thing we ought to go in for. You could come over to see him, perhaps, if we decide to take. About those people down the road, she says that they are a very bad lot. He used to, be a prize-fighter and the women are the lowest of the low".

"Did she say anything more about the pie-works"? Bob asked.

"Yes, they have piemen with barrows all about the place, so that all little eating houses find it hard to compete".

"Well, what do you think, Mother, about taking? It's near the Works; it's not near anything else; it's not a bad house; and I see one thing. If we WERE great successes, we could put the kitchen down below and have all the floor for an eating room; with a sort of lift down to the kitchen".

"Are you for it, Bob"?

"On the whole, yes, I am. It's putting all the eggs into one basket; but that's what you have to do in life. We shan't get better for what we want to try".

"O, Bob, it's a frightful responsibility, with your father not here".

It was raining really hard now. They were near the

city's western gate. "Look, Bob", Tryphena said, "there's a little church over the arch; that must be St. Wirren's over the gate. Let us go in and ask for guidance".

The church was perched on the top of the arch or tunnel in which the gate had stood. You entered up a stair at the side of the road. Twenty steps brought you into a cheery little church gay with painting. It had been built by a knight who had done rather well with the ransom of prisoners during the French wars of the fifteenth century. Bob knew what was meant by asking for guidance. He had used the method himself, more than once, in times of doubt, with results which had been a puzzle to him. He had asked the Lord, among other things, whether he ought to give up sugar in Lent. The text "vouchsafed" had been "Baalah and Iim and Azem", and on repeating the enquiry the answer had been, "How thy garments are warm, when he quieteth the earth by the south wind".

Tryphena knelt down and after asking for guidance, shut her eyes and asked Bob to lead her to the lectern. Here she said in a low voice, "Lord, if it by Thy Will, suffer my right hand to find a text to guide me".

She then closed the Bible, and slowly opened it, so that her right thumb lay upon a text.

"Bob", she cried, "this is very wonderful. Come to see what the Lord has sent to us".

The thumb rested on Psalm 78, verse 54:

"And he brought them to the border of his sanctuary, even to this mountain, which his right hand had purchased".

This was none too clear to Bob, but like revelation to Tryphena, who had now no doubts whatever. They determined, therefore, to take No. 27, Tyler's Road. A woman who was tidying the vestry of St. Wirren's directed them to the agent's office. Other omens were propitious. As they walked, the rain ceased; a pale light struggled with the clouds. The agent's office was opposite a splendid red-brick Georgian building, inscribed:

STANCHESTER TOWN HALL, 1765

Over the door of the hall was the city clock, the pride of Stanchester, made by a local genius, who had been promised a thousand pounds for it, but had been fobbed off with seventy. As supporters to it, standing one on each side of it, were the two legendary figures of Stanchester, life-sized and more than life-coloured, St. Wirren and King Stanno, the Pagan, who was said to eat horses.

Just as mother and son halted opposite this splendour, the clock struck the hour. St. Wirren, lifting his sword, struck the first note; King Stanno, lifting his club, struck the second. At their feet, some tubby little angels without any bodies, but with hands and wings, beat out a chime on a dulcimer. Those citizens who had gathered to watch the miracle now smiled at each other, saying, "There it is. It's two o'clock by St. Wirren".

Alongside the Town Hall was another big building inscribed:

PUBLIC LIBRARY

All these things seemed good omens to the Mansells. As they entered the agent's office, the sun shone out.

"You see", Tryphena said, "the Sun of Joshua. That's the very voice of the Lord".

It was soon agreed, that they should take No. 27 from early January, on a yearly tenancy, for the carrying-on of an unlicensed dining-room or eating-house. As neither mother nor son knew anything about the sort of meals needed by the pipe workers, Bob went again to Stanchester to talk with some of them and to pick the brains of the watchman of whom Miss Lypiatt had spoken. The workers gave him useful advice. The watchman gave him the whole art and philosophy without pretence.

"So you want to start an eating-house here, do you? Well, listen to me. I can tell you about starting an eating-house, who better, for I've run one. It's not the trade it used to be. It was like the Guinea Coast, but now it's more like Workhouse Bay. Still, I don't want to discourage you. I'm free till the whistle blows. I can tell you what to do and what not. But one thing I warn you, don't try to be expensive. These lads can't pay much and won't. They've got the pie-works over in Glove Walk or Glovers Walk; their barrowmen will sell 'em pies at a penny; good pies, too, sausage rolls and that, at a penny. You couldn't make such pies at a penny and cop a profit. It can't be done. They make 'em a hundred at a time. You'd only make 'em twenty at a time.

"Remember what these Works lads are. They never pay more than twopence for a dinner, if they don't bring it with them from home; they can't. Most of them like a big penny tart for their meal, with jam on it; or they might like a bit of farm-cake, as they call it, what will stay by you if it won't fetch more than a penny; or they might like a faggot. If it should come on cold, a faggot is the thing they would like best of all.

"Now, as to a faggot. You'll have to go every Saturday

night the very last thing, to Mr. Evans, the pork-butchers, or some other pork-butcher. Just before closing time, you'll find these Saturday market men will almost give the stuff away rather than keep it over the week-end. You'd be surprised the nice bits you can get, and bits of liver, too, and that stuff lights, what you give to cats. Then, on Sunday, you chop all these things up with fat and herbs and bread crumbs, and put a dash of pepper and a nick of mustard and do 'em up tasty. Then in the week, you serve 'em up hot and hot. And in the pork season, when the weather's nice and cold, one lot will do you all the week.

"Now, as to drinks. You aren't in the licensed trade? No. Well, then keep out of it. Unless you're born to it, you can't make anything out of that. But you'll want some drinks. Not cocoa; never have cocoa, for that's a prison drink. But tea and coffee. You make 'em both the same. You get some bread crusts and burn 'em black, that's the foundation. Then for coffee you get what they call a bottle of coffee essence; and for tea you get a tin of what the grocers call Counter Tea; you can get it from most grocers. It's the stuff that falls on the counter when they're weighing tea. It all goes into a tin and you can get that for very little. Now, milk comes expensive, so it's best to have condensed milk. And you mix it in every week, or every two days, into your urn, coffee or tea, whichever you are making.

"Now, as to sweetening. Don't go to have sugar, as some folks do, in bowls on the table. That's just asking for trouble. All these folk have very sweet teeth, and they'd break the Bank of England in sugar. They'd steal every lump you put out. No; you put in dark treacle for the coffee; it helps to colour it, and golden syrup for tea, that does the same. Serve them both all ready sweetened.

"Now, pease pudding you could do a good deal with; but it must be hot and hot, and they won't give you more than twopence, even for that. But where you would find your account would be in the sweet line. You catch the girls that way. You see, these girls they don't care about getting dinner in the middle of the day; they are all out then to joke with the fellows; but they like to have a bit of a good stick-jaw or a brandy ball to eat while they're at work. You'd be surprised the profit there is in this. It's only getting a bottle of Peppermint Essence, as costs sixpence, and boiling it up with sugar.

"One thing you'll be surprised at is the way men will come in to you to ask for a sup of black tea with a stick in it, or what they call here 'a bit of tape'. These are the lads who go around at nights and come to work, as they say, with their tongues like blacksmith's rasps. They'd give a lot for a dram on the quiet; to make them up to their work; but they wouldn't go into a licensed house so near to their work. But, of course, if once the police catch you at that game selling sticks without a license, you'll be for the mat in the morning. But you say from the first that you don't touch that business, and you'll not be bothered.

"Another thing; don't you never put on table cloths. The men'll wipe their knives on them and run their forks through them and the girls'll steal 'em under your noses and sew them into underclothes. And don't you have metal spoons and that. The kind of lad here, he means no harm but he'll take spoons, salts, anything you have. You'll be surprised the things you'll lose: plates, knives, anything. And if you allow smoking the girls and the older men won't come; and if you don't, nobody else will.

"Oh, and then, mats; I was forgetting mats. You'll need mats on all the floors, for it's swimming with mud here when it rains. And another thing, you'll have to screw the mats in and unscrew them to clean, or you won't have a mat left to you. They'll take them. They'll take anything. They don't mean any harm, but young fellows, you know, they think it's sport.

"And then, another thing; that's vinegar. A lot of these girls, they like to try to keep slim. And you tell your mother to look out for them. They'll come to her quietly for vinegar, just pure vinegar out of a cup. They'll drink down two or three pints a day, they say. So you tell your mother to get her vinegar by the keg. It's nothing but sour wine, that's gone wrong, and these girls'll pay any money for it.

"And another thing, about washing up. The heavier you can get your china, the less you'll smash. Oh, and I was forgetting about the prairie oysters. You'll find a lot of sore heads in the Pipe Works on Monday in the mornings. Lots of men'll come to you for prairie oysters. Just raw eggs in a saucer of vinegar; and they daren't look at it, but just shut their eyes and down it".

This man helped the Mansells more than anyone, though he made their hearts to sink. They were to try to skin a living off the poor food of the poorest livers in the land.

Just before Christmas, they sold off some of their things in Condicote, and did well; some of the furniture fetched good prices; the horse went for seventeen pounds, the van for fifteen. After the sale, they had more than a hundred and twenty pounds to face the world with.

"Come, Mother", Bob said, "that's more than Adam and Eve had".

They practised the making of faggots and of pease pudding, the exact amount of jam to put in a jam puff, and of ham to go in a sandwich. They worked out costs, and did sad chemical experiments in the name of coffee.

Soon the little boys and girls of Muck and Fever Alleys began to go round from house to house after dark. Standing in groups, they would gabble:

> *"Ile uv jeez uz,*
> *Ile uv jeez uz,*
> *Ile uv jeez uz,*
> *Cozzy fuzz lumm Ee.*
> *Juicy cruicy Fie dim,*
> *Juicy cruicy Fie dim,*
> *Juicy cruicy Fie dim,*
> *Dungim monner tree."*

Then they would knock at the door and say they were carols please and it would be a hapenny.

It was a sad Christmas for the Mansells, for they had never before had a family Christmas without the baker. They saw him in the week after Christmas. He was looking ill, but hoped to be with them in February.

On the twentieth of January, they set out from Condicote and so came to the new home in Stanchester to prepare it as Mansell's Cosy Dining Room at Popular Prices. They put notices on the walls and red geraniums in the window. Bob put a placard in the window:

OPENING DAY
THE
27TH. JAN.
AT 12. NOON.

Twelve noon being the time of the Works knocking off for
dinner. The night before the opening, Bob bought a few
threepenny calico flags, which he festooned inside the window, about a notice in red:

LOOK HERE
MANSELL'S COSY DINING ROOM
OPEN TODAY. 12 NOON.

WALK IN.

He and his mother noticed with joy, that at least forty
of the pipe workers looked at the notice as they passed the
shop in the gas light of the early morning.

At a little before twelve, Bob put on a clean check apron
which belonged to his father, and went outside the door,
to act as chaunter. He had not before spoken in public;
his knees were knocking together below him when the
whistle blew, and the flood of young men poured·out from
the green doorway, cheering, screaming and snatching at
each others' caps.

"Walk in, Ladies and Gentlemen", Bob cried. "Try our
dainty dinners. Walk in. Walk in".

A wild young man stopped in his race, looked at Bob,
and called out,

"Go put your head in a bag".

Another snatched a friend's cap and flung it in Bob's

face. But these were the racers, who did not stay to pursue their quarrels; in a few seconds the steadier lads were there, and of these four shy ones came in, and though much abashed at the neatness of everything did take seats, and ordered each a penny tart and a cup of coffee, for which feast each paid twopence. Tryphena asked them to tell their friends, and to come again, which they said they would do. After they had gone, Bob saw that the sugar basin which Tryphena had insisted on putting on each table, had been emptied at that table. It was a whole pennyworth of lump sugar gone; the night watchman's warning had been wise. The boys had only been there ten minutes.

After they had gone, three girls came in, who had a cup of tea apiece and then had some brandy balls to suck while at work. As they were sitting over their tea, looking at the brandy balls, two men came in for two-pennyworth of pease pudding each. While the men were being served the three girls went off without paying. Bob ran after them and asked for the fivepence. They tried to face him down, but finding that did not serve, they made up the money between them, paid it, told Charlie, as they called Bob, to run home and chase himself, and then strolled off along Tyler's Road, shouting at their gentlemen friends, who were not without ready answers.

Just as the hooter blew for the end of the dinner hour, the lady, Joanna Maria, with her sister and man, came in. They ordered a sandwich, a blob of pease pudding, a tart and a cup of coffee apiece, a big fivepenny meal each, one-and-three-pence for the three of them. Bob did not like the looks of the three; and Tryphena who saw them from the inner room, was horrified at having to serve such people and having them within her house. However, they had to serve them and to listen to the comments of the three on the fittings and the food. When they had finished their meal, the man pushed past Bob, so that he could look into the inner room and make sure who was there. Seeing that Tryphena was alone, he said,

"It will be all right, if I settle at the end of the week. You know me. I'm just down the road".

"No", Tryphena said, "I don't know you and this is a cash house. The notice is on the wall there".

"I did not see any notice", the man said, "and, as a matter of fact, haven't any money on me. It will do at the end of the week".

"Oh, no it won't", Bob said. "Don't ask for tick here. It hurts our feelings to refuse".

"You go to hell, boy", Joanna Maria said.

"I'll go for the policeman just along by the corner there", Bob said.

As it luckily happened, a policeman did saunter to the corner at that instant, and stood there, looking down Tyler's Road. Joanna's sister suddenly rolled up her skirt, and produced from under a dirty and ragged garter a shilling. Joanna, rolling up her skirt, produced from a similar purse a threepenny bit. They tendered these, and then, with some rude comment from the man, the three went off.

Tryphena said after they had gone, that she had almost told them not to come again. Bob said, that he did not think that they would come again.

The takings for the dinner hour had been two-and-eightpence, of which eightpence might be profit, but against this eightpence was a pennyworth of sugar stolen.

The sevenpence remaining might pay for their own food during the day, but did not promise to do much towards paying the rent, the rates and clothing; or providing against old age and sickness.

No one came in during the afternoon, but when the whistle blew at night, eleven young men came in and sampled Mansell's Famous Faggots. Bob could not make out what the lads were; they were friends and free with their money; they spent three-and-ninepence altogether, and thereby raised the profits of the day to one-and-six-pence-halfpenny. Tryphena was in despair at the smallness of the takings, but contrived to hide her feelings from Bob. Bob thought that they would do better as time went on, and contrived to give this courage to Tryphena. But during the next three days they came to know what they had not before considered, that Tyler's Road was without life of its own; it was the approach to the Pipe Works; other people did not use it. Mother and son were committed to a place where only pipe workers passed; if they could not draw in the workers they might shut up shop.

After the evening whistle, a few of the better men from the works dropped in to eat faggots, drink hot coffee and to play dominoes, for which some of them had asked. At seven o'clock these all set out for home. Bob and Tryphena would then close the shutters and clear up for the night. The road was still enough after that, except that a little later Joanna Maria and her sister would go out upon their cruise together, and would perhaps return later, with or without prey. Sometimes, after their return, there might be a dispute down the road between their prey and Joanna's man.

Joanna and her two friends sometimes came in for

meals. They were not pleasant guests and Tryphena hated having them there. One evening, the man came in with a much younger man, who was dark and sideways and downwards whichever way you looked at him. Bob, who served him, was sure that he was there for no good purpose, but could not refuse to serve him. The two sinister heads were whispering close together, and both pairs of eyes roved about the shop and premises. They went out, after a time, but Bob saw them outside looking at the upper windows.

"I'll just put an extra bolt on that outer door", Bob thought. "I don't at all like the looks of those two birds".

The business grew slowly; day by day they did better. They discovered what the different clients liked. Before the first week was over, they had their habitues who liked particular chairs and expected their fancies to be known. It was interesting work to mother and son, yet galling to their pride. They had been independent almost, as bakers; now they were at the beck and call of everybody.

They kept saying, "Very soon now Father will be back. He'll have ideas of how we can improve it, or get more people to come in".

The frost set in at the end of their first week; they found that hot treacle possets made a good line. Then a letter came from the baker saying that he was to be released the next day, and that though he was really all right he would feel glad if one or other of them would be there to help him home.

The two debated which should go. Bob did not like leaving his mother alone there for the night; and Tryphena did not like to leave Bob to do the breakfasts by himself. It was arranged that Bob should go. Both were uneasy about it. Both felt that the chances were that the baker was more ill than he said.

Bob went to Tatchester that night, so as to be there betimes. A policeman in the town took him to a sixpenny lodging house, where he engaged a bed for the night. The policeman advised him to sleep with his boots tied round his neck, which Bob did; they were not stolen. In the morning a cab driver took him to the Discharge Gate of the prison.

"See there", he said, "over the gate there. Those are the leg-irons worn by the famous highwayman Benjamin, before he was hanged. Forty pounds apiece, they're said to weigh".

After admiring these works of art, he was admitted to his father, who looked and was a sick man, but so over-joyed to be free that the sickness did not matter to him. They took train together through Condicote to Stanchester, talking nineteen to the dozen.

"Open the window, Bob", the baker said, "and let me have the free air and see the fields again. Lord, it's good to feel a draught on one's face".

"Don't you get too much draught", Bob said. "It's cold. You've not been used to it, and a chill is easily caught in one of these trains".

"Don't you tell me. It's like drinking great draughts of freedom to have this blowing in".

He looked out eagerly for every familiar land-mark, and spoke excitedly about each one.

"There's the Camp. There's the row of poplars. There's the mill where we used to be millers. In one of the rooms there they used to have the heights of all the Mansell children pencilled off on the wall where they were measured. Now we're away from Condicote. The New Life lies before us. Hurray".

However, he coughed a good deal. Towards the end of the journey, he was less excited. He shut the window, and said that he was rather afraid that he had taken cold.

"I was wrong and you were right, Bob; a draught is a risky thing when one's been penned up like I have".

He didn't talk any more. "I'll tell you all the news when I'm at home and your mother can hear", he said. "I've got a lot to tell which she must hear".

Presently, they were at home, and he could begin his work as the proprietor of Mansell's cosy dining-room.

When the mid-day dinner had been cleared, he said,

"I want to tell you now of what I've known. I shan't ever allude to it again, and I want you never to. But first, I want to say what a wonderful new home you've made for me. I've brought deep waters over you two dear ones; and done no one good by it, neither poor Magpie nor myself. They put the poor Magpie and Rapp away, as you know. It won't bear talking of. We used to cry out to them in Chapel, as we were singing in the hymns. 'God bless you, Rapp and Magpie'. They heard some of it. Well, they are out of their misery now, and in the woods of the New Jerusalem perhaps, where the game is free to all.

"Ah, I've brought grief to you two; but I'll make it up to both of you, you'll see.

"I shan't speak of the prison again. I used to think that a lot of Old England was rotten with wrong, but I didn't guess how wrong till I saw the kind of remedies they were applying. Still, one can't spread Christian feeling by shewing un-Christian feeling. All that's over now.

"And now, do you know I feel I can't talk any more; it makes me cough and I feel that I've got a fever. I ask you both to forgive my hasty un-Christian way that brought all this shame and misery on you".

He went up to bed then, coughing and shaking. "I've caught a chill as Bob said I should", he said. "I'm not fit to be let out alone anywhere. I'm Tom Haste, who brought all to waste". ·

Later that night he began to cough what Tryphena thought was blood. He tossed and tumbled in bed. About midnight, Tryphena could not understand what he was saying, and called Bob, who said that he was delirious. The Doctor, who came next morning, said that it was lobar pneumonia, a typical severe case. As to danger: yes, there was always danger; that is, it is not a thing to trifle with anywhere, and in this case the patient had been a "flour and furnace man", which was not a good preparation for this disease. Still, if they kept his strength up and nursed him carefully . . . It would be about a week before any turn came.

It was a hard week for the Mansells, mother and son. For the first five days, the· baker, though very ill, was cheery; he talked a little of going over to Tatchester to shake hands with one of the warders who had been a beast to him, and taking the Governor, who had once stopped his meat for three days, a pork-pie of Tryphena's make. She had been famous for them once. He took nourishment, too: beef-tea, jelly, and sweet chocolate, saying that a man had to go to prison to learn the taste of food. At the midnight of each night he used to became a babbler, but this light delirium lapsed in the mornings, when the temperature dropped.

But on the sixth morning it did not drop. He remained talking incoherently about the Magpie and others, with some mention of golden streets. The Doctor, who was a young and cheerful man, said that he would come in later in the day. He had not said that hitherto. He reassured Tryphena, with the remark that the baker would have to be worse before he could be better. He went away with a confident air, having left confidence behind him; but Bob, all busy as he was with the countless jobs of washing and serving, had within him now a recurring wave of terror that kept surging up across his mind, that his father was going to die.

The Doctor came in again that evening, and looked at the sick man, who was babbling with a high temperature, coughing uneasily, and in pain.

"Well, Mrs. Mansell", he said, "you are one of the best of nurses. Keep on as you're doing; keep the sponge going".

"I'm afraid it's a bad case", she said.

"Pneumonia always looks bad", the Doctor agreed. "Perhaps it looks worse than it is, but this is a sharp attack".

"I do wish that dog outside would stop howling", Tryphena said. "He's been outside howling like that all day, on and off".

"Whose dog is it"?

"Nobody's. It does not belong here".

"I'll see if I can?t get it away", the Doctor said. "It may keep him from rest".

He gave some instructions to Tryphena and then came downstairs. Bob, who was waiting for him, saw that he was graver than usual.

"Let's see if we can't get this dog to the police station", the Doctor said. "Can you spare me a bone, to lure him away"?

Bob brought a bone, and followed the Doctor out of doors.

"I wanted to speak to you, Doctor", he said. "I believe that that dog is howling for my Father's death".

"You mustn't hold superstitions like that, you know", the Doctor said.

"It isn't all superstition", Bob answered. "But let that be as it may. Doctor, I know you want to spare mother, but how ill is my father"?

"He's very ill", the Doctor said.

"Will he get better"? Bob asked.

"He may take a turn", the Doctor said. "It's all in his favour that he's at home, being looked after".

"He's not so well as he was", Bob said.

"No, he's not quite so well", the Doctor answered.

"Is he going to die"? Bob asked.

"I'll do my level best to pull him through", the Doctor said, "but we aren't magicians. We can only assist Nature".

"Then, you think my father is going to die"? Bob said.

"Your name's Bob, isn't it"? the Doctor answered. "Well, Bob, I'm awfully sorry for you, but, you see, you're going to be a man, and you will have to be prepared for anything that life may bring to you. But don't frighten your mother".

Bob went away, feeling his heart wrenched in two with terror. His father was going to die.

Late that evening, he took his basket as usual, to buy cuts of meat for faggots and a bit of beef for beef-tea for

his father. It was a little after ten. The market stalls always shut at half-past. He was shaken to the soul by the
thought of his father dying and of his mother's despair.
How would they manage? They were all alone. They had
no friend in Stanchester; nor anywhere else in the world;
they stood alone. Death would come and take the poor
baker, and leave his mother desolate; then horrible men
in black, all smelling of spirits, would come up the stairs
and the poor body would be carried to the cemetery, perhaps the one in Condicote, near to that tomb of little
'Phosie which he had so loathed as a little boy when he
was taken there on Sunday afternoons.

He made up his mind to it. It was a part of this life
into which he had somehow come. He was tied to the
stake and had to stand what came. It would come and then
perhaps presently it would go. In the meantime he would
have to look out carefully, that he was not diddled over
the beef for his father. The old chap had sold him a very
poor bit as a prime cut, two nights before.

As he passed out of the Tyler's Road, he saw a man
loitering on the other side of the way. Something dark and
slinky in the figure reminded him of the man who had
supped the other night with Joanna's friend. He did not
heed the figure. He thought, "Well, we've closed for tonight, so we shan't have the pleasure of your company
tonight, thank the Lord". It occurred to him afterwards
that this man was joined by another; he half saw it. But
he was oppressed and in a hurry to get along towards the
market. He enjoyed the night marketing. The stalls were
brightly lit with naphtha flares. Some of the stall-holders
made their stalls gay with paper zinnias, stuck in the corners of the stalls and in the cracks in the pavements near

them. There was always a good deal of bustle and excitement, if the night were fine; the stall-keepers cried, "What d'ye like, now. What d'ye like, now". The cheap-jacks would blow their squealers. Sometimes a woman would sing there, to a mandolin, or one of the pipe workers, supposed to be the best concertina player in the district, would come there playing either "Annie Laurie" or "Won't you buy my pretty flowers"?

On this night, the concertina player was there with a penny-whistle player. Somebody said that he would get a pound a night, playing like that, in London. Bob well believed it, for he was fond of music, and could not keep from listening, all worried as he was.

It was twenty minutes to eleven when he started back from the market, and about ten minutes to when he turned into Tyler's Road. It was at this point that he noticed that something was amiss with No. 27. The front door was ajar, so that a ray of light came from it across the pavement.

His first thought was, "Something has happened to Father and she has run out for help". He ran down the pavement to the door. His mother had closed it after him, on his leaving; he was certain of that. Now it was open a foot or more. He was shocked at its being open like that, for his mother had had a fear of prowlers, and had always kept the door locked or on the chain, whenever they closed for the night. He stood at the entrance an instant, and then called "Mother" softly, fearing to lift his voice lest his father should be asleep. He had no answer from his mother, but from the room above there came a moaning noise and the sound of his father's cough. The light in the dining-room was from a lamp without a glass. Someone had lighted it without putting the glass shade over the burner. It was now flaring angrily, with a lot of black smoke. His mother would never have done that. By the light he saw that the place had been pillaged. He listened lest the pillagers should still be upstairs. He turned down the flaring wick and lifted the lamp. "The robbers have gone", he thought.

He put the chain on the door. Holding the lamp, he went swiftly upstairs to his father's room. A night light was burning in a dish there as always. As he entered, a coal in the fireplace broke, with a little rush of flame which gave a good light. He saw his father apparently dead on his bed and the figure of his mother bundled up in a table cloth and tied with a length of her own clothes-line to a chair. The room was in disorder. Drawers had been pulled out and the contents flung anyhow. Some swift and brutal hands had been busy there in the last half-hour.

He put down the lamp; his mother was moaning under her bandages. He cast loose the line and flung away her swaddlings. She moaned and was not quite conscious. He flung some water in her face; she shuddered, opened her eyes, said "Oh", shuddered again and then fainted. His father said suddenly,

"Is that you, Bob"?

Bob said, "Yes. It's all right, Father; don't you worry. I'm back".

"How's your mother"? the baker asked.

"I think she's all right, Father. Don't you worry. Don't talk".

He fetched some more water and splashed his mother's face, which was swollen from a blow. She was shaken and trembling. He reassured her and comforted her, that all was now well; that it was over. She was in a state of twitter and shudder. He got her to lie down on her bed, (it was Bob's bed usually, but now that the baker was so ill Tryphena slept on it and Bob slept on a mattress on the floor). He gave her some of the brandy which he had refused to Engels.

The baker began to talk about floating about with the moon and being sometimes right up above it, looking down on it. "It's like a big orange", he said. "No, no".

Bob gave some more sips of brandy to his mother. He was sure that they had been robbed of all their wealth; but with his mother all bruised and banged, and his father dying, that seemed not to matter much. Gradually his mother came to herself, and said that men with masks had done it. After this she became so hysterical, that he had to beg her not to worry, not to try to speak, since it was all right now.

He never knew much of what had happened; but the results of the men with masks were clear enough.

The baker and Tryphena had both strong views about the iniquity of usury and, therefore, never used a bank. They kept their savings in old stockings in two or three hiding-places. At Condicote, Bob had not known where these were, but at Stanchester he had become an active partner: they had been shewn to him. Two of the three hoards had been found and pillaged. Their wealth had gone at a blow. The only hoard not found by the thieves was the little one in which they kept the money for daily and weekly expenses. This had in it at the time four pounds, seventeen shillings and sixpence. This was now all their money. The thieves had taken nearly a hundred and fifteen pounds in money, as well as most of the baker's clothing and the easily carried mats and table cloths from the shop. They had taken Tryphena's brass candlesticks and the clock given to her on her marriage by the parish workers at Yockford. It had not gone for a great many years, but she treasured it.

It was all dead loss. The two had always refused to insure, saying that that would be not trusting the Lord.

Tryphena was fairly well the next morning, though very tired. She said that soon after Bob had gone out, she heard him give his tap outside. A signal tap had been arranged between them. Bob, on returning after night shopping, tapped twice, paused and then tapped a third time. Thinking that he had returned, she came downstairs, undid the chain and opened the door. She was so sure that it was Bob tapping that she was not certain if she asked, "Is that you, Bob"? On opening the door, two or three men rushed in, flung something over her, and hit her hard. She cried out and ran upstairs. They came after her, hit her again and tied a rug over her. She did not see who they were. She could not swear how many were there. She was inclined to think they were three young men, all silent and very active. They could not have been there long. She knew that they tore the cupboards open, and had everything topsy turvy in a very few minutes. They had come upon the money, for she had heard them give a low whistle of joy. What with pain from her blow, terror lest they should make the baker even more ill than he was, and another terror lest Bob returning should be murdered by them, she lost consciousness.

"I kept fainting", she said.

Bob thought of the man on the pavement. He was one of them, no doubt, and had been watching for his

going out to shop. Probably the thieves had been watching
the shop for some time. Very likely they had had meals
there and seen all the lay-out of the house, the fittings of
the door and windows, and the ways of the inhabitants.
As the old night-watchman had said to him, "You'll find
all sorts in the pipe works, except the sort to give trust
to for meals".

They had paid the first quarter's rent in advance; but
now, with the baker ill and the money gone, how were
they to pay the second quarter? They were living from
hand to mouth, barely making their keep from the shop.
What more could they do? Tryphena said that they must
take a lodger; but where could they put a lodger, and how
could they look after a lodger, when the sick man and the
shop together kept them busy all day and far into the
night? Bob said, that it would pay if he were to get a
job in the pipe works, work there during the day and bear
a hand in the shop before and after hours. With some of
his weekly makings, he said, Tryphena could pay for a
woman to come in by the day. This might have been a
help, but unfortunately the works did not want any more
boys of Bob's age. They needed strong lads of eighteen.

The one bright spot in the trouble was that the baker
was better, quite strangely better. The Doctor was late in
coming to them, but when he came he said that he was
better.

"But, Mrs. Mansell, what have you done to your face"?

"We had thieves in", she said, simply, "and I know not
how we're to pay you, Doctor".

"Never bother about that", the Doctor said. "But I'll
just step around to the police about the theft, for that
must be reported".

There was no doubt about the baker having become

better; yet Bob, all depressed by the run of the luck, wondered whether it were not that clearing of the faculties which sometimes precedes death. He wondered, but had the work to do. The police came in, later on, and took what statements he and his mother could make. Bob said, that it might be well to call at Joanna Maria's.

Later that afternoon, he sat at a table in the shop, drying some pease-pudding bowls, which he had just washed in the sink in the kitchen. His father was sleeping uneasily; Tryphena, who was worn out, was sleeping heavily. He was thankful that they were resting.

He wondered whether someone would invent a machine for drying towels. His own was wet. Coal was scarce with them; it was difficult to get the towels near the range when the meals were preparing; and when the towels were wet, as these were, the job of washing up became ten times more difficult than it should have been.

"What would be nice", he thought, "would be a sort of endless chain, with catches for the dishes, to take them all under boiling water, then rinse them, and then put them under cloths, so that they wouldn't be touched by hand at all. Well, when I'm less busy, that's the kind of thing I'll invent. And the machine will have a mechanical hand attached to put the dishes on the dresser when they're dry".

He tried to think of the hot, humming machine, with its dishes proceeding from the tap to the dresser untouched by hand; but he could never think of it for long. Every few moments a wave of mingled fear and horror came over him, saying,

"Your father is going to die, and he is the peg which holds your home together".

As he rubbed and wished that the towels were dry so

that he could do the work, he noticed a four-wheeled cab pulling up the road outside No. 27. He judged that someone had come on business to the works and wondered why the cabman had stopped there instead of going across the road to the main gate or office door. The cabman got down from his box, came up the steps to the pavement and opened the door. Bob now thought that the cabman had come for a cup of tea, and rose to greet him. He recognized the man as the driver who had brought his father home from the station a few days before.

"Is your name Mansell"? the cabman asked. "But I see it is over the door. A lady's here to see you. An old lady. She's down in the cab".

Bob wondered what lady could be there to see him. He stood up. The cabman said, "I must look to that horse of mine", and went down to do so. Bob wondered if this were some new dodge of thieves to get what little was left to them. He went to the door, and there saw a little old lady climbing the steps of the raised pavement. She had a radiant face, all alive with light and goodness. She was dressed in black silk, with a little mauve velvet at the throat and wrists. She wore a plain gold cross as a brooch and a very long gold Albert chain was round her neck. Bob did not know her: she was not anyone from Condicote; he had never seen her before.

"Have I come to the right house"? she asked. "You are Mr. Robert Mansell"?

"Do come in and sit down", Bob said. He dusted and placed a chair for her. She sat down, smiling upon him curiously. She had very bright eyes which seemed to take in all things; her little, thin body was still strong and active. "Do you want to speak to my mother"? Bob asked.

"She's asleep at the moment, resting. Perhaps you will tell me if I can do anything? I don't want to wake her. She's been up all night".

"How is your father"? the lady asked.

"Why, better than he has been, but I'm afraid he's very gravely ill", Bob said. "Would you care to leave a message"?

The lady shook her head. "There is no hurry", she said. "I will wait for a while, if I may, and then speak with your mother".

She kept looking at him shyly and curiously. There was something familiar in her look; he could not quite say what.

"May I stay a little while"? she asked.

"Certainly, madam", he said. "I'll move these bowls out into the kitchen. Perhaps you would prefer to sit in the kitchen; there's a fire there".

"No, no", she said, "this place will suit very well, thank you. But you are wondering who I am? Did you ever hear of your great-aunt Dixon"?

"Only just", he said.

The old woman was trembling, her eyes were full of tears.

"You are my great-nephew", she said. "And you are just like my sister, Louisa, when you turn to the light like that".

She turned quickly from him, so that he might not see her tears.

"I doubt", she said fiercely, "I doubt you will know who my sister Louisa was"?

A memory of what Engels had told him months before came back to Bob.

"She was my grandmother", he said.

"She was a fool", the old woman said, with the quiet intensity peculiar to her. "But she seems to have caused a nice grandson".

All this time, they were speaking in low voices, as Bob wished not to disturb the sleepers. He was somewhat afraid of her, because of the power of her spirit.

"I doubt", she said again, "I doubt you will have heard of Miss Dixon"?

"I have just heard a little", Bob said.

She had a walking stick in her left hand. It was an elegant stick made from some heavy black African wood, with a little gold binding near the handle. The handle was crooked in a peculiar way, which Bob, owing to some picture seen in childhood, always associated with a witch and witchcraft. There was something witchlike in the lady's bearing. The delicate nose and chin shewed a tendency to hook; the eyes, very bright for one so old, had unnatural power in them. He looked at her, being fascinated. On close examination, the first impression that she was old fell away; she was not old, but seemed frail, as though not long before she must have passed through illness.

"I doubt you have heard much good of me", she said.

Bob had no doubt on the point. His face shewed it.

"My boy, Robert", she said, "nothing but a visit to the doors of Death will soften the heart of pride".

Bob was even then visiting the doors of Death; he felt the truth of the remark, but wondered even more on what had brought the woman there. She was very beautiful, he thought, being so clearly cut in feature, so elegant in bearing, so erect, and so swift in feeling. But why had she come? What did she want? The cabman was waiting there in the road. He was taking a fill of tobacco, while his horse ate from the nosebag.

"My boy, Robert", she said, "come to me. I would like to kiss you. It is the first time for many years that I have kissed anyone of my kith and kin".

Bob was aghast; he was not used to being kissed; besides he was all damp from washing up, and wearing an old, rather dirty check apron. However, he took the old lady's hand and kissed it. She was touched by this, and kept his hand and patted it.

Bob remembered how his father and mother had mentioned this Miss Dixon. His father had said, "She's the King of Prussia's Dragoon, that old lady".

She seemed to divine something of his thought.

"It will often happen", she said, "that pride forbids a friendship which life intended to bring to be. The first attempts may be disastrous. Then Time passes and pride gets chastened. Sometimes a pair that quarrelled worst are the best of friends late in life".

She produced from her bag a little book or case of puce-coloured leather, clasped with gold. Inside it she shewed some miniatures.

"See, my boy, Robert", she said. "These are the Dixons. This is my father, this my mother, and this one, here, is my dear sister, Louisa, who became your father's mother".

Bob looked at the beautiful face. He did not know that that very miniature had been given by Louisa to the man with whom she had eloped, who had sold it later, when hard up, for what an old admirer offered.

"Louisa was ten years older than myself", the old lady continued. "She looked after me when I was little. She was very much more than a mother to me, for my mother was weary of children by that time, having had nine before I was born. I do not approve of the ways of parents; they assume the powers of Deity without the attributes. But for Louisa, I should have been neglected. And for Louisa there was nothing in that great, empty, soulless house of pride and more pride.

"My sister Louisa ran away with a sporting adventurer. I was forbidden to see her or write to her. Though I tried to do both, it was useless. It was drilled into me that she had disgraced the family. Years later, when I had to see your father, it was on a matter of business, to which we both brought pride and more pride. It was not a happy meeting.

"Lately it chanced, that I was ill, and near to Death's door, which caused me to shed some pride perhaps. I felt that my sister Louisa wished me to find you. Sickness will do that perhaps. It will lessen the barriers to the other world for us. It was then that I learned of some of your troubles, and of your father's gallantry with the egg. I know the Judge. I wish that your father had made a better shot. I should have come before, but this has been an inclement winter, and not the weather for travelling. But I am here now to make what friendship I can between the two branches of the family. Do you think that your father and mother will help me to bury the hatchet for my sister Louisa's sake"?

There was a slight noise in the kitchen. Tryphena came in to the dining-room. She was looking very beautiful, because her bandaged face hid all her poor features and made her eyes look superb.

"Miss Dixon", she said, holding out her hand, "let us bury any hatchet. Any that there was was of our forging,

God knows, and there's nothing like sorrow for shewing the madness of it".

The two women shook hands.

"About Robert", Miss Dixon said. "May I see him"?

"Come up", Tryphena said, "but forgive the untidiness of things".

"Everything is beautiful", Miss Dixon said.

As they came into the sick room, the baker wakened from his sleep.

"This is Aunt Dixon", he said, "come to forgive her nephew".

"No, to ask forgiveness", she said.

"I've been dreaming of this", the baker said. "It is all in Ezekiel". He lay still for a while, then went on. "It's a text in Ezekiel: 'When the prince shall prepare peace offerings voluntarily unto the Lord, one shall then open him the gate that looketh toward the east . . . then he shall go forth'. You find all topsy and turvy, Aunt Dixon".

"You're going to get better", Aunt Dixon said.

"Yes", the baker whispered. "I'm going to get well. I'm got through Jordan. You've opened the gate and I'm going forth".

"The property that should have been your mother's, Nephew Robert", the old lady said, "came unjustly to me. I come to make restitution and amends. You will not deny an old aunt the pleasure of trying to spoil a nephew".

"I'll deny no one the joy of forgiving a sinner", the baker said.

"When you are a very little better then", the old lady said, "we will have you away from this to stay with me, till we can see. Now, in the meantime, you are all worn out with watching. I am therefore going to the hospital, to find nurses, to take the watching from you. To go on with your Ezekiel, who is my favourite prophet, too:

" 'This is the place where the priests shall boil the trespass offering and the sin offering' ".